BLACK BUCK

Black Buck

BLACK BUCK

MATEO ASKARIPOUR

THORNDIKE PRESS
A part of Gale, a Cengage Company

GALE
A Cengage Company

LIBRARY OF CONGRESS CIP DATA ON FILE.
CATALOGUING IN PUBLICATION FOR THIS BOOK
IS AVAILABLE FROM THE LIBRARY OF CONGRESS.

ISBN-13: 978-1-4328-8835-0 (hardcover alk. paper)

Published in 2021 by arrangement with Houghton Mifflin Harcourt

Printed in Mexico
Print Number: 01   Print Year: 2021

*To all of those who have ever
been made to feel less than
I see you*

The most unprofitable item ever
manufactured is an excuse.

— JOHN MASON

AUTHOR'S NOTE

There's nothing like a Black man on a mission. No, let me revise that. There's nothing like a Black *salesman* on a mission. He's Superman, Spiderman, Batman, and any other supernatural, paranormal, or otherwise godlike combination of blood, flesh, and brains. He can't die. Don't believe me? MLK. Yes, Martin Luther King Jr. was a Black salesman. In the same way used-car salesmen hawk overpriced hunks of metal that break down once an unsuspecting customer drives off the lot, our man ML to the goddamn K was a salesman to the highest degree.

Not only did he sell Black people on the vision of a unified America, but he also sold the United States Supreme Court, which at the time contained nine white men — the hardest decision makers for any Black man to convince.

MLK, Malcolm X, James Baldwin, Jean-

9

Michel Basquiat, and Frederick Douglass were all salesmen. Hell, Nina Simone, Rosa Parks, Harriet Tubman, and every other Black woman who achieved any leap of success was a saleswoman. Oprah "hide a BMW under your seat" Winfrey is a saleswoman. You get the point. Each and every one of these people was selling something more precious than gold: a vision. A vision for what the world could look like if millions of people were to change their minds — the hardest thing to change.

How do I fit into all of this? When will I shut up and get to the point? Don't worry, I'm getting there. I am a Black man on a mission. No, I am a Black *salesman* on a mission. And the point of this book — which I'm writing from my penthouse overlooking Central Park — is to help other Black men and women on a mission to sell their visions all the way to the top. So high up that I'll have to crane my neck, like one of those goofy white people in films deciding whether a superhero is a bird or a plane, just to catch a glimpse of them before they're out of sight. *Whoosh! Bang! Poof!* The great disappearing act of success.

My goal is to teach you how to sell. And if I'm half the salesman every newspaper, blog, and hustler in New York City says I am, then you are in luck. With my story, I will give you the tools to go out and create the life you want. To overcome every seemingly impossible obstacle. To fix the game. Which game, you ask? We'll get there. But before we do, I'm going to ask you to do three things.

1. Let down your guard and open your mind to what I'm going to tell you. I know we're strangers right now. You're likely asking yourself why you should trust me. The good thing is that you already bought this book, so you trusted me enough to part with $26. I won't let you down.
2. Understand that I want all people to be successful, but in the same way that Starbucks can't just give out Mocha Frappuccinos to anyone who doesn't have $14, I can't help everyone. So, I am starting with Black people. If you're not Black but have this book in your hands, I want you to think of yourself as an honorary Black person. Go on, do it. Don't go don blackface and an afro, but picture yourself as Black. And if you want, you can even give yourself a fancy Black name, like

11

Jamal, Imani, or Asia.

3. Say, "Every day is deals day," and clap your hands. I know it's strange, but do it. And when you do, think of the number one thing you're working toward. It may be a new car, a promotion, someone's affection, or an expensive pair of shoes. Whatever it is, think of it and say, "Every day is deals day," and clap your hands as loud as you can. As you'll find out, every day *is* deals day. A day without deals is like a camel without humps; it doesn't exist.

At this point, your heart's beating and there's a twinkle in your eye. I know because I've given this speech before. I've given it to myself. I've given it to thousands of people wanting to change their lives. And I've given it to people who didn't know they wanted a change but needed it. A long time ago I was one of these people. I was like you. Ambitious but afraid. Intelligent but impotent. Curious but cowardly. I was all of this and more.

But freedom, true freedom, the kind where you do what you want without fear, comes at a cost. It's like my urban-corner-philosopher-cum-fairy-god-uncle Wally Cat used to say, "You can change the hands of a clock, but you can't change time." I can give you the tools to change, but only you can change yourself.

And if I am successful in teaching you how to sell and fix the game, I ask that you buy another copy of my book and give it to the friend who needs it most. Who is stuck like I was and in need of a way out. Who is blind to the game but has potential, just like you. Does that sound fair? If so, and if you can do the three things I outlined above, then we have a deal. And if we have a deal, it's time for you to do one last thing.

Turn the page.

Happy selling,
Buck

■ ■ ■ ■

I.
Prospecting

■ ■ ■ ■

In the middle of every difficulty lies
opportunity.
— ALBERT EINSTEIN

1.

1

The day that changed my life was like every other day before it, except that it changed my life. I suppose that makes it as important as a birthday, wedding, or bankruptcy, which is why I celebrate the twentieth of May every year like it's my birthday. Why the hell not?

As with any other day, my alarm went off at 6:15 a.m. The buzzing interrupted an unremarkable dream that left me with morning wood. But instead of rubbing one out, I kissed my photo of my girlfriend, Soraya; straightened my leaning tower of books; said good morning to my posters of *Scarface, The Godfather,* and Denzel as Malcolm X, and stood in front of my mirror, taking stock of the person staring back at me.

I didn't know it back then, but I was, and am, an attractive Black man. At six two, I'm taller than average, and my skin, comparable to the rich caramel of a Werther's Original, thanks to my pops, is so smooth you wouldn't believe it's not butter. My teeth are status quo and powerful, also known as white and straight, and my hair is naturally wavy even though I usually keep it short with a tight fade. Goddamn! The kid looked good and he didn't even know it. I took a deep breath, hopped in the shower, and began my morning routine.

The house smelled as it always did at 7 a.m. — like coffee. It made me want to puke. After years of being surrounded by it, I could tell where a bean was sourced without even tasting it, which I would never do because I hate coffee. Yes. I. Hate. Coffee. It's black crack. Nothing more. Anyone who drinks coffee craves it, needs it, and shakes, scratches, jerks, and twerks for it every minute it's not coursing through their collapsed veins.

A "café" is a euphemism for a crack den. But instead of lying on a moldy sofa cushion stained with blood, sweat, and semen, folks with names like Chad, Kitty, and Trip sit down on plush leather-backed chairs licking the sweet white foam off of a seven-dollar venti, caramel, mocha, choca, cock-a-doodle-do, double-espresso long macchiato. But I digress.

This morning's narcotic of choice was an Indonesian blend from Sumatra if my nose was right. When it comes to coffee from a far-flung location, your normal run-of-the-mill American addicts either fall in love with the high-body, caramel, and chocolaty explosion of flavor or hate it.

"Coffee?" Ma asked, smirking as she filled her favorite "Coffee's for Christians" mug.

"Funny," I said, planting a kiss on her cheek and grabbing a banana.

"Darren," she said, staring at the banana. "You're forgettin' somethin'."

I stared at the banana, then at her, then at the photo of her, Pa, and me on the living-room wall. "My bad, Ma." I crossed the hardwood floor from the kitchen to the living room, leaned over, and kissed the glass protecting Pa's smiling, tanned, and clean-shaven Spanish face. "Mornin', Pa," I said, before returning to the kitchen.

Ma looked at her watch and sat next to me, staring. She was fifty but didn't look a day over forty. Her hair was always shoulder-length and relaxed. And with makeup, which I almost never saw her wear, she could pull off thirty-five. Back in the day, she was prom queen and had plans of being Miss America until her parents dissuaded her. But Ma's magic wasn't in her appearance, which used to get me into fights on the regular. It was in her ability to make you think you were meant for more, and almost believe it, just with a stare.

"What?" I asked.

"What *what*?" Her eyes smiled at me, ready. I turned my body into rubber, bracing for impact.

"When're you goin' to quit that job and go to college, Darren?"

Knew it. She'd asked me the same question for the last four years, in different forms. Like the time she told me how useful LinkedIn was for finding internships. Or when I found a new white button-up, brown leather belt, shoes, and khakis neatly folded on my bed with a note that said, "For campus visits!" *If she only knew why I stayed home, she wouldn't ask that question and do these things,* I thought. *But I'll die before I tell her.*

"I dunno. Jus' waitin' for the right opportunity, Ma. You know that. Plus, why you tryna get me up out the house, hmm? Gotta new man I dunno about?"

She sucked her teeth. "Don' be silly. You know I only have room for one man in my life. But I swear, if you jus' keep waitin' for the right opportunity, as you always say, and don' put that big ole brain to good use, it's

gonna get you in trouble. Mark my words."
She bent over, coughing like something serious was stuck in her throat.

I rubbed her back just like she did to me when I was a kid. She gripped my other hand and smiled.

"I'm okay, Dar. Don' worry 'bout me."

"But I do worry. You been coughin' like this for a month, Ma. Mus' be all those chemicals you messin' with at the factory."

"Well, let's make a deal," she said, wiping her mouth. "I'll stop messin' with all those chemicals when you get rich enough to take care of me. How's that sound?"

She was always looking to make a deal. I should've seen it back then — that Ma was the best saleswoman I knew. She'd made deals with me ever since I was a kid. A deal for me to go to bed by a certain time. A deal for us to take a trip to some random island if we ever won the lottery. A deal. A deal. A deal. Every day in my house was deals day; everything was up for negotiation.

"Deal," I said, kissing her forehead before jetting out.

It's important for you to know that we weren't poor, that not *everyone* living in what some white folks think is the "hood"

21

is poor. Thanks to Ma's parents, who passed when she was twenty, we owned a three-story brownstone in the heart of Bed-Stuy. And even with the rising property taxes, we made enough between the two of us to avoid the Key Food on Myrtle. We weren't middle class, but life isn't that bad when you own your home and earn side income from tenants.

Just as I did every day, I jumped down the stairs of 84 Vernon Avenue, jogged down the street, turned right on Marcy, and headed for the G train.

"Morning, Darren!" Mr. Aziz, the Yemeni owner of the corner bodega, shouted as he beat the living hell out of a speckled floor mat like it was a badass kid.

"Sabah al-kheir!" I shouted back, always trying my best to connect with local folks, both old and new.

But inner-city diplomacy was hard. Factories, restaurants, and every other building with a few cracks in it were being torn down to make way for high-rises and the influx of Bed-Stuy's newest, pigment-deficient residents, which is why I always found hitting the corners next to the G a fresh breath of air. No matter how early or late it was, the usuals were there, like gargoyles on a Gothic church.

"What's good, Superman?" Jason said, as our hands connected, palms popping and fingers snapping.

"Not much, Batman. Jus' headin' to work, you?"

He laughed, slapping his hands against his jacket. Even though it was May, it was already heating up, and I imagined him sweating like a suckling pig under there. With his baggy jeans, spotless Timberlands, and durag topped with a bucket hat, my man looked like an original member of the Wu-Tang Clan. We were both twenty-two, with the same athletic build, but somehow people always thought he was older. Must've been the manicured moustache and goatee.

"Already workin'," he said.

Man, this guy was a trip, but he was my best friend. Had been for more than seventeen years, when some clown was trying to press me for my Ninja Turtles backpack and Jason knocked him upside his head. When I asked him why he defended me, he just shrugged, and said, "Jus' 'cause someone wants somethin' doesn' mean they gotta take whatchu have." From then on, we were Raphael and Donatello, Batman and Superman, Kenan and Kel. But if I had known that being boys with him was going to land me in the deepest of shits, I may have just

23

laid him out then and there.

"What?" he asked, noticing my stare. "You ain' the only one tryna get up outta here."

"I'm not tryna get up outta here, man. I'm jus' waitin' for the right opportunity, tha's all. And when I get it, I'm not gonna switch up and bounce. You'll see me grabbin' a slice from there," I said, pointing at the Crown Fried Chicken next to Mr. Aziz's bodega. "There," I repeated, pointing at Kutz, the barbershop next to Crown Fried Chicken. "But you for sure won' see me there or there," I said, nodding at the new hipster bar and condo building that just went up.

Jason laughed. "Yeah, tha's what all them say until they leave yo' ass for a white world."

"I'm good where I'm at, Batman, and with the company I keep. Like your wack ass. But I gotta bounce. Whatchu readin' now, anyway?"

"Williams."

"Tennessee?"

"You buggin', son. John A. You?"

"Huxley."

"You need to stop readin' them old white writers, nigga."

"Aight, bro. I'll catch you later."

"Bet."

Wally Cat sat on an overturned plastic crate on the corner across the street reading the newspaper. I was rushing into the subway when I heard him say, "Aye, Darren!"

Something told me to ignore him and descend into the damp, urine-smelling subway, but I didn't listen.

I crossed the street. "What up, Wally Cat?"

"How's yo' momma?" He licked his lips like a sweaty pervert.

If I'd had the balls back then, I would've told Wally Cat that if he didn't stop asking about Ma I'd put him in a casket quicker than a steady diet of Double Big Macs with supersize fries could, but I didn't. Partly because I was shook, but mostly because I liked him.

You see, Wally Cat was the definition of an oldhead. But not the kind that just reminisced about all of the stuff they coulda, woulda, or shoulda done "back in my day." No, at sixty with a Hawaiian shirt, low salt-and-pepper afro, immaculate fedora, and burgeoning paunch, Wally Cat was a millionaire a couple times over. As Ma tells it, this guy used to live on a farm and study horses — their weights, temperaments, the way they moved and ate — then just roll up to a racetrack and almost always pick a winner.

One day he was scanning the upcoming races in the paper and noticed all these new companies popping up on the stock market. And that was that. He stopped betting on horses and started betting on companies. But the way he'd do it was by going to a company's office and speaking with the janitors, who always had the scoop on the CEOs, VPs, whether a company was sloppy or clean, punctual or late, and more. He turned a couple thousand into a couple million in less than a decade. All on his own. And then he started buying up property. But the thing is, what Wally Cat loved most in the world was just sitting on the corner, reading the newspaper, and watching people go by. Plus, he still used coupons.

"She's aight," I said, sitting on the crate next to him. Parents with children too young for school and too energetic for home arrived at the playground behind us, Marcy Playground, and let them loose. Screams filled the warm air.

"Good, good. You know, back in the day your momma was the finest woman in Bed-Stuy. So fine she didn' mess with no niggas like me. She had to have that high-quality, knowwhatImsaying? Like yo' daddy. He was one of those clean, *suavamente* Spanish nig-gas who had girls all over him, but he was aight." He removed his fedora, patting his sweaty forehead with a handkerchief.

"Yeah, man. I know." Not wanting to hear Wally Cat continue panting over the memory of Ma, I changed the subject. "Hey, Wally Cat. Why do they call you Wally Cat again?"

He sucked his teeth and looked over his shoulders. "Boy, don' ask me questions that don' *concern* you. You betta be askin' questions that give you information you can use in yo' own life. And no 'yes or no' questions. I'm talkin' the open-ended ones that'll crack your mind in half. Like why would the valedictorian of Bronx Science be wastin' his life away workin' at a damn —"

Reader: Wally Cat is many things, but a fool he is not. What he told me that day was a sales lesson in disguise. The quality of an answer is determined by the quality of the question. Quote that and pay me my royalties.

I was across the street before he could finish. I usually enjoyed chopping it up with Wally Cat, but on this day, the day my life changed forever, I just wanted to go to work, get back home, kick it with Soraya, and sleep.

After transferring from the G to the L at Metropolitan Avenue, I felt a tap on my shoulder. Thinking it was an accident, I turned my music up and closed my eyes. The bass from Meek Mill's "Polo & Shell Tops" invaded my ears like American troops in Iraq.

Another tap, this time more forceful. Whenever this type of thing happened, I just ignored it. But then a manicured hand grabbed my wrist and pulled it back, bringing me face-to-face with a slim Korean girl with curly brown hair and a jean jacket that fit just right.

"Darren Vender, the ghost of Bronx Science," she said, glossy lips breaking apart to reveal a Colgate smile.

I removed my earbuds. "Adrianna, what's up?"

"Not much, heading to Midtown. What about you?"

"Yeah, same. How've you been?"

"Oh, you know," she said. "I graduate from NYU next week. Actually on my way to an interview right now."

"That's awesome," I replied, shaking off the Bed-Stuy in my voice. "What's the interview for?"

"I'm sort of embarrassed to say, but it's one of those entry-level marketing positions at a startup."

Jesus. If she's embarrassed by an entry-level marketing position, especially before graduating from NYU, then I'm fucked.

"I'm sure you'll crush it," I said.

Thank God she didn't have X-ray vision. If she did, she would have seen the black apron in my backpack. Thank God twice that the train arrived at Union Square, ending the conversation.

"Thanks, I'll see you around," she said, taking off. A second later, I realized we were both hopping on the 6, so I headed to the opposite end of the train.

It's funny. Back then I didn't pay any attention to running into Adrianna; ghosts from the past always reappear in New York City. But now that I think back on it, maybe seeing her had something to do with the wild shit that happened next.

2

3 Park Avenue was its own world. Part office building, part high school, the forty-two-floor behemoth stuck out like a sore geometric brick thumb. Twelve elevators. Thirty companies. One Starbucks. One Darren Vender toiling away inside of that Starbucks for coming up on four years. Yes, after nearly four years, I was still in the same place. But at least I wasn't making the same drinks or even wearing the same lame green apron. The drinks became more ridiculous with every year. People were no longer satisfied with familiar flavors like gingerbread, pumpkin, and peppermint; now they needed Grasshopper Frappuccinos. Fucking grasshoppers.

As for the uniforms, well, most people don't know it, but Starbucks treats its aprons like martial-arts belts. Green aprons for beginners, black aprons for coffee masters, and purple aprons for gods. I was a black apron. After working there for four years, I was certainly the Head Nigga in Charge. But to be honest, this didn't mean much.

"Hey, Darren!" Nicole said, tying the straps of her green apron behind her back. Nicole was a large white woman with a pretty face. She was probably thirty-five and always in a great mood no matter how rough customers were.

When I came out, the place was packed. Carlos, Brian, and Nicole were filling cups, making change, and serving pastries as if it were a five-star restaurant. They were a motley crew — Carlos was an ex-con who'd committed a crime he wasn't allowed to discuss, Brian had charcoal skin with a face full of acne and a side of Tourette's, and Nicole, though well-meaning, only saw the world through rose-colored glasses — but I molded them all into soldiers. They were never late, always professional, and knowledgeable about every newfangled drink that corporate handed down to us. But most of all, they were just good humans. I don't have any siblings, so they were the closest thing to it. And even though I was the youngest, they saw me as an older brother.

As the line of morning addicts stretched out the door, I hopped into action. Now

I'm not trying to brag, but I was what you'd call a Starbucks prodigy. No one except Carlos, Brian, and Nicole knew it, but that didn't matter. I could remember someone's order from three months back, mix and match drinks to accommodate special tastes, and while doing all that, man two registers at once, shuffling back and forth like I was Billy Blanks or Richard Simmons.

We halved the line within ten minutes, and I hadn't even broken a sweat. Then I saw him. He had started coming in two months ago after his company moved in. Early mornings, he'd enter alone, always on the phone. At ten, he would return flanked by a group of men, all resembling Dobermans. In the afternoon, he'd come in again with a few younger people who beamed at him as he laughed, and he'd tell them to get whatever they wanted. Then late afternoon would arrive, and I never knew what to expect.

His appearance changed depending not on the time of day but on whom he was with. When alone, he was pensive; with his Dobermans, he was focused; with his young disciples, he shined brighter than the sun itself. He'd never order food, and despite his athletic build, well-groomed hair, and healthy olive complexion, I was sure he ran on nothing but coffee.

I can't tell you why I did what I did next; I suppose I just wanted to be helpful. He walked up to the counter, earbuds firmly in his ears, his face twitching in frustration. But instead of getting him his regular Vanilla Sweet Cream Cold Brew — I waited. He nodded his head, then finally said, "I know, I know. It's going to be fine, trust me. I've got the board handled."

I served customers on the adjacent register until he looked up, and said, "Hey. Vanilla Sweet Cream Cold Brew. Like always. You remember, right?"

By now, the last of the morning customers had grabbed their drinks, and it was just us at the counter.

"I don't think you want that today," I said.

I didn't know why my heart was furiously beating against my ribs. But looking back on it, I realize my body must've known that this was a pivotal moment in my life, that these supernatural turns of fate are rare.

Reader: What you are about to see is what happens when intuition overrides logic, which is the mark of any salesperson worth their salt. People buy based on emotion and justify with reason. Watch.

"Yeah, hold on," he said into his mic, staring at me. His eyes burned with anger. "Why wouldn't I want that today?" he asked, growing larger, like a lion with its prey in reach.

"Because I always hear you on your phone talking about efficiency. And the Vanilla Sweet Cream Cold Brew isn't built for that. You want something like —"

He laughed, but it wasn't the kind where someone actually finds something funny; it was the type where you're so pissed off, you're about to snap. He took a deep breath, slowly releasing it. "Listen, I'm good on whatever you're selling, just give me my regular. I don't have time for this."

Just give him his regular. Stop fucking around. But I didn't listen. What I said next had to be divine intervention because I didn't know where it came from.

"That's what the last five customers also said to me, until I gave them another option that solved a problem they didn't know they had."

He clenched his jaw and leaned toward me like he was going to Tyson my ear off.

"Because," I continued, too committed to stop, "believe it or not, when you come here and order something, you're not ordering a drink, you're ordering a solution. A solution to fatigue, irritability, and anything else that a lack of coffee means to you. So, if you'll indulge me, I'm confident that the Nitro Cold Brew with Sweet Cream is what you *actually* want. It has ten grams less sugar than your regular, forty fewer calories, and one hundred forty milligrams more caffeine. But at the end of the day, those are just numbers. So if you buy the Nitro Cold Brew and don't like it, you can come back, and I'll give you your regular free of charge. What do you think?"

Silence. Ten full seconds of silence. If you don't think ten seconds of silence is long, just count it out while picturing a grown man staring directly into your eyes as if he's going to snatch the black off you. *One. Two. Three. Four. Five. Six. Seven. Eight. Nine. Ten.* I was tempted to tell him to forget it, that it was my bad, but something told me not to. I just stared back into his eyes until he said, "Did you just try to reverse close me?" He relaxed his jaw and his eyes softened with curiosity.

It was then I realized Carlos, Nicole, and Brian had been staring at us the entire time. I felt their hearts collectively skip a beat when the guy spoke, and I remembered the color of the apron I was wearing, and that I was *the* HNIC. "I suppose I did," I said, nodding at Brian to make the guy's drink.

"What's your name?"

"Darren. Darren Vender."

"Rhett Daniels," he said, extending a hand over the counter. I quickly wiped the sweat off mine before gripping his.

"Nice to meet you, Rhett. I see you in here every day. Well, a few times a day, actually."

He laughed. Genuinely this time. "Yeah, I run on coffee. What do you do besides work here?"

"Read, watch movies, hang out with my girlfriend. Normal stuff guys get into in the city."

"And how much do you make?"

Damn, how much do I make? This guy was going in deep. I shrugged.

"Your drink is ready," I said, nodding toward the far side of the counter.

Rhett slowly walked over, never taking his eyes off me, grabbed the drink, and took a sip. "This is delicious. Thanks for the recommendation, Darren."

"No problem." I felt uneasy. Something had shifted.

"Listen, I gotta get to work. But here's my card. Why don't you swing by the office after your shift?"

Swing by the office? I had no clue what this guy was talking about. "For what?"

36

"An opportunity."

"What kind of opportunity?"

He was already walking out the double doors leading to the lobby. "Come by and you'll find out."

"So did you meet him?" Soraya asked, a film of sweat spreading across her naked body thick with curves all over. She twisted her long curly black hair into a knot.

My heart was still beating from our lovemaking session. I took a big gulp of cold water and collapsed back onto the pillow. "Nah."

She propped herself up on an elbow and raised a thick eyebrow at me.

"Why not?"

" 'Cause the whole thing was strange and mad fast," I said, distracted by her beautiful brown areolas. "Plus, I was jus' messin' around. I dunno what made me do it, but I sorta wanted to see if I could actually change this powerful white guy's mind."

"And you did," she said, tracing my chin with a slender finger. Shit gave me chills.

"Yeah, but I was jus' messin' around. I dunno what this guy actually wants. Plus, I'm too busy with everything else."

"Everything else like what, D? You're always sayin', 'I'm jus' waitin' for the right opportunity.' Isn' this it?"

"Nah, this isn' it. At least not what I envisioned."

"And what did you envision, Cassandra?"

I sat up. "Man, quit that Cassandra shit." I had to give it to her; like Ma, she knew how to push my buttons. We'd met when we were seven. She'd just moved to the States from Yemen, and Jason saw her at Marcy Playground playing alone. He ran to my house, and when I opened the door, he said he'd found an alien, pushing her in front of me. When I said, "Hello," she said, *"As-salamu alaykum!"* "See," he said, nodding in self-satisfaction.

We brought her up to show Ma, and Ma slapped both of us upside the head, and said, "She's not an alien, silly boys. She's jus' new. You better treat her like a queen." I'll skip the corny romantic shit, but we became best friends, and then, around middle school, became more than that, and have been together ever since, minus a few minor breakups. She was my Wonder Woman.

She laughed. "You know what my dad said about you?"

"Nah, what'd Mr. Aziz say about me?"

"He said you're a smart guy with a bright future. And, jus' from lookin' at you, the way you actually listen to people, and are always curious, that you're not like the other guys around here. That you're different."

"Different how?"

"I don' know. Jus' different. So keep it real with me. Is it really jus' not the right opportunity, or is it somethin' else?"

I turned away from her. She had the type of eyes that saw through you. "Somethin' else like what?"

"Like you bein' afraid of what could come of it but disguisin' that by sayin' it's not the right opportunity 'cause you wanna stay here and take care of Mrs. V when she's the last person who needs to be taken care of. Plus, she knows you're holdin' yourself back for her, D. She jus' wants you to get started with your life."

Damn. The pro of being with someone for more than half your life is that they know you better than you know yourself. The con of being with someone for more than half your life is that they know you better than you know yourself.

"I have started. What would I be afraid of?"

There was a knock at the door. "Dar, I brought some pizza home for us all to eat."

"Thanks, Ma. But who's us?"

She sucked her teeth behind the door.

39

"Don' think I don' know Soraya's in there. Hi, baby."

Soraya shifted under the covers, wrapping her naked body as if Ma had X-ray vision. "Hi, Mrs. V."

"Mr. Rawlings is comin' up to join us, so get dressed and come on out."

The good thing about living in a three-story brownstone was that there was plenty of room. Mr. Rawlings lived on the garden floor, Ma's bedroom was on the first, we had a large living room and kitchen on the second, and I had the entire third to myself. I'd told Ma I could stay on the first floor with her, to make room for another tenant, but she said that I was grown and that grown men need their space.

Even though we all had access to the back garden, Ma and I rarely went. First thing, Mr. Rawlings *loved* that garden. He tended it all day and night, even in the winter when he'd put up frost blankets, bedsheets, and heat lamps. It blew my mind to see radishes, broccoli, turnips, kale, spinach, and other vegetables sprouting when there was snow on the ground.

Second, the man was about as old as the earth itself. He was in his late seventies back then and had lived at 84 Vernon for decades before Ma inherited it. I'd never heard him talk about family, so I assumed he didn't have any. But after Ma's parents passed only months apart when she was twenty, he treated her like a daughter, and then when I came along, he treated me like a grandson. All this made Mr. Rawlings the man — a Bed-Stuy veteran to be respected.

Soraya and I entered the kitchen. "Hi, Mr. Rawlings," she said, planting a wet kiss on his bald, liver-spotted head. He was wearing his usual outfit: the Old Geezer™ starter kit equipped with soft-soled black leather shoes, gray slacks, and a tucked-in plaid shirt with a navy vest over it. Sometimes he exchanged the vest for suspenders. Yes, suspenders. His rosewood cane rested on the arm of his chair.

"Good evenin', Jasmine," he said, winking at her. Jasmine, of course, being the princess from *Aladdin.*

She pinched his cheek. "Don' start, old man." Like I said, the man was a Bed-Stuy veteran to be respected, but if you're going to dish it out, you also got to take it.

"Take a seat and let's say grace," Ma said from the head of the table, still rocking the clothes she always wore to and from work — a loose fitting white blouse tucked into blue jeans — smelling like chlorine. I knew breathing that shit in all day wasn't good for her, but she refused to quit, saying that she was good at her job and needed to feel good at something.

The four of us held hands and Ma prayed. "Dear Lord, thank you for your unconditional love, the opportunity you've afforded all of us to be able to sit down with one another, eat good food, not have to worry about where our next meal is goin' to come from, and —"

She pulled her hands away, her whole body convulsing like the cough was coming from somewhere deep inside of her. As if a monster had wrapped its phlegmy tentacles around her insides.

"Ma," I said, rubbing her back. "Spit it out. Whatever it is, spit it out. You'll feel better afterward."

"Thank you, baby. I'm alright. Let's finish up."

We grabbed hands again. "Sorry, Lord. Had a cough." The four of us chuckled. "Thank you for the opportunity to see another day. Dear Lord, I pray that you help Darren find his path and that you use him as an instrument to help others in the ways we all know he's intended to. I pray that Soraya continues to grow her father's empire of bodegas to the farthest edges of your green earth, and that Mr. Rawlings's garden continues to produce delicious vegetables and flowers for all of us to admire and enjoy. Amen."

"Amen."

"You know, Mrs. V," Soraya started, plopping a piece of pizza onto my plate. "You mentioned opportunity in your prayer tonight. What's funny is that D has jus' been presented with one but doesn' plan on takin' it."

The three of them glared at me as if I had been accused of a crime. I just kept eating.

"Well, boy, go on," Mr. Rawlings said, hitting me with those stank eyes only wrinkly-ass Black men know how to do.

"Yeah, Dar. Go on," Ma said, gripping the hell out of my hand.

"Ah, c'mon, Soraya. Why'd you have to bring it up? It's nothin', Ma. Some guy at work today, you know those white techie guys? He asked me to visit his office to talk."

"Whatchu mean, *talk*?" Mr. Rawlings asked. "What kinda *talk* he wanna do, askin' you to *talk* outta the blue like that?"

"It wasn' outta the blue," Soraya explained, jumping into the entire story. The double registers, what Rhett was like, how I convinced him to buy a different drink, the reverse close.

"Reverse what?" Mr. Rawlings asked.

"Sounds like one of those newfangled sex positions y'all young folk be pretzelin' yourselves into nowadays."

"Percy!" Ma shouted, slapping Mr. Rawlings's wrist. "And what, Dar? You didn' go to his office after work?"

"Nah," I said, preparing for whatever she was about to lay on me. But instead, she just pulled her hand away and looked down at the white crumbs on her plate. Then the sniffling came.

"C'mon, Ma." I felt like shit. Mr. Rawlings grabbed another slice of pizza, muttering to himself. And Soraya looked at me like she messed up, which she did.

"In the middle of every difficulty lies opportunity," Ma said, staring down at her plate. "You know who said that?"

I took a breath, shaking my head.

"It's somethin' your father used to always say. Whenever we were goin' through a tough time, or somethin' jus' wasn' workin' out like it was supposed to, he'd turn to me, and say, 'In the middle of every difficulty lies an opportunity, *amor*.' I always believed him. And he was always right. It's what I told myself when he passed and what I still tell myself today."

"Look here, boy," Mr. Rawlings said, staring me down.

44

I quickly looked up, then away.

"I said *look* at me," he repeated, sounding more serious than the time I accidentally crushed his English peas. "Young Black folk, even mixed-up Black and Spanish folk like yourself, don' get this type of opportunity too often.

"Back in my day, when a white man gave you an opportunity, it came at a cost. You could be his chauffeur, but had to always be available to drive him around no matter if you had plans with your family or not. You could vote, but someone would break your legs if you didn' vote for the candidate they wanted you to. But either way, an opportunity was an opportunity, and if you took it, and learned how to play their game, you could be successful."

But I don't want to play their game. I was fine doing my own thing. Working at Starbucks wasn't so bad. I had plenty of time to kick it with Soraya. And most important, I was there for Ma whenever she needed me. But it wasn't until she turned to me, tears running down her cheeks, that I actually considered seeing Rhett.

"Promise me you'll at least give this a chance. Whatever it is," Ma said. "That man must've seen somethin' in you, Dar. Somethin' that everyone in Bed-Stuy sees in you.

You owe it to yourself to follow up and see what he wants. Promise me."

I crossed my fingers behind my back and looked into her eyes.

"Aight, Ma. I promise."

3

I lied. I lied because I didn't want Ma to feel like I wasn't trying to better myself. I lied because of the stank eye Mr. Rawlings gave me as a string of cheese clung to his lip for dear life. But most of all, I lied because I was afraid. You see, it's easy for someone to walk around telling everyone that they're "jus' waitin'" for the right opportunity," but an entirely different thing when they actually receive it. An opportunity means change. An opportunity means action. But most of all, an opportunity means the chance of failure. And it's the potential for failure, more than failure itself, that stops so many people from beginning anything. Back then, I was no different.

When I walked into work the next morning, I received a roomful of applause. The room only contained three people, but it was a roomful of applause nonetheless.

"Man, you really gave it to that gringo,"

Carlos said, giving me a hearty dap and bringing it in so close I almost blacked out from the thick fog of vodka, weed, and cheap cologne.

"Uh, it was nothing," I said and headed to the back before noticing Nicole's wide-eyed look.

"Come here, Darren," she said, wrapping her thick, plush arms around me. "Where did that come from? It was like you transformed into someone else. Like the Hulk!"

"The Black Hulk, *hermano,*" Carlos added. "I knew somethin' was comin' when you hopped on both registers. You had this look in your eye, like you was the same person but sorta different. Like a superhero who sees the city burnin' down and you had to step in to help out. Except this Starbucks isn't like a city, but, wait, maybe it is; if you think about it, we gotta —"

"Yeah, I get what you're saying, Carlos," I said, deciding whether to call him out for being high, drunk, both, or something else. But every soldier deserves a break, so I dropped my bag, threw my apron on, and unlocked the front door.

When the room fell silent — that crisp silence before the first person walks in *clip-clopping* their expensive leather shoes like a horse — someone tapped my shoulder.

"Hey, Darren?" Brian said, looking in every direction except at me.

"Yeah?"

"You think you could, uh, you think you could — *shit!* — sorry. You think you could" — he quickly brought a hand to his mouth, muffling a still discernible *"Penis!"* — "Sorry, sorry."

Now, not everyone with Tourette's involuntarily curses like a sailor with syphilis. It's called coprolalia, and only about one in ten people with Tourette's has it. Brian Grimes — age twenty-six, born in Virginia, raised in Connecticut, avid Dungeons & Dragons player, and spectacular barber — was that one. And even though I'd never sat around a table and battled mythical beasts with him, we often bonded over comic books and our shared ironic hatred of coffee. He also gave me lifesaving shape-ups once in a while.

I put my hands on his shoulders, and said, "Close your eyes and take a deep breath."

I should also mention that, even though he was older than I am, Brian — perhaps because I was a Black man like him except with a little power — looked up to me. So, being the HNIC, I did my best to make him comfortable, put him at ease, and let him know he was doing a good job.

49

"Thanks, Darren. What I wanted to ask was if you think you could teach me what you did yesterday?"

"What did I do, Brian?"

"How you, uh, how you —"

"Take a breath, man. You know I'm here to help."

"How you did mind control on that guy? To buy the Nitro Cold Brew instead of his regular?"

I laughed. "It wasn't mind control, Brian. I don't know what it was, but it wasn't that."

"Yes, it was! The dude came in here wanting one thing and walked out with another. Not only that, but he *enjoyed* the other thing. It was like you put him under a spell. And I'm not saying I want to be a wizard or anything like that, or that I want to control what people drink, but I just want to be able to" — he paused to scratch at his face — "to be persuasive, you know? Like maybe if I can learn how to do that, I can get a girlfriend or something like that?"

I didn't want to break the bad news to him, but the power of persuasion probably wasn't going to do the trick as long as his face looked like a burnt pizza.

"Listen, Brian. I don't know how to do mind control, nor do I know how to be really persuasive. It was just something that happened in the moment. I'm sorry I can't be of more help, but what I can do is make sure you're as good a barista as possible so you can woo women with your coffee-making skills."

"Yeah, okay. But I just want to say one last thing."

"Go for it." The first *clip-clops* of the day walked in. Nicole and Carlos were handling them but would need backup soon.

"Most superheroes don't know they're superheroes until they get caught up in a moment, just like you. Something either overcomes them, showing them a glimpse of their hidden powers, or they're pushed so far past their limitations that they have no choice but to succumb to whatever makes them most special."

"Thanks, Brian. I'll keep that in mind. Now let's get to work." But in that very moment, his eyes went wide, his mouth fell half-open, and he raised a zombielike finger toward the door.

I turned around, and there was Rhett Daniels. He was walking in just like any other day, but unlike any other day, he didn't have earbuds in nor was he looking at his phone, chatting with his Dobermans, or trailed by faithful followers. He was staring at me.

And he was pissed.

He waited in line with the other addicts. But when he got to me, he just kept staring. I looked away.

"Can you come for a walk?" he asked, his voice calm.

"Uh, no, I need to man the Starbucks." I was starting to sweat.

"No, Darren, it's fine. We'll man the fort while you talk," Nicole chimed in out of nowhere.

"Yeah, man, we got you," Carlos added.

Rhett winked at them, then looked at me. "So?"

Fuck it. I untied my apron, put it down on the counter, and followed him out the door and through the lobby.

"Where to?" I asked, realizing I hadn't been outside 3 Park Avenue at 8 a.m. on a workday in years. Twenty-first-century yuppies walked through the revolving doors like worker bees returning to the hive.

"Wherever you want. You hungry?" He scanned his phone before slipping it into his pocket.

"No, I'm good." I didn't owe him an explanation or an apology. But for some reason, I felt like I did. It was as if he had a gravitational pull, and if you got too close, it was impossible to escape.

"Great, let's get pancakes."

We walked for only a few minutes, but our silence made those minutes feel like days.

He opened the door to a diner named Bobby's Big Breakfast, BBB for short, and we sat down in a booth in the back.

"So, pancakes," he said, ignoring the menus in front of us.

"Pancakes." I nodded, avoiding eye contact. *I'm trapped, but it'll be over soon.*

An eager blonde waitress appeared with pen and pad in hand and stared at him — his unblemished skin, his defined jawline with light black stubble — as though she were hypnotized. *I know this guy is attractive, but damn. Snap out of it!*

Rhett ran his hand through his tousled brown hair, no doubt achieved through relentless scrunching and spritzing, and smiled. "Hi."

"Oh," the waitress replied, waking from her daydream. "Sorry, what'll it be?"

"Two black coffees and a stack of banana pancakes for me. And blueberry pancakes for my friend," he said.

"Can I get you anything else?" she asked, drooling over him now like a dog outside a butcher shop.

He flashed a flirtatious grin. "No, that'll

be all. Thank you."

"Suit yourself," she said, and walked away.

"You cool with that, Darren?"

"Um, yeah, sure."

More silence. Exactly one and a half minutes of silence until our coffee came out, and another six and a half minutes until our steaming plate of pancakes arrived, a mountain of chocolate chips on both of them.

"Something a little extra for you boys," the waitress said.

I sat there, wrinkling and flattening my pants. The aroma rising from the coffee entered my nostrils. Guatemalan.

"You haven't touched your coffee," he said, nodding at my cup.

"Uh, yeah, I —"

"Take a sip, it's delicious. It's not Starbucks" — he smiled — "but it's still good."

I stared at the black pool in my cup, saw my watery reflection. *No fucking way.*

But Rhett nodded at the cup again.

I looked back down into the mug. *Fuck you.* I lifted it to my lips and took a sip. *Fuck you to hell!*

"Pretty good," I said. I was surprised; it wasn't half bad.

He laughed. "What did I tell you? Also, has anyone ever told you that you look like Martin Luther King?"

"Uh, no. You're the first."

He leaned back. "Well, you do. So, where are you from?"

"Bed-Stuy."

"Chris Rock, nice," he said, clearing all of the melted chocolate chips from the top of his stack before cutting it up piece by piece.

"Most people only know it for Jay-Z," I replied, surprised.

He continued to cut his stack into little layered triangles. "Most people only know what other people talk about. But what about school? Where'd you go?"

"Bronx Science. I was valedictorian."

He stopped cutting his pancakes and looked up at me. "So you're either incredibly smart or just someone who knows how to do what's asked of them incredibly well. Which is it?"

I looked down at my leaning tower of pancakes, suddenly hungry. "I'm still not sure."

"And what about college? Where'd you go?"

"I didn't go to college."

"Why not?"

"Just wasn't for me." I wasn't about to tell this guy my life story no matter how deep into his gravitational field he pulled me.

"College wasn't for the valedictorian of

one of the best high schools in America? C'mon. Don't give me that."

"It wasn't. I had — I have other priorities."

"And what did your mom and dad think about these other priorities?"

"Well, my dad is dead and my mom wasn't too happy about it. Still isn't, really," I said, taking a sip.

"Sorry about your dad. What happened, if you don't mind me asking?"

"It's fine. He died when I was two. He was a handyman and, after years of saving up, finally had enough to start his own business. He bought a van, and on the same day he got it, he was speeding home when a bus slammed into the driver's side."

Rhett took deep breath. " 'If we live, we live for the Lord; and if we die, we die for the Lord. So, whether we live or die, we belong to the Lord.' "

"What's that?"

"Romans 14:8. But I'm sorry. That must've been tough."

"More for my mom, yeah. I didn't really know him."

"And do you have siblings?"

"No, it's just me and my mom." I saw a brief flicker in his eyes, like he saw something he couldn't see before, an answer he was looking for.

"So you didn't go to college because you didn't want to leave your mom alone at home. And you work at Starbucks because it keeps you busy, especially since you're the boss. But it doesn't demand too much of you. So you're still able to get out of the house and feel productive, but there's a large part of you that can't help but ask, 'Is this really it?' "

The fuck? It felt like the guy jumped inside my head, looked around, took a shit, and left. If Brian thought I was capable of mind control, I wanted to see what he'd make of Rhett. I took a bite of my cold pancakes, shifting in my seat until I mustered up the courage to speak.

"Yeah. Maybe."

"But you still haven't been tested, so you just tell everyone you're 'waiting for the right opportunity,' right? So here it is. What if I told you that you could learn how to do what I do?"

Ah, we've finally arrived. Here is what this entire breakfast has been building up to.

"And what is it that you do, Rhett?"

"Deals, Darren. I do deals and I sell the one thing that everyone wants."

"Which is?"

"A vision."

57

"What kind of vision?"

"A vision for the future. I sell people on the opportunity to live their lives to the fullest, and I'll tell you, people will pay an absolute fortune for that. But beyond that, what we do up there," he said, pointing toward the upper floors of 3 Park Avenue, "is help people. We're changing the world through what we do, making a positive impact, and having a blast while doing it."

"So why do you need me?"

"I don't need you, but I want you. What I saw yesterday was something I haven't seen in years: raw talent, confidence, and the ability to make me think differently. You convinced me to buy what you were selling because my choice would benefit *me*, not *you*. Having you up there," he said, nodding at 3 Park Avenue again, "would have a large impact on my organization and an even more life-changing impact on you."

My heart was racing. My mouth went dry. I gulped down half a glass of water. "I don't know, Rhett. What happened yesterday was just me getting caught up in the moment. I don't think I'm the type of person who could sell whatever vision you're talking about."

He reached over and grabbed my shoulder. Hard. "Listen to me, Darren. You were meant for more than pushing caffeinated water. Do you want to sell that shit for the rest of your life, or do you want to come with me and change the world?"

While the prospect of changing the world sounded great, I still wasn't sold. Like he said, I was comfy. I had Soraya, Ma, Mr. Rawlings, Jason, a whole brownstone floor to myself, a decent salary; and I wasn't in need of anything I couldn't afford. I felt like I was already making a difference for those who mattered most no matter what he thought. But I would've been lying if I said I wasn't curious about why Rhett selected me, about what he actually wanted.

"I'm sorry, Rhett," I said as he paid for our meal. "But I'm not the person you think I am."

Once we got outside, he wrapped his muscular-but-not-beefy arm around me as a best friend would. The embrace was strange but comforting, especially when paired with his cologne, which was woodsy with hints of lavender, as if to say, *I'm manly, but that doesn't mean I can't cry.*

"You're right, Darren. You're not the person I think you are. You're probably a lot better. But let's do this. Just come up to the office and see what the vibe is. If you don't like what you see, you can jump in the elevator and leave. I'll go back to being the guy ordering coffee from you, and you'll go back to being the guy who's getting it for me. Sound fair?"

Reader: Ending a pitch with "Sound fair?" is a common sales tactic. Most people don't want to be viewed as unfair or unreasonable, so they're more likely to give in, especially when what someone is pitching does sound fair enough. Give it a try and let me know how it goes.

If I had known where that question would lead me, I might have thought twice about going up to the office. I might have shrugged his arm off my shoulder, and said, "Thanks, but no thanks," returned to my soldiers, and put my black apron back on. I might have also just hopped on the subway, went to Bed-Stuy, and buried my face in Soraya's chest, seeking refuge somewhere safe. But I didn't.

"Yeah," I said. "Sounds fair."

We crossed Park Avenue and entered the building. But instead of cutting left for Starbucks, I went straight: across the lobby, past the security guards, and into an elevator headed for the thirty-sixth floor.

4

We entered the elevator. A woman already inside pressed the button for the thirtieth floor. On seeing Rhett, she smiled.

"Which floor?" she asked, beaming like a firefly's ass.

"Thirty-six, thanks," Rhett said, grinning at me.

She folded her arms, squinting. "So you're the floor making all of the noise and having the best parties, huh?"

Rhett backed into a corner, raising his hands in surrender. "Guilty."

"Rumor has it that you have to pay the security guards not to call the cops when you all get too rowdy."

"The truth is that it's usually the security guards who are the rowdiest when they hang with us."

The elevator bell rang, signaling we were at her floor. She walked out but not before looking back at Rhett.

"So, are you going to invite me to one of your parties?"

"Every Friday at six," he said, giving her a mock salute.

As the elevator climbed, the sound of bass-heavy music shook the cab like a mild earthquake. The higher we went, the more violent it became. My heart beat irregularly at the thought of cables snapping and me plummeting thirty-six floors to my death.

"What is — ?"

Rhett placed a soft finger on my lips. "This is where men and women are made, Darren. If you don't just survive but thrive here, you will be able to do anything."

The doors opened to an elevator bay with see-through glass doors to the left and a pair with frosted glass to the right. Through the transparent doors sat a young white girl with short hair, glasses, and sharp features. A blond guy, who could've been her twin, leaned over her desk and caressed her face before she slapped his hand away. But it was the frosted doors to the right that the noise blared from.

Fuzzy silhouettes moved beyond those doors: jumping, running, and whizzing by all to the sound of Wiz Khalifa's "We Dem Boyz." Something small and round, like the Golden Snitch from Harry Potter, ricocheted off the glass.

Rhett turned to me. "You ready?"

I straightened out my shirt and nodded, unsure of what I had to be ready for.

The minute Rhett opened the door, something flew at his face, and before I could register what it was, I found one in my hand.

"Whoa, the brother can catch!" someone shouted from the lawless scene in front of us.

Brother?

"Good reflexes," Rhett said, pointing to the purple stress ball in my hand.

Everything happened so quickly, I hadn't even realized someone had thrown one at me. I turned it over and saw the word SUMWUN in white cursive. When I looked back up, my eyes readjusted to the chaos in front of me.

A sea of people ebbed and flowed, spilling out of every corner, entering, leaving, standing on desks, huddling in offices, sitting under tables with fingers in their ears as mouths moved at hyperspeed, throwing balls at one another. *Is this real or was there something in those pancakes?*

People zipped by on scooters with mugs of hot coffee in their hands. Clusters of guys and girls wrote on floor-to-ceiling windows overlooking the East River like they were in

63

A Beautiful Mind. Dogs barked and chased one another. A few people wielded purple-painted Louisville Sluggers behind others sweating on phones, as if they would bash their heads in for saying one wrong word. There was a girl walking around with a piglet in her arms, petting it as she laughed into the headset nestled in her orange-red hair.

I turned to Rhett, who was casually scrolling through his phone. "What is this?"

"This?" He shrugged, smiling at me. "This is the sales floor at 9 a.m. What else?"

"But how can anyone work?" I swung my head around, searching for an answer. "People are on the phones, but there's music blasting from — where's the music even coming from?"

"Everywhere. We had speakers installed in every room, even the gym. It's good for parties, but it also lets everyone know when we're celebrating a new deal, like now."

"Gym?"

"Yeah, you wanna see?"

"Sure."

"Twenty K, Rhett!" an indistinct voice yelled from the void.

"Throw it up!" Rhett said, pointing toward the whiteboard nailed to the wall next to us.

"Already did!"

We took a right and walked down a narrow corridor until we arrived at a door with a workout calendar on it. Rhett opened it. Inside was a small spotless gym with weight benches, dumbbells, treadmills, a flat-screen TV, and other meathead paraphernalia. A white guy with Mediterranean features — black hair, chestnut eyes, olive skin — and more chiseled than Adonis and Hercules put together abused a leather punching bag.

"Mac, Darren. Darren, Mac," Rhett said.

I had seen Mac in Starbucks before, accompanying Rhett on some of his afternoon coffee runs, so I stood there waiting for him to recognize me as the "Starbucks guy," but he just pulled off his gloves and extended a calloused hand. I extended mine and he squeezed it, almost bringing me to tears, but I didn't relent. I just held his stare until he laughed and smacked the shit out of my back.

"Good man! Thought you would've backed down after a few seconds, but you didn't. Solid."

"Darren," Rhett said, stretching his hands around. "This is the gym. Mac's our in-house personal trainer. We have locker rooms with showers, soap, towels, and anything else you need. Let's continue.

"The office is one large bisected circle," he explained as we passed a quiet group with their heads down in their laptops.

"This is where marketing sits. They usually spend the day writing copy, emails, working on ads, and supporting sales."

A pale white woman with brown hair and freckles looked up, waved to me, then focused back on her computer.

"Jen," Rhett said, causing the woman to look up again. "Meet Darren. Darren's going to be one of our new SDRs."

"New what?" I asked.

Jen stood, grabbed my hands, and got so close to my face that I swore she was about to kiss me. Like Mac, I had seen Jen in Starbucks on dozens of occasions, to the point that I knew she preferred soy milk over whole, yet when she looked into my eyes, it was as if she were seeing me for the first time. *How does no one recognize me?*

"It's so nice to meet you, Darren! We can't wait to have you on board. If you're getting the royal treatment from the king himself, you must be special. By the way, has anyone ever told you that you look like Sidney Poitier?"

"Um —"

"Really?" Rhett said, incredulity in his voice as he stared at Jen.

Finally, we can stop all this bull —

"I thought MLK," he finished.

"No." Jen shook her head. "Definitely Sidney."

"Uh, no, never got that before. But thanks."

We walked on, passing offices featuring different scenes like flipping through TV channels: white people huddled around a table, shouting into a phone; the blond guy from earlier writing on a whiteboard as white guys and girls nodded along; two white guys doing push-ups, slapping their hands together after each one; a pack of white girls eating salads.

"Hey," I started to ask, "where's all the Bla—"

"Heads up!" someone yelled before two scooters flew past us.

We came to the far side of the office, where there was a meeting room that ran the length of the hallway.

"This is Qur'an, the main conference room," Rhett said, opening the heavy wooden doors and pulling out a leather-backed chair for me. I took a seat in front of the long mahogany table.

"Sort of corporate, but we like it. Makes us feel more serious." He pointed to the table studded with triangular conference

67

phones. There was a large flat-screen TV on the wall across the room, and we were surrounded by glass. Glass floor-to-ceiling windows, like the ones on the sales floor, and clear glass walls. *But why the hell is it called Qur'an?*

Before I could take it all in, a small, sweaty, red-faced guy with hair sticking out in every direction burst in.

"Rhett," he said, breathing heavily.

"What is it, Chris?"

"Lucien called. He wants to chat. Now."

Rhett waved him off. "I'll call him later. Don't worry about it."

"But, Rhett —"

"Dammit, Chris. I said I'd call him later. Stop worrying, will you? It'll all be fine. I promise."

"Stop worrying? How in the world can we stop worrying when the board is breathing down our fucking necks, Rhett? You tell me how and I will."

Rhett didn't say anything. He just looked at him. Chris nodded and left as quickly as he had come.

"So," Rhett said. "What do you think of all of this?"

"I don't even know what all of this is, man. Is this some kind of illegal operation or an insane asylum?"

He laughed, squeezing my bicep. "Definitely not illegal, but I can't say the same for this not being an insane asylum. Most of us here are crazy, crazy enough to think we have what it takes to change the world and all of that other startup bullshit. But here it's true. You saw it for yourself, Darren. The burning passion, the unrestrained madness, the electricity. Can you feel it?"

I'd be lying if I said I couldn't. There was something like lightning in the eyes of everyone I saw. It burned through each of them, like it would destroy them if it wasn't put to use. It was something I also used to feel before I allowed myself to become complacent.

"I can," I said, looking down the length of the table. "But I definitely don't have that spark, Rhett. At least not anymore. I don't even know what you do here."

"I told you; we sell a vision."

"Yeah, but *what* vision? What does the company actually do?"

"Don't worry about that yet. I want you to be as pure and pristine for your interview as possible. We can discuss specifics afterward. I promise."

"Interview? What're you talking about? I need to get back downstairs, man. The Starbucks could be on fire and I wouldn't even know."

He yanked me up by my elbow and pushed me toward the windows. "What do you see, Darren?"

I looked down and flinched. Gridlocked taxis, buses, and trucks flooded the street below us; cyclists wove in and out of them like threadless needles; smoke rose from food carts on the corners; men and women hurried across the avenues, some likely wondering if the babysitter would work out, others worrying if they'd be able to make rent. From where I stood, I felt like God.

"I see New York," I said. "It's messy as hell but beautiful."

He stood behind me, holding my shoulders. "Then if your precious Starbucks was on fire, right now, and the whole building was going down, wouldn't you at least want to be up here with the view?"

"Uh."

He pressed a button on a conference phone.

"Hello?" a voice answered.

"Yeah, Clyde. Qur'an."

Seconds later, the tall blond guy who had been caressing the receptionist's face strode in, a smirk slowly forming on his face.

"Clyde, Darren. Darren, Clyde."

I extended my hand. "Nice to meet you, Clyde." His deep-blue eyes resembled whirlpools ready to swallow me at a moment's notice.

"Oh," he said, grinning from ear to ear as he shook my hand. "*This* is going to be fun."

"I'll leave you two alone," Rhett said, patting my shoulder before walking out.

I turned to Clyde, who was sitting at the head of the table. "Where's he going?"

"Doesn't matter," he said, crossing his legs, laying his hands flat.

I wasn't sure what the hell to do. The guy just kept staring. After a few endless minutes, he took a deep breath and slapped the table.

"Where are you from, Darrone?"

"Bed-Stuy. And it's Darren."

"Sure. You're quite a ways from home, no?"

"Where are you from?"

"Greenwich."

"Then I'd say you're even farther from home than I am."

He laughed, then nodded, never taking his eyes off me. "It sure doesn't feel like that. So how do you know Rhett?"

"We recently met. I can't say I really *know* him, but he seems like a nice guy."

"Yeah, he *is* a nice guy. Crazy, brilliant, and manic, but nice nonetheless. Where did you meet?"

I didn't want him to know anything about me. He reeked of privilege, Rohypnol, and tax breaks, which rubbed me the wrong way. But instead of making something up, I figured telling the truth could be in my favor since Starbucks was a common place where people in the pigment-deficient world met.

"Starbucks."

He clapped his hands and threw his head back. "I knew it! Here I was, trying to place you. I knew you looked familiar, but I wasn't sure if it was in the way most Black people look alike. Not in a racist way, of course. You're the dude downstairs who works at Starbucks, aren't you? Frankly, I almost missed it. I doubt anyone else here will even recognize you without your uniform."

Shit. I knew I'd seen him somewhere before, no doubt walking in with Rhett and ordering some disgusting drink. But I wasn't sure. In the same way Clyde claimed that all Black people looked alike, I couldn't tell one tall blond WASP from another. It was as if they were agents straight out of *The Matrix.* But instead of wearing black suits, they wore Ralph Lauren polos, Vineyard Vines pullovers, Easter-egg-colored slacks, and brown leather belts with matching Sperrys.

"Yeah, that's me." There was no use hiding it now. I had been found out. And weirdly enough, I felt relieved. This whole hallucination was about to end, and I could wake up and return to my normal life.

He looked me up and down. "Has anyone ever told you that you look like Malcolm X?"

"Uh, no," I said. "But I recently got Martin Luther King and Sidney Poitier."

"Hmm. Well, you do. Where do you like to go out?"

Is this a joke? I thought that after discovering I worked at Starbucks he would've pressed a little button on one of the phones and called Rhett to escort me out.

"I don't really go out much. I'm usually at work, home, or hanging with my girlfriend."

He raised an eyebrow. "Girlfriend? How long have you been dating?"

"It's hard to say. We've been on and off for about nine years now if middle school counts. But I guess I'd say six years since that's when we first became serious."

He slapped the table. I flinched. "On and off, huh? I know how that is, brother. I've been on and off with a handful of girls. Where's she from?"

"Yemen, originally," I replied, unsure why he was so interested in Soraya. But the way he was acting made me feel like I was just chopping it up with someone instead of being grilled.

"Arab, nice. I had one of those once. From Lebanon. You'd think they'd be all covered up and shy, but I gotta tell you, she wasn't a hijab-wearing Muslim, that's for sure." He winked.

I swallowed the anger bubbling up in my throat.

He leaned in closer. "Listen, I'm not allowed to ask certain questions during interviews. At least that's what I was told. You can't ask things about race, gender, age, blah, blah, blah. But," he said, pointing at me, "*this* isn't really an interview, is it, Darrone? More like a chat between two dudes getting to know each other, right?"

"Uh, I guess so." It didn't feel like any interview I'd had before. I didn't even know what the job I was not interviewing for was. Or what the company actually did.

"Good," he said, leaning back and putting his feet on the table, inches from where I sat. I could see dirt in the cracks on the soles of his Sperrys and noticed that he wasn't wearing socks. It was warm out, but *shit.*

"How old are you?" Clyde asked.

"Twenty-two."

"Nice, I'm only two years older than you." I nodded.

"How did you end up at Starbucks?"

"I needed a job and applied four years ago. Been there ever since."

"Christ, you've been slinging coffee for four years? Couldn't you have gotten another job?"

"I guess, but it's easy and leaves me time to do other things."

"You guess," he said, slowly turning the words in his mouth as if they were hard candies. "You guess. You keep saying you guess. Why do you keep saying that?"

"Um, I don't know."

"And those 'uhs' and 'ums.' " He swung his feet off the table and pointed at me. "And the way you're sitting, slumped over, twisting your hands under the table. I can see your wrists moving. Are you nervous?"

I hadn't noticed I was twisting my hands, but when I looked down, I saw that I was. *What the hell is going on?*

"Uh, I don't think so."

"There it is again!" he said, like he'd found a stain on his favorite pair of Dockers. "The 'uhs' and you not being sure about yourself. How can you not know if you're nervous? It's your body, isn't it? At twenty-two, do you not know your own body?"

"Well —"

"Well what? You're not making coffee anymore, *brother.* Tell me what we do here."

"You, uh —"

"Cut out the 'uhs' and 'ums,' brother. They make you sound retarded. You're not retarded, are you?"

My knee was bouncing up and down so hard that I thought I was going to break through the floor. I curled my hand into a fist, ready to either knock this WASPy mother-fucker out cold or just leave without looking back. But that's what he wanted, and I wasn't going to give him the satisfaction of getting it.

"You sell a vision," I spat.

He rolled his eyes, waving his hand around. "Anyone can say that. You probably heard Rhett say that. But what is it, *exactly,* that we do here at Sumwun?"

"I don't know."

"You don't know? Then why the fuck are you sitting in front of me, taking up my precious time?"

"Because Rhett brought me up here," I said, running out of air. "I didn't even know

I was going to be interviewed for something today. I'm supposed to be at work."

"First off, this isn't an interview, remember? Second, you'll be back making me drinks in no time. Don't worry about that, *brother.* I just have a few more questions, then we're done. Tell me what you think Rhett sees in a kid from Bed-Stuy who sells coffee."

"I don't know," I said, wondering the same thing. I didn't belong there. I wasn't one of those people, and I damn sure didn't want to sit in front of this future white-collar criminal anymore.

"I'll tell you what I do know, Darrone. Or rather, Buck. I'd call you Starbucks, but it's too long, so Buck will have to do. You don't mind, do you, Buck? No, I didn't think so. So I'll tell you what I do know. I know that Rhett likes to take a shot on people like him, hustlers, kids he thinks are doing nothing with their lives but just need a chance. Sometimes it works out; most of the time it doesn't. You, Buck, would be one of the times it doesn't. Trust me. So I'll spare you the agony and walk you out."

He stood and opened the heavy door of the conference room, waiting for me to leave.

But I didn't get up. I stared down at the

table, the knots of wood frozen in polyure-thane coating like prehistoric bugs in amber. "You don't fucking know me." I was en-raged.

It would've been easier to forget every-thing and go back down to Starbucks, but I couldn't. This motherfucker had no idea who I was, anything about my life, and what I was and wasn't capable of. In that mo-ment, it wasn't about proving anything to him; it was about proving everything to myself. That I could do more. That I didn't have to be held down by my fear of the unknown and *what-ifs.*

He looked over his shoulder. "Excuse me?"

"I said" — I stared him in the face — "you don't fucking know me. You have no idea who I am and what I can or can't do. You sit up here on your precious thirty-sixth floor looking down on people like me, people who you think are hopeless and wasting the air you breathe. But you don't know me. I can outwork you and anyone on this floor. It doesn't matter if I don't know what the company does or even what I'd have to sell. I know that I can do what you do and do it better. Because, Clyde, you probably never had to work for anything in your entire fucking life.

"You're from Greenwich, one of the richest towns in America. I grew up in Bed-Stuy, *brother,* where most people fight, struggle, and claw to pay rent that's rising because of trust-fund babies like you who want to buy bigger apartments at half the price. So don't tell me you know me, because you don't."

He closed the door and I felt trapped, ready to swing on him if he tried anything slick.

"There it is," he whispered, swinging around and grinning wider than when he first came in. "There it fucking is, Buck!"

He gave me a round of applause, walked over to a phone, and pressed some buttons.

"Yeah?" It was Rhett.

"He's ready," Clyde replied, shoving an open hand toward me.

I still didn't know what the company did or what I would be doing for them, but I grabbed his hand and shook it. Deep down, I knew Clyde was right. Whatever happened next, I was ready.

■ ■ ■ ■

II.
QUALIFYING

■ ■ ■ ■

Most people want to avoid pain,
and discipline is usually painful.
— JOHN C. MAXWELL

II

wash, a stranger to the wives of minimum
wage. Then he told me they'd pay me
$40,000 a year with at least $5,000 on top
of that if I hit my goals.

"What? $45,000 a year? You bout to be
richer than that cracker kid in Home Alone
bout." Mr. Rawlings shouted, banging his
redwood cane on the floor and spittin'
charred hamburger all over the table.

5

"And then what happened?" Ma asked, tearing a piece of flesh off her signature well-done-but-really-almost-burnt-to-a-crisp burger and cracking it in her mouth.

Mr. Rawlings, Soraya, and Jason were over, likely wishing Ma had ordered out. As far as anyone was concerned, our home was their home, and in some ways, the family you choose can be stronger than the one you're given or, in my case, missing.

"Then the other guy, Rhett, walked in and slapped me on the back so hard he knocked the wind outta me. He sat down at the head of the table, and the white boy, Clyde, sat across from me. Rhett asked how much money I was makin'. I told him about $9 an hour. Around $19,000 a year. He looked at Clyde, then back at me, and asked how the hell I was survivin' in New York City.

"He ran his hand through his silky hair, like some movie star, you know, and said he wasn' a stranger to the woes of minimum wage. Then he told me they'd pay me $40,000 a year with at least $25,000 on top of that if I hit my goals."

"What? $65,000 a year! You 'bout to be richer than that cracker kid in *Home Alone,* boy!" Mr. Rawlings shouted, banging his rosewood cane on the floor and spitting charred hamburger all over the table.

"That's more than I make, baby," Ma said, grabbing my hand with tears in her eyes. "And I've been workin' at the Clorox Company for over two decades."

I knew she was happy for me, but I can't lie, something felt strange about making $65,000 a year for sitting in a room and talking on the phone while Ma, a chemical process operator, stood on her feet all day breathing in God knows what.

"I'm proud of you, D," Soraya said, rubbing my dick under the table. I spit bits of charred burger all over.

Ma brought out a cheap bottle of champagne and poured everyone a glass. "You want one, Dar?"

"No thanks, Ma."

"Ah, c'mon, boy," Mr. Rawlings pressed. "Nothin' wrong with a li'l bubbly every once in a while. It's not like you 'bout to go lose your damn head and gamble your life savin's away."

That's oddly specific.

Everyone raised their glasses. I toasted with a cup of Mountain Dew. "To my baby, Dar," Ma said. "Thank the Lord for puttin' his hands on him and settin' him on the path of success, like we all knew he was destined for. Cheers."

"Cheers," everyone echoed. Except Jason.

"So what is it you gon' be doin' anyway?" Mr. Rawlings asked, topping his glass off.

"Well, I don' really know," I said, realizing I still had no idea what Sumwun did.

Mr. Rawlings hit me with the stank eye. "You *don'* know? How you gon' be up in there making $65,000 a year without knowin', boy? Is this one of those Wall Street scams where we gon' find you on TV one day, reporters sayin' you played old folks for their pensions?"

The table shook with laughter. "Nah, I don' think so, Mr. Rawlings. After I signed some papers, they said I was gonna get unlimited vacation, health benefits, one thousan' stock options, and a 401(k), though. There's also a gym, you can bring pets, and they play a lot of music. I'm sure I'll find out more on Monday."

"Things have changed," Ma said. "Back in my day, no one was gettin' unlimited

85

vacation or had gyms inside of offices. I'm sure it's gonna be quite the place to work, Dar."

"Who the hell needs a gym in a damn office?" Mr. Rawlings asked, twisting his head around. "And animals runnin' all up in there like it's a damn farm? Sounds funny to me." He stuffed his face with potato chips, washing them down with more champagne.

"Aye," I said, turning to Jason. "You sorta quiet, bro. You good?"

He grabbed a second rock-hard patty and took a brave bite. "Yeah, bro. Jus' don' forget *those* people ain' *your* people. It's easy to get it twisted. Damn, Auntie, these burgers are type delicious."

"Eat as many as you like, baby," Ma said, as she walked into the living room. "And since we're all talkin' news, I got somethin' interesting in the mail today." She returned with an envelope.

NEXT CHANCE MANAGEMENT was typed on the front. "What's this?" I asked, removing the letter.

Ma smiled. "Read it."

Dear Mrs. Vender,
    I hope this letter finds you well.
    My name is Richard Lawson and I'm

86

writing to you on behalf of Next Chance Management, a real estate firm specializing in high-value properties throughout New York City, including Bedford-Stuyvesant. We've worked with folks like yourself for years, helping them sell their properties in order to move somewhere more comfortable.

If you should ever want to discuss selling your property, especially in today's climate, where folks want to live in up-and-coming neighborhoods such as your own, please give me a call at 212.781.9258 or email me at r.lawson@nextchancemanagement.com.

To be frank, the market won't stay like this forever. As time goes on, your property taxes will rise, making remaining in the neighborhood more financially difficult than it has been to date. We're currently in conversations with a few of your neighbors, Mr. Jones, Mrs. Williams, and others, and would be happy to run you through some numbers.

Again, feel free to reach out at your earliest convenience, but we'll also be in touch should we not hear from you.

Sincerely,
Richard Lawson
Next Chance Management

"Frederick and Maisal are sellin' their houses?" Mr. Rawlings shouted. "Have they lost their goddamn minds?"

"Ma, you're not gonna reply to this, are you?"

"Of course not, Dar. But it's good to know we have options in case it ever comes to it."

My heart beat faster than when I was with Clyde. I couldn't imagine Ma selling the house; the house I grew up in; the house Pa repaired from top to bottom with his two hands. "If it ever comes to what?"

"I'm jus' sayin', if we ever needed the money, it's good to know we'd be able to get it."

I grabbed her hand harder than I wanted to. "Ma, we will *never* need to sell the house. With my new job, I promise that. Promise me you won' contact that man. Promise me."

She patted my hand. "I promise, Dar. There's nothin' to worry about. It was jus' a letter."

After dinner, Soraya and I made love, and I never felt like I needed it more. Her curly hair, the curves of her body, the way she touched me, all of it. The day was more eventful than any other I'd had in years, and she seemed to sense this, doing all she could to help me release my tension and stress through loving her.

"I'm goin' back to school," she announced. She curled her fingers around mine like ivy.

"School?" I sat up. "You already did four years at Hunter. What do you want more school for?"

"To be a nurse, D. You know I've always wanted to be one."

"Then why'd you get a business degree? Sounds like a waste of money."

"Because I thought it'd be more practical, so I could help my dad with his shops. And now that that's goin' well, it's time to follow my own dreams."

I raised her chin and looked into her eyes to see what was going on beneath the surface. "Have you thought about her lately?"

She rested her head on my chest, hugging me tighter. "She would've been eighteen last week, D."

"You were nine, Soraya. You can't keep beatin' yourself up over that," I said.

When they were kids, Soraya's younger sister died from a horrible disease that ate her organs from the inside out. I remember Soraya being out of school for long stretches at a time back then, and when she was in school, she'd randomly burst into loud sobs that seemed to never end. Her ESL teacher would send her to the nurse, then the nurse would send her home. It was a pattern that went on for what felt like forever. Her mom, unable to process, moved to Harlem and started a new life, leaving Soraya and Mr. Aziz to fend for themselves.

Years later, Soraya told me that the only happy memories she had from that time were hanging out with Jason and me at the playground, playing pranks on Mr. Rawlings, or Ma giving her a hug and a snack.

"I know," she whispered. "I'm tryin'. But becomin' a nurse will help, I know it."

"So what's the plan? Am I gonna have to make you ramen, force you to take study breaks, and bring you jugs of black crack again for another four years? Because . . ." I paused and she looked up at me, upset. "Because you know I will," I said, smiling at her.

She laughed and ran her hand over my chest hair, which she claimed felt like grass. "Well, you'd only have to do it for eighteen months this time. I'd go to the accelerated program at NYU. Then I could get a job at Woodhull and still live at home with my dad, so he wouldn' get lonely."

I kissed the back of her hand. "Whatever

makes you happy makes me happy, *habibti.* Same team, same dream, you know that."

She grabbed my raw dick, slowly rubbing it up and down, making me hard again. "You know I can't resist you when you speak your broken Arabic to me."

I winked. "Why you think I'm speakin' it?"

"Jus' promise me one thing," she said, flipping herself on top of me, inserting me inside her.

"What?"

I already knew my answer would be yes. It was hard to negotiate with a girl when you were inside her. I mean, Soraya was my one and only, but I imagined it was the same whenever anyone had sex.

"Don' change when you become a big shot, okay?"

I laughed, scrunching my face up. *What's she talking about? Me? Big shot?*

She leaned in closer, no longer smiling, as if one of us were about to disappear.

"Promise me."

I gripped her ass and filled my lungs with her sweet smell. "I'm not gonna become a big shot, Soraya. You have nothin' to worry about."

"Yes," she said. "You will. And if you don'

promise me, we might as well break up right now."

"Damn. Okay. I promise. Happy?"

Reader: Believing that you can some-how prevent change is the surest way to fail. Whether in life or sales, nothing ever stays the same.

"We'll see," she said, as she thrust her hips into mine. Soon, I no longer knew where her body began and mine ended.

6

My alarm went off at 5:30 a.m. I slapped my clock, hopped out of bed, and jumped into the shower. It was Monday, my first day of work. And I couldn't be late.

Before leaving the office on Friday, Clyde told me that I had to be in at 7 a.m. *sharp.* "Is it cool if I'm a minute or two late?" I asked, hedging the fact that I couldn't control subway delays or Greenpeace workers who just wanted "one minute" of my time.

"Of course, no problem," he'd replied. Given how intense the place was, I was relieved they weren't *too* militant.

I walked into the empty kitchen, grabbing a banana and a bowl of cereal. It was only 6 a.m., but I wanted to arrive early and make a good impression. So I scarfed down my Cap'n Crunch like a rabid beast and tossed the empty bowl into the sink.

Ma walked in sporting her pink terry-cloth

robe, tight multicolored head wrap, and white slippers, a finger scratching the top of her head.

"You're up early, Dar. Ready for your first day of work?"

"You know it, Ma. Can't be late."

She looked me up and down, and shook her head, laughing.

"What's so funny?"

She swept her hand in front of me. "You look like a Mormon, son."

I looked at my white short-sleeved button-up with two pens in the front pocket, black slacks with a black belt, and black leather shoes to match. *Shit.*

"But it was you who bought me these clothes last year!" I said, panicking. I couldn't go to that office looking like a Mormon. They'd laugh me out the moment I walked in, probably telling me that I showed up for the wrong sales job, that church would be in session at eleven.

"Go get one of your plaid button-ups, denim jeans, and throw some clean runnin' shoes on," she ordered, as she turned the coffee maker on.

"Ma, I don' think that'd look right."

"Dar, from what I've read, it's better to dress casually at these startups. If you come in lookin' stiff, they'll think you're uptight.

Trust me."

I thought back to my visit on Friday and remembered seeing people rocking everything from holey hoodies and sneakers to starched slacks and sweaters. She was right, so I changed as quickly as I could.

"Thanks, Ma." I kissed her forehead.

"Dar?"

"Yeah, Ma?"

"I'm proud of you, son. And I'm happy you've finally found somethin' that makes you want more outta life. You have so much to give, and now's the chance to show the world. I know your father would be happy too."

Pressure. That's all I felt. Not happiness from making Ma happy. Not a rush of excitement about my first day. *What if it didn't work out? What if I wasn't who people thought I was? Who did people even think I was?*

"Thanks, Ma. I'll do my best," I said, running out of the house.

6:15 a.m. Forty-five minutes to make it. If everything went right, it was doable. I jumped down the stairs, jogged down the street, turned right, and saw Mr. Aziz unlocking his store's roll-up gate.

"Morning, Darren! Soraya tells me you're starting a new job today," he said, as I ran

95

past him.

"*Na'am,* Mr. Aziz! Running late!"

"Go get 'em!"

I saw the gargoyles on the corner and figured that even though I was late I could give them a minute total just to say what up. Jason gave me a quick nod before turning away.

"No dap?" I asked, moving closer.

He pulled his hood lower and pushed his hand out.

"You good?"

He nodded, but I got closer. Under his hoodie, his face was swollen, red and glossy like a cheap Halloween mask. I pulled his hood off, exposing a blown-up eye, puffy cheeks, and a split lip. "Yo, J, what happened, man?"

"Get the fuck off me, B!" he yelled, shoving the shit out of me.

I walked back toward him, my hands raised. "C'mon, Batman. It's me, bro. Talk to me."

"Ain' nothin'. Got robbed last night, so out here tryna make it back up for Malcolm."

"Damn, J. I didn' know you were messin' with Malcolm, man. Shit's dangerous."

He hocked a loogie. You could hear it hitting the concrete.

96

"Why you think I'm out here this early? Gotta push this weight."

"Weight? It used to jus' be bud. Yo, you gotta get outta this shit ASAP. It's only gonna end badly."

"Whatever. The less you know the better, son. And I don' need you out here tellin' me what to do like you're my daddy. Jus' 'cause you gotta new job don' mean shit."

"Aight, man. But what's your plan?"

"What's my plan? I'm out here tryna be a man and get my momma out the projects, nigga. Tha's the plan. Now please get the fuck up out my face, drawin' all this attention so the jakes scoop me up."

Jason was my best friend, my brother, and we knew each other better than anyone else. But in that moment, it felt like we were worlds apart. He was the type of person to laugh instead of cry — he pierced tension like a needle. As I stared into his broken face, I knew there was an interior world he was hiding, even from me. And to keep it real, it hurt.

"Aight," I said, grabbing his shoulder. Wally Cat waved me over, but he'd have to wait. There was no chance I'd risk being late.

6:25 a.m. The train pulled up and I had thirty-five minutes left. *I can do this.* I hopped on, put my headphones in, and closed my eyes, listening to Nas's "Hate Me Now."

6:35 a.m. I caught the L right before it took off. My heart was working overtime. Everything was happening so fast. Meeting Rhett, the office, Clyde grilling me. *Stop thinking. The minute you slow down, you're gonna get whiplash.*

6:50 a.m. By the grace of God, the 6 train was sitting with its doors open. I jumped the stairs two by two, just making it. Sweat ran down my forehead, and I gripped the cold metal pole so hard, I thought I'd dent it.

"Hey, Darren." I turned around. It was Brian. Wearing his green apron on the train. *There's no hope for this guy.*

"Heard you're not working at Starbucks anymore?"

"Uh, yeah, man. Sorry I wasn't able to give you all a proper goodbye. Everything happened so quickly, and I ended up taking a job with that guy who came in the other day. Rhett Daniels."

"It's okay. I knew you were meant for bigger things. Don't get me wrong, you were the best boss we ever had, but you were sort of too smart to be a shift supervisor. That's like, I dunno, Professor X teaching elementary school."

He was staring at one of those shitty poems on the wall instead of me. I couldn't tell what he was feeling.

"I appreciate that, Brian. Working with everyone was fun, man. I'm gonna miss you all. Is Jared taking over my shifts?"

"Yeah, Nicole was crying when he told us, and Carlos was smiling, like he was proud of you or something. You'll still stop by though, right?"

I looked down at my phone. 6:56 a.m. and we were at Twenty-Eighth Street. *One more stop. If I run, I'll make it.*

"Of course," I said. "Jared's an asshole, so I'll see you all around as much as —"

The train jerked to a stop, throwing bodies into one another.

A voice came over the intercom. "Apologies, ladies and gentlemen, but we are experiencing delays due to a sick passenger on the train ahead of us. We hope to be moving shortly."

Sick on the train ahead of us? Fuck! What they actually mean is someone threw themself on the tracks. Who would be so selfish to commit suicide on a Monday at 6:57 a.m. and make everyone else late? Kill yourself on your own time!

"Hopefully they didn't throw up all over

99

the place," Brian said, still staring at the poem.

The train pulled into Thirty-Third Street at 7:01 a.m. I bolted up the stairs of 3 Park Avenue, through the revolving doors, and into an elevator right before it closed. I hit thirty-six, praying it wouldn't stop on a lower floor.

As the elevator climbed, all I heard were cables pulling, stretching, and shaking. No music. No mayhem.

I jumped out and looked to the right, but saw no commotion beyond the frosted doors. When I looked left, my heart dropped. The conference room was packed, and everyone inside was staring at something.

Me.

I stood in the elevator bay without a clue what to do. There I was in the plaid button-up, denim jeans, and Saucony running shoes Ma had picked out for me. I took a breath and opened the doors.

The sharp-featured receptionist smirked and clicked her tongue. "Bad move, Buck."

Why the hell is she calling me Buck? But I had no time for questions. I was shaking worse than Jack at the end of *Titanic.* And there would be no one to save me either.

I walked toward the heavy wooden door on the left. But before I opened it, Rhett shook his head, pointing to the other side of the room. I walked the length of the glass wall, everyone's eyes still on me, and opened the other door.

Every single leather-backed chair around the mahogany table had an ass in it. Every inch of the marble counter below the flat-screen TV was occupied. Every heater in front of the windows had someone on it. Some people smiled, others covered their mouths in horror, and a few seemed to be praying for me. And, I shit you not, every single person was white.

I looked across the room at Rhett. Clyde sat next to him, beaming.

"Why are you late?" Rhett asked.

"This is going to be good," one girl whispered to another.

"Um, the train. Someone got sick on the one in front of me." I looked around the room to see if it was an acceptable answer.

He closed his eyes and nodded. "Ah. Got it. The train. No worries. Take a seat and we'll begin."

I wiped the sweat off my forehead and sat on the floor.

"Get the fuck up!" Rhett yelled, charging toward me.

I shot up and braced for impact. What I knew even then was that this office was not a normal office, that this company was not a normal company, and that these people were not normal people.

"Are you out of your fucking mind? We start at 7 a.m. sharp. Every single Monday of the year. Not thirty seconds late. Not one minute late. And sure as hell not three minutes late. Where the fuck do you think you are? The first floor?"

My mouth went dry. I couldn't do anything except look at my feet.

"Look at me!" Rhett shouted, red in the face with a vein jumping around his forehead and threatening to explode into an aneurysm.

"If you are ever late to a Monday-morning meeting again, I mean point-two nanoseconds late, every single person in here, all fucking one hundred five of them, will have to do push-ups until their arms are so sore, they won't be able to pick up their phones. And you'll have to watch them until they collapse. And then, after that, I'm going to fire your ass. Understood?"

I nodded so hard that I almost snapped my neck.

"Now," he said, straightening out his shirt and walking back to his chair. "Everyone, this is one of our four new SDRs, Darren Vender."

"Buck," Clyde corrected, smug as hell.

"Why Buck?" a pasty white girl across the room asked.

"Because if he does his job, he'll make us each a million bucks," Clyde replied, winking at me.

"Right," Rhett said, nodding. "This is Buck. Are our other three SDRs here?"

Three people seated on the floor below me, two white guys and a tall blonde girl, raised their hands.

"You see?" Rhett said. "*They* made it on time. Did you three take the subway?"

They all nodded.

"*And* they took the subway! Just like you, Buck. Except they weren't late. You three, stand up and join Buck."

They stood and looked around the room — nervous sheep who'd just seen one of their own slaughtered.

"State your name and one fucking fun fact about you," Rhett commanded.

"I'm —" White Guy Number One's voice cracked, and the room roared with laughter.

"Did your balls just drop, kid?" Rhett asked. The room's laughter shot up ten decibels, and he got red in the face and started clearing his throat over and over again like he'd swallowed a chicken bone. The laughter became louder and louder.

"Go on, speak," Rhett said.

White Guy Number One's shoulders folded, and he leaned over like he was going to puke. But instead of blowing grits all over the floor, he grabbed his bag, pushed me out of the way, and ran into the stairwell.

Rhett laughed. "That's going to be a long walk down."

White Guy Number Two, who'd just been promoted to White Guy Number One, puffed his chest out, and said, "I'm Arnold Bagini. I played D1 football at Notre Dame and came in third for two-hundred-twenty-five-pound reps at the NFL Scouting Combine."

"Third place?" someone shouted. "You suck ass, bro!"

A blonde girl in front of us turned around, and said, "Bagini? Sounds like Bilbo Baggins from *The Lord of the Rings*!" Everyone erupted in laughter again, and someone yelled, "Frodo!" to which the whole room replied by chanting, "FRODO! FRODO! FRODO!"

But Arnold Bagini didn't sweat. He just closed his eyes and nodded in different directions, like he was listening to music. Eventually, he opened his eyes, and shouted,

"My name . . . is Frodo!" The whole room clapped in approval.

"Great, Frodo is here," Rhett said. "Next."

"Claire Vanderbilt," the tall blonde girl sporting a white dress and brown leather belt said, straight-faced, with determination in her eyes. "I'm from Darien, Connecticut. And I'm a Vanderbilt."

The room fell silent. Then someone shouted, "Dutchy!"

"No," someone else said. "The Duchess!" Everyone nodded in agreement at Claire's new name, and she nodded before taking a seat.

"And you, Buck," Rhett said. "Your name is already Buck, so what's your fun fact?"

After being screamed at, then witnessing what happened to the original White Guy Number One, I tried to think of something good but couldn't.

"Um." Seconds stretched into eternity. Someone loudly knocked on the table. *Tap-tap. Tap-tap. Tap-tap. Fuck it.* "I can freestyle."

Everyone's eyes widened. Including Rhett's. "Well, go on," he said. "Give us a demonstration."

"Uh, I can't."

It's not that I couldn't, but I didn't want to start my career, especially as the only

Black person in the room, as some wind-up monkey that would bang his cymbals whenever white people wanted him to.

Sensing my hesitation, they all flung a series of boos at me as if they were throwing rotten apples, peanuts, and other circus trash.

"It's the least you can do for being late," Clyde said.

"Yeah," a girl insisted. "C'mon, Buck."

"Buck, Buck, Buck," everyone whispered, raising the volume until they were screaming. "BUCK, BUCK, BUCK!"

Then I heard a *tap. Tap-tap-tap. Tap-tap.* Coming from the table. *Tap. Tap-tap-tap. Tap-tap.* All of them did it in unison.

My mouth went dry again. I couldn't breathe.

"He's going to choke like B-Rabbit in *8 Mile!*" someone shouted.

Fuck. There was no time to weigh the costs of being Flavor Flav versus the benefits of being Jesse Jackson. I'd already made a fool out of myself, and I couldn't let it happen again. Thank God I wasn't dressed like a Mormon. I took a breath and opened my mouth.

"Aight I'm really sorry, for doin' that thing you hate. I'm sayin' comin' in with excuses, jus' a li'l late. Got two hundred and ten eyes on me, and nah, it don' feel great, but it's sure better than that guy who ran out barfin' what he ate. It's true I may be new, but I promise I got potential. Words and verbs coalescing into proverbs comin' straight up at your mental. It's my first day, but if there's one thing I can say, it's that my man Frodo, the Duchess, and me are gon' kill it, like a turkey on Thanksgivin' Day."

Silence. All two hundred and ten eyes stared at me.

"Holy shit," a girl said. "Buck can actually rap!"

The room thundered with applause, pale hands surrounding me for high fives.

Across the room, Rhett gave me a look that said, *There he is. There's the guy I hired.*

Reader: If you are a Black man, the key to any white person's heart is the ability to shuck, jive, or freestyle. But use it wisely and sparingly. Otherwise you're liable to turn into Steve Harvey.

Rhett raised his hand and slowly curled it into a fist until a dense silence fell. I sat on the floor next to the Duchess, who scooted as far away from me as possible.

"What week is it?" Rhett asked.

"DEALS WEEK!" everyone shouted.

"That's right. And for the uninitiated, can someone please explain what Deals Week is?"

A blonde girl raised her hand.

"Deals Week is the most important week of the month. It's when every single member of the team is doing absolutely everything in their power to ensure we hit our MRR goal."

"And what's MRR?" Rhett asked.

"Oh," she said, looking at us new hires. "Monthly recurring revenue. The amount of closed-won cash we assume will repeat every month after. It helps with the financial model and adjusting our CAC, which, of course, impacts the LTV of our customers."

Everyone in the room nodded, as if she had delivered some prophecy. To me, it just sounded like she was speaking in tongues.

"Thank you, Tiffany. She's right," Rhett said, standing. "But she left out a few things. Can anyone tell the new folks why we have a Deals Week to begin with?"

The girl with orange-red hair, the one I'd seen yesterday with the piglet in her arms, stood. She had this far-off look in her eyes, like she was peering into another dimension. "Because it's a crazy fun time?"

"It is that, Marissa," Rhett said. "But that's not *why* we have a Deals Week.

Anyone else?"

A stocky kid with a full beard who was sweating through a plaid button-up raised his hand.

"Tell us why, Charlie," Rhett said, walking the floor.

"Because we've achieved twenty-five percent month-over-month growth for the past eleven months, and if we don't achieve our goals, our growth will suffer."

"And what happens if our growth suffers?"

Charlie paused, surveying the room. "All this goes away. Everything we have, everything we are. We will no longer be the best."

"Fuck that!" someone yelled.

"Yeah, fuck that!" another voice echoed.

Rhett stopped in front of me, my eyes level with the backs of his knees; his denim jeans were obviously tailor-made, his suede Chelsea boots unblemished.

"That's exactly right, Charlie. Thank you. Now," he said, rounding the back of the room, stepping over people, occasionally resting his hand on someone's shoulder. "Are we going to let that happen?"

"Hell no," a few responded.

"No? I thought I heard a few of you," he said. "But I didn't hear all of you. I said, Are we going to let that happen?"

109

"No!" more people shouted; some of them proceeded to beat their white hands on the table until they turned red.

"Not good enough. You call yourself Sumwunners? If you actually mean what you say, I need to hear it. So again. Are. We. Going. To. Let. That. Happen?"

"NO!" the entire room screamed, banging on every surface they could get their hands on. Someone flung a Moleskine at the glass behind me. I ducked just in time.

"FUCK NO! FUCK NO! FUCK NO!" they chanted. You could see the fire in their faces, the madness mixing like cement behind their eyes.

Dozens of nonsales spectators formed a crowd outside the room, throwing their hands in the air, stomping their feet to a beat only they knew. These people, who I assumed were semi-intelligent and sane, were hooting and hollering like a pack of savages beating their chests as a herd of mastodons approached. I was waiting for them to take out whips branded with Sumwun's logo for self-flagellation.

"We have Deals Week because being the best means that we *need*" — Rhett thrust his finger into the air — "to crush our goals every month. And I'll let you in on a little secret, it's not just selling. It's not just putting numbers on the board, because if we do our jobs this week, we will make history. Yes, history.

"So let's be clear about what we're *not* doing. We're not fucking selling shitty pieces of cardboard and calling it furniture. This isn't IKEA! We're not fucking selling greasy, heart-attack-inducing poop on a stick that kills billions of people every day. This isn't McDonald's! And we're sure as hell not fucking selling overpriced, low-quality pieces of burlap sacks assembled in Bangladeshi sweatshops halfway around the world. This is not fucking American Eagle, Hollister, Aéropostale, or any of those lame-ass fucking brands that are making the world a worse place to exist in.

"We are Sumwun. And what Sumwun does is help people live better. Be better. Coexist better. We give people hope: the hope that tomorrow will be a brighter day, the hope that someone out there understands them, and the hope to continue living with purpose. 'God is not unjust; he will not forget your work and the love you have shown him as you have helped his people and continue to help them.' Hebrews 6:10. Now go stretch and let's get this Deals Week fucking started. First person who closes a deal gets a thousand dollars. Cash."

I thought the whole scene was extreme and straight out of *Any Given Sunday,* but I'd be lying if I said my heart wasn't pounding. No way in hell had I bought into their madness, but the energy in the air crackled like static.

"Stretch time!" Clyde shouted.

We filed out of the room one by one. As I waited in line, I noticed that everyone wore the same straight face with hard eyes and clenched jaws. They didn't have war paint, AK-47s, or fighter jets, but they were soldiers all the same.

And truth be told, they were ready for war.

I followed the sea of people into the "event space." Purple couches and wooden tables had been pushed to the side of the room, and the hardwood floors looked as if they'd just been polished. I looked out the floor-to-ceiling windows and took in the unobstructed view of the East River. Then I noticed an orchestra-size gong suspended from the ceiling. *What the hell is that for?*

The smell of French toast, pancakes, sausage, syrup, and fresh fruit filled the air. Two dozen aluminum trays, heavy with food, sat on a large white marble island toward the back wall. Behind the island, against the far wall, were refrigerators, fruit baskets, moneyless vending machines, cereal dispensers, and taps bearing different labels, like Joyride Coffee Cold Brew, Blue Moon, and Health-Ade Kombucha.

The nonsales crowd toasted bagels, mixed oatmeal, and sliced bananas, never laying a finger on the trays, almost as if they didn't even see them. The whole thing was like an adult version of Neverland Ranch.

"Circle up," Clyde said. The salespeople got into formation. "And not a word."

This is it. The moment of human sacrifice. If I see someone sharpening a knife and licking their lips at me, I'm running. With this decided, I joined the circle a few people away from Clyde.

"To the right," Clyde commanded. Everyone reached across their chests with their left arms in one swift motion, holding them in place with their right forearms.

"To the left," Clyde said. Everyone was so used to the motions that his instructions were only a formality; the movements and pace ingrained in them like biological code.

"Smile time," Clyde said, making the most menacing smile I'd ever seen. His eyes popped out of their sockets, and his mouth stretched so wide I thought he'd tear his lips. But when I surveyed the circle, everyone was smiling like a gang of killer clowns.

"Why aren't you smiling, Buck?" Clyde asked through clenched teeth.

"Oh, sorry," I said, exposing my teeth like a feral animal.

Clyde then told us to close our eyes and "breathe it out." But before I closed my eyes, I noticed that the spectators were watching with increased enthusiasm. Jen from marketing waved at me. Mac from the gym threw up a Black Power fist when our eyes connected. It would've been more comforting if Mac was actually Black.

"Keep your eyes closed," Clyde ordered. "Today is day one of Deals Week, which means we need to do everything humanly possible to hit our goal ASAP."

The room fell silent.

"We have four hundred and fifty thousand dollars to close this week. I know it sounds like a lot, but we've done that with less time before."

"Damn right we have!" Frodo shouted.

Clyde saluted him. "That's right, Frodo. But aside from what we need to hit, I want you all to empty your minds and picture yourself a year from now. Where are you? Maybe you're taking a vacation with your girlfriend in the Caribbean, lying down on the beach, cracking open a fresh lobster. Or you're hiking Machu Picchu, smelling the ancient Peruvian jungle beneath you as you climb higher, poking your head through dense clouds. What are you wearing?"

To be honest, as he spoke, I couldn't stop picturing Soraya and me having hot, sweaty sex and ordering pizza afterward. The good thing was that I wouldn't have to wait a year for that to happen. I'd just need to make it through the day.

The floor creaked as people shifted, all of them prophesying piles of hundred-dollar bills and gold ingots falling from the sky.

"Now come back here, to this building, this floor, and this office. Imagine yourself closing that deal you need, throwing it up on the board to a room of applause. Imagine smashing the crap out of the gong, knowing you didn't just hit your number, but that you also helped your team hit theirs."

I wasn't sure if we were still supposed to have our eyes closed, so I cracked mine open. Every single person in the circle had their eyes shut and heads bowed; they all were nodding and whispering to themselves. I shit you not, some even had tears streaming down their faces. If there was a Church of Sumwun, Monday morning of Deals Week would have been Sunday Mass.

With closed eyes, Clyde extended his arm in front of him and pointed at different parts of the circle, directing his energy. He was a privileged son of a bitch, but he actually *did* believe in what he was saying and what the company stood for. I had to give him that.

"Every time someone tells you no, hangs up on you, or says 'maybe next month,' I want you to dig deep and do everything not to be discouraged. I want you to pick up the phone again and make the next call no matter how much rejection you face and how many nos you hear. Remember, if you are saving them money and time, there should be no reason they don't sign."

Reader: I hope you're taking notes. Clyde was a maniac, but this is Sales 101. Repeat: if you are saving them money and time, there should be no reason they don't sign.

"And if you see someone getting down, pick them up. Hitting this month will mean we've hit our number for a full year, which is unheard of. So I want you to open your eyes, scream as loud as you can, clap your hands, and slam your foot so fucking hard that people on the ground floor think there's an earthquake."

Everyone opened their eyes, bodies tense

like sprinters awaiting the starting gun's blast.

"Every day is deals day on three," Clyde shouted. "One."

There was something on their faces.

"Two."

It took me a second to realize what it was.

"Three."

Rage.

"EVERY DAY IS DEALS DAY!" they shouted, clapping their hands and slamming their sneakers, heels, boots, and clogs onto the ground so hard that the floor really did shake.

"Get some food and let's get to work!" Clyde ordered.

They descended on the trays of food like vultures. And then I felt a hand on my shoulder. Clyde.

"Let's go. You and the other two are training with me today. But I'll show you to your seat first."

"Okay."

We arrived at the sales floor, a long rectangular room containing ten rows of desks.

He pointed to two desks facing each other. "The Duchess and Frodo, you'll sit there and there."

"You," he said, gripping my shoulder, "will sit here." He slapped the desk closest to the frosted doors, in the same row as the Duchess's and Frodo's.

Moments later, everyone poured onto the floor balancing plates and bowls overflowing with food from the breakfast buffet. Most of them hurried to their desks. But a few of them, the ones whose desks were closest to mine, seemed to be taking their sweet time.

"Take a seat," Clyde said. "And get settled in. Then we'll begin training."

When I pulled out my chair, a downpour of paint pummeled me, covering my desk, chair, and body in a white blur. When I looked up, I saw a dripping bucket hanging from the ceiling, apologetically swaying from left to right.

WHAT THE FUCK?

The entire floor burst into laughter. Some people snapped photos; others, whose desks were closer to mine, smirked as they wiped off flecks of white paint before sitting down.

With paint on my clothes, in my hair, and even in my nose, I turned to Clyde. He was smiling.

"Got you, Buck! Ha-ha! I thought the white would help you fit in better," he said, smacking my back. "Don't look so shocked. It's just a little welcome joke. You're not mad, right?"

Not mad? I couldn't speak. I wanted to ram my fist through his face, shattering his abnormally straight LEGO castle–looking teeth.

"Well," he said, waving his hand around the mess. "Clean this up and meet us in Bhagavad Gita. Training starts in ten."

I should've known from the Middle Passage to never trust a white man who says, "Take a seat." It could be your last.

7

In addition to being an ancient Hindu text, the Bhagavad Gita was a nondescript meeting room on the thirty-sixth floor of 3 Park Avenue. It featured a brown wooden table with brown chairs, floor-to-ceiling windows, and walls made of dry-erase material. It had the same corporate vibe as the conference room, but stuffier.

The receptionist, Porschia, procured a white T-shirt and sweatpants for me, but I still had white paint stuck in my hair, eyes, eyebrows, fingernails, and other places I couldn't see but felt. If this, a little white-boy fraternity hazing, would be the worst of my time at the company, I figured I could manage.

"Sit," Clyde ordered us three new hires, as he wrote something on one of the walls.

He capped his dry-erase marker and moved to the side, exposing what looked like a family tree. Rhett's name was at the top; dotted and solid lines poked out of it, leading to other names and boxes.

"What is this?" Clyde asked.

"An org chart," I said.

"One point for Buck. We have Rhett at the top, since he's the CEO and founder, Chris to the right of him, as cofounder and CTO, and beneath each of them are the teams they own. As you can see," he said, pointing to his name, "I'm the director of sales."

Frodo looked left and right, like he was about to cross a street, and raised his hand.

"You don't have to raise your hand, Frodo," Clyde said. "You're an adult now."

"Oh, right," Frodo said, slicking his hair back. "I just noticed everyone below Rhett was a VP or C-something except you. Why's that?"

Clyde went beet red and balled his writing hand into a fist. "Well, we had a VP of sales, Frodo, but he sucked and got the boot. And as you so astutely pointed out, there's now a vacancy, which I plan to fill."

"When will that happen?" Frodo asked, a goofy, dreamlike smile dancing on his face.

"As soon as you stop asking stupid questions and start putting numbers on the board. That's when."

Frodo's smile disappeared.

"And when can we start doing that?" The Duchess asked, admiring her manicure.

"Once you earn the right to do so," Clyde said, writing numbers next to everyone's name. There was a 108 next to Clyde's and a 208 next to Rhett's.

Frodo raised his hand again. Clyde sighed and rubbed his eyes. "Yes, Frodo?"

"How come so many people report to Rhett? Seems a bit odd that he, uh, owns all of these different departments."

"How many companies have you built, Frodo?"

"Uh, none, I'm just trying to —"

"Exactly. None. Zero. Zilch. If you haven't noticed, Rhett likes control. He likes it because he's the best at every single function below him. MBA from Harvard, master's in organizational psychology from USC, number one salesman for every year he worked at Salesforce, director of product at Google for two years, and inventor of seven products marketed and sold on HSN, QVC, and those commercials that air at three in the morning. We're not supposed to know about those, but I'll just tell you that one of his products rhymes with 'slam cow.' "

Frodo's eyes widened. "Rhett invented the sham —"

"Don't say it!" Clyde said. "Again, we're not supposed to know. But, yes, he did. Moving on. The sales team," he said, slapping the chart, "has three parts. Account executives, known as AEs. Account managers, known as AMs. And sorry-ass sales development representatives, known as SDRs, which is what you three are. Who can tell me what an SDR does?"

The Duchess rolled her eyes. "We call new companies, qualify prospects, and hand them off to the AEs to close."

"More or less, yes," Clyde said, erasing the chart. "But not exactly. SDRs are the lifeblood of the sales team. Without you, there are no deals or branded hoodies, no food or kombucha on tap, or any of that other crap. If you don't do your jobs, and I mean if you don't fucking produce, the company ceases to exist. So, beyond qualifying and handing people off to the AEs, your role requires blood, sweat, and tears of enthusiasm that I'm frankly not seeing in any of you right now."

Tears of enthusiasm? It was nine in the morning and I was already exhausted. Exhausted from trying to get to the office on time, from the stress of the morning meeting, and from smelling like Bob Ross's studio. I didn't even notice I was nodding off until . . .

"Stand up!" Clyde shouted, centimeters from my face. "You want to sleep? On day one of training? Not on my fucking watch. Tell me what Sumwun is. Now."

I had googled the company over the weekend and finally found out what it did, or at least what I thought it did. "Sumwun is a platform that connects individuals with what are known as 'assistants' from around the world to discuss their various issues, life problems, and challenges in an effort to —"

"ANG!" Clyde shouted. "That sucked. Take a seat. You obviously don't know how to spit. The Duchess. Go."

She stood, straightening out her wide leather belt, and said, "Through live video sessions, two-way texting, and visual reporting, Sumwun gives individuals the support to overcome their issues and achieve their goals."

"ANG!" Clyde yelled. The Duchess cut him with her eyes. "Sit!"

Frodo shot up, and said, "Sumwun is, uh. Sumwun is about, uh, giving people the power to, um —"

"Sit the fuck down," Clyde said, shaking his head. "All of you sound like robots regurgitating what's on the website. No, you sound like retarded robots, like you didn't

124

make the cut and should have had your plugs pulled." He went back to the wall, and the three of us sat there awkwardly as Clyde wrote out the entire pitch, reading each word aloud as he did.

"There are more than seven billion people on earth, meaning there are at least seven billion people with their own struggles, challenges, and ways of living. Seven billion people, like you, who wake up, go to work, spend time with family, eat, love, and sleep awaiting a new day. But as the population grows, the stresses, difficulties, and anxieties that people face grow with it. Long gone are the days when traditional, one-size-fits-all therapy worked. In fact, it has never worked, but no one has had an alternative, so people have ended up paying insane prices to speak with so-called therapists, and wasted thousands of dollars on self-help books that have helped no one except the authors who pocketed the cash. Or they've ended up suffering silently, eventually harming themselves or others.

"Realizing this, we created Sumwun to empower individuals to receive assistance that is personalized, tailored, and customized for their needs, all while removing the stigma around seeking help. By offering a growing team of over two thousand assistants from around the world, who have different ways of life, subscribe to different beliefs, and apply different methods of therapy, we guarantee that you and those closest to you will find someone who is able to speak to your own challenges in a way that is geared toward finding a solution, rather than someone who will profit off of your pain by keeping you on as a patient.

"With individual and corporate clients in more than 150 countries, Sumwun ensures that you will always have someone to talk to whenever you need someone to talk to.

"That," Clyde said, slamming his hands on the table, causing us all, even the Duchess, to flinch, "is what we do here. Now I want you all to stand up and say it out loud until you believe it. Because if you can't say those words with confidence, enthusiasm, and vigor, you might as well walk the hell out right now. I'll be back in one hour. I said stand up!"

We stood up. He walked toward the door, paused, and said over his shoulder, "Oh yeah, no one's allowed to leave, or even sit, until I come back. If you do, you're fired. And if you think I'm bluffing, take a seat or open the door and see what happens."

The three of us jumped to our feet and began walking around the room like monks in prayer. *Shit.*

It was harder to say those words with real chutzpah than it was to memorize them, especially with a full bladder and a neo-Neanderthal next to me stumbling over the same word for ninety minutes at this point. Every time he got to it, Frodo pronounced "population" as *pope-ulation.* I just took a breath and tried to focus on the script.

" 'Realizing this, we created Sumwun to empower individuals —' "

Frodo stopped pacing and looked at me. "It's *encourage* individuals, not *empower* individuals, Buck."

"It's *empower,* Frodo. The word is right there on the board where it's been for the last ninety minutes. And don't call me Buck, man. My name is Darren."

"It's *encourage,* Buck. And why shouldn't I call you Buck? Everyone else does. Plus, you call me Frodo, and my name is, uh —" For the record, Frodo, formerly known as Arnold Bagini, almost forgot his own name.

"Arnold. My name is Arnold," he said, sighing with relief.

"The difference is you like being called Frodo; you even admitted that it's your new name. I don't like being called Buck; I just let everyone else call me it because it'd take more energy to fight it."

"So why are you fighting me?"

He had a point.

Frodo turned to the Duchess, who stood in the corner, staring out the window. "What about you, the Duchess, do you mind your new name?"

She didn't turn around.

"Uh, the Duchess, I asked —"

"I heard you," she said in a tone as dry as the Gobi Desert. "I don't care what someone calls me. All I care about is seeing whatever people call me at the top of the board, which, one way or another, will happen."

Damn, she's cold as hell. The Duchess reeked of old money and blood-splattered gallows. I pictured her at an auction in the 1800s, pushing her cuckolded husband aside and prying open the mouths of the "beasts," "savages," and "barbarians" imported from Africa.

"Well, I just wanna make my dad proud," Frodo said, staring at her back. "When I was growing up, he was a used-car salesman. Before he lost his job and got to drinking, I always liked hanging out on the lot with him, watching him talk to people, make them smile, and shake their hands after handing them the key to a new car. I want to do that."

"Handing them keys to a *used* car, you moron," the Duchess said, still staring out the window.

"What?"

"You said 'handing them the key to a *new* car,' but your father was a *used-car* salesman. So the keys he handed them were to *used* cars."

"But the cars were new for them . . . even if they were used."

"So" — she spun around, a small smile on her face — "if I wear a pair of sneakers for five years, sweat in them, get dirt on them, and tear them to shreds, will they be new or used when I hand them to you?"

"Well, I guess that —"

The door burst open and Clyde walked in with a group of salespeople. "Frodo, go," he ordered, shutting the door.

"There are seven billion people on earth, meaning there are seven billion people," he started, missing a few words but not sounding too bad.

"Seven billion people, who wake up, go to work . . ."

He was getting closer now, and I really hoped he wouldn't mess up.

"Spend time with family, eat, love, and sleep awaiting a new day. But as the *pope-*

ulation —"

"Hold the fuck up," Clyde said, looking at the crew he brought in. "What the hell is a *pope-ulation?*"

"Uh," Frodo said, redder than a Russian, "I meant *population.* I'm sorry. I'm, uh, I can go again."

"No," Clyde said. "You can't. If you do that on the phone, people will think we hire retards. In fact, they'll think *I* hire retards. And then they'll hang up and laugh — at me, Rhett, and what this entire company stands for. You want that, Frodo?"

"Um."

"Don't fucking 'um' me, you worthless sack of pigskin. I asked if you want that to happen. If you want people to laugh at me and Rhett."

"No," he said, looking down at the table and picking healthy skin off his fingers, causing them to bleed.

"That's what I thought, now sit. The Duchess, go."

"There are more than seven billion people on earth, meaning that there are at least seven billion people . . ." She recited the whole thing and didn't miss one word. Clyde's gang looked at him expectantly.

"Not bad. You need to sound a little more human, but good work."

She just nodded, took a seat, and folded her hands as if nothing had happened.

"The best for last, right? Let's get it, Buck," he said, smiling.

"There are more than seven —"

"Christ!" Clyde shouted. "What the fuck is that?"

"What's what?" I asked, confused.

That," he said, pointing a finger so close to my eye, I flinched. "That was worse than Frodo's. You had no spirit, spoke with no conviction, and frankly sounded as flat as a deflated sex doll. Again."

I took a breath. *There's no way in hell mine was worse than Frodo's.*

"There are more than seven billion people on earth, meaning that there are at least seven billion people with their own struggles, challenges, and ways of living," I said, making sure I enunciated every word. "Seven billion people like you, who wake up, go to work, spend time with family, eat, love, and —"

"ANG!" he yelled. His gang chuckled, shaking their heads.

"You're trash, brother," he said, staring directly into my eyes. "You need to smile as you speak. When you're on the phone with someone, they can't see you and don't know if you're wearing a three-thousand-dollar

131

suit or whatever Payless shit you have on now. So your voice is your appearance. A shitty voice, like the one you just spoke in, will make them think you buy your clothes from the clearance rack at Kmart. A strong, passionate voice will make them think you're wearing Gucci, Versace, or whatever you and your *dogs* are into. Got it?"

Reader: That second-to-last sentence was racist as hell, but the previous ones were good advice. Write that down.

Breathe. Breathe. Breathe. If Ma had been there, watching this mayonnaise-loving, *Seinfeld*-watching, Columbus Day–celebrating asshole speak to me like that, she would've held me by the wrist and told me to breathe. So I did.

He walked behind me and brought his lips so close to my left ear, he was almost kissing it. "Again," he whispered.

"There are more than seven billion people on earth —"

He thrust a hand into the air. "Wait! Something's not quite right. Again."

As I started, he took his iPhone out and showed one of his lackeys something. She laughed. I paused.

"Did I say to stop? Keep going."

I continued.

"A little better," he interrupted. "But still off. I'm going to level with you, Buck. I don't think you believe the words you're saying. Actually, I just don't think you care. We're going to stay here all day until you convince me that you do. Again."

When I tell you that this went on for eight more hours, I mean that this went on for eight more hours. The Duchess, Frodo, and I did not take turns; they, along with different groups of sales reps, listened to me recite the same 266 words over and over and over again until my voice was hoarse. Toward the end, Clyde had me write the script from beginning to end until it covered every inch of Bhagavad Gita's dry-erase walls.

A large part of me knew that none of this was right — that I was being targeted — but I wasn't just doing this for myself, I was doing it for Ma, Mr. Rawlings, Soraya, and everyone else who believed in me. I just had to man up and take it.

After the sun set and the sounds of the office quieted down, Clyde looked up from his laptop and nodded. "One last time."

I said the words. All of them. For what was likely the thousandth time that day.

Frodo nodded off, and the Duchess, with arms folded across her chest, looked at me, infuriated.

I finished, and Clyde clapped his hands. Frodo woke and the Duchess sat up. "You're almost there, Buck. Not quite, but almost. Either way, I'll give you a pass. Tomorrow the real fun begins. Role-plays. After stretch, just come straight here. You're all dismissed."

As Frodo and the Duchess filed out, Clyde called out to me.

"Hey," he said, nodding at a chair.

With everyone out of the room, Clyde — wearing what I would come to know as his signature outfit of a Brooks Brothers checkered button-down with a black or blue Patagonia vest, khaki Dockers, and penny loafers or boat shoes — looked up at me with guidance-counselor-like concern.

I opted to stand. "Yeah?"

"You sure this is for you? I'm asking as a friend because I know it's not for everyone. Some people just aren't suited for it, you know?"

I stared him dead in the eye. "I'm sure."

"Okay, get some rest. Believe it or not, today was easy."

Once I stepped into the elevator, someone yelled, "Hold it!" I caught the door, and

Rhett jumped in. Despite it being the first day of Deals Week, he somehow retained his otherworldly sheen, as if nothing could faze him.

"Thanks, Buck."

All of the day's stress rushed out of me and I smiled. "No problem."

He placed a hand on my shoulder, bringing us eye to eye. "Hey, Buck. Sorry about this morning. I just can't go easy whenever anyone is late to a Monday meeting. Or not on their A game. It wasn't personal."

"Yeah, I didn't think it was. I understand."

"Cool. How was your first day?"

I widened my eyes and shook my head.

He laughed. "That bad, huh? I know it's tough, but I guarantee that this will be the best professional experience of your life, Buck. Seriously."

"I hope so."

"I *know* so. You'll see."

We split in the lobby. I headed out the door and Rhett went into the Starbucks. It was the first time in twelve hours that I'd tasted the sweet fresh air of May and heard the sounds of the city up close again.

I don't remember much of the subway ride. But I do remember getting home, passing out, and hearing Ma crack the door open to ask if I was all right.

"Yeah," I said, half-asleep.

"How was your first day?"

I can't recall what I said, but I do remember thinking, *If that was only day one, what the hell will the others be like?*

8

Except for Mondays, work started at 8 a.m. But I was traumatized, so on day two, I got up at 6:15 a.m., took a quick shower, and headed into the kitchen.

Ma was in there sitting at the table reading a newspaper with a strong, frothy cup of coffee. The smell was sweet, like a tangerine, yet spicy with bright notes of acidity. *Definitely a Salvadorian blend.*

"Mornin', Ma." I planted a wearied kiss on her cheek. Even though I'd slept for almost ten hours, I was still exhausted, which made me fear for the long day ahead.

"Mornin', Dar." She folded her paper. "You were sleepin' like a corpse when I got back from work. If I hadn' gotten a response from you, I was gonna shake you to make sure you were alive."

I laughed, pouring myself a bowl of cereal. "Yeah, I felt like a corpse."

"So, how was it?"

What I wanted to say was *Help me, Ma! They forced me to rap, pulled some KKK tar-and-feather shit on me, and made me write on a board until my fingers bled. Please, please, please don't make me go back!* But I couldn't. Jason was out on the corner trying to provide a better life for his mom. I had to swallow my feelings. Ma had played mom and pops for my entire life, and it was time for me to take care of her.

"It was okay," I said, taking a seat. "There's three of us new hires. Well, there were four, but one kid left. And now we're all workin' hard to get some script down."

"What happened to the other kid?"

I thought back to him, realizing I never knew his name. I saw sweat pouring from his red face, the desperation in his eyes as he looked around the room for help like a frightened animal.

"Jus' wasn' right for him," I said with a shrug, and inhaled my bowl of cereal.

"Well, no matter how hard it gets, remember why you're there, Dar. To become somethin' and show the world what you're made of. To let your light shine and be all I know you can be."

"I know, Ma. I'll try." I grabbed my bag and headed for the door.

"Oh, and Dar?"

"Yeah, Ma?"

"I was thinkin' we could have another dinner on Friday. Me, you, Soraya, Jason, and Mr. Rawlings. To celebrate the end of your first week. I'll cook some extra spicy turkey chili for you."

"Sounds good, Ma. I love you," I said, and rushed down the stairs so I wouldn't be late no matter what.

When I rounded the corner, Soraya was sitting on a bench outside of the shop and wearing a black hoodie with HUDA SHA'ARAWI: GOOGLE HER on it. She was reading from a small stack of papers.

"Hey," I said, surprised. "What's up?"

"Helpin' my dad open up," she replied, her eyes glued to the papers. "Gotta new shipment of African black soap."

"Oh *really*?"

She laughed. "Don' worry, one already has your name on it."

"*Shukran, habibti.* And what're those?"

"Application papers. To be accepted to NYU's accelerated nursin' program I have to take six prereqs. I already did three at Hunter, but I'm gonna take summer courses for the rest and hope they accept me."

"They will." I lifted her chin toward me and our lips quickly connected. "When's it due?"

139

"If I wanna start in the fall, I need to apply by June fifteenth. So a coupla weeks."

"Okay," I said, and kissed her once more. "Lemme know if you need any help."

"I will. And wait, you never texted me last night. How was your first day?"

"I'll tell you later!" I shouted, jogging toward the gargoyles.

"Come here, boy!" Wally Cat called.

I ignored him for the moment and gave Jason a quick dap. "You good?"

"Yeah, bro. How I look?" he said, still bruised but smiling.

"Like you got fucked up, but not bad."

"Good lookin'. Tryna play some chess?"

"Nah, I gotta head to work."

"Aight. I wouldn' wan' it wit' me again if I was you either. But don' forget what I said."

"About what?"

" 'Bout those people in that fancy office not bein' *your* people. Shit'll get you got."

"Whatever, man. Peace."

I jogged over to Wally Cat and sat on a crate, checking the time. 6:58 a.m. *I'll be fine.*

"What's good, Wally Cat?" I noticed he was wearing a particularly bright Hawaiian shirt.

"How was your firs' day?"

140

"Hard. They got us workin' on some script, and today we'll be role-playin'."

"What those white people even have you sellin' over there? Whenever I read up on these new tech companies and all that Mark Zucker-who shit, even my head spins. I know they gotchu on some crazy shit."

"To be honest, I'm still not sure. It's like a platform where people can talk to other people around the world to get help with their problems. You know, therapy without all the bullshit."

He threw his hands up and sucked his teeth. "Without all the bullshit? That shit ain' made for no Black people, Darren. Tha's some rich white women shit, nigga. Ain' no Black people need no therapists, 'cause we don' be havin' those mental issues. OCD, ADD, PTSD, and all those other acronyms they be comin' up with every day. I'm tellin' you, the only acronyms Black folk need help with is the NYPD, FBI, CIA, KKK, and KFC, 'cause I *know* they be puttin' shit in those twelve-piece bucket meals to make us addicted to them. All that saturated fat, sodium. That shit crack, but —"

"Aight, man. I gotta go, Wally Cat. Can't be late. But thanks for the talk."

"Aye, I gotta piece of advice 'fore you go.

I been on this corner long enough to see tens of thousands of transactions go down. And what I learned is that either you sellin' somebody on yes or they sellin' you on no. No matter what happens, some nigga gon' be walkin' away worse off than the other nigga, so you gotta figure out how tha's never you, you feel me?"

Reader: Pay attention to what Wally Cat just said, minus all the acronym BS. Whether you sell someone on yes or they sell you on no, a sale is always made.

"Word, good looks," I said, dapping him up and heading into the subway. I checked my phone: 7:05 a.m. I'd make it.

It was 7:40 a.m. when I got to 3 Park Avenue, so I figured I had enough time to say hi to my old soldiers.

Carlos mopped the floor as Nicole made drinks. "What's up, guys?"

Carlos looked up and threw his hands in the air, the broom slapping the wet floor. "Ayo, Darren! What's good, *hermano*? Thought we'd never see you back here now that you're all fancy up in the penthouse, bro."

"Never that." I dapped him up and surveyed the area. Everything looked as I had left it except for the cardboard cutouts on the counter advertising a new heart-stopping concoction.

"Darren!" Nicole shouted behind the register. "I'd come and hug you, but I gotta get these drinks out," she said, wiping sweat from her brow. Part of me missed her — all of them. I missed the familiarity, I missed being the real HNIC with no one else to tell me what to do or hurl insults at me like I was a stray dog.

"All good, Nicole!" I shouted back over the coffee machine's whir.

But when I was about to head upstairs, I realized something was off.

"Hey, Carlos. Where's Brian?"

He nodded at the back room. I approached and heard shouting behind the door. I opened it and found Brian sitting in a chair, his face soaked in tears, as Jared loomed over him like an overseer ready to bust his ass.

"What the fuck is going on here?" I asked, looking from Jared to Brian.

"What're you doing here?" Jared asked, surprised. "You don't work here anymore."

"Why is he crying?"

"It's none of your business, guy," Jared said, pushing me out of the door.

"Touch me again and I'll break your hand."

"Well, maybe you should've taught this kid how to make coffee. He keeps burning all of the beans and spilling shit. I don't know what's up with him."

I grabbed Brian's arm, helped him up, and walked him out, leaving Jared standing in the room.

"What's going on, Brian?" I patted his face with a napkin.

"I don't know. It's just — FUCK! Sorry. It's just that without you here —" He quickly covered his mouth and held his hand there until he snuffed out the next expletive as if he were suppressing a sneeze. "I'm sorry, Darren. Without you here, it just feels like I'm sort of alone. And I'm just distracted."

I took a long look at Brian and wondered what would happen to him. When I was the HNIC, my concern stretched as far as making sure he was happy and focused, but I never wondered where he'd go from here. Even so, he'd always looked up to me, which maybe was where part of the confidence I had to pitch Rhett that day came from. I had to be there for him.

I grabbed his shoulders. "Listen, man. I'm just trying to figure out this new job myself,

144

but maybe I could give you a referral or something like that. Once I get settled. I'm not saying you'd get hired, but I could at least put in a good word in a month or two."

He smiled, exposing beautiful teeth that looked like pearls in black velvet, and his eyes threatened to jump out of his skull like a cartoon character's. "You would do that for me?"

"Sure, man," I said, as I patted his shoulders. "I gotta go, but keep your head up. Do your job and don't get fired."

"I will!" he said, straightening out his apron. "You're the best, Darren!"

With everything under control, I bid my soldiers farewell and checked the time. 7:55 a.m. *Shit.*

I jogged into the elevator bay and saw one closing. "Hold it, please!"

But no one held it open. And as the doors inched closer, I saw Clyde inside, pointing to his watch with a smirk on his face. *Motherfucker.*

I joined the circle at 7:59 a.m. Clyde gave the same pump-up speech, made the same threats, and fostered the same tension as the day before. Afterward, I was the first one through the door of Bhagavad Gita. I sat in a chair at the short wooden table, and my knee jumped up and down like it contained an automatic spring. *Today is my day. Be the man Ma needs you to be.* Clyde walked in trailed by Frodo and the Duchess, and went straight to the whiteboard.

He laid out what he called the "anatomy of a cold call" — intro, rapport, discovery, presentation, objection handling, qualification, and handoff. "If you do each of these seven things well, you'll succeed. If not, your career at Sumwun will die a quick death."

Then he told us about what our entire week of training would come down to: a formal role-play on Friday. "But it's nothing big. It'll just be me, Rhett, and Charlie, who's going to manage you once training is over. If you pass, you'll get on the phones on Monday. If you don't, you're out the door." He mimed kicking someone out the door with his shiny loafer.

Reader: This is important. If you can master the following, you'll be able to call any stranger up and get what you want. I guarantee it.

For the remainder of the session, Clyde explained the steps one by one. A good intro, he said, is based on simplicity. You say who you are and kick the call off on an upbeat. With rapport, you're looking to quickly establish a connection between you and the prospect. To do this, ask how they are, what their plans for the weekend are, if they caught a popular TV show the night before, etc.

"But," he said, "for God's sake, never bring up the weather. Everyone and their mother brings up the goddamn weather. The point here is to make yourself familiar to them ASAP. The quicker you do that, the more likely someone will let their guard down. And once their guard is down, you can make them do anything you want."

The Duchess perked up at that, asking the best way to get someone to let their guard down.

"By your confidence and tone," Clyde replied. "You never want someone to feel like they're being sold to. Instead, they should view you as a friend, relative, or trusted advisor. *Not* someone looking to get something from them. So while you don't need to give a fuck after the call is done, you need to deeply care for the ten, twenty, or thirty minutes you're on the phone with them. If their dog just died, you console them. If they're excited about some geeky Renaissance fair, you ask them if they're dressing up as an elf or a knight. Get it?"

Everyone nodded.

Frodo raised his hand, then quickly dropped it. "How do we, uh, get paid?"

"By generating sales-qualified leads, aka SQLs. If you pass the prospect off to an AE and the AE says it's good, you get paid. Same works for if those SQLs turn into deals. Other questions?"

Not a word. All of the acronyms and steps made my head spin. Frodo was writing down as much as possible, literally sweating. And the Duchess was, no lie, filing her nails.

"Good," Clyde said, smiling. "Let's begin."

"Frodo, I'm Jack Durft, director of HR at Cold Stone Creamery," Clyde said. "Give me a ring."

"Uh, who's Jack Durft?" he asked, turning to the Duchess and me.

Clyde pinched the bridge of his nose and took a long breath. "Frodo, I just told you. He's director of HR at Cold Stone Creamery, fuck. Call me."

"Okay, um, hello?"

Clyde slammed his hands on the table. I jumped. "Ring the fucking phone, you idiot!"

"Oh, right," Frodo said. He formed his hand into the "hang loose" sign, and brought it to his ear. "Ring ring."

"This is Jack."

"Uh, yes, Mr. Jack, this is —"

"*Click!* Why are you calling him *Mr.* Jack? Be familiar. Would you call your friend *Mr.* Alex?"

Frodo shrugged. "I guess it depends on if he wanted to be called Mr. Alex."

"You must have some weird fucking friends," Clyde said, shaking his head. "But for the purpose of this, let's assume your friends didn't ride the short bus. Call me again."

"Ring ring."

"Good morning, this is Anna."

"Anna? I thought you just said you were Jack?" Frodo asked, getting red.

Clyde swooped down on Frodo so viciously that I thought he was going to punch him in the face. Instead, he got real close to his ear, and whispered, "Do not ever, under any circumstances, break character. Understand?"

Frodo gulped loud enough for us to hear and nodded into his lap.

Clyde stood. "What? You think you're always going to get the person you're calling? You'll have days where you make two

149

hundred calls without ever speaking to someone. And if you do get through, you might speak with Anna the secretary, a gatekeeper whose job it is to keep incompetent salespeople like you from taking up their boss's precious time. It's your job to plow through them like a gang of starstruck groupies."

Reader: This is true. It's the twenty-first century, so secretaries are no longer just women, but regardless, a large part of getting to the right person is by befriending the gatekeeper so they pass you along, give you information, and become an ally — not an enemy.

Frodo smirked. The Duchess yawned. I felt like I was going to be sick.

"Buck."

Shit. Oh no. It felt like I was tied to a railroad track waiting for a bloody collision as a train hurtled toward me, its lights shining through the dark.

"I'm Harry Johnson. VP of people at McDonald's. Call me."

I took a breath. Without doing any of Frodo's stupid hang-loose shit, I said, "Ring ring."

"Harry here."

150

"Hi, Harry, this is Darren calling from Sumwun. How are you?"

"Hi, Darren, I'm great. How are you?"

"Pretty good, enjoying the nice, uh, nice —"

"Nice what, Darren? Hello? Are you still there? Were you just about to talk about the weather? The FUCKING WEATHER LIKE I KNOW YOUR BOSS TOLD YOU TO NEVER TALK ABOUT BECAUSE IT'S BORING AND ONLY DISCUSSED BY BORING PEOPLE? Fuck!" Clyde grabbed my elbow hard, yanked me up out of my chair, and walked me over to the windows.

"Look outside, Buck," he ordered. "What do you see?"

"Buildings." I was now officially ill.

"That's right," he said, patting my back. "If you ever bring up the weather again, I'm going to throw you through this fucking window and make sure you never see *those* buildings from *this* view again. Understand?"

Clyde somehow resembled Jack Nicholson in both *The Shining* and *One Flew Over the Cuckoo's Nest*. His teeth were bared, gelled clumps of blond hair hung down over his eyes, and he was breathing like a feral animal.

I had never let anyone speak like that to me before, and while I didn't want to let it fly, I knew, as Mr. Rawlings said, that it was all a part of the game and that real men were judged by how much they could withstand. So I nodded.

"The Duchess. Call Harry. Same guy Buck felt compelled to discuss the weather with."

Her performance was flawless.

Clyde, finally satisfied, dialed a few numbers into the phone on the table.

"Hello?"

"Yeah, it's Clyde. Grab Eddie and Marissa, and come to Bhagavad Gita."

Marissa, Eddie, and Tiffany, senior SDRs who'd already hit their numbers, stood at the head of the room and inspected us as if we were cattle. With arms crossed, Tiffany grinned, and asked, "Who's first?"

"Wait," Eddie said. "Let's get a temperature check. How're you all doing?"

Frodo and I shrugged. The Duchess said, "Fine, how much longer do we need to be in here?"

"As long as it takes, rich bitch," Tiffany snapped. "You three must be the most pathetic group of SDRs I've ever seen."

The rest of the session was traumatizing.

By lunchtime, I felt as if I'd been mauled by Mike Vick's dogs. Fortunately, lunch was catered.

The event space's marble island overflowed with yellow rice, pinto beans, spotted tortilla shells, chicken, steak, sautéed onions, lettuce, tomatoes, and green peppers. The three of us returned to Bhagavad Gita without a word. Frodo had taken double of everything, and it barely fit on two oversize plates, the Duchess had made herself a small taco salad, and I went with a modest steak burrito.

"So, how'd you all hear about Sumwun?" Frodo asked, as a mouthful of salty juices trickled down his chin.

"I met Rhett at Starbucks," I said, trying to be casual.

"Is that what happened?" the Duchess asked. She impaled pieces of chicken and lettuce with her fork, likely performing culinary voodoo on someone.

"That's what I said, didn't I?"

"What were you doing at Starbucks?" she asked.

"How did *you* get here?" I deflected.

"My father plays squash with Clyde's father at the Greenwich Country Club," she replied, like I should have known. The truth is, I hadn't known squash was anything other than a vegetable until I was fifteen.

"And?" Frodo asked, pausing to swallow an overambitious mouthful.

"And Clyde told me about the role, gave me some guidance, and now I'm here with you two specimens of excellence."

"Guidance?" I asked. "Like what?"

"Like how to role-play and do the job, what else? Nothing special."

Nothing special. No wonder she wasn't getting destroyed in the role-plays. She had *connections.* Connections, like treasury bonds, are issued to every rich white person upon exiting the womb. Whenever one of them gets high and crashes their parents' car, whenever they get busted for buying coke from an undercover, whenever they get caught messing with the wrong gangsters on vacation, they make a call, send a text, or whip out their AMEX.

Reader: One of the most important keys to success in sales is focus. Never let anything or anyone throw you off track, especially people who seem to be born with it all.

Frodo, having managed to swallow more than he could chew, breathed with relief. "Yeah, my recruiter also coached me.

Sumwun was actually the sixth place I interviewed at. When Clyde saw I was a D1 tackle at Notre Dame, all he asked was if I was prepared to work harder here than I had on the field. After I said yes, I got the job. By the way," he said, setting his dripping taco down and turning to me, "has anyone ever told you that you look like Dave Chappelle?"

The cards are stacked against me. I didn't have a daddy to play squash with the director of sales' pops. No recruiter to lay up five interviews for me to bomb until someone took a chance on me because I was an athlete. The only thing that got me there was a momentary flash of courage — courage that was growing weaker by the day.

The day repeated in cycles of different SDRs grilling us nonstop. By the end of it, I was spent. Thank God Clyde never came back.

I grabbed my bag and headed for the elevator when I heard shouting. My curiosity outweighed my exhaustion. When I got closer to Rhett's office, the door swung open and Chris, the small, sweaty, red-faced cofounder, rushed out like a hurricane.

"If you don't take care of this, I will!" he shouted over his shoulder as he stormed

155

past me.

I peeked in and found Rhett seated on a leather couch with a glass of gin in one hand and his forehead resting in the other. His pressed white button-up was wrinkled. I quietly backed away until he looked up, our eyes connecting.

"Oh, Buck, I didn't know you were here. Everything alright?"

His eyes were bloodshot, and his olive complexion looked paler, as if someone had ripped off a few sheets of his skin to reveal the sallow, vampirelike inverse of his daytime self.

"Uh, yeah," I said. "Sorry for interrupting. I've just been stuck in Bhagavad Gita all day and heard screaming so . . ."

He waved a hand and smiled, bringing the color back to his face. "Ah, don't worry about that. Just boring startup stuff. Take a seat."

I dropped my bag and grabbed the other end of the couch. His office was massive, about half the size of Qur'an, and had two long black leather couches, a full-size pool table, a desk made out of an old door, and, of course, floor-to-ceiling windows.

He slowly rose from the couch, and walked toward shelves full of books and bottles of bourbon, whiskey, vodka, and more.

"Drink?"

"No, thanks, I don't really, uh —"

"No worries. I probably shouldn't as much as I do. But there's something about a cold glass of gin at the end of the day that makes me feel more human." He laughed. "Does that make me an alcoholic?"

"I guess it depends."

He sat next to me. "On what?"

"On if you still feel human without it."

He looked into his glass, as if there were answers at the bottom. "Clyde tells me you're having a hard time."

"It's okay," I said, admiring his books. Daniel Pink. Dale Carnegie. Eric Ries. Andy Grove. All part of the standard startup CEO guide. "You like to read, huh?"

He laughed. "You could say that. But you still didn't give me a straight answer. How're you doing?"

"This shit's tough, man," I said before I could stop myself. "I feel like Clyde's going harder on me than the others. Like I'm always a step behind."

He set his glass down and nodded. "This is normal, Buck. If you feel like he's going hard on you, he probably is. But it's only because he secs your potential just like I do. This," he said, waving his hands around, "means nothing if people aren't pushed past

157

the limits of who they thought they were. And, believe it or not, I *know* who you truly are, how great you can become."

Damn. This guy believes in me more than I believe in myself.

Reader: Everyone thinks the key to succeeding in sales is motivation. Wrong. Motivation fades in an instant. But inspiration? Man, that'll sustain you longer than accidentally overdosing on Viagra. Rhett, as you'll come to see, embodied inspiration. He hooked me — even blinded me.

"And what about you?" I asked.

"Me? Ah, all's well. We just need to hit this number. What you'll learn, Buck, is that every single problem you have disappears," he said, clapping his hands, "once you hit your number."

I didn't know where the time went, but it was 8:30 p.m. and my exhaustion returned like a dormant case of the clap. "It's getting late, Rhett. I gotta go."

"This?" he said, laughing. "Late? By next week, eight is going to be early for you. Go home, rest up, and be ready to kick some ass tomorrow. But I want you to promise me something, Buck. I know we haven't known each other for long, but if you promise this to me, I'll promise it to you."

I waited for the guy to get down on one knee and profess his love to me, but I was thankful that he just said, "Promise me that you'll always be honest with me, Buck. That you'll never hide anything from me. And I promise to look out for you. To mold you in my own image and make sure you succeed."

He stretched his hand toward mine. I knew that taking it into my own meant making a promise I couldn't turn away from — a handshake I couldn't undo. Like I said, I was already a minor planet in Rhett's gravitational pull, and I liked the feeling. I took a breath and grabbed his hand. A small smile appeared on his face.

"I promise."

9

After waking up with a headache the size of Kanye's ego, I headed into the kitchen. But there was no sign of Ma. I walked downstairs and found her door closed, which was unusual. She normally slept with it open.

"Ma," I said, tapping the door. No answer. "Ma," I repeated, louder. No answer. When I opened the door, I found her lying on her back, out cold. Seized with terror, I slowly crept toward her, thinking she'd died in her sleep. Tears had begun forming in my eyes when I kicked over a glass she'd left on the floor. She bolted upright, her black sleeping mask still over her eyes.

"Thank God," I said. I picked up the glass and wiped my tears. "I thought —"

"What time is it, Dar?" She removed her mask to reveal dark rings under her eyes.

"6:40 a.m., Ma."

"Oh, I must've slept through my alarm. I've been so tired, baby. I think I may jus' call out."

This was the first time Ma had ever called out. She always managed to put the coffee on and make it to work — no matter how bad she felt. She even went to the factory the day after Pa died because she said it felt good to be needed even when you were just one out of thousands. I was worried, but I figured the best thing to do was get to Sumwun, knock it out of the park, and trust that she'd feel better soon.

"Can I get you anything before I leave, Ma? You want some more water, coffee?"

"No, thank you, baby." She closed her eyes and grabbed my arm. "Have a good day at work, Dar. I'll see you when you get back. And don' forget about Friday. I'll be better by then. It'll be nice."

I bent down and kissed her cool forehead. "Okay, Ma. I'll be there."

Down the stairs. Turn the corner. Wave to Mr. Aziz. The gargoyles were parked in their same spot. Jason wanted to talk, but I had no time, so I just ran past him and saluted Wally Cat before entering the subway.

Like Ma, I should've called out sick.

Clyde was working on a deal with someone in London, so Charlie, the Paul Bunyan-looking guy from Monday who explained why we needed to hit our number, and my future manager, led the stretch.

At the end, Rhett walked into the center of the circle. He was no longer pale and shrunken like he had been the previous night. He was brighter, fuller, more like the guy I pitched at Starbucks.

Everyone stopped moving; the only sounds were rain pattering against the window and far-off voices on the sales floor from people trying to close overseas deals. Rhett closed his eyes and stood in silence for two full minutes.

"Let me ask a question," he said. "A simple one. Two years ago, what did we raise in our Series A?"

"Seven million," someone said.

"And our Series B?"

"Twenty million," another added.

"All in all, including a seed round, we've raised twenty-eight million dollars. Take a second to imagine what a room full of twenty-eight million dollars looks like," he said, turning around the circle. "Someone, tell me what they see."

"A room full to the brim with hundreds," someone called out.

"Gold bars in a bank vault," another said.

"What else?" Rhett asked.

"A garage full of Bugattis!" a voice

shouted.

"Sure, it could be all of those," he said. "But when I think of a room of twenty-eight million dollars, what I see is all of you. I don't see this office, with our perks, the MacBooks with our Mac monitors, or even Mac Jackson our trainer, though he is a stud."

Mac, among the kitchen spectators, waved to the circle and everyone smiled.

"I see a room of people. And I'll tell you, when family, friends, and investors gave us that twenty-eight million, the money was only a symbol. A symbol of the belief they had in us. In each and every one of you." He pointed around the circle. "And what matters most is that we hit this month and show them that they made the right move betting on us even when everyone said we were crazy to think we could disrupt the world of therapy.

"They said no company cared enough about their employees to pay for modern therapy. They said no one in their right mind would log on to a computer to speak with a stranger halfway around the world, opening themselves up like cracked fortune cookies. But here we are. The darling of New York City. Putting Silicon Alley on the map."

Clyde entered the circle. "Good news?" Rhett asked, everyone watching, tense.

"Two hundred thousand from Virgin!" Clyde shouted, and raised his fist to a room full of applause.

"FUCK YEAH!" Rhett said, picking him up and twirling him around.

The room got quiet, and Clyde parted the sea of people, making his way toward the gong. He grabbed a rubber-tipped mallet and faced the crowd.

"It's just a pilot program, but Virgin is going to have one thousand of its lowest-performing employees across its subsidiaries use Sumwun to increase performance. They've assured us that if it works they'll roll it out to ten thousand in the next year!"

"We love you, Clyde!" a gaggle of girls shouted.

"Yeah, us too, bro!" a horde of guys wearing backward snapbacks echoed.

"I love you too, I do. I know it's been a tough month" — he ran his hands through his hair — "and that they don't get any easier. But I just want to thank all of you for how hard you're working, and Rhett for helping get this deal over the line."

"It was all you, Clyde. Please, I was just along for the ride."

It was then that I first saw it. I don't know

if I can say it was the look a father gives a son or an older brother gives a younger one, but what I can say is that it was true love. The love that is exchanged between people who would do anything for each other. And, for the first time, I saw a humanity in Clyde that I didn't know he possessed.

"Now hit that shit!" Rhett ordered.

Clyde cocked his hand back like a pitcher about to throw a ball at ninety miles an hour and struck the gong with a force that made the ground shake.

"ABC, baby!" Rhett shouted. "Always. Be. Closing!"

"That's how you fucking do it!" Clyde screamed, strutting into Bhagavad Gita like a colonizer.

Frodo held his hand up for a high five. "Nice one, Clyde. Can't wait to be able to close a deal like that."

"Okay," Clyde said, ignoring Frodo. "Plan for the day is to role-play with me. Then one-on-one role-playing with a senior SDR until the end of the day. Now's crunch time, so don't fucking slack off. Frodo, you first. Stand up."

Clyde was Karl Schmitt, CEO of Schmitt Dogshit. And Karl schmitted all over Frodo. He even said, "You're almost worse than

165

Buck, and that's an achievement." Aside from "having less of a brain than a mummified corpse," Frodo's main undoing was ending statements with a question mark, which Clyde said introduced doubt into the conversation.

Reader: This is one hundred percent true. If you talk like this? People will think you don't know what the hell you're saying? So, when speaking, picture ending everything you say with a period. Periods = confidence. Confidence = success.

When it was the Duchess's turn, Clyde told her to stay seated because she'd pass on Friday without any more sessions. "But you" — he kicked my chair — "get up. I'm Tyrone Williams, VP of people at Imperial Tobacco."

"Ring ring."

"Tyrone."

"Hi, Tyrone, it's Darren calling from Sumwun. How are you?"

"I'z good, Darren. Hey, now dat sound like a brother's name. You a brother?"

Ignore it. I wasn't going to let him get to me.

"Yeah, Tyrone. I'm a brother. And I'm

calling you today to learn more about what you're all doing over there to increase employee wellness."

"Huh, dat a funny question, Darren. Never tawt about dat one. Gez not much."

"Great, sounds like it's a good thing I called. We're working with companies similar to your own to help increase employee productivity through a more balanced, healthier state of mind. How's that sound?"

"Gez it sound awright to me, suh! Aye, you ever have a Philly Blunt?"

"No, Tyrone. I don't smoke."

"You don' smoke? What kinda brother 'r' you? We over here at Imperial Tobacco make 'em! I don' think I can do business wid someone who's never had a Philly Blunt befoe."

Fuck this. He wouldn't do this to anyone else. Hit him and walk out. No, don't. This modern-day minstrel show is irritating, but you can take it. Think of Ma. Think of Ma. Think of Ma.

"Well, how about this? I get a little more information from you, Tyrone, and then whenever you're in New York, we'll spark up a Philly together?"

"*CLICK!* What the fuck was that, Buck? You'll smoke a blunt with him? Christ."

"They're also cigars, man. I didn't mean a blunt."

"No, you did. What else do you all use them for? Learn the difference between getting familiar and getting *too* comfortable. What if Tyrone was recording that and posted it online? You'd bring the fucking company down with how unprofessional that was."

"You were the one acting like a stereotype."

"Are you calling me a fucking racist, Buck? You better watch it."

My hand was ready, my heart was ready, and my frustration, reaching magma-level intensity, was there.

"Please do it," Clyde said, eyeing my fist. "I want you to. It'll make this easier for everyone."

"Buck." Frodo grabbed my elbow. "Chill out."

Clyde walked toward me and didn't stop until our noses were touching. He smiled that same fucking smile, with those same sky-blue eyes, and that same stench of self-entitlement. "Sit," he ordered.

I was tempted to splatter his brains against the dry-erase wall, but that same voice from before said I needed to choose my battles, keep my eyes on the prize, and all of that other *Rocky* "Eye of the Tiger" bullshit. So, I sat.

Reader: No matter how much it hurts, never let short-term frustration disrupt long-term gain. Sales is a marathon, not a sprint.

"Good boy," he said, walking toward the door.

Doubts ricocheted inside my head. *Is this really what Ma wants? What was so wrong with who I was last week?*

"Buck?" Clyde said, pausing in the doorway.

"What?"

"The next time you threaten me, you won't just be fired. I'll also have you thrown in jail. You got that?"

No, I don't fucking got that, you David Duke–worshipping, NRA license–carrying, "Take Me Home, Country Roads"–singing motherfucker!

But I stayed silent.

He turned around, amused. "I want to hear that you got that, Buck. No, I *need* to hear it in order to feel safe, to know you're not *dangerous*."

I closed my eyes, imagined getting up and slamming my fist through his face, his nose cracking like ice in a plastic tray. But then I pictured Rhett staring at me with the same look of pride that he'd given Clyde that morning, the same look he'd given me after I rapped in Monday's meeting. I don't know why that vision held so much weight for me, but it did. And it was enough to make me swallow any trace of pride I had.

"Got it," I said, hating myself.

"Welcome to Torah," Eddie said with outstretched arms. Torah, like every other room in the office, bore no cultural resemblance to its namesake.

"Another religious text, cool," I said.

Even though I'd had only a few interactions with Eddie, I liked him. The whole hipster-punk-rock look — black ear gauges, goatee, wire-frame glasses, holey Metallica T-shirt to go with his black skinny jeans and leather combat boots — didn't match his glittering personality, but I appreciated that I couldn't really place him in a box.

"Mm-hmm. When we moved offices, the almighty Rhett decreed that each room be named for one of the sacred books of our assistants' various religious beliefs."

"So how does that work? The assistants, I mean. Do they find us or do we find them?"

"A little bit of both, but we have what we call community managers who sign them up. They're not like licensed therapists, but are totes certified in their various belief systems and can speak credibly about them. For example, our community managers may find a prominent Hindu practitioner in India via a blog post or video, then reach out to see if she'd like to become an assistant. After she accepts, her time becomes available to book for employees of the organizations who use us. And while the woman may not be certified by our American standards, her different outlook on life could still be useful to people going through hard times here or in other places around the world."

"I see. But are there ever any issues? You're finding strangers online and people are paying to speak with them. They can't always be good, right?"

He stroked his goatee. "Yeah, of course. There're always a few bad eggs who get into trouble, but users can review, report, or leave comments so we can kick them off the platform ASAP. But it's obviously not in the assistants' best interest to be assholes. They want to make money and help people."

"Got it."

That session with Eddie was the day's silver lining. I learned that "no one's going to stay on the line with someone as interesting as C-SPAN," that "what and how you pitch depends on who you're pitching to," and that the point of speaking with someone is to have a conversation, not to conduct an interrogation. But best of all, I learned how to have fun on the phone.

Reader: All of that is critical advice. No one is going to listen to someone who sounds like they'd rather be doing something else. And when you're trying to convince someone of anything, you need to tailor your message to the person you're speaking with so it resonates as powerfully as possible.

At the end, Eddie smiled, and said, "You might just get this." And no matter how corny this sounds, it felt like one of those movie scenes where the skinny white nerd begins to grow muscles, run faster, and lift more weights right before he knocks the shit out of his bully. Or shoots up the whole school. But you get the point.

For the first time in my life, *I* was the skinny white nerd.

When I swung by Rhett's office, he was in the same spot as the night before, alone with the lights low, nursing a glass of gin. His eyes were closed when I entered, as if he were praying.

"Anything good?" I dropped my bag.

"The usual." He opened his eyes and patted the couch. "How was your day? Any better?"

"Uh, sort of. At least role-plays were. Eddie set me straight."

"Good one. Drink?"

"No, thanks."

"Then pool. Get up."

He chucked a stick at me and racked the balls.

"Break," he said, bloodshot eyes glaring at the illuminated triangle.

I'd always thought pool was reserved for white guys with tattoos, leather jackets, and asthmatic Harley-Davidsons, which led to one unfortunate outcome: I couldn't hit a ball to save my life.

"The aim is to hit those balls in the center of the table, Buck. Not do all you can to miss them," he said, shaking with laughter. "Again."

I took aim and caught the bottom corner of the triangle. Fifteen balls inched away.

"I'll tell you one thing," Rhett said. "I sure hope you sell better than you play pool."

"This game's fixed," I said, after he

whooped my ass. Any game where one white ball can beat the living crap out of every other non-white ball on the table has to be rigged.

"It's not fixed, Buck. You just need to change your approach. All you need is a coach."

"Yeah, whatever," I said, plopping down on the leather couch. "Like God, right? The ultimate coach? Is that who you were chatting with before?"

He grabbed a bottle off the shelf and poured himself another glass. "I guess, yeah. Are you a believer?"

"My mom used to bring me to a Seventh Day Adventist church when I was little but stopped after I kept complaining about having to go to church on Saturdays."

"Brat. Does she still go?"

"Once in a while, yeah. After my dad died, she said God and me were the only men she had time for."

"And what about you?" he asked, racking the balls. "You still haven't answered my question."

"I don't know, man. Not really."

"So what happens after we die?"

"I have no idea. I mean, I hope this isn't it. But if it is, can't really do anything about it, right? What about you? You a 'Man of God'?"

He struck the balls so hard that I swore they would all roll into the pockets just to escape his wrath. "I grew up poor, Buck. And from the sounds of it, worse than you. Poor people and God usually go hand in hand because it's easier to explain why some people have so much and others have so little when there's a master plan.

"My parents used to bring me and my younger sister to church every Sunday without fail. We'd dress up in the only pair of decent clothes we had and walk a mile to the church, holding hands the whole way. But when we'd get in, my mother would light up like it was Christmas. She'd glow, and you'd never know that she scrubbed floors for a living or sometimes went nights without dinner so her kids could eat."

He continued driving balls into the pockets, one by one. Red solid in the corner. Purple and white in the side. "You still haven't answered my question," I said.

"Yeah, I believe in God." He rounded the table, getting a better angle. "Even if I'm wrong, there's no harm in believing. When it comes to any gamble, I always hedge my bet."

"Even with me?"

He laughed and chipped a ball off the table, sending it soaring toward my face. I caught it just in time.

10

When I woke, the kitchen was just as I had left it the night before: a solitary plate and mug resting in the sink, all of the chairs pushed to the table's edge, no Ma.

"Ma," I said, knocking on her door. I hadn't noticed that she wasn't awake when I got home. I just shot into my room and passed out. The same fear of finding her frozen in some last, clawing gasp for air prevented me from opening the door. I knocked again.

"Come in, Dar," she whispered.

I found her in the same position I'd left her the previous morning: slightly curled to the side with blankets pulled to just below her eyes. The blinds were shut, and the room gave off a sour smell, like it was rebelling against whatever was going on with her.

I sat next to her. "Ma, what's goin' on?"

"Still a bit tired," she said, sitting up. "What time is it?"

"6:47 a.m. You been in bed since I left you?"

"No." She grabbed a glass of water from her table. "I went to the bathroom, got some water, and walked around. I tried to wash what was in the sink but couldn't."

"Don' worry 'bout that, Ma." I placed my hand on her forehead. "Is it a cold or somethin'? Doesn' feel like a fever."

She grabbed my hand, brought it to her cheek, and smiled. "Salesman. Doctor. What else are you gonna become, a politician?"

"Nah, probably not, Ma," I said, laughing. "I'm not much of a leader. Except for at Starbucks."

"Mm-hmm. That's what you say. But I know what you are. I've always known."

"Oh yeah? And what's that, Miss Cleo? All you're missin' is the Jafaican accent."

She sucked her teeth and pushed my hand away. "Don' play with me. I may be weak, but I'll still show you who's boss."

"So what am I?" I asked. "What have you always known?"

"That's for you to find out, Dar. Not for me or anyone to tell you. When you get to wherever you're goin', you'll know. And I'll be there, watchin' from afar, proud as a peacock."

I felt her forehead again to see if she was

178

feverish. She wasn't, but something didn't feel right. My gut told me to stay with her and walk her to the doctor's, but the thought of Clyde thinking I quit overpowered my gut. *Let's make a deal.*

"Ma." I grabbed her hand. "I won' lie; I don' wanna go to work today with you feelin' like this."

"Darren Vender, if you don' get up and get to work, I'm gonna be sicker. Trust me."

"Okay, but only on one condition."

She closed her eyes, shaking her head. "What is it?"

"You ask Mr. Rawlings to bring you to the doctor today jus' to make sure this isn' anything serious. Deal?"

"Deal," she said, smiling. "Now go on and don' be late. I'll be alright. May even get my stuff together and go to work. I'm already feelin' a bit better."

I took a long look at her and got up. "Aight, Ma. I love you."

"I love you, too, Dar," she said. "I'll grab Percy in a minute and go. I promise."

Down the stairs. Turn the corner. Wave to Mr. Aziz. Dap up Jason. Say what up to Wally Cat. That's the way it went on most days, but on day four of Hell Week, Jason, wearing military fatigues from head to toe, acted like he didn't see me when I held my hand out.

"What's good, Batman?" I asked, waiting for him to look at me. "You good?"

He pulled out his phone and plugged in earbuds, nodding to whatever he was playing.

"Yo," I said, ripping one out.

He punched me in the chest, knocking me onto the ground. "What the fuck, man?" I asked, looking up at him, his hand still in a fist.

"Don' fuckin' touch me," he said. "I don' let no stranger touch me."

I got up and dusted the sidewalk off my ass. "You're buggin', J. What's goin' on?"

"What's goin' on is that you out here runnin' past me every day like you don' even see me. Like I'm not the nigga who watched out for you when older niggas tried runnin' your backpack, sneakers, or clean clothes your momma bought with money from her good job. But I'm buggin', right?"

I moved to grab his shoulder until he backed away. "I already told you 'bout strange niggas touchin' me. Next time it won' be a fist."

"Are you jealous or somethin'?" I asked, seeing real hate in his eyes. "That I'm movin' up and you're stuck on this corner?

Is that it? I could try and get you a job, bro. Jus' say the word."

The hate in his eyes melted, and he laughed. "A job? You so lost you can't see that you doin' exactly what I am. Because no matter how you package it up and sell it, weight is weight. Except you pushin' weight for the white man and your corner is an office. But you ain' one of them. And when they find out you a nigga, jus' like me, they gonna kick you to the curb. Watch."

"Aight, man," I said, tired of his shit. "Only difference is my weight won' land me in jail. I'd say maybe I'll catch you tomorrow, but I know I will, right here on this fuckin' corner."

I crossed the street to Wally Cat, who sat shaking his head. "You li'l niggas shouldn' have no beef," he said, patting the crate next to him. "All this Black-on-Black shit. Nigga, we gotta come together, like a community, 'specially when all these white folks comin' in. Shit, you probably know some of 'em now, don' you?"

"Whatever, man," I said, rising from the crate.

"Sitchyo ass back down," he ordered, and he pulled me down so hard I almost tripped. "Have some respect for an OG like Wally Cat. How's yo' girl?"

I shot a rope of spit into the street just like I used to see Wally Cat do when I was younger. "She's straight."

"And yo' momma?"

"A li'l tired, man. But she'll be aight."

"Yeah," he said, looking up at the sun, shielding his eyes. "She strong. Always has been. What about yo' new sales hustle? You makin' millions yet? You know when you do, you owe me. Nothin' large, jus' a couple thousand, somethin' small for all the knowledge I been droppin' on you over the years."

I stared at him, wondering if he was kidding, but I couldn't tell. "I'm not makin' shit, man," I said, spitting again. "Got all these white people, 'specially this one white guy, tellin' me I can't do it, that I'm not good enough."

"Fuck 'em," Wally Cat said, fanning himself with his fedora. "Everybody doin' somethin' got people tellin' 'em they can't do it. If you doin' somethin' and people ain' tellin' you that you can't do it, truth is, you ain' doin' shit!" he said, doubling over the crate, laughter rocking his whole big-boned body.

"Tha's the truth, nigga! And also" — he grabbed my shoulder — "in any game, you gotta have a short-term memory. Someone tell you some shit you don' like? Forget it

182

the minute they mouth close. Someone tell you some shit you do like? Man," he said, sucking his teeth so hard that I swore he was about to swallow them, "you betta forget *that* shit even quicker."

Reader: Highlight that whole paragraph, it'll save you years of pain.

"Only thing that matters is this," he continued, extending a thick, level hand in front of my eyes.

"What, your hand?" I asked, remembering I had to hit the train.

"Nah, nigga. A balanced mind, jus' like this here balanced hand. I knew they ain' teach you shit at your fancy-ass school."

I dapped him up. "Good looks for the lesson, Wally Cat. I gotta jet," I said, heading for the subway.

"Oh, and Darren!" he shouted from across the street. "Never, under any circumstances, fuck a snow bunny. Never! You'll have bad luck for seven years! Why you think I'm out here on this crate?"

I didn't pay those words any mind, but maybe I should have. A great fall would come, and I still wonder if it's because I didn't listen to Wally Cat.

"No deals," Clyde said. "It's Thursday, and we haven't had a deal since Virgin."

The circle was as frozen as an Inuit's titty.

"That means we have two hundred and fifty thousand to go find in" — he looked down at his bare wrist — "less than two days. And normally, you all know, I'm as cool as a cucumber. But every single one of you" — he swung his finger around the circle as if it were a Death Eater's wand — "better haul ass today. If I don't see money on the board, heads will roll. Understand?"

Everyone nodded.

"Good. Because, while I can't guarantee that we're going to hit our number even though we've hit every fucking number for the last year, I *can* guarantee that if we don't hit I'm firing someone. *No,*" he said, his eyes ablaze with visions of fire and blood. "I'm firing a group of you. The fat. And after you're gone, there will only be meat. Sweet, delicious, savory, and delectable meat. Now go," he commanded. The circle scattered like roaches when the lights are turned on.

"Frodo, Buck, the Duchess," he shouted. "Book of Shadows. Now."

Book of Shadows? I imagined dark screeching spirits flying out of an oversize leather-bound book, forcing their way down our throats, overtaking our souls.

This can't end well.

We shuffled in one by one, and once the door closed, we were bathed in ultraviolet light. It made Clyde and the Duchess, with their glowing white manes, brightly colored skin, and piercing eyes, look like alien nobility. Intricate illustrations of pentagrams, moons, horned man-beasts, and candles glowed on the carpet, and we all sat in a circle cross-legged, kumbaya style. Clyde explained that the designers had come up with the room to scare people.

Skipping Frodo and the Duchess, Clyde role-played with only me. He was Marshall, CEO of Marshall Bakeries, and even though he made it nearly impossible by saying he wasn't interested, repeatedly telling me he had to go, and even calling me "boy," I ended up fully qualifying him. But after we hung up, there was silence. It floated throughout the room like smoke, stopping to caress my face before growing deadly.

"It astounds me," Clyde said, pausing, "how much you fucking missed."

"Missed? I qualified you!" My voice was rising.

"The guy was obviously yessing you to death to avoid being impolite. Dude wouldn't have showed up to the next meeting if you offered him a million bucks."

My whole body shook, but I wasn't going to give in. Not when I was almost on the other side.

"Let me ask you a question," Clyde said, dragging himself across the circle. "What did you do the first time you tried to fuck your girlfriend? When you put your hand down her tight little jeans. You didn't flinch, did you?"

I dug my fingers into the carpet.

"Because if you flinched," he continued, his teeth shining like turquoise Tic Tacs, "she would've slapped your hand away. And you would've never fucked, right?"

Do not give in. Do not give in. Do not give in. I repeated it like a prayer, like it was the only thing that would prevent me from finally hitting him or running out the door.

"Yes or no?" he pressed.

Think about the future, when you're on an island with Ma, Soraya, and maybe even Jason and Mr. Rawlings. None of this will matter.

"Yes," I whispered through gritted teeth.

"What?" he said. "I couldn't hear you, *brother.* Speak up. It's dark in here, but you don't have to be so quiet. C'mon."

Be the man Pa would've wanted you to be.

"Yes," I repeated, louder.

"If you can't speak up for yourself, those leads will swallow your ass alive. Speak the fuck up!"

Man up, man up, man up.

"Yes!" I repeated, even louder. I felt like I was about to throw up.

"Just pack your shit up and leave. You won't last an hour out on that floor. I said SPEAK THE FUCK UP!"

"YES!" I shouted, heavy tears staining my cheeks. "YES! YES! YES!" I stopped caring. I no longer gave a fuck. About Clyde. About proving that I could do it or anything else. I was done. They had won. I bent over and the tears continued to fall; my body shook as I struggled to breathe.

"*Shh.* There you go," he whispered, gently rubbing my back. "Finally, a broken Buck."

"Hey, you coming back?" Frodo asked, as I waited for the elevator.

"Don't know."

"This is all just, uh, part of it, you know, Buck? It was like this when I started playing for Notre Dame. You gotta go through the pain to get to the pleasure. Can't let 'em get to you or else —"

"Word," I said, entering the elevator.

I crossed the lobby, pushed my way out into the sunlight of a hot May day, and texted Soraya, asking where she was. She replied in seconds: At the shop, where else?

I knew she'd be there. She was always there during the week. But I couldn't think straight. The only thing I knew was that I needed her. Can you meet me in Washington Square Park?

On the way, she replied.

The entire twenty-eight-block walk to Washington Square Park was a blur. I can't tell you what the city buses advertised on their sides. I don't remember the tunnel of smells I encountered as I navigated through Murray Hill, Gramercy, and Union Square, down to the Village. The panhandlers with outstretched cups, the businessmen and women, and the dog walkers were all as faceless as storefront mannequins. But what I do remember, finally, is the park.

A shaggy pianist busting out old-time rhythms; nations of Black, Hispanic, and Asian nannies pushing blonde-haired and blue-eyed surrogates in $1,500 strollers; skateboarders abusing Garibaldi when they should've been in school; the fountain, like a humpback, spouting water into the sky, catching the light's reflection. Washington's words forever inscribed in the arch, built over the bones of the natives buried beneath: LET US RAISE A STANDARD TO WHICH THE WISE AND HONEST CAN REPAIR.

Sounds like a confession, I thought, sitting inside the fountain, out of the water's reach.

A shadow appeared, blocking the sun's heat. "Come here often?"

I looked up and saw her sweet, smiling face. Beneath her acid-washed jean jacket, I could make out a white T-shirt with one of Frida Kahlo's self-portraits on it. For the briefest moment, I forgot why we were there. "Occasionally," I said, reaching my hand out to help her climb in next to me.

"So." She grabbed my face with her smooth hands and planted a kiss on my forehead. "What's up?"

"Nothin'." I watched little white kids running through the fountain. *To be that free, man. That's the dream.*

"Nothin', huh? Okay," she said, getting up. "Guess I'll go back to Brooklyn then. Bye."

"Wait!" I grabbed her hand. "Aight, aight, aight. It's work, what else?"

She sat back down. "What about it?"

"I can't do it, Soraya. This shit's jus' not

189

for me. These people, almost all of them, I feel like they're targetin' me."

"Targetin' you how, D?"

"This guy Clyde. The one I told you about. He goes in on me durin' role-plays and gives everyone else a pass. He tells me all day about how I'm not good enough and how I'm gonna fail. And then this girl I'm trainin' with, the Duchess, is OD pretentious. And the other kid, Frodo, he's mad dumb but not too bad. And Rhett, he's the only reason I'm there, but even he can't save me. It's all jus' messed up. I'm done. They won."

"Whoa." She pulled my head onto her shoulder, the smell of cinnamon and cocoa butter almost calming me down. "Slow down, slow down. All these names. All these people. Isn' this the whole point of Hell Week, D? For them to make your life, I dunno, hell? In order to see if you can take it?"

"Yeah, but I can't. This is why you don' see minorities in these places. We're not built for this shit. Forreal."

"So what?" she said, lifting my chin. "You're jus' gonna give up, huh? You're seriously gonna, what, go back to bein' a shift supervisor at Starbucks? C'mon, D, you're smarter than that."

I pulled away from her, my pulse rising. "What the fuck was wrong with bein' a shift supervisor at Starbucks? You were my girl when I was there, and I never heard any complaints."

She pulled my hand to her chest and I could feel her heart beating. "Chill out, D. It's me. Same team, same dream, remember? Always have been and always will be, you know that, but let's jus' slow down."

I closed my eyes, took a big breath, and let it out. The sounds of the city surrounded us: taxis honking; kids laughing; heels clacking on the concrete; the piano mixed in with stray guitars, saxophones, and trumpets.

"I know, my bad. It's jus' that I'm tired of all these mind games. Every day is a test, and it all jus' seems mad unfair, you know? Like why do I gotta be twice as good?"

"You gotta play their game to be able to win it, D. And it doesn' matter if you gotta be twice or three times as good. What matters is that you don' let them beat you once, and say, 'Game over.' 'Cause if you quit now, it's gonna be much harder to get back up."

What she said was true, but I didn't care. I was tired. Tired as hell. Frodo and the Duchess weren't going through half of what I was, and it all felt so unfair. Like my skin came with a bull's-eye.

Reader: Contrary to popular belief, "fairness" has no place is sales. It is not a meritocracy. Every salesperson comes into the game with a different set of advantages and disadvantages, but it's knowing how to double down on what makes you special that will help you get ahead.

She rubbed my cheek. "You remember when my parents split, and I planned to run away?"

"Yeah," I said. "Right after your moms moved to Harlem, you came to my house, at like midnight, with a packed bag, all ready to go."

"And then what?"

"I wen' inside, grabbed my backpack, and we headed to Penn. We were some stupid-ass twelve-year-olds, though." I laughed. "Thinkin' we could grab the Amtrak to Hersheypark at one in the mornin' with no money."

"And what did you say to me, D? When I was cryin' on your shoulder back to BK?"

"I said that everything happens for a reason. And that sometimes, when you run away from somethin', you miss an opportunity to grow."

"And what else?"

"And that no matter what happened, I'd always be there for you."

"Sounded like pretty good advice to me back then," she said, wrapping her arms around me, pulling me closer. "Sounds like pretty good advice now."

I kissed the top of her head and held her, the two of us clutching each other while the city's lifeblood rushed all around us.

"Habibi," she said, looking up at me. *"Habiiiiiiibiiiiii,"* she repeated, stretching it out. I couldn't prevent myself from smiling. *"Habiiiiibiiiiiii,"* she said again, intoning the words like the morning calls to prayer from Mr. Aziz's collection of religious CDs we listened to when we were kids. She rocked me back and forth, repeating *"Habibi, habibi, habibi"* until I busted out laughing.

We stayed like that for an hour, with her updating me on her nursing application and the goings-on at the bodegas.

"I gotta head back," she said eventually.

"So what now?" I climbed out of the fountain.

She squeezed her eyes and cheesed like a kid making a funny face in a school photo. "First. A kiss."

I leaned down and brought my lips to

hers. "Now what?"

"Now go back to work and kick some ass."

Finally, the big day was here. I stood in front of my mirror, figuring out what to wear. I needed something to give me an extra boost of confidence. So I put on my boxers, placed my head through the ring of my black Starbucks apron, tied its strings in the back, and threw on a T-shirt and jeans, concealing the apron like Clark Kent's Superman outfit. *Hell yeah,* I thought, admiring myself. *Let's get it.*

The smell hit me before I entered the kitchen, and with it came an ocean of relief. It was clean, with a hint of blueberries and oranges, freshly roasted, and a bright, almost winelike acidity. *Kenyan.* There's no coffee around the world as beloved as Kenyan coffee. I also smelled maple syrup, buttermilk, cinnamon, and vanilla.

"Mornin', Dar," Ma said. There was a steaming pile of pancakes on the table, fresh maple syrup, and, best of all, Ma sitting with a cup of coffee in her hand.

"Mornin', Ma. What's all this for?"

"For you, baby, who else? It's your big day, so I figured you'd get up early and wanna get somethin' in you."

My intestines were doing all kinds of acrobatics, and I kept on feeling like I had to take a crap. But given how tired she'd been for the last few days, I couldn't leave Ma hanging.

"Thanks, Ma. They smell delicious. You mus' be feelin' better, huh?"

She smiled. I reached over and grabbed the pot of coffee.

"What are you doin'?" she asked, her eyes growing wider.

"Pourin' myself some coffee, what's it look like?"

She leaned forward, squinting. "*You* drink coffee? Since when?"

"Since now," I said, and took a sip.

"Well, look at you, becoming a grown man right before my own eyes."

I pinched her cheek. "So funny, Ma. You'd give Richard Pryor a run for his money. I gotta go, though."

"Okay, Mr. Grown Man, but don' forget about tonight," she said, as I headed for the door. "Soraya and Mr. Rawlings will be here 'round eight, so you'll have time to relax a bit before we eat. It's too bad Jason can't make it, said he was busy."

Busy? He's really taking this shit far.

"Sounds good, I'll be there." I held the door open. "Aye, Ma?"

"Yes, baby?"

"I'm happy you're feelin' better. I, um, was worried for a second."

She held her arms out, as if she had just completed a magic trick. "You know you don' need to worry about me, Dar. God's got my back, as always. Yours too."

I'm gonna need it today, that's for sure.

Down the stairs. "Come 'ere, boy!" Mr. Rawlings shouted from the backyard. "I know tha's you, always stompin' down the stairs like a damn elephant. You're lucky I get up early. Door's open."

I entered his apartment and encountered a strong smell of sour fruit, incense, and eggs. A trumpet blared from an old record player, and no lie, there were insects flying around. One landed on me — a ladybug. Another one led me to a picture frame bearing the photo of a beautiful dark-skinned woman cradling a baby. She had a smile that'd make even the devil cry.

"Hey, who's this?" I asked, bringing the photo with me through the back door. Mr. Rawlings kneeled in front of a mess of green

197

hairy vines, his rosewood cane within arm's reach. The cuffs of his light blue cardigan were rolled back, and I imagined the knees of his brown slacks to be covered with black dirt.

When he looked up, his face went from confusion to anger. "No one. Put that away. *Now.* This is why I don' be invitin' you to my place. You're too nosy. Kids have no sense of privacy nowadays."

"Sorry." I put it away. "What's up?"

"Your momma tells me you have a big test today."

"Yeah."

"And that them white boys been beatin' you down."

"Yeah."

"Well, come 'ere."

I walked over to the tangle of vines and kneeled beside him.

"Go on, put your hands in the ground."

I placed my hands on the soft black earth, but he put his hands over them and pushed them deeper than I knew the old man still had strength for.

"What do you feel?"

"Dirt?"

"Of course dirt, boy. Stop bein' so simple. What do you *feel*?"

I closed my eyes and moved my hands

through the soft dirt, grabbing roots, running into what I guessed were worms. "Roots, worms, and other stuff I can't see," I replied.

"Life, boy. You're feelin' life. And can' nothin' grow without fertile soil or the right hands for it. This right here," he said, touching a dusty finger to my temple, "is soil. Jus' like this garden. And only you can decide what grows and who you allow to get their hands in it. Understand?"

"I do. Thanks, Mr. Rawlings."

"You're welcome. Now go on and get outta here and don' touch none of my stuff on the way out."

Turn the corner. Wave to Mr. Aziz.

"*Bit tawfiq,* Darren!" he shouted.

"*Sabah al-kheir,* Mr. Aziz. But what's that mean?"

"Means 'good luck,' " he said, holding a broom. "Soraya tells me you have an important exam today."

"*Shukran jazeelan,* Mr. Aziz."

It was early, but the gargoyles were there. Jason didn't look at me. Wally Cat waved me over, but I tapped my invisible wristwatch before diving into the subway.

With Kid Cudi's "Pursuit of Happiness" bumping in my ears, I closed my eyes, allowing the lyrics — about never letting up, doing what you want, and only focusing on the future even if it includes failure — consume me.

Easier said than done, Cudder. Easier said than done.

The circle assembled and silently followed Clyde's movements. I looked around, wanting to see what Frodo's and the Duchess's game faces looked like; Frodo, wearing a red T-shirt with some football team's logo on it, was covered in sweat, and the Duchess, in a beige kaftan, looked as bored as ever.

"Seventy-five left to go," Clyde said, barely louder than a whisper. "Losers lose; winners win. It's as simple as that. And we don't hire losers."

He uttered the famous Maoist/musketeer maxim, "All for one, and one for all," and said that we were going to hit our number "because we're scrappy, resourceful, and more tenacious than fucking HIV in Africa." I was the only one who cringed.

Rhett appeared outside the circle wearing the same look from a few days ago: pale, with dark rings under his eyes, and hair like a bird's nest. He was biting his fingernails and tried to go unnoticed, but Clyde looked in his direction, and asked, "Any words, Rhett?"

He coughed and entered the circle slowly. "No, not really. But as we all know, we've had three new hires start this week — the Duchess, Frodo, and Buck — and in true Sumwun fashion, today is day five of Hell Week. So you know what that means."

Smiles, smirks, and other forms of fervor appeared on every face like stars becoming visible in the night sky. The air in the event space, building off Clyde's energy, surged, sparked, and snapped. It was some real Dr. Frankenstein shit.

"Oh, that's *right,*" Clyde said, tapping his forehead. He entered the circle with outstretched hands. "Who should go first?"

Go first? Are we doing this in public?

The circle shouted our names until the chaotic screams settled on "Frodo!"

"Frodo, enter the circle," Clyde commanded. "And Tiffany."

Tiffany rubbed her hands together, smiling diabolically, as Frodo, visibly shaking, wiped his sweaty red neck with a paper towel and entered the circle.

"Wear this," Clyde said, shoving a small football helmet into Frodo's chest.

"Uh, why?" Frodo asked, struggling to get the helmet over his wide head.

Clyde laughed, pounding the helmet in place. "To get you focused, why else?"

Tiffany circled him like a snake ready to strike.

She had her fun with him, but Frodo, despite his stuttering, asked the questions he needed to, and it ended without too much bloodshed.

Clyde entered the circle, stretching out his thumb sideways, like Commodus in *Gladiator,* and held it there. It wiggled toward the floor, then toward the ceiling, like a bipolar magnet, then back down, then finally, up. Frodo sighed with relief, and the circle chanted, "Frodo! Frodo! Frodo!" Everyone clapped and laughed, clearly more *at* him than *with* him, but *tomayto, tomahto.*

"The Duchess and Eddie. Go," Clyde ordered. "But first," he said, procuring a bedazzled plastic crown, "wear this."

The Duchess stared at the crown in Clyde's hand as if he'd gotten it out of the garbage. I thought she was going to refuse, but she rolled her eyes and placed it on her head to everyone's delight.

Their role-play was short and efficient. Eddie wasn't an asshole; the Duchess put on a fake smile and went down her checklist of questions. Clyde entered the circle and swiftly flipped his thumb up as if it were a mailbox flag. The circle didn't chant her name or erupt in applause. She just quietly removed the crown, swiftly broke it in half, and tossed it into the garbage.

"Okay, the best for last," Clyde said. Everyone in the circle focused their eyes on me. My heart felt like it was going to explode. *At least if you die, you won't have to go.* I prayed to God that Clyde wouldn't pair me with Tiffany or one of the other sadistic AEs. *Eddie would be perfect. Even Marissa would do.* But no, I got . . .

"Me," he said. "You and me in the circle, Buck. Let's go."

My mouth went dry. I tried to think about Soraya telling me to fight, about Mr. Rawlings's dirt, about Ma and her prophecies of greatness. But none of it helped. The only thing that relaxed me was remembering that I was wearing my black Starbucks apron and that I was once the best Starbucks shift supervisor in the city, maybe even the world.

"Before we begin," Clyde said, smiling like a hyena on heroin, "put this on."

I froze when I saw what it was: a black cap with STARBUCKS embroidered in white lettering with that almost invisible ® at the end of it. But it wasn't just the hat that made my heart stop; it was also the squarish green pin with the Starbucks mermaid and the words CERTIFIED BARISTA next to it, which could have meant only one thing.

"I got it off one of the people who works downstairs," he said, tickled. "Black kid with the gross pimples? Paid him twenty bucks and he was incredibly grateful. Told me to tell you hi."

He wants to throw me off and make me fail. Fuck him. I grabbed the hat, placed it on my head, and said, "Who am I calling?"

"I thought you'd never ask. You're calling Deborah Jackson, VP of HR at Starbucks."

What a maniac. Instead of making someone up, he was using a real person, someone I actually knew. But Starbucks was my domain, so there was no way he'd trip me up. I smiled and said, "Ring ring."

"Hello, this is Debbie!"

"Hi, Debbie, this is Darren calling from Sumwun, how are you?"

"Oh, hi, Darren! I'm swell, thanks for asking. Just another day over here in paradise. Grabbed my morning cup of joe, so I'm ready to go! How're you?"

"I'm great, thanks for asking. What are you drinking?"

"One of our new blonde roasts — can't get enough of it! How can I help you today?"

"That's a delicious one. I've heard that

folks love the hint of lemon. Anyway, I'm calling because we've been working with other VPs of HR like you to drive employee productivity through increasing happiness and —"

"Wait, sorry to interrupt. You said your name is Darren, yes?"

"Yes, that's me."

"This may be random, but you're not Darren Vender, are you?"

"Um, yes, that's me," I replied, suspicious. "Maybe you've seen one of my emails? We tend to send a lot," I said, laughing.

"No, no. Darren, it's me! Deborah Jackson, remember? Gosh, we haven't spoken in about, what, a year? You were such a hard worker, stacking boxes and serving coffee the last time we spoke. How are you?"

Where was this going? What the fuck was he doing?

"I'm fine, Debbie. Didn't notice it was you, actually. So, like I was saying —"

"Gee, Darren. I didn't even know you left Starbucks. Four years was quite a while, though. Which location were you at again? The one at 3 Park Avenue over in Manhattan?"

I looked around the circle. People stood with confused faces, whispering to one another, finally realizing I wasn't just a faceless Black guy but that I was *that* faceless Black guy from the Starbucks downstairs.

"Yes," I said, taking a deep breath. "That's the one."

"And now," Debbie said, "you're at this company called, um, Sumwun? It's so good to see you're doing well. For someone who didn't even go to college, no less! Are you still living with your mom in, where was it, Bed-Stuy?"

I was sweating, sinking, and shrinking into a dark hole like a circumcised dick. Clyde dramatically extended his arms and looked around the circle, pretending to be confused.

"Helloooooo? Darren, you there? I asked if you were still living with your mom."

I'm done. This is too much. But then I heard a voice. One of those voices people hear in movies that all of a sudden give them strength to fight on. It's cliché as shit but true. And it wasn't the voice of God. It was none other than Wally Cat's rich baritone: *"In any game, you gotta have a short-term memory. Someone tell you some shit you don' like? Forget it the minute they mouth close."*

I forced myself to forget all of Clyde's bullshit and smiled. "I am, Debbie. It's nice to still be able to see her even with my busy

206

new job. But let me give you the quick, thirty-second pitch on Sumwun, and if it's a fit, I'll set up some time for you to speak with my colleague and very best friend Clyde."

The circle laughed. I loosened up and told "Debbie" about how Sumwun would be an incredible way to invest in her employees' happiness and mental health.

"Sure, Darren. That all sounds good, but you still haven't told me what Sumwun is. I'm sorry, but I also can't get over how cute it is that you're calling me up and giving me your little pitch!"

"I guess it is, Debbie. Everything has come full circle. Anyway, through our platform, Starbucks employees can speak with what we call assistants, who are folks around the world who specialize in different ways of life. They're like therapists without all the stuffiness. People can speak with them by phone, computer, or even text. How's this all sound?"

According to "Debbie," it was hard for her to trust a company she'd never heard of, especially one that allowed people who didn't complete college to work there. It was "too much of a liability."

"That's what people said when they first heard of Starbucks, Debbie. That buying coffee from a no-name brand was a liability. But in the same way people took a chance on Starbucks, someone here took a chance on me even though I don't have a college degree. You obviously have the budget, there's a real need, and you're the one who calls the shots. So I'll introduce you to my colleague, you check out what we have to offer, and if it's not a fit, we can just stay friends. Sound fair?"

Reader: I know; I killed that shit. *This* — the perfect close — is what we sales-people live for. Give me five on the black-hand side!

Silence. Clyde's eyes locked onto mine, and the circle became still, no more whispering, jittery legs, or coughing. I couldn't feel my heart beat and wondered if I was dead and didn't know it.

"Alright, Darren," she said. "Let's set it up. But only because I know you."

The circle applauded even louder than they had for Frodo, and I smiled because I had won; I had beaten Clyde at his own game. I had gone through hell and come out the other end — bloody, bruised, and beaten, sure, but still breathing. *That was for you, Ma.*

"Yeah, Buck!" Rhett shouted from outside the circle, clapping like I'd won the Super Bowl.

Clyde, staring at Rhett, looked as if he smelled a fart. He turned back to me, straight-faced, and stretched out his thumb. But instead of flipping it up, he twisted it down, shaking his head. "Not good enough, Buck. Not good enough at all. Go again."

This can't be happening. "Again?" I said, looking around the circle. "But you, I mean Debbie, agreed to the meeting? Didn't I pass?"

"No, I'm afraid not." He shrugged. "You set up a dud. A lemon. There was no shot that Debbie was going to show up to the next meeting. You were serving up dogshit hoping it would stick."

"I think he was fine," Eddie said from outside the circle.

"Good thing it doesn't matter what you think," Clyde snapped. "Tiffany, in the circle with Buck."

I was shaking. I'd thought it was over, that I had passed.

"Okay," she said, out for blood. "I'm Nora —"

"No," Rhett said. "Let him go; it was fine."

"He needs to go again," Clyde said, without looking at Rhett.

209

"C'mon, Clyde. If he has any issues, he can just work them out on the phones."

"There's no way we can let dogshit on the phones, Rhett. He's going to make us look bad. Plus, it's my decision who passes, right?"

Rhett, looking ill again, closed his eyes and took a breath. "He passes."

"But he's not one of us!" Clyde shouted. "He doesn't belong here."

"I think he does," Rhett said, winking at me. "But let's let the team decide. Does he pass or not?"

Everyone stood still, two hundred eyes darting around to see if anyone would make a move, Clyde's wrath filling the air. But then Frodo, of all people, stepped forward. "If I passed, Buck passes. He's better than me."

"No," Clyde said. "You're an idiot, but *you're* more of a fit than he is."

"Pass him," Eddie said, stepping into the circle.

"Pass him," Marissa repeated, also stepping into the circle. Clifford, her piglet, followed.

"Pass him," others, whose names I didn't know, said as they stepped into the circle. They chanted, "Pass him, pass him, pass him," until it became deafening.

"Alright," Clyde said, waving them off. "You're all fucking wrong, but it won't be my fault when I fire him. You want me to pass him? Fine. He passed."

Before I knew what happened, Frodo threw me onto his shoulders and everyone was clapping, whistling, and chucking shit at me like I just got married. I didn't know why they went to bat for me, but I was grateful.

As Frodo spun me round and round, with dozens of hands slapping my back, I caught a glimpse of Clyde standing with his arms crossed away from the crowd. When our eyes met, he mouthed two words that were as loud and clear as if he had shouted them: *Fuck. You.*

"You're one of us now," Charlie, our manager with the mountain-man aesthetic, said as he handed us brand-new MacBook Airs, hoodies, iPhone cases, pens, sunglasses, socks, slippers, hats, tote bags, mugs, water bottles, notebooks, stickers, T-shirts, and backpacks, all purple, all with SUMWUN printed on them in white cursive.

"No way!" Frodo shouted, putting on every piece of gear in seconds. "I've been waiting for this my whole life!" He looked like a walking billboard.

"You've been waiting your whole life to be handed a ton of branded startup gear?" the Duchess asked, pushing all of her swag into a wastebasket.

"Uh, no, but I mean, this is all, it's just really cool to be a part of this and walk around with our logo and stuff. It's like our uniform," Frodo said, deflated by the Duchess's lack of enthusiasm.

Charlie said a lot of things, including that marketing was going to set us each up with a list of leads to call on Monday. But the most important thing he said was about a "sort of tradition." He leaned back in his chair before resting his tall leather moccasins on his desk. No lie, I was waiting for him to pull out a beaver pelt and tell us how he snared it.

"I want you to come up with a wish list of three people you don't know or have any connection to. And who are well-known, even celebrities."

"For what?" the Duchess asked.

"One second, I'm getting there. If you successfully qualify and hand off any of the people on your list, you'll automatically be promoted to AE."

"Seriously?" I asked. "Just like that?"

He snapped his fingers twice. "Just like that."

"Even if we do it on our first day?" Frodo asked, looking like a fool. The guy was even wearing Sumwun socks and slippers.

Charlie nodded. "Yeah, but no SDR has ever done it. And I have to approve your list. So take a few minutes and let me know."

Frodo picked the head of the NFL, the president of Ford Motors and, after Charlie told him he couldn't put down a no-name Southern girl band, the head of HR at Wendy's. The Duchess picked the heads of Yves Saint Laurent, Chanel, and Hermès.

"What about you, Buck?" Charlie asked. "Who do you got?"

I blanked and said the first three people who came to mind: "Bernie Aiven, head of Hinterscope Records; Stefan Rusk, head of SpaceXXX; and Barry Dee, that guy all over YouTube who owns that big media company, DaynerMedia."

"Okay, it's settled. You all have your wish lists, you'll get your leads on Monday, you got your gear, you passed your role-plays, and best of all, you got me. So we're set."

"Do we have a team name?" Frodo asked, struggling to pull a sticker off his sunglasses.

Charlie slapped his forehead. "Oh, yeah! How could I forget? All of you are now proud members of NWA."

My hand instinctively curled into a lead

fist, and I had to consciously uncurl it before I popped Charlie, who, up until that point, I thought was an all right guy. All I managed to say was "What?"

"Oh, right," he said, covering his mouth. "No, it's not what you think, Buck, I swear. It stands for Negotiators with Attitude. Each team adapted names from different hip-hop groups to be salesy, you know, like a fun way of switching things up. C'mon, the last thing anyone here is is racist." He placed a hand on my shoulder, awaiting absolution.

I just stared at him. He went on to explain what the other SDR teams were named.

1. Prospect-tang Clan
2. Tupac ShaCall
3. A Tribe Called Qualify
4. De La Sales
5. LauRing Hill

Christ. This is what happens when you have a company with zero Black people in it.

"Okay. Now what?" the Duchess asked.

"Now," Charlie said, running a hand through his hair, avoiding the Duchess's eyes lest she turn him to stone, "you can review our systems, shadow some calls, and pray we hit our number."

214

Five o'clock arrived, and we still had forty-eight thousand left to go.

The sales floor, which was usually louder than Times Square on New Year's, quieted down, and a dense fog of anxiety descended.

Rhett would come out of his office, stare at the whiteboard, bite his fingernails, then walk back in with a different closer, no doubt doing everything in his power to hit the number.

"It's never taken this long," Marissa said, walking past our row of desks with a baby bottle in Clifford's snout. "Three, maybe four-thirty the latest, but never five on a Friday. What if —"

"Don't say it," Eddie said.

"I'm nervous, Buck," Frodo said across from me. "Real nervous." I'm sure he was, but it was hard for me to take him seriously in his Sumwun sunglasses, hat, hoodie, slippers, socks, and backpack. Yes, he was sitting down but he still wore his backpack.

I turned to Charlie, who was next to me. "Hey, Charlie," I whispered, tapping his shoulder. "Are we going to hit?"

"I don't know," he said, typing away. "It's never gone this late, and the fact that Rhett or Clyde hasn't said anything makes me worried."

Around six, Clyde came out of Rhett's office, shaking his head. He walked to his desk, which was, by the grace of God, rows away from mine. When he picked his head up, the entire floor looked away.

"Listen," he said, standing. "We knew it was a long shot and that we were trying to do something most startups frankly never even get close to doing. So I'm just going to say it right now. We didn't hit."

The entire floor moaned. Tears welled up in their eyes. Even Frodo, who had taken his sunglasses off, was sobbing.

"This isn't happening," someone said.

"Yeah," Charlie muttered. "This can't be real. If it is, we're all in trouble."

Trouble? I knew hitting twelve months in a row was an important milestone, but damn.

"I'm sorry to say that it is happening," Clyde said, walking around, grabbing shoulders, consoling his constituency like a benevolent priest. "We'll still have a small celebration, though. For effort, because we all worked hard this month. I know we did."

"Fuck that!" Rhett shouted, yanking his door open with an arm around Chris. "Month twelve, baby! We hit it!"

Instead of throwing papers in the air, jumping around, and clapping until their wrists snapped off, the entire floor looked at Rhett in disbelief. He walked over to the board, erased the $48,000 under the LEFT TO GO box in the center, and put a big fat $0!!! in its place. Everyone audibly exhaled.

When he capped his marker, the floor exploded. The Black Eyed Peas' "Let's Get It Started" bumped from the ceiling speakers. Porschia and her team walked out with carts bearing bottles of champagne and branded glasses.

Rhett gripped a microphone. *"Woooooo!"* he shouted. "We almost didn't make it, team. We seriously almost didn't make it this month."

"But we did!" someone shouted, violently chucking a purple stress ball directly into his face. He remained unfazed, like he enjoyed it.

"That's right!" he said. "That is fucking right. And we did it because people believe in us. Because of each and every one of you beautiful, brave, and ballsy people," he said, aggressively grabbing a fistful of his testicles.

"You. All of you are the definition of Sumwunners. I know that we cut it close and you were nervous but that," he said, beating his chest, "in your soul you believed.

That you KNEW! Someone, hit me with a ball!" Dozens of people obliged him. A shower of balls hit his body at warp speed.

"Now I want you all to forget the month. Forget how hard we worked. Forget the tears, sweat, and, in some cases, blood. I want you to head to the event space, grab a drink, food, and get ready for the night of a lifetime. Lucien from Poplar Capital called, and he gave us the green light to go insane. So put on your fucking dancing shoes and finest threads, because we're hitting the club! 'Clap your hands, all peoples! Shout to God with loud songs of joy!' Psalms 47:1, motherfuckers!"

Everyone rushed into the event space. I sat glued to my chair, trying to fathom what the hell just happened. The insanity of the week had paralyzed me.

Rhett stood next to the whiteboard removing Silly String from his hair, and Clyde walked over to him. They embraced for minutes, Rhett whispering into Clyde's ear, Clyde silently nodding and, I shit you not, sobbing. Rhett held Clyde's head and kissed the top before they walked off the floor.

The event space was full of people downing shots, doing keg stands, and swaying off rhythm to music with bass heavy enough to make your heart shake.

"Buck," Rhett said, opening his arms with a smile that automatically made me smile. "Come here."

He wrapped his arms around me more affectionately than any man ever had. He was warm and held me until his head fell on my shoulder. "We did it, Buck."

"Yeah," I said, unsure of what to say. "I mean you did, Rhett. You did it."

He shot up and held me in front of him. "No, Buck. *We.* You are as much a part of this as anyone here. And you're going to be better than all of them, I know it. So stop acting like this isn't you," he said, jabbing a hard finger into my chest. "And that you're not one of us, okay?"

"Okay," I said. Tears began forming in my eyes. I don't know why I was so emotional. I looked around the event space, saw all of the people laughing, dancing, and hugging, all of the real, tangible love, and I started to believe. To believe in the Gospel of Rhett. In the Church of Sumwun.

Clyde waved me over from across the room. *Fuck. Everything's going so well, what could he want?*

"Hey," he said.

"Hey."

"Listen, Buck. I know I was hard on you this week, but it's my job."

I stared at him, thinking about the torture he put me through. The embarrassment and humiliation. All of it.

"Rhett likes you. And if Rhett likes you, I like you. So what do you say?" He extended a porcelain, blond-knuckled, manicured hand. "Truce?"

Didn't this guy mouth Fuck you *to me hours ago?* I had no plans of becoming "best bros" with Clyde, but I figured it was better to let bygones be bygones than be the "angry Black man" at Sumwun. And as crazy as it sounds, seeing how he was with Rhett and watching him console everyone earlier made me believe that he wasn't a complete asshole; he was just someone who wanted to make his mentor proud.

"Yeah," I said, shaking his hand. "Alright, man. Truce."

"Good," he said. "Now chug this."

This was a red Solo cup filled to the brim with beer.

"No, thanks," I said, pushing the cup toward him.

"C'mon, Buck," he said, staring at me with a childlike smile. "We're friends now. So let's make it official with a drink. Is it against your religion or something?"

"No, I just don't drink. It's not for me, you know. Makes people lose their minds."

220

"One drink won't hurt," he insisted, pushing the cup toward me. "I promise."

"I'm good, thanks."

He thrust the cup into the air. "HEY, WHO WANTS TO SEE BUCK CHUG THIS?"

Everyone looked up, already possessed by liquor, greasy food, and God knows what else, and screamed, "CHUG! CHUG! CHUG!"

I started to shake. The week, the screaming, the pressure, all of it became too much and I wanted to shut it out. I grabbed the cup and drained it in one gulp. The coppery liquid gushed down my throat and pounded into my stomach, and I bent over in pain.

"YESSSSSSS!" they all shouted.

"*Now* you're one of us," Clyde said, patting my back. "Welcome to Sumwun."

One beer led to two, and two led to beer pong, and beer pong led to shots of tequila with salt on my hands and lime wedges in my mouth, which led to me stumbling out of 3 Park Avenue and Rhett pulling me into a black Escalade, and saying, "Buck rides with us." Chris, Clyde, Porschia, and two women I'd never met were already inside.

The Escalade took us to the Meatpacking District, right near the Hudson. We hopped out, plumes of smoke slowly rolling around us like magicians appearing out of thin air — except these magicians were high out of their minds and trashed. Including me.

Before we entered the club, I took my phone out to check the time, but Rhett grabbed and pocketed it. "No you don't. No phones, ever. We're celebrating, Buck, and we don't want to worry about anything going up on social media. You get it, right?"

I nodded, drunk. The line in front of us stretched around the block: guys dressed in crisp white shirts and slim-fitting blazers; women wearing dresses and heels, exposing a healthy amount of ass cheek.

Rhett walked to the head of the line and spoke with the bouncer, who then let us in along with the other Sumwunners piling out of taxis, Ubers, and Lyfts behind us. I felt like I was floating on a cloud. Like we were celebrities or some shit.

A hostess showed us to a section in the back, and people — bottle girls, random guys, some of the models from the line — swarmed us. Someone handed me a screwdriver that burned going down my throat. The music, the people, all of it was making my head spin. Rhett pulled me onto a leather couch.

"What do you see, Buck?" he asked. Blue and indigo lights flashed around us. It felt like an underwater dream.

I saw Porschia grinding on Clyde, Frodo and Marissa locking lips, Eddie and some guy holding hands. "I don't even know, man," I said, my eyes feeling heavier. "This is all some wild shit."

"This is the life you were made for, Buck. People who are smart," he said, touching my temple, "and work hard don't deserve to grind day in and day out at a place like Starbucks. They, you, deserve to have it all. And I promise that this is only the beginning. Do you believe now?" he asked, staring at me with half-closed eyes. "Do you believe that you're one of us?"

"I am" — the was room spinning now — "a believer, Rhett. I am."

"Good."

I got up and pushed my way through the crowd. "Where's the bathroom?" I asked a bouncer brandishing a metallic flashlight as if it were a baton. He nodded down a hallway, and I stumbled into the room.

My knees dropped, and I hurled all of the beer, tequila, orange juice, greasy food, and everything else into the toilet. It kept coming till I was heaving just air into the bowl. The last thing I remembered was washing my mouth out and grabbing a towel, then, I don't know how much later, there was banging on the door.

"Open up!" someone screamed. It sounded like the bouncer.

Damn, this guy bangs harder than Ma. Wait. Ma. Soraya. Panic wrapped its arms around me and squeezed.

Ripping the door open, I sidestepped the bouncer and pushed my way through the crowd. "Hey, watch it, motherfucker!" someone shouted.

When I got to our table, I saw Rhett speaking with Clyde and Porschia. "Buck, my man!" he said, reaching out. "Where have you been? We were just talking about you. Sit, sit. You okay?"

"My phone," I said, sobering up.

"What?"

"Give me my phone! Please!"

He fumbled around in his pocket and handed it over. "Fine, but no photos. Remember."

The seconds it took to turn on felt like eons. The time. It was no longer six or seven like it was back in the office. Time, with a mind of its own, had crept all the way to one in the morning. I looked around the club, trying to figure out where the hours, minutes, and seconds had gone.

Then a hard shiver in my hand turned into a full-blown seizure. Three missed calls from

Ma, eight from Soraya. Two voice mails from Ma. Five from Soraya. Ten texts total.

From Ma:

Hey Dar, puttin the finishin touches on your celebration meal!

Dar, youre probably still busy at work. Its 8:30 now so text or call to let us know how late youll be.

Baby you okay? We havent heard from you in a while and its 9:30 now. Everyones hungry. Mr. Rawlings and Soraya have been waiting for you.

PLEASE CALL ME BACK ONCE YOU SEE THIS. It's midnight and Soraya and Mr. Rawlings are gone. Everyone left already, but Im worried. This isn't like you.

From Soraya:

I hope your day went well, D! Can't wait to see you later. It's 8:15 and you're late, MISTER! You better be on the train. Mr. Rawlings is about to do some voodoo on you if he doesn't get his hands on some of this chili soon.

D? Where are you? Why aren't you answering any of our calls? Seriously?????

WHERE ARE YOU! I swear to god, if you're in the hospital or something happened to you, I'm going to bring you back to life just so I can kill you for making us all worry.

This isn't like you D. I hope you have a good excuse for this. Your mom is worried sick and crying.

Going home. I hope whatever you did tonight was worth it.

Rhett stood and placed a hand on my frozen shoulder. "You don't look so hot, Buck. You okay?"

I stood there motionless, my phone resting in my hand like a gun I'd just killed someone with: heavy, cold, and unaware of the damage it had done.

■ ■ ■ ■

III.
DISCOVERY

■ ■ ■ ■

Success has a price. If you aren't
prepared to pay it, you shouldn't expect
to achieve it.

— DAN WALDSCHMIDT

■ ■ ■ ■

III.

12

12

3 MONTHS LATER

I never expected to be where I am today. Living on the penthouse floor of a ninety-eight-year-old building, worth millions of dollars, and admired by people from Brooklyn to Brazil. If you'd told a younger me that I'd be here, I'd have said you were smoking rocks. But here I am, and there you are, looking in from the outside and hopefully getting what you paid for. I worked hard to get here, and if you continue following me, I'll help you better your life and the lives of those you love most. I guarantee it.

In the world of tech startups and sales, three months, aka a quarter, is a long time. A lot can happen. And for me, it did.

On the first Monday in June, the first workday after Hell Week, when we achieved our goal for the twelfth month in a row and partied like savages, the newest members of

NWA — Frodo, the Duchess, and I — hit the phones. On day one, the Duchess shot from the bottom of the almighty whiteboard to the top. She had a few of her father's friends — CEOs, titans of business, and other suspects of questionable character — lined up to qualify and hand off, which meant she hit her goal in a few hours. She piled on more SQLs and deals throughout the month.

Even Frodo had a few connections — like trustees of Notre Dame who fondly remembered Arnold Bagini, the right tackle who often played through multiple concussions to bring their university glory. He qualified one of those on day two and added a few more. He didn't end the month at the top of the board, but he was somewhere safe and comfortable in the upper middle.

And what about your boy Buck, you ask? Well, I made more than one hundred calls a day for two weeks but couldn't get anyone on the line. Most of the numbers were fake, went directly to foreign voice mails, or led to receptionists who told me so-and-so was dead.

When I brought it up to Clyde, he said, "Part of the game, Buck. Welcome to the show," before patting me on the back and telling me to keep at it. But when I eventually told Charlie, he looked at my list and realized that I, yes, only I, was being sent leads from the "Do not call, they're absolute shit or dead" pile. If you're wondering who was in charge of marketing's lead distribution, it was Clyde. So much for a truce.

All of this is to say that I ended the month with a big fat, uncooked, and likely salmonella-infected goose egg. I earned nothing in commission; Frodo earned $535 dollars, and the Duchess, of course, earned over $1,500. It's funny how the rich always somehow end up richer. Fortunately, no one had come close to qualifying anyone on their "Advance to AE, collect $200" wish list. Even the Duchess and all of her incestuous wealth connections couldn't swing that.

The rest of the months followed the same pattern. Only after getting better leads with Charlie's help did I start generating opportunities, which moved me a few spots up from the absolute bottom of the board. I even earned a couple hundred bucks in July and August, which I used to celebrate Soraya getting into her nursing program and pay for a dinner for her, Ma, and Mr. Rawlings at a fancy Manhattan restaurant as an apology for missing my Hell Week celebration dinner. Jason, still saltier than a sailor, declined the invitation.

Aside from that, all was cool on the home front except for two things. One was that Ma missed a few more days of work due to fatigue. I kept pressing her to go to a doctor, but she said she already had and that they said it would pass, that it was all part of the aging process. She hit me with the same line over and over again: "Jus' focus on work, Dar."

The second thing was that the real estate company that had sent Ma a letter in May, Next Chance Management, called every few weeks until I picked up and said if they didn't lose our number, I'd have to "take care of them." An empty threat, but it worked.

Which brings us to day one of September. A time when the jungle-like heat of New York City begins to settle down, when yoga-pants-wearing, Pumpkin Spice Latte–drinking, and basic-as-free-cable Beckies emerge from their Southampton vacation homes like bedazzled cockroaches. A time when the whole city looks back at the summer like one long acid-laced dream that possibly couldn't and absolutely shouldn't have happened. A time when the Church of Sumwun, and all of its constituents, came under grave threat. Before long, we would be taking fire from the media, investors, and even stale talkshow hosts clinging to their dwindling viewers like Southerners and their "It's not racist, it's tradition!" Confederate flags.

In short, we were about to enter an all-out war.

It was the first Monday of September, and the war started after lunch. Frodo and I were discussing the merits of being born in summer versus winter and whether the time of year you were born actually had an effect on your character.

"It definitely does," Frodo declared, drinking an entire can of Sprite in one gulp, letting out a stinky, hamburger-laden belch. He wore a T-shirt that read: EVERY DAY IS FIRST DOWN.

"Shit, Frodo. That smells," I said, shoving him into the elevator.

"Sorry. But like I was saying, if you're born in the summer, you're fiery, like the sun. And if you're born in the winter, then you're cool, like the snow. Maybe even more relaxed."

"You do know that Kim Jong-il was born in the middle of February, right?"

"I don't know who that is. But most people I know named Kim are really nice, like my babysitter, my uncle's wife, and Kim Possible."

When the elevator opened, the floor sounded louder than it should have for a Monday at 12:30 p.m. People were shouting into their phones until they were red in the face, some of them were crying, and a few were pacing in circles, squeezing purple stress balls.

"What's going on?" I asked Charlie, who sat with his head in his hands.

Without moving, he muttered, "The beginning of the end, Buck. The real beginning of the end. It's all over the news."

I flipped my Mac open and googled "Sumwun." The first page was plastered with articles from every major news outlet: "Sumwun is now for no one," "CEO Rhett Daniels declines to comment on murder," "Assistants or assailants?," "Tech darling of NYC drowning as we type," "Psychologists or psycho killers?"

"Yes, that Sumwun, but I one hundred percent promise it's nothing serious," Eddie said into his phone. "These things happen. No, I know. Yes, it shouldn't have. I assure you we're doing everything in our power, Jack, so let's just schedule some — fuck! He hung up. No one is giving us a chance to speak. Everyone knows."

"Knows what?" I asked, still confused, staring at the headlines on my screen.

Reader: Every great salesperson has to go through tough times in order to find out what they're made of. The best thing to do is to try to come out as unscathed as possible but to never forget the experience. Pain is a powerful teacher.

"Oh, Buck," he said, grabbing me. "One of our assistants in China. He convinced a noncorporate user, some depressed sixteen-year-old girl from Arkansas, to go to China and meet him for a face-to-face session. Her parents and friends hadn't known she went until they forced us to break our user confidentiality agreement and release her sessions' transcripts. They called the Chinese authorities, and the cops found the assistant's apartment. But when they got there, the girl was tied up and dead on the floor. They're looking for him now."

Holy fucking shit. "So what happens now?"

"Everyone's canceling. And every deal we forecasted for September is now down the drain. No one wants to sign their employees up for a service that could get them killed."

Rhett walked out of his office and the floor

went silent. His skin was whiter than I'd ever seen, as if he'd just thrown up the previous day's breakfast, lunch, *and* dinner.

Porschia handed him a microphone, and he stood in front of the almighty whiteboard with Clyde on his right. The Holy Trinity. He gripped the mic and closed his eyes.

"Listen," he said, taking in a lungful of air. "There are no two ways about it. And frankly, I'm not going to sugarcoat anything. What the media is saying is true. One of our veteran assistants preyed on a user. And he murdered her."

He dropped his head to his chest. Clyde placed a hand on his back. Everyone had tears in their eyes, including me. And what's messed up is that I don't think the majority of the tears were even for the poor girl; they were for Rhett, for Sumwun, for us.

"It's my fault," Rhett said, taking a tissue from Porschia and wiping his eyes. "I take full responsibility. We should have instituted better check-ins, a tighter vetting process, and not been so lax, especially with younger folks who have serious mental issues. I'm sorry."

I'd never seen Rhett look so defeated, not even when we almost missed our number during my first Deals Week. Fear spread over everyone's faces, and it truly did, as

Charlie said, feel like the beginning of the end.

"What are we going to do now?" Marissa asked, stroking Clifford's back. No longer a cute piglet, he was now a full-grown, stinky, market-weight pig.

Rhett, cheeks glistening, looked out over the sea of solemn salespeople who, though we were in our early twenties, were like his children. After a second, like Dr. Jekyll transforming into Mr. Hyde, he straightened his back, gritted his teeth, and balled his hands into knuckle-ripping fists.

"We are going to fight," he announced. Everyone looked up, wiping their tears away. "Because this is war. And the only point of war is to win. Everyone who was on our side before, including the board, doesn't want to touch us with a ten-foot pole. They say we had it coming all along, that we were growing too quickly, winning too much, and believing in what we were doing too hard."

"BULLSHIT!" I screamed.

"Yeah, fuck that!" another shouted.

"That's right!" Rhett roared into the microphone. "It *is* bullshit. Everyone wants you when you're hot but drops you once you're not. But you know what?"

"WHAT?" we shouted, as if we'd just gotten a shot of steroids.

"Fuck 'em! We don't need 'em. We never did. Even the board. They want us to quiet down, to not speak with the press or do any interviews, but forget that. This isn't something that'll just blow over, and it's sure as hell not something I'm going to let take us down. Will you?"

"NO!"

"That's absolutely fucking right. Because we're the best fucking salespeople in this entire fucking city, and we have proven it time and time again. So we are going to sell everyone to death. The prospects who want to pull out. The clients who are trying to cancel. The media, and even the board!" he yelled, a crazed look on his face now, like *he* had murder on his mind. "The true salesman," he continued, pointing at us, "is a god! And God, not man, makes the rules! And we all know what happens when man tries to conquer God, don't we?"

"Tell us, Rhett! Tell us what happens!" someone shouted, egging him on.

He laughed. He laughed so hard and so long, I thought he had lost it, that his company crumbling right before his eyes had broken him. But no, he stopped laughing, became very still, and brought the microphone closer to his mouth.

"He drowns, burns, and turns them to stone with less energy than it takes to breathe. And that is what we will do to our enemies. Because, as the Book of Nahum says, 'The Lord is slow to anger but great in power; the Lord will not leave the guilty unpunished.' "

The clapping went on for so long that it felt like it would be easier to continue clapping forever than stop. And while I couldn't admit it then — because I didn't want to see it — when I looked at Rhett breathing heavily in front of the crowd, something on his face made my heart plunge. Something that betrayed everything he had just said. Something more man than God.

Desperation.

13

I woke before my alarm went off. I was twenty-two years old and had never served in a war. I didn't know any military drills, tactics, or strategies. I'd never read *The Art of War,* played Battleship, or even held a toy gun — Ma didn't allow those. But I was ready to fight for Sumwun, to do whatever it took to win.

Reader: Salespeople are often separated into two camps: those who love to win and those who hate to lose. Before joining Sumwun, I was one of the latter. But once you taste what it feels like to win, to *really* win something meaningful — like your spot on the dream team — you will do everything to protect that feeling. Be careful of winning, it's one of the most dangerous things you can ever do.

Ma wasn't in the kitchen. She insisted on what the doctors had told her — that everything was fine — but she continued missing days of work and didn't seem like herself. I knocked on her door. A hoarse voice said, "Come in, Dar."

"You aight, Ma?" She was curled up in bed watching reruns of *Judge Hatchett.*

"Better than this one." She pointed to the skinny teenager with tight cornrows being ridiculed.

"What'd he do?"

"Same as all these kids. Thought he was grown until he realized he wasn't. Kids these days doin' all types of things they never woulda dreamed of doin' in my day. They need a healthy helpin' of God and someone to slap them upside their heads."

"Word, Ma. Not goin' to work today?"

She took a sip of water and sat up, eyes fixed on the television. Her hands shook so much I had to take the glass from her.

"Ma," I said, grabbing her hand. She weakly tried to grip my own but failed.

"My supervisor told me to take a coupla days off, Dar. Saw me coughin' up a storm and I had a little blood on my mouth, so . . ."

My face got hot. "Blood, Ma? This can't be right." Either her doctors were lying to her, or she was lying to me. "You've been missin' more days of work than before, you're coughin' up blood, and you're losin' your voice every other day. Plus, you can barely hold a glass of water. C'mon, Ma. What's goin' on?"

"Nothin', Dar. Don' worry 'bout me. It's jus' old age. The doctors say I'll be fine in no time. But if this gets worse, I'll head to the hospital. Deal?"

"Aight," I said, still skeptical but not wanting to push the issue and make her feel worse. "Deal."

A commercial flashed across the screen and then I saw it: a news clip featuring the photo of a smiling young girl with braces. I froze. The screen cut to another of an older Chinese man with a straight face and over-size glasses. The types you see pedophiles wearing in their mug shots.

"Sixteen-year-old Donesha Clark from Little Rock, Arkansas, suffered from depression. Her parents heard about a New York City tech startup called Sumwun, which they hoped would help her since traditional therapy wasn't working. Her parents say that after a year of therapy with a Chinese man named Jiao-long Lee, Donny, as they called her, began to turn back into the smiling girl you see here. But all of that ended when Donesha flew to China behind her parents' backs. Authorities say Donesha was lured by Mr. Lee, her therapist or, as Sumwun called him, her 'assistant.'

"Donesha thought she was meeting him for a few days of in-person sessions, but Mr. Lee had other plans. After the FBI contacted Chinese authorities, they raided Mr. Lee's home to find little Donny Clark tied up and dead, with multiple knife wounds, internal bleeding, and blows to the head from what may have been a lead pipe or hammer. Chinese authorities say Mr. Lee is still at large. Later today, we'll speak with representatives from the company at the center of this controversy, including CEO Rhett Daniels."

Ma shut the TV off and stared at me for a long time before saying anything. "Dar, you know 'bout all this mess?"

"Yeah, Ma. But we're gonna take care of it. They're tryna make us out to be bad people, but we're not."

"I know that, baby, but I don' know if you wanna be caught up in all of this. It could end up hurtin' you."

I kissed her forehead. "Don' worry, Ma. I'm not caught up in this. I'm jus' someone who works at the company doin' my job, tha's all. I love you."

"Love you too, Dar."

I grabbed my bag and headed out. Down the stairs. Turn the corner. Wave to Mr. Aziz. But when I passed his bodega, he waved me over.

"*Sabah al-kheir,* Mr. Aziz. How's it going?"

"*Kullu tamam,* Darren. Everything's fine. But Soraya is inside and said she just saw something on TV about your company. Maybe head in there for a second?"

I walked in, the doorbells clanging.

"Darren!" Soraya yelled, wearing tight blue jeans, red flats, and a black T-shirt with NINA SIMONE FOR PRESIDENT written on it. I know it'll make me sound soft, but every time I saw her felt like I was seeing her for the first time, like the earth only orbited the sun so it could see her from all angles.

Behind the transparent plexiglass display, surrounded by all kinds of colorful candies, beef jerky, and lotto tickets, she swung around and pointed to the tiny flat-screen TV in the corner of the store.

"I jus' saw Channel Seven, D. They're sayin' some crazy stuff about Sumwun and that little girl who got murdered. What do you know about it?"

"Not much, really," I said, snapping back

to reality. "Shit's crazy over there right now and we got all of our clients cancelin'. Rhett says it's war."

"You okay?"

"Yeah," I said. I made sure Mr. Aziz was still sweeping before bringing her in for a kiss. "I'm aight. What's good with you, Miss Nurse?"

She smiled and pointed to a thick textbook on the counter. "Gettin' a head start now, but I'm sorta nervous about —"

The bells clanged, and a tall white woman dressed in black leather from her head to her patent leather Doc Martens walked in. She looked like she was about to hit either an early morning BDSM session or a neo-Nazi rally. "Got any American Spirit rolling tobacco?"

Soraya stood on her tippy-toes, scanning the overhead rows with her hand. "Yeah." She placed a light-blue pack on the counter.

The dominatrix looked down and scrunched her face. "The *organic* kind," she said.

"We don't have that one," Soraya replied. "But this is just as good."

The heavy-metal hippie grabbed the pack and threw some cash on the counter. "Jesus. You people have nothing in this fucking neighborhood," she said, before stomping out and bumping Mr. Aziz with her shoulder.

"What the fuck is her problem?" I asked.

Soraya popped open the cash register and placed the money in with a smile, shrugging. "Who knows. A lot of them are like that. But a lot of them are also really nice and like to make small talk. It's fine. You wanna hang later?"

"Yeah," I said, looking at the time. 6:45 a.m. "We'll see. I gotta go, *habibti*." I leaned over for a kiss, but she turned around and began arranging candy in the window display.

Mr. Aziz walked in, my cue to leave.

Once I got to the corner, Jason hit me with a nod and I nodded back. *Word, a peace offering.* We hadn't really spoken since we got into that argument a few months ago. Some days he'd hit the corner with bruises all over his face, other days he was shining like he'd made a million bucks. Today was one of the former. Various shades of red bloomed all over his face like ripe plums.

"You aight?" I asked.

"What it look like?"

"Looks like you got fucked up."

"Aight then, why you askin'? Should jus' keep mindin' your own business like you been doin'. Chump."

The way I saw it, people, no matter how close you once were, could grow apart. And maybe that's what was happening to us.

"Yo, tha's your problem right there," I spat, pointing in his face. "Always blamin' people for shit instead of lookin' at yourself. Thinkin' you're too smart to get a real job. You're a loser, bro."

He brought his hands up, jerking his head at me. I flinched. He laughed. "Yeah, tha's what I thought. If a loser can make you shook, what does that make you?"

"Aye, Darren!" Wally Cat called. "Where yo' momma at, boy? Ain' seen her in a minute."

I stared at Jason, spat on the ground, and walked away. *He's just jealous I'm moving up and he's moving backward.*

"She's still sorta sick," I said to Wally Cat, plopping my ass down on a crate. "But she'll be aight."

"Mm-hmm, tha's right. Faith, nigga. Always gotta have it. What's new in the WWW?"

I burst out laughing. WWW is what Wally Cat had started calling Sumwun a couple months ago. "The World White Web is aight, man. I mean, nah, not really."

He scooted his crate closer. "What's goin'

on? You didn' fuck no snow bunnies, right? Remember what I said. They is trouble. They will steal yo' fuckin' soul if you let 'em."

"Nah, man. It's not that. It's worse. Some girl — hol' up."

My phone was ringing. Rhett. He never called this early in the morning.

"Yo, I gotta take this. I'll be back."

"Aight, don' forget."

I picked up. "Hello?"

"Hey, Buck. How are you?" He sounded anxious.

"I'm okay, Rhett. How're you? I saw the news, man. You're about to be on *Rise and Shine, America,* right?"

"Yeah, yeah," he said. "About that. You've spoken with an assistant or two before, right?"

"Yeah," I replied, my heart fucking racing. *Was someone trying to implicate me in this?* Thinking I was going to faint, I walked to the park and sat down on a swing too small for my ass.

"Great, that's good. Listen, Buck. This is going to sound weird, but you know we're at war, right?"

"Of course, Rhett. I know."

"And you know we gotta do whatever we can, right?"

"Yeah," I said, unsure.

"Exactly. And they just fired their first shot this morning. ABC, NBC, Fox, MSNBC, CNN, all of them. They're coming down hard and trying to make an example out of us."

"But why would they do that? What have we ever done?"

"It's like I said yesterday. We were winning too much. We represent the future, and people are afraid of the future, so they do all they can to maintain the status quo. And now it's time for us to hit back. Starting with going on *Rise and Shine, America* and letting the world know who we are instead of having others tell them."

"Hell yeah," I said, swinging back and forth, shaking the rickety swing set.

"And this is where you come in," he said. "I need you to go home, change into something nice, and take an Uber to Times Square Studios. I'll pay for it."

I fell off the swing and landed on my face, dropping the phone onto the rubber playground tiles before scrambling for it.

"You there?" he asked.

"Yeah. But what's this all about, Rhett?"

"It's time for us to hit back, Buck. You and I. We're going to go on *Rise and Shine, America.* Together. I'll tell you why when you get here. Now hurry."

Morning traffic in Manhattan was slower than loading porn with dial-up in the nineties. The Uber driver with skin the color of midnight and eyes as yellow as egg yolks kept looking at me in his rearview mirror.

"Excuse me, sir."

"Yeah?"

"Are you somebody?"

Good question.

"Nah." I looked down at my white short-sleeved button-up with two pens in the front pocket, black slacks with a black belt, and black leather shoes to match.

"Oh," he said, disappointed. "It is just that you look like somebody, you know? You have that look."

"Sorry to let you down, man," I replied, twisting in my seat. My phone vibrated. Rhett.

Where are you Buck? Starting in 15. Hurry!

There was a huge television screen on the building with the words RISE AND SHINE, AMERICA plastered on it, headlines flashing on the banners below. "Sumwun CEO to speak." "Sumwun got some explainin' to do." "Tensions rise in Libya."

The driver turned around before I hopped out.

"Hey," he said, exposing teeth that matched the color of his eyes. "You are going to be somebody, I know it."

"Thanks, man," I said, showing him the five-star rating on my phone. "I appreciate it."

After arriving on the second floor, I saw an audience full of white women and Sandra Stork, the beautiful tall Black TV host Ma loved. A group of lights and cameras faced windows looking out on Times Square.

"Thank God," Rhett said, hugging me. "You, uh" — he looked me up and down — "sort of look like a Mormon, Buck. I don't know if that's the look we want. But maybe it is. Friendly and harmless." Rhett wore a sharp beige suit with a white button-up and light-brown dress shoes.

"Thanks, I think. So what's going on?"

"You and I are about to go on national television to hit back, that's what," he said, pointing to the cameras. "Just be yourself, answer questions as they come, and don't, I repeat, don't get defensive. We have nothing to hide."

"*Okay,* but why am *I* here with *you*? Why not Chris, Clyde, or someone else?"

He shook his head. "No, we all went through that already. Everyone thinks it's best for you to come on with me. For optics, you know?"

"Optics?"

"Yeah, optics, you know?" he said, smiling as he play-punched my shoulder.

"No, I don't know, Rhett. What do you mean?"

"Listen, Buck. You know I love you like a brother. Everyone thought it'd be good to have a younger member of the sales team with me who won't come off as a holier-than-thou white frat bro, you know?"

It took me a second, but I got it. Donesha was young and Black. I was young and Black. Rhett, Clyde, Chris, and everyone else on the team were white, which, I guess, meant they weren't optimal for *optics.*

Reader: There's a difference between *saying* you'll do whatever it takes to win and *doing* whatever it takes to win. The true salesperson is a doer.

"Yeah," I replied. "I get it."

Rhett exhaled. "I knew you would. It's war, Buck. We all gotta play our roles."

Sandra walked over wearing a sleeveless slim-fitting blue dress, and I was surprised to see that she was even more radiant in person. She also had a commanding presence — she was obviously the HNIC here, which was impressive since everyone else, including the audience, was whiter than the proverbial light at the end of the tunnel.

"Everyone ready?" she asked.

I turned to Rhett. He nodded at me. A chubby guy who smelled like the inside of a high school locker room mic'd me up, and Sandra walked us to three tall chairs behind a curved desk.

"Just relax and be natural," she said, smiling into the cameras. "I won't throw any hardballs. Just a few light ones to let the world know everything is under control, okay?"

Rhett and I nodded. The chubby stinker gripped the main camera in front of us, counting down with his grimy fingers.

One.

I glanced at Rhett. Having looked like he was going to throw up a moment ago, he now had a fake smile plastered to his face and appeared as cool as a Klondike bar.

Two.

My hands were sweating, and I really wished I didn't look like a Mormon. *Do Black Mormons even exist?*

Three.

"Today we have a *Rise and Shine, America* exclusive interview with the CEO of Sumwun, Rhett Daniels, and Sales Representative Darren Vender, who will tell their side of this truly tragic story. As you probably know, Sumwun, a New York City tech startup with more than three hundred employees and twenty-eight million dollars invested from some of tech's biggest players, including Lucien Quartz, has been at the center of controversy since the story broke yesterday.

"To recap, it was Sumwun's platform that connected young Donesha Clark — also known as Donny — with her therapist, Jiaolong Lee. Lee lured the depressed and unsuspecting Donesha to China to brutally murder her. Donesha's parents say their little girl had plans to attend college and become a dentist in order to brighten the world with more smiles, but now, she'll never smile again."

Damn. This is how she kicks this shit off?

"Gentlemen, many people are saying that you should all be thrown in jail, just like Mr. Lee, for allowing this horrific death to happen. What do you have to say to that?"

So much for no hardballs. I turned to Rhett, who was still wearing that superficial smile.

"Well, Sandra, I first want to say that the entire company is devastated by what happened. Each one of us is someone's sibling, child, or parent, so we understand how deeply unsettling this is. Second, this is the first time anything like this has ever happened, and more than ninety percent of our assistants, which is what we call the people who users speak with, have five-star ratings."

"And about these people, Rhett," Sandra said. "A majority of them aren't licensed, are they? I mean, they're not actually certified therapists who have been trained and passed exams in order to be qualified to help anyone, correct?"

This was an ambush.

"Well, I can't speak for all of our assistants, Sandra. They hail from different countries with different interpretations of what it means to be certified. But truthfully, I'd say that many of the licensed therapists here in America aren't qualified. The only thing they are qualified to do is charge astronomic prices to vulnerable people in order to get them hooked on useless therapy instead of actually helping them."

Boom. The audience watched with excitement, and one woman even broke out a box of Milk Duds. Popcorn, no doubt, would be next.

"And," Rhett continued, "we have a strict vetting process and review system. This means that if a user feels uncomfortable with an assistant they can notify us immediately and we'll look into it."

"Got it," Sandra said. "So you're blaming the victim."

"What? No."

Sandra assumed a menacing smile — her first taste of blood. "Let's switch gears. I have a question for you, Darren. As a young Black man, how are you able to go into work and sell a product you know has the potential to kill young women, especially young Black women, like Donesha Clark?"

"Um," I said, coughing so hard and for so long that Sandra handed me a bottle of water. *How the hell could they let a twenty-two-year-old wing it on national television?* I kept coughing, trying to buy time, but then it hit me like Muhammad Ali knocking out George Foreman in Zaire: this was a role-play. Sandra was playing the role of a tough prospect, and I was playing the role of a salesperson — selling her, the live audience, and everyone watching at home on our side of the story.

Reader: What you are about to see is all of my training put into action in the world beyond Sumwun. If you ever needed proof that what I'm teaching

you is more about life than just about sales, this is it. Hold my drink.

"Platforms like Sumwun don't kill people, Sandra," I said. "People do. And that's what happened here. Yes, a man killed someone, but people have done that since the beginning of time and will continue to long after we're gone."

Sandra's smile disappeared. A faint rage flashed in her eyes. "That sounds an awful lot like what right-wingers say about guns, Darren. Any tool can be turned into a weapon, no?"

"Sure, but any reasonable person understands that it comes down to intention. The end result of pulling a trigger is always harm, even at the cost of protecting yourself and others. In all cases, except for this outlier, the end result of using Sumwun is happiness and well-being."

"But your platform enabled the murder of an innocent, depressed young woman," Sandra replied. "If Sumwun never existed, Donesha Clark would still be alive today. What you're saying is completely irresponsible."

"How do you get to work, Sandra?"

She shifted in her high seat, confused. "Excuse me?"

257

"How do you get to work in the morning? Like today, how did you get to the studio?"

"I took a taxi, but sometimes I take the subway."

"Why did you take a taxi, and why do you sometimes take the subway?"

She laughed, sipped from her *Rise and Shine, America* mug, then said, "Because it beats walking! You try treading through Manhattan in Manolos." The audience laughed.

"Exactly, Sandra. This year alone, more than one thousand people have died in car crashes and subway-related accidents. So, by your logic, we should take cars off the road and stop the subways because those one thousand people wouldn't have died if cars and subways had never existed, right?"

She opened up her mouth, then closed it. "It's different, Darren. You may be too young to know the difference, but things that are more helpful than harmful are good for society."

She's done. This was nothing compared to Hell Week.

"One person died, Sandra, which, I agree, is a tragedy. But we have hundreds of thousands of users who log into Sumwun daily and decide to live another day because of the help we provide. And if that counts

258

for nothing, then I truly feel sorry for a society that would rather focus more on some random, senseless act of violence than on the lives we save."

The audience nodded, and I knew if I'd convinced a bunch of middle-aged white women that we'd done no wrong, the rest of America watching us from the comfort of their couches would also agree.

After that, Sandra lost her spark. The other questions she threw at us — "Where does Sumwun go from here?" "How are you going to prevent this moving forward?" "Anything you want to say to the family?" — were the softballs we'd expected.

By the end, she clenched her jaw and looked into the camera, putting on her million-dollar smile. "There you have it, ladies and gentlemen. Two representatives of Sumwun. You have the facts, so it's up to you to decide what you make of them. Thank you for your time, gentlemen."

The stinker came over and unmic'd us. Sandra stood up, impressed. "Fair play," she said, shaking Rhett's hand, then mine. "Especially you, young man. If you ever get tired of sales, give me a call."

"Thanks."

Rhett and I headed for the elevators. Once inside, he wiped thick beads of sweat from his forehead then took my face between his hands. "You crushed it, Buck!" he shouted, and kissed my forehead. No man had ever done that to me before. "Just like we knew you would. It was exactly the type of offense we needed. Time to go back to the office and see if things are settling down."

We hopped in an Uber. Stopping at a red light, the driver looked in the rearview mirror and smiled. He was a pale kid, maybe my age, with cheap sunglasses, and some flag I couldn't place stuck to his dashboard. "I saw you two coming out of that big building where I sometimes see celebrities. You guys somebody?" he asked, his voice heavy with excitement.

Rhett laughed and elbowed me in the rib. "I don't know about myself, but this guy sitting next to me? He certainly is."

14

Two days later, things were finally returning to normal. Prospects weren't hanging up after hearing, "Hi! This is so-and-so from Sumwun, how are you?" Clients weren't frantically canceling. And the tension we all felt, while still being very real, slowly dissipated. Even Lucien, our main investor, relaxed, and the media latched on to some story about a Justin Bieber–worshipping cult in Oklahoma kidnapping "non-Beliebers" and eating them. It felt like we were in the clear.

"I still can't believe how hard you destroyed Sandra Stork," Eddie said, sitting across from me in the event space.

"Yeah, Buck," Frodo added, as he inserted a piece of raw steak into his mouth. "It was like, I don't know, like she didn't know what to do."

"Can you not eat that in front of Clifford?" Marissa asked, patting her pig with

261

one hand and offering him a palm full of potato chips with the other.

"What? What's wrong with this?"

Eddie pinched his nose. "It's fucking raw meat, Frodo. Why on earth are you eating a raw steak for lunch?"

"Oh, uh, I'm on the Paleo Diet. So, if a caveman wouldn't eat a certain type of food that exists today, like those potato chips Marissa's feeding Clifford, I won't eat it. It's supposed to be healthy."

"But why *raw* meat?"

Frodo smiled, gripping Eddie's bony shoulder with his beefy paw. "Because cavemen didn't have stoves, Eddie. Come on."

"Buck, is that you?" Marissa asked, pointing to the flat-screen TV across the room. "Hey!" she shouted. "Turn up the TV; it's Buck!"

I looked up and instantly froze. It was a photo of me at Starbucks smiling as I served a customer while Carlos, Brian, and Nicole watched in delight — a professional photo corporate took for promotional material. But I didn't know why it was being plastered across PSST News.

"Turn it up!" I screamed.

A standard male TV voice spoke. "But who is he really? A few days ago, Sumwun CEO Rhett Daniels appeared with this no-

262

name sales kid in an obvious PR stunt. He acted cute for the camera, had some clever answers for Sandra Stork, but how credible is he? Here at PSST News, we decided to search for answers, and what we found was startling. Before working at Sumwun, where he's been for only three months, he was a shift supervisor at Starbucks. And before that, well, he was just someone who never even went to college. We have Bonnie Sauren on the ground in Bed-Stuy, which sources say is where the young man is from. Over to you, Bonnie."

My photo with a superimposed question mark switched over to an attractive blonde girl in a white dress and heels walking out of the Myrtle-Willoughby stop on the G train — my subway station. The same subway station I entered every morning and exited every evening. The subway station across from Wally Cat's corner and right in front of . . . *wait. No. No. No.*

"Thanks, Chet," Bonnie said, smiling with teeth as white as her dress. "This afternoon I'm in Bed-Stuy, home of the random boy who Sumwun paraded around on national television a few days ago. What we know is that he's worked there for only a few months, and before that, he was a Starbucks barista after graduating from Bronx School of Science as the valedictorian."

"Whoa, Buck," Frodo said, as everyone in the event space stared at me. "You were the valedictorian? Why didn't you say?"

"Uh," I groaned, and focused back on the TV.

"But the public wants more answers. So we're here to get them today. I have with me Jason Morris, a friend of Darren Vender who says he's known him longer than anyone else."

Fuck. Oh fuck.

The camera focused on Jason, who was wearing a black balaclava, black hoodie, and baggy black pants with his underwear exposed.

"So, Jason," Bonnie said. "If you don't mind, could you remove the ski mask so we can see your face?"

"Nah," he said. "I don' wan' no feds being able to identify my ass."

"But, Jason, we've already said your full name on national television," Bonnie said, looking nervous.

"Whatever, man. Then I ain' gonna make it worse by showin' my face."

"*Okay.* So, Jason, what can you tell us about your friend Darren Vender?"

"Friend? Nah, you got me *BLEEP* up. Darren Vender ain' no friend of mine. He's a punk-ass *BLEEP* who think he's better than everyone around here. He think he comes from, iono, wherever you're from."

"Bismarck, North Dakota?" Bonnie asked, confused.

"Yeah," Jason nodded. "He think he from North Dakota, Beverly Hills, or some *BLEEP*. Guy's been on his Hollywood ever since he gotta job wit' those white people in Manhattan. Walkin' 'round here like he ain' grow up hittin' a lick or two on an ice cream truck."

"Hit a lick on an ice cream truck?" Bonnie said, pushing the microphone closer to him. "What is that? Hitting a lick?"

"You know," Jason said, pulling his balaclava down farther, looking over his shoulder. "Robbin' *BLEEP* for some candy, a little ice pop, or some change."

"Excuse me, Jason. Just for clarification, are you saying Darren Vender used to rob ice cream trucks with you?"

"I ain' sayin' *BLEEP*," he said. "Ain' nobody snitchin' out here. I'm jus' sayin', dude think he smooth, politickin' and *BLEEP* on television. That *BLEEP* ain' *BLEEP*."

I couldn't believe it. I thought my body was going to spontaneously combust where I sat. I knew we had our issues, but I didn't

265

think he'd do me like that on television. I was hurt, but beyond that, I was furious. I would've never betrayed him like that no matter what.

"Thank you, Jason," Bonnie said, shaking his hand then wiping hers off on her dress. "And there you have it, America. Darren Vender. Salesman. Starbucks barista. Thug. Our sources also say Jason Morris was arrested a few years ago for grand theft auto and served twelve months. It sounds like Sumwun still has more explaining to do. Back to you, Chet."

Eddie grabbed my shoulder. "Buck."

"Don't," I said, digging my nails deeper into my thighs. With dozens of eyes on me, I got up, grabbed my bags, and headed for the elevator.

I felt exposed. Like every single person — security guards, people entering elevators, postal workers — were all staring at me and wondering, *Is that the kid?* I hurried across the lobby and shoved my way through the revolving doors.

"Hey." Someone running up behind me tapped my arm.

"What!" I screamed. It was Brian with his green Starbucks apron over a black short-sleeved button-up.

"Sorry, Darren — *SHIT!* I just saw the

news. Everyone's talking about it. You okay?"

"I will be," I said, walking down the steps.

He jogged after me. "Hey, Darren. Can I ask you something?"

"What?"

"Um, it's just that, uh, you said you would try to get me a job at Sumwun, right? Doing what you do. And I know that it didn't work last time, but, um — *COCK!* Sorry, uh, maybe you could talk to Clyde and ask for a do-over?"

"I don't have time for this, Brian," I snapped, my voice soaked in rage. "I got you an interview a month ago, like I said I would. I vouched for you, like I said I would. And you fucked it up, like you said you wouldn't."

"But —"

"But what, Brian? You think I'm just some endless well of opportunities? You think I can just, as you say, 'Talk to Clyde and ask for a do-over?' Life doesn't work that way. Sometimes you get one shot at the game," I said, jabbing a finger in front of his face. "And if you fuck it up, you're done. And it doesn't mean it's right, but that's just how the game is. But it's a good thing you didn't get the job. Because, frankly, you don't have what it takes. You would've been eaten alive,

267

and it would've been more of a waste of your time than the time I'm wasting with you right now. So just stick to Starbucks, okay?"

Tears welled up in his eyes and slowly crawled over the pimpled and pockmarked surfaces of his face. He nodded, walked back up the stairs, pushed his way through the revolving doors, and disappeared.

When he saw me exiting the station, Wally Cat stood up from his crate, eyes wide in fear. Today his Hawaiian shirt featured red, blue, and yellow parrots on various tropical leaves. "Aye, don' do nothin', Darren! It's not worth it!"

Jason was where he always was: on his corner, wearing the same black hoodie with the sagging black pants and rolled-up black balaclava from TV. He was on the phone, waving a hand full of cash in the air. Before he could turn around, I rammed my fist into his face, knocking him to the ground. His phone bounced off the concrete and the wad of hundred-dollar bills exploded like confetti.

"Yo, what the fuck?" he shouted, eyes knocked into the back of his head.

"What's good now, son!" I said, crashing heavy fist after heavy fist into his face. Left eye, right eye, left cheek, right cheek, nose, chin, upper lip, bottom lip. My hands knew no boundaries, traveling freely from place to place like migratory birds.

He scratched and clawed at my face, doing anything to make me stop, but I was already on top of him, the weight of my body planted on his chest, my feet firm on the concrete.

"Big man now, huh?" I shouted, pummeling his face like a raw piece of meat, unable to feel the tears flying out of my own eyes. "I'm not shit, right? Said I forgot where I come from, right?" I beat his mouth so many times I felt teeth break right out from his gums, heard his nose crack to the left, then straighten to the right, saw blood pooling in his mouth so dark and red, it resembled oil.

"You're gonna kill the nigga!" someone shouted.

"WORLDSTAR!" another said, cell phone cameras flashing as if I were surrounded by paparazzi.

I didn't care. Nothing hurts worse than betrayal from someone you love.

"D! Stop!" someone yelled. I looked up, and in the dense crowd that swarmed the corner, I saw Soraya, a hand covering her mouth and her face wet with tears. Unable to continue, I got up, wiped my eyes, and walked over to her.

When I looked back at Jason, he was choking on his blood. Wally Cat turned him over and pounded his back. Blood splattered all over the corner, filling the cracks in the concrete.

Police sirens grew louder, and the crowd dispersed in every direction. I stood still. The wind blew a strong smell of cinnamon and cocoa butter toward me; I allowed it to fill my nose and spread throughout my body.

"Let's go!" Soraya pulled me away.

I looked back and saw Wally Cat holding Jason in his arms, rubbing his head.

As we passed the bodega, I waved to Mr. Aziz, but he just stared. We turned the corner and bolted up the stairs.

"I don' understand," Ma said, dabbing my face and hands with alcohol.

"Ow!" I shouted. "That hurts, Ma!"

"Well maybe it should hurt more. I don' understand how you and Jason went from bein' Batman and Superman to fightin' on the corner like animals."

"You saw the interview, Ma. You saw how he did me, didn' you?"

She pressed the alcohol harder into my cuts, bringing the pain to an all-time high.

270

"How he *did* you?" She sucked her teeth. "What's gotten into you, Darren Vender? You're startin' to sound like one of those prepubescent gangbangers on *Judge Hatchett,* talkin' 'bout street justice and other nonsense I raised you to steer clear of."

Soraya walked into the living room, waving my phone. "It's ringin', D."

I swatted Ma's hand away and sat up on the couch. Rhett. *Fuck.*

"Hey, Rhett," I said, trying to sound normal.

"Jesus, Buck. What did you do?"

"What do you mean?"

"Buck," he said, spitting my name out. "The video is all over every news channel. Why did you do that? I thought you had more sense. I thought you knew what was at stake."

Shit. "I don't know, Rhett. I wasn't thinking. I just saw what he said about me and lost it. I'm sorry, man. I'm really sorry."

He drew a lungful of air. "Sorry doesn't work here, Buck. Not at all. We were counting on you. You never get emotional in war, Buck. Ever. Listen" — he paused — "don't come to work tomorrow."

My heart stopped. And when I say that, I truly mean it. For a moment, I couldn't feel it. While the idea of dying on the couch in

271

our living room was bad enough, the thought of my career ending at Sumwun was infinitely worse.

"Are you — are you saying I'm fired?" I asked, afraid of the answer.

Silence. Silence that likely lasted only a few seconds but sprouted legs and ran far and hard.

"I should fire you, Buck. It's what the board wants."

Salty tears gushed from my eyes, stinging my cuts. Whatever I had eaten in the morning started to reverse its trajectory through my intestines, and the room spun around me.

"But no, Buck," he said. "I know that what happened today won't happen again. I promised you that as long as you're honest with me I'll always have your back, remember? But you need to lay low over the next few days until this blows over, okay?"

All I could do was sigh with relief. I grabbed the paper towel from Ma and wiped my eyes with it, forgetting about the alcohol. I didn't care.

"Okay, Buck?" he repeated. "Promise me that you're not going to give the news anything to write about. Nothing."

"I promise," I said, still crying but shedding tears of relief now. "Thank you, Rhett.

I'm sorry. Nothing like this will ever happen again."

"I know, Buck. It's going to be fine. You know I see you as my brother, right?"

"I know, Rhett. I see you as my brother too. Forreal."

"Good. So here's what I want you to do. Take tomorrow off and go to Shangri-La Palace. It's on Thirty-Second and Sixth."

"Alright, but for what?"

"To relax, Buck. What else? I'm sure you look like shit right now. I'll book a body scrub, facial, and massage — the works. You wanna take Soraya?"

"Sure," I said, unsure of everything. I just wanted the day to be over.

"Great. I'll book it for two. My treat."

"Okay. Thanks, Rhett. I appreciate it, man. Everything."

"Of course. Love you, Buck. Rest up and see you at seven sharp on Monday. We'll keep fighting, but we need you in top shape."

"Love you too, Rhett. See you on Monday."

15

"You happy?" Soraya asked, storming into my bedroom and throwing a pile of papers at me.

"What?" I quickly sat up.

"The papers." She pointed to the mess at the bottom of my feet.

"What are you talkin' about? I see the arts section about some new play hittin' Broadway, some shit about baseball and politics."

"This!" she shouted, shoving one of the sheets in my face.

It was me, well, a close-up of that Starbucks photo of me, with the words YOUNG THUG HITS BACK plastered in bold white lettering. *Fuck.*

She crossed her arms, cradling her breasts as if they were ripe melons. "Well?"

"Well what?" I threw the front cover to the floor and lay back down.

"Are you happy with yourself? With all this publicity you're gettin'?"

"*Habibti,* c'mon. You know I'm not. It was my bad. Can we forget about it?"

"Forget about it, D? This isn' somethin' you jus' forget about. You better go and apologize to Jason."

I shot straight back up. "Apologize? That motherfucker was comin' at me on national television. We're even now and I don' feel sorry about a damn thing."

"Alright, D. If you say so." She quietly gathered the papers and threw them in the trash before heading for the door.

"Wait." I jumped out of bed and grabbed her hand. "Where you goin'? Let's go to the spa, relax, and have a good day. I don' have to go in, remember?"

She yanked her hand away and opened the door. "Good for you. Now you'll have plenty of time to think about how wrong you are. Peace."

"C'mon, Soraya, don' be that way. I'm the victim here. I got people comin' at me from all angles and you're takin' their side? What is this? I thought it was always me and you."

She paused at the door, inhaling deeply before facing me. "It is, D. And if you think I'm takin' someone else's side, then you're more messed up than I thought. So what I'm gonna say is this: either you grow up and apologize to Jason, or I'm not gonna see you for a very, very long time. *Hal tafham?*"

I closed my eyes and saw Jason with Bonnie Sauren, wearing that black balaclava with that black hoodie and those saggy black pants. Talking shit about me. My heart banged against my chest like a stranger in the night. Harder. Faster. Louder. And my jaw became so tight, I swore I was going to split my teeth in half. But when I opened my eyes, Soraya was gone. The door downstairs slammed shut. In my boxers, I ran down the stairs and out the door after her.

"Okay, okay, okay," I said, snatching her hand. "I'm sorry. I'll do it. I'll get dressed and say sorry to him on the way to the spa. Deal?"

Satisfied, she cracked a smirk and pointed to the house. "Go."

"Damn, boy. You lookin' more naked than a jaybird," Mr. Rawlings said from his window. "Put some clothes on 'fore the police arrest you for prostitution. Yeesh!"

"Aight, aight," I said. "Mornin' to you too, Mr. Rawlings."

"Also, your momma feelin' better?"

"I think so," I said, running up the stairs before the police actually did stop and ask what the hell I was doing. "She went to work, so probably."

"Mm-hmm. You better keep outta trouble now," he said, shutting his window.

Minutes later, I was dressed and jumping down the stairs. We walked toward the corner. No Jason. Just Wally Cat sitting on his crate.

"Aye, come here!" he shouted.

"Hang here for a second," I told Soraya. "Let me see what he wants."

"Wassup, Wally Cat?"

"*Wassup?* Nigga, you almost killed someone yesterday, tha's *wassup*. If it wasn' for me, he would've bled out on the street right there. I seen that shit too many times on this corner to be seein' it again. What got into you?"

"I know. My bad, man. We jus' had some trouble and I lost it. You know tha's not me."

"I do know, which is why I'm not beatin' your ass right now. Servin' up some street justice like we used to do back in the day. All those reporters runnin' 'round yesterday. I heard what he said, but you kids can't always be throwin' hands like that. It's what they want," he said. "You hearin' me?"

"Yeah, man. I'm listenin'."

"I didn' ask if you was *listenin'* to me, nigga, I asked if you was *hearin'* me. The media feeds off of black blood like vampires. They want more of it, and they'll pit us

277

against each other jus' to see it fly like firecrackers on the Fourth of July. And you know what? You gave it to 'em. You played into their hands. And now that boy is in the hospital, messed up as a duck."

"Which hospital?"

"Woodhull, whatchu think?"

"Bet," I said. "I'll check you later, Wally Cat."

"The devil finds work for idle hands, Darren!" he shouted. "Don' forget that!"

"You can come in now," a nurse said, scanning her clipboard.

"I'll wait here," Soraya said. She kissed me on the lips and grabbed a magazine in the waiting room.

I followed the nurse down a series of mazelike hallways and arrived at a closed door. "Bed closest to the window," she said. "But try to keep it down. He's not the only one in there and he just woke up."

I placed my hand on the doorknob, trembling. *Damn, Jason. Of course something like this would happen.*

I turned the knob and walked past beds with curtains wrapped around them, various machines beeping and buzzing like insects in the night. I arrived at his bed and gripped the side rails and just stood there, watching him rest. His lips were busted and swollen like halves of a tomato, and his eyes straight up resembled a raccoon's: thick black circles that almost looked like they were painted on his face. A thick piece of white tape stretched across his nose.

"Yo," I said. He opened his eyes slowly. When he saw me, he just stared, then looked away.

"Yo, Jason," I repeated, louder. "Can you hear me?"

"Yeah, nigga," he said through a clenched jaw. "I ain' deaf."

Thin strips of metal crisscrossed his teeth like telephone wires. "Damn, son. They got your jaw wired shut like fuckin' Kanye. You 'bout to spit a verse?"

"Fuck you, nigga," he said, exhausted. "Whatchu want?"

I tapped on his guard rail, internalizing the question. I knew what Soraya wanted and why I felt forced to go there, but what did *I* want?

I watched green lines rise and fall like the Dow Jones on a monitor next to his head. "I dunno."

"Then why you here?"

"I dunno."

"Then leave before I fuck you up," he said, wincing.

"Listen, man. You shouldn' have gotten up on television and said that shit about me."

"It was true though, wasn' it?" he said, staring at me. Through me, really. "That you been walkin' all over these streets like you suddenly own them, lookin' down on me like I wasn' the same nigga who used to protect you from older niggas tryna steal your bike or makin' fun of your light skin, that fancy-ass school, and havin' a Spanish daddy. Nigga, I was even the one who introduced you to Soraya."

He squeezed his eyes tightly as he sat up, then eased his lips around a thin straw sticking out of a Styrofoam cup.

"But you don' remember any of that, right? So you get a little tight when I speak the truth. Think you big comin' on the block and sucker punchin' me? You ain' even had enough respect to square up like a fuckin' man. You lucky I don' fuck you up right now, with all these wires and shit."

I grabbed a chair and looked out the windows at cars going by in every direction; doctors on smoke breaks, laughing, puffing, and smiling; trains rumbling over the elevated tracks across Brooklyn and Queens. We used to ride that shit like it was a roller coaster, racing from one end to the other,

280

pushing people out the way, jumping all over like it was a jungle gym to try to earn a few bucks.

"I didn' forget," I said, still staring out the window. "I didn' forget any of it."

He sank back into his bed. "Good."

"I'm sorry, Batman. For everything."

"Sorry don' fix my jaw, nigga. Or the fact that Imma be off the corner for a minute now. My momma can't eat 'sorry.' "

"I know, but —"

"But nothin', son." He turned toward the window. "When you see me in the street, don' try dappin' me up, talkin' to me, or even lookin' at me. I meant what I told that white girl on TV. You still over here steady thinkin' you one of them. But you'll see. You ain' shit, and now you less than shit. You dead to me. Now get the fuck up outta here before I tell my nurse to get security on your bitch ass."

"I guess we have to buzz up," Soraya said, as she scanned Shangri-La Palace's directory. The door clicked open and we packed ourselves into a claustrophobic elevator.

"You okay?" she asked.

"I'm good."

"We don' have to do this if you don' want to. We can jus' chill."

281

"I said I'm good, Soraya."

The elevator bounced before it came to a stop and opened on a reception area. Sounds of flowing water, birds, and a harp filled the humid air.

"How may we help you?" a smiling Korean woman asked.

"Um, we have a reservation. Darren Vender?"

The woman scrolled through her computer and frowned. "I'm sorry, we have no reservation under that name. We do have one for Buck Vender, though, made by Mr. Daniels?"

"Oh, yeah, that's me. That's my, uh, other name."

"Okay, perfect. Mr. Daniels put you down for a body scrub, facial, massage, and couples jacuzzi. Does that sound right?"

I raised an eyebrow at Soraya. Her brown eyes grew larger. She mouthed, *Seriously?*

"Yeah, I guess that does."

"Okay, follow me, please." The woman led us down a set of stairs to a changing room with lockers, sinks, and what looked like an operating table.

"Please place your belongings in the lockers and change into these," she said, handing us each a white robe and slippers. "You can also freshen up with a warm towel, if you'd like."

"Thank you," Soraya said.

We changed in silence, and even though we wore robes, I felt naked under Soraya's stare.

Someone knocked on the door. "What would you like to do first?" the smiling woman asked. "Couples jacuzzi, body scrub, facial, or massage?"

"Massage," Soraya declared, pushing past the woman into the hallway.

Getting the hell beaten out of me by an older Korean woman was *not* relaxing. All I could think about was the front page of the *Daily News,* how fucked up Jason was, and the fact that I came within an inch of being fired — losing everything I had worked so hard for.

"Okay," she whispered after what felt like an hour. "Body scrub time. Please follow us."

Soraya silently rose from her table, took a sip of her iced water with orange and apple slices, and left.

The "body scrub" was more of a "body flay." The women threw buckets of hot water on us, applied copious amounts of cold gel, then went to work with coarse mitts, scraping off thick pieces of skin that looked like folds of grated cheese.

After the torture ended, the women moisturized our bodies with yogurt lotion. I cautiously glanced at Soraya, who was admiring her skin. No bullshit, it glowed like brown suede — so slick, it reflected the blue tiles. With her hair wrapped in a towel, face massaged and polished, she was sculpturesque.

A woman led us to a door and said, winking, to take our time. Without a word, Soraya pushed the door open. In the center of the room was an oversize circular jacuzzi. Across every wall were recessed shelves that held lit candles. A table next to the jacuzzi bore chocolate-dipped pineapples, strawberries, apricots, a bottle of champagne in a bucket of ice, and two glass flutes. At the front of the room was a flat-screen TV.

Soraya dropped her robe as she walked toward the table. She delicately brought a chocolate-dipped strawberry to her mouth and turned on the TV. Her body, thick, smooth, and tight, was irresistible, but I couldn't even allow myself to enjoy the moment.

"The TV, really?" I asked, grabbing a piece of pineapple.

"You obviously have nothin' to say, so why not?" She poured herself some champagne and settled into the jacuzzi.

I took a swig straight from the bottle. "Whatever, man."

"Whatever is right. Look at you. Since when did you start drinkin' champagne?"

I pointed at her hand holding the glass above the water. "Tha's funny. So what? You can drink and I can't?"

"You know that's not what I mean." She set her glass down on the jacuzzi's edge. "You used to be so against drinkin', sayin' it wasn' for you and was never gonna be for you, but once you start workin' at this company, you suddenly drink. If you ask me, *that's* funny."

"Yo, what the *fuck* is your problem? We get this expensive-ass spa day, which, by the way, is from the CEO of my company, and you're tight the whole time. Shit makes no sense."

"You're right, D. It doesn' make any sense. You're the one who's been all tense. You haven' said anything about Jason or if you even apologized. It's like you're all shut up inside."

"I *did* apologize to him, jus' like you told me to. And now I got you here ruinin' my fuckin' day of relaxation."

"Sorry, D," she said, tapping her forehead. "I forgot you were the only one with problems. Like I don' have my own worries,

285

tryna get my nursin' degree, managin' my dad's shops, or havin' to prevent you from killin' someone. You're right, D. I'm sorry."

I stood there and took large swigs of champagne and stared at her. *What happened to her?* She used to be my ace, my ride-or-die, and lately she was just getting on my last fucking nerve, like she was blind to all of the shit I was going through. I silently stepped into the jacuzzi and closed my eyes. The champagne lifted me, and I finally relaxed.

We stayed like that for a while until I felt splashing water on my face. I opened my eyes and she was eating a fig, smiling.

"Oh, so now you wanna play?" I flicked water back at her.

She jumped across the jacuzzi and landed on top of me, causing the water to overflow and her flute to shatter on the floor. I grabbed her and held her on top of me. Her hands gripped my face and our tongues rolled over each other to a rhythm only we knew. She moaned, and I was harder than a diamond. I kissed her neck. She bit my lip. I entered her. She thrusted, thrusted, and thrusted on top of me like she was possessed.

Someone banged on the door, but we didn't stop. "Is everything okay?" they asked. "We heard glass breaking."

"Yes!" Soraya shouted as the water sloshed and spilled over the jacuzzi's edge.

I gripped her tighter, going deeper. She threw her head back, screaming toward the ceiling loud enough for the receptionist upstairs and the men selling salty hot dogs and roasted nuts outside to hear. I squeezed my eyes shut, pleasure overtaking my body like an exorcism.

"Faster," she said, pushing against my chest. "Faster."

I opened my eyes and pushed her off of me.

"What the hell, D?"

I jumped out, scrambled toward the flat-screen, and turned the volume up. There was a white man with white hair, pale-blue eyes behind rimless glasses, and translucent skin exposing rivers of blue veins. He exited a black limousine and reporters surrounded him. Words scrolled at the bottom of the screen: "Sumwun's lead investor, Lucien Quartz, speaks."

"Darren, are you serio—"

"Sh!" I said, glued to the TV.

"Well, it's all very troubling, very troubling indeed," Lucien said in a posh English accent. "Believe it or not, I've advised Rhett Daniels to close up shop, just for a bit, in order to respect the dignity and pain of the public. But he refused. I was the lead investor of Sumwun because I saw how much promise it had, but now I not only doubt the direction and overall strategy of the organization but also Rhett Daniels. That will be all, thank you."

As he headed up a set of marble stairs somewhere in San Francisco, reporters followed him shouting, "But, wait, one more question, Mr. Quartz!" "Please, Mr. Quartz, tell us about . . ." "Mr. Quartz! Mr. Quartz!" Without another word, he disappeared through a pair of revolving doors.

"Fuck," I said, sliding down the wall onto the soaked floor.

"You gotta be kiddin' me, Darren," Soraya said, sitting in the jacuzzi.

"I know." I shook my head. "I can't believe any of this. I dunno what we're gonna do. It's like —"

"No," she said. "*You* have gotta be kiddin' me. You can't think about anything other than that company. Not even while we're havin' sex. How do you think that makes me feel? Do you think it makes me feel special?"

"What are you talkin' about? Didn' you jus' see the TV? Don' you know what's goin' on? This isn' about you, Soraya, and I

288

frankly don' know why you're makin' it about you."

She threw her hands in the air, laughing. "*Frankly.* Since when did you start sayin' that? I *honestly* don' know who you are, Darren. You and Rhett sayin' you love each other? You jus' met the guy three months ago and you don' even tell me, your *girlfriend,* that! If you ask me, you need to get the hell away from Sumwun."

"Good thing no one asked you," I mumbled.

She got out of the jacuzzi and grabbed her robe. "You're right, Darren. No one did ask me. But if someone did, I'd say that maybe Jason wasn' so wrong about what he said."

I jumped in front of her, water dripping off my body, my face so close that I felt her breath.

"What?" she asked, looking me up and down, chuckling. "You gonna hit me? Beat me up like you did Jason?"

I just stared at her, grinding my teeth, my knuckles choking against taut skin.

"Yeah," she said, opening the door. "That's what I thought. If you find the old Darren, gimme a call. I miss that guy."

The door slammed behind her. I grabbed the bottle of champagne, sank into the jacuzzi, and chugged until it was empty.

"Fuck the old Darren," I announced to the empty room. "I'm Buck."

16

A week later, Rhett ordered us to offer steep discounts to close more deals, but that didn't work. PSST News aired an interview Bonnie Sauren did with the chief of police of Little Rock, where Donesha Clark was from. In it, the chief revealed that before working for Sumwun, Jiao-long Lee had spent five years in Qincheng Prison, a maximum-security prison in Beijing, for domestic assault, armed robbery, and voluntary manslaughter — which exposed Sumwun's negligence. If we'd been in deep shit before, we were drowning in it now.

A bouquet of chocolate, peanuts, and caramel drifted toward me as I entered the kitchen on Friday morning. *Brazilian.* Likely a robusta from the state of Espírito Santo. Ma was at the table with a cup of it in one hand and a newspaper in the other.

"Smells good, Ma," I said, and took a seat across from her. It was early, but she was already dressed for work, which made me happy.

"Mm-hmm," she said, reading her paper. She took a slow sip of coffee, struggling to swallow, as if she were drinking liquid concrete.

"You okay, Ma? You look like you're about to choke."

"I'm okay, Dar. Jus' a sore throat, that's all."

"I didn' know sore throats made you choke on coffee."

She put the newspaper down and finally looked at me. "Seems like you don' know a lot these days, baby."

"What's that mean?"

She went to the sink. "I raised you to have more sense, Dar. To stay away from trouble. But all I'm hearin' nowadays is about your company and the trouble it's causin'. Maybe it's time you took a break."

"Took a break? Ma, this isn' somethin' you jus' take a break from. You been talkin' with Soraya?"

"No, I haven't, but you need to give that girl a call. I haven' seen her around here in too long, and Wally Cat tells me you and Jason still aren' talkin'."

I sucked my teeth. "That guy stays runnin' his mouth, man. Wally Cat needs to mind his own fuckin' business."

The plate fell from Ma's hands and bounced around the sink. "I don' wanna hear any of that disrespect in here. Wally Cat is your elder, and I raised you better," she said, wet hands gripping the sink. "I jus' know how these people use us. One day they have you on TV defendin' them, then got you out all hours of the night, comin' back smellin' like a whiskey barrel."

"No one is usin' anyone, Ma. Trust me, I got this. Plus, you're the one who wanted me to do this in the first place. You kept tellin' me to go and show the world who I was. To not let these people get to me. To be more than who I was before."

"I didn' say *be more,* Dar. I said give yourself the opportunity to *be yourself.* That's all. Who you are has always been enough."

"Nah, tha's not what you said, and you know it. So if you think I'm not who I used to be, it's because I'm not. Jus' like you wanted."

She turned toward me. "Dar."

"Nah, Ma. I gotta go. Have a good day at work."

"I love —"

Down the stairs. Turn the corner. Soraya was walking out of Mr. Aziz's bodega, but I

293

kept going.

"D," she called. I stopped.

"What up."

"Listen, I know things haven' been good with us, but we gotta work it out."

"Why do we *gotta* work it out? Seems like you worked it out fine when you left the spa."

She closed her eyes, rubbing her shoulder. "My dad invited you over for dinner tonight. He saw what happened with Jason and knows you're goin' through a tough time, so he wants to cook for you."

I'd been to Soraya's house a handful of times, but never when Mr. Aziz was there. He'd always been nice to me, and he obviously knew Soraya and I were more than friends, but he always just treated me like one of his customers.

"So I think," she continued, noting my surprise, "that it'd be a good reset for us, you know? You can get to know my dad more, and he can get to know you as more than jus' some guy from the neighborhood. We can work it out."

I took in a big breath of Bed-Stuy and held it. I'm not gonna lie, I was still upset about the things she'd said and how she'd been acting, but we'd been through shit before and always got over it. "Aight."

"Aight?" she asked, smiling.

"Yeah." I nodded. "Aight."

"See you at seven then."

I passed Jason's empty corner as Wally Cat shouted, "Aye, Darren! Aye!" But I put my head down and descended into the station, preparing for whatever the day had in store for me even though no amount of preparation could've helped with what happened next.

"Hello?"

"Hi, Dawn! This is Darren calling from Sumwun, how are you?"

"Oh, hi, Darren. I'm sorry, but, um, this really isn't a good time."

"No problem, but I thought you said to call Friday at two? Should we reschedule?"

"Um, no Darren. We just, I, um, I just don't think we're going to need your services."

I rubbed my eyes, exhaling. "Dawn, I don't mean to come off as a pushy salesperson, so please forgive the persistence, but you told me two months ago that Sumwun was *exactly* what you needed to battle your millennial turnover. Are you not experiencing turnover anymore?"

"Darren, I *did* say that, and we *are* still experiencing turnover, but I'd rather have people leaving Chuck E. Cheese than pay to have them murdered."

"But, Dawn —"

"Goodbye, Darren. Please don't call again." *Click.*

"Fuck!"

Charlie looked over. "Sorry, dude. It's happening to everyone. Those marketing videos we put out yesterday with the young girls saying how we've saved their lives and shit were supposed to help, but I guess not."

Frodo chimed in. "I think we need Magic Johnson."

"What?" Marissa asked. Clifford was ramming his fat head into the back of her chair, rocking her up and down.

"Magic Johnson," Frodo repeated, standing up. "Whenever anyone is in trouble, they get, like, uh, a celebrity spokesperson, you know? Someone famous to be the face of the brand. And Magic Johnson could be that for us."

The Duchess walked through the frosted doors, sipping a smoothie, and dropped her bag at her desk. Even during Sumwun's horrible economic downturn, she managed to generate meeting after meeting, coming and going as she pleased. She no longer spoke to us, even to put us down.

Frodo nodded in Eddie's direction. "What

do you think, Eddie?"

Eddie was glued to his phone, furiously swiping left and right on photos of buff guys. "Yeah, good idea, Frodo."

"Um, thanks," Frodo said, scratching his head. "Hey, what's that app? Looks fun."

"Well —"

Charlie slowly rose from his chair and pointed to the frosted doors. "What the fuck?"

I turned around and thought I was hallucinating. Dozens of men and women in navy jackets poured out of the elevators in every direction.

"FBI! Everyone stop what you're doing and put your hands where I can see them," a pale man in a blood-colored tie and white button-down shouted as he shoved open the frosted doors. "Now!"

They flooded the entire floor, walking single file throughout the rows and around the corners, looking out the floor-to-ceiling windows as helicopters moved across the sky.

Clyde stormed toward the pale man but froze when the agent gripped his holster. "Make another move and we'll arrest you!"

"I hope you bastards have a warrant," Clyde said. "If not, get the fuck out of here! We know our rights."

The pale man reached into his jacket, procured a folded piece of paper, and handed it to Clyde.

"Court authorized," the pale man said, smiling. "You think you guys can just get an underage girl killed and not be investigated? This falls under violent crimes against children, online predators, and maybe we'll find more, but who really knows? Now sit down and shut up!"

Clyde didn't sit down. He stood there and read, gripping the paper so hard, it looked like he was going to tear it in half.

"I said sit!" the pale man roared into Clyde's face. Clyde wilted into his seat. *Pussy.*

"Now," the man said, as he turned around the room. "Where's your fearless leader?"

Rhett walked out of his office looking like he'd just seen a ghost. "What's going on?"

"What's going on" — the pale man grinned — "is that Sumwun is under investigation. Give us everything you got. And I mean *everything.*"

I exited the subway. The sun had set, but the humid heat of summer still clung to the September air. There were still trees on the sidewalk with leaves that refused to turn brown, as if change didn't always win in the end.

I charged past Wally Cat and Jason's empty corner, looking through the bodega's windows to make sure Mr. Aziz and Soraya weren't there.

"Hey, Darren," Waleed, Soraya's cousin, said from behind the counter.

"What's good, Waleed."

I walked to the back and grabbed a bottle of sparkling cider.

"This for tonight?" he asked, ringing me up.

"Yeah, how'd you know?"

He laughed. "Soraya was nervous about you actually makin' it, but I knew you would. I'm ten bucks richer now. Good looks."

I cut left down Myrtle Avenue, passing Crown Fried, Kutz, and the laundromat before hearing rock music blasting from a bar. I stopped at the window and saw only white people inside, playing pool, drinking cold glasses of beer, and jerking their elbows and knees wildly — what I guess they considered dancing. *Shit is changing. No doubt about that.*

I buzzed, then heard Soraya's sandals slapping down the stairs.

"I didn' think you'd come," she said, unable to hide her smile. She wore a modest black dress and looked incredible.

"Which is why I made sure I did," I said. "It's been a long day."

"I bet. Is that for me?"

"Oh, yeah." I handed her the bottle and followed her upstairs, watching her ass shake with each step.

Like us, they owned their home. They rented the bottom floor to relatives and occupied the others. Soraya had the top floor to herself and Mr. Aziz lived on the second, where the kitchen and living room also were.

"Darren, *marhaban,*" Mr. Aziz said, gesturing to a small wooden table set for three.

I hadn't been there in a while, but it was exactly as I remembered: brown suede couches; flat-screen TV with a foreign cable box; glass cupboard full of colorful plates, bowls, and utensils; an oversize photo of Soraya's little sister, destined to be five years old forever.

"Thank you, Mr. Aziz. It smells amazing in here."

He laughed. "Well, I wasn't sure what you'd like, but Soraya said you eat everything, so there's *maraq,* which is a delicious soup made from goat meat broth; *mandi,* which is spiced rice and slow-cooked lamb made in a traditional tandoor; *shafoot,* which is a spiced yogurt; and, of course, salad and different types of pita. Please, dig in. I hope you like it."

An hour later, I was stuffed. The care that Mr. Aziz put into the meal was obvious; every single bite was different from the last. After we discussed the changes in the neighborhood, Mr. Aziz's plans for expansion, and the rising cost of living in Bed-Stuy, Mr. Aziz put his drink down, and said, "So, Soraya and I saw the news about the FBI and Sumwun. What's going on?"

"It's nothing to worry about, Mr. Aziz. We have it under control."

"It doesn't look like it. People are saying your company should be shut down and that your pompous CEO should be in jail. What do you think?"

I gritted my teeth, beginning to regret not blowing off the dinner. "I'd prefer to not talk about it, Mr. Aziz. If that's okay."

He shot a look at Soraya, then back at me. "Darren, you're a smart guy. I've known it since I first saw you. So why do you want to be mixed up in this? Maybe it's time to move on."

I turned to Soraya, whose eyes were full of concern, like I was a dopehead in need of an intervention. Then I faced Mr. Aziz and forced a smile. "Thank you for your concern, but trust me, everything will be fine."

"Will it?" he asked, ripping a floury piece of pita in half. "You need to cut your losses before it's too late. I'm sure there are plenty of other places where you could work, and with people more grounded than that so-called CEO of yours. He reminds me of —"

"Mr. Aziz," I cut in, past my breaking point. "With all due respect, you don't know what you're talking about."

Soraya coughed, rising from the table. "Tea? I think we need tea."

"I came to this country with nothing and made something of myself, Darren. So I believe that I do know what I'm talking about. It's obvious the company you work for has done more harm than good, so why not take your talents elsewhere? Someone like you can —"

"Take my talents elsewhere? Mr. Aziz, Sumwun is where I belong, and Rhett gave me an opportunity when I needed it most. We help people want to live another day. And if you call that 'harm,' then you're as crazy as the people who believe everything the news says."

"Darren!" Soraya shouted, dropping the saucers onto the table. "Apologize to my father right now. He's trying to help you.

302

We all are."

Mr. Aziz raised his hand in Soraya's direction. "It's okay, Soraya. Your boyfriend is what we uneducated and crazy people would call brainwashed. It usually happens to the ones who think they're too smart to be tricked."

Soraya, horrified, looked from Mr. Aziz to me and back to him, no doubt trying to figure out how to fix this. But it was too late.

In a situation like this, the old me wouldn't have said anything — he would've apologized and tried to smooth things over, but the old me was gone, and I was happy about it, because he was a boy and I was finally a man. A man who took shit from no one.

"You know what, Mr. Aziz? You're the one who's brainwashed. You came to this country thinking that buying a house and setting up a chain of cheap bodegas meant you'd be successful, when selling a bag of chips for ninety-nine cents has never changed the world. You wouldn't know what innovation was if it slapped you in the face."

Soraya rounded the table and knelt beside me. "This isn't you, D. This isn't you at all. Please apologize to my dad and let's just have tea. It'll be fine, right, *baba*?" she asked, turning to Mr. Aziz.

"No, Soraya," he said, staring at me. "I'm sorry, but I don't think it will be."

"Funny," I said, getting up from the table and heading for the door. "We finally agree on something."

17

"Darren!" Someone was banging on my door. "Darren Vender, wake up! Are you alive in there?"

My head felt like it had been run over by an eighteen-wheeler carrying elephants and cement. I opened my eyes, my blurry vision slowly focused, and I tried to respond, but my throat was drier than a nun's vagina.

"Darren! Do you hear me? If you don' get outta bed and open this door in five seconds, so help me God I will break down this door and beat you awake."

After I'd left Soraya's, I grabbed drinks with Eddie and Frodo, drowning my anger in vodka, rum, gin, and beer. But hangover or not, I leapt out of bed and opened the door before she reached zero. "I'm up, Ma," I said, blinded by sunlight pouring into the room. "What's up, the house on fire?"

She was dressed in black leather flats, black stockings, a black blouse under a black velvet jacket, and a wide-brimmed black hat to top it off: funeral attire.

She stared at me — long curly hair matted to one side of my face and nothing but a pair of boxers on — and sucked her teeth. "If the house was on fire, you'd be burnt to a crisp, son. You smell like a pub and look like somethin' the cat dragged in. Get dressed."

"Dressed? For what? Somebody die?"

"For church. And if you don' come, you'll be the dead one."

I coughed a few times, bending over. I was about to throw up. "Nah, Ma. No church for me. I'm feelin' sick today."

"Which is exactly why you need to be gettin' up and goin' to church, boy," someone said from the hallway.

"Mr. Rawlings?"

"Ain' no damn Mister Rogers. Get dressed, we gon' be late now."

"I really can't," I pleaded.

"Come on, baby. Please come with us. It's goin' to be a nice sermon, everyone over there hasn' seen you in years and I jus' . . . I jus' need you there with me."

There was a desperation in her voice, but I ignored it. My head was pounding, and all I wanted to do was go back to bed. "Why today, Ma? You been goin' to church for years without me. So why do you need me now?"

She looked at me like she hadn't seen me in a while. "Baby, it's jus' —"

"Sorry, Ma. I jus' can't. You know what's goin' on at work, and I need as much rest as I can get."

"Okay, Dar. It's okay. Get some rest," she said, gently closing the door, defeated.

I got back into bed and curled up with my phone. There was a text from Soraya.

If you don't apologize to my dad, never talk to me again. We're all just trying to help you!

I didn't have time for any of that or anyone who thought that fighting for what you believed in meant you were brainwashed.

The room was spinning, and I covered my face with a pillow, trying to make it all stop. More knocking at my door. It was the Saturday morning from hell.

"I can't move, Ma. I'm gonna throw up."

"Tha's what happens when you can' hold your damn liquor, boy," Mr. Rawlings said. "But if you don' open up, I'll beat the rest outta you."

I crawled to the door and opened it. "What's up, Mr. Rawlings?"

"Since when you start drinkin'? Jus' a coupla months ago I couldn' even get you to

307

have a li'l champagne."

"I dunno, Mr. Rawlings."

"Sheesh. Get dressed and come to church with me and your momma. It'll mean a lot to her."

"Mr. Rawlings, I get it, but you don' understand, I'm in no shape for church." I closed the door until his hand stopped it.

"I don' know what's goin' on with you, boy. I don' know if it's who you're associatin' with, if you're losin' yourself to the bottle, or somethin' else, but what I do know is you only got but one momma. And you only got her for a bit of time in this world, so you should do what any self-respectin' man would do and make her happy while you can."

He sold me. I got dressed and went to church. We filed into the rickety wooden pew one by one, and after I kissed and hugged a hundred people, explained where I'd been, and answered questions with yes, that was me on TV, and no, I don't work for the devil, the minister's sermon began.

I'm not going to lie; I fell asleep with my head down fifteen minutes in. No one bothered me since I looked like I was praying. It was perfect until my phone vibrated. Rhett.

Meet me at my place now. I'll call you an Uber.

"Jesus," I said.

A woman behind me gripped my shoulder, and whispered, "He soon come, honey. Soon come indeed."

I looked to the left and saw Ma with tears in her eyes, gripping Mr. Rawlings's hand. "Glory be to God!" she shouted in response to something the minister said.

I couldn't bear to interrupt, so I quietly got up and walked out without turning back.

Rhett lived on one of those quaint, tree-lined streets in the West Village with cobble-stones, celebrities walking their dogs, and boutique shops that need to sell only two pieces a month to survive. He had the entire floor of a brick townhouse all to himself, but he always had people — models, bottle girls, and other glamorous socialites — inside.

"Yo," he said, opening his door in nothing but a pair of plaid pajamas. His eyes were bloodshot.

"What's up, man?" I dropped my bag and sank into his soft leather couch.

"I'm losing it and didn't know who else to call," he said, arms crossed as he paced around the room. "We're getting eaten alive.

By everyone. The media. The board. Celebrities. Do you know what Mark Zuckerberg said about us? Mark fucking Zuckerberg of all people. That we're the reason tech startups are getting a bad rap. Can you believe it? *Us?* When Facebook's been stealing users' information from fucking day one. I ought to find him and beat the shit out of him."

"Whoa, slow down, man. This is war, remember? This shit happens, and we can't let it get to us, just like you've said this whole time."

He sat down on the polished hardwood floor, his head in his hands.

I walked over to the kitchen and grabbed some expensive faux-gourmet coffee and put it in the machine.

"It'll be okay," I said, watching his shoulders shake up and down. He was sobbing. Loudly.

"Get up." I picked him up and threw him onto the couch. "And drink this." I handed him a cup of the over-roasted sludge.

"Thanks," he said, wiping his eyes. "Lucien and the rest of the board said that if we don't close a significant amount of cash this month I'm out."

"What do you mean *out*?"

"Fired, Buck. They said I'm fired at the

end of the month if we can't pull it together. All of this shit, it's just the excuse they were waiting for to get me out. They've always hated us, and I knew it, but now I really know it."

"But how can they fire you, Rhett? Don't you and Chris own a majority of Sumwun?"

Rhett tried to muster a smile. "Sometimes I forget you're still so young. Of course we don't own a majority of the company. All of those millions we raised came at a cost. The more money we needed, the bigger the piece of the pie we gave away until we were left with less than them. Plus," he said, sinking deeper into the couch, "Chris is on their side."

I reflexively took a sip of my coffee and spit it out. "Hold on, Rhett. So why don't we say fuck them? After all of the cash we've closed over the past few months, can't we just survive off that?"

"No, Buck." He shook his head. "That's not how it works. Plus, we don't have any cash. We've been living from hand-to-mouth for the past quarter."

"Hand-to-mouth? We've closed over a million dollars a month since I started. We've been hitting the numbers."

Rhett threw his head back, letting out something between a sigh and a growl. His ceiling was a graffitied version of the Sistine Chapel's, coincidentally spray-painted by an artist who also went by the name Michelangelo. He said it was cheap, but I don't see how it could've been.

"Rhett."

He just lay there staring at the multicolored men and women wearing tight-fitting skirts, baggy jeans, basketball jerseys, Timberlands, and other "urban" clothing you'd see in a nineties rap video.

"Rhett," I repeated, standing over him now, blocking his view.

"What, Buck? What the fuck do you want to know? That we were never really closing as much cash as I said we were? That whenever we *just made it* at the last minute, the last fucking second of the month, we actually didn't? That I spent a good chunk of the money we raised on all of this?" he said, stretching his arms around the room. "Tell me, Buck, what do you want to know? Just tell me." He rolled off the couch onto the floor, sobbing again.

"Rhett," I whispered. "You can't be serious."

"As serious as lung cancer, Buck."

I sat on the floor next to him and closed my eyes. The room was spinning, and all I could do was rock back and forth, breathing in and out. Trying to figure out what Rhett had just said. Because it sounded like he said that we'd been living a lie. That everything I believed in was nothing more than a myth.

"Do you have any ideas?"

"No, Rhett," I said in disbelief. "How could I have any ideas?"

"I don't know, Buck." He sighed, smaller now. "It's what I hired you for. When you pitched me that drink, I swore I saw a purer, smarter, more courageous version of myself."

"And what do you see now, Rhett?" I asked, afraid of his answer.

"Well, Buck," he said, getting up and walking to his bedroom. "Frankly, I don't know. Everything is a blur."

18

Not much had changed by Wednesday. The media was still replaying clips of the FBI raid; everyone at Sumwun was tense, making calls into the abyss to keep the floor humming; and Rhett was looking worse with each passing day.

It was still early, but I decided to head home and see Ma. She had gotten upset when she realized I'd left church in the middle of the sermon, so I was doing all I could to make it up to her. I figured heading home and ordering pizza before she got there would be a good move.

But when I got home and opened the door, something felt off, like the house was heavier. Muffled masculine voices came from the kitchen. And with each step I took, the voices got louder. There was laughter, a thick smell of Javanese coffee, and the *click-clack* of hard rubber heels. *What the fuck is going on?*

I swung the door open and found Ma at the kitchen table, pieces of paper spread out in front of her, and two men dressed in the same shit-colored brown suits leaning over her shoulders like mini angels in cartoons. Except they were both devils.

"Oh, hello," the blonder one with a wrinkled, tanned face said, looking up. He smiled as he walked over with an outstretched hand. "You must be Darren."

I just looked at it, noticing the gold watch hanging off his wrist before seeing the shock on Ma's face. She was wearing a white T-shirt tucked into a blue denim jean skirt, which made her look twenty years younger.

"Dar," she said, quickly shuffling the papers. "I didn' know you'd be home so early, baby. Why didn' you let me know?"

I looked from the man's hand to Ma, then to the other blond man pouring himself a fresh cup of coffee like he owned the place.

"Who are these people?" I asked, ignoring the men.

Ma looked over her shoulder, and said, "This is —"

"Richard Lawson," the blonder man said, taking the papers out of Ma's hands, flipping through them. "And this is Harry Richards." He nodded at his associate.

"So many dicks," I said, still stuck in place.

"Darren!" Ma shouted.

It hit me. Richard Lawson was someone I'd spoken to months ago; the real estate agent from Next Chance Management who sent that letter to Ma and kept calling about buying the brownstone.

"Ma," I said, slowly walking toward her, shoving both Richard Lawson and Harry Richards away from the table. "What are they doing here?"

"Calm down, Darren."

I snatched the papers from one of the dicks' hands and leafed through them. One was the deed to the house. The others were copies of the floor plans. Another was a contract to sell.

I slammed the contract on the table, sending a coffee mug crashing to the floor, drenching the dicks' leather shoes.

"Answer me, Ma!"

"We need to get things in order, Dar. Nothin' is finalized. But jus' gettin' things in order, you know?"

"No," I said. "I *don't* know."

My heart was pounding and I could feel my veins bulging, threatening to tear and leave me bleeding out on the floor. The room was spinning worse than during a bad hangover, and all of it — Ma, the dicks, the smell of coffee, the sun slowly disappearing over the horizon — turned into some un-identifiable Picasso-like painting.

"Do we need the money, Ma? Are you sick? Is this what all the coughin' and missed days have been about?"

"No." She wrapped her hand around my clenched fist. "I jus' wanna know how much everything is worth. That's all."

"You promised," I said, ripping my fist out of her weak grasp. "You promised that you wouldn' reply to these, these fuckin' parasites."

"Darren, please." She feebly stood up and reached for my arm.

I ran up to my room, stuffed clothes in my bag, and headed for the door.

"Baby, don' leave me," she begged, blocking the doorway. "Not now, baby. Please, not now. You don' understand." Thin streams of tears traveled down her cheeks, filling the dry wrinkles around her mouth.

"I do understand, Ma," I said, moving her out of the way. "I understand that we made a deal, and you broke it. I understand that you're a fuckin' liar."

Down the stairs. Scream my lungs out. Turn the corner. Shatter my phone. Hit the subway. Wipe my tears.

On Friday, I woke up suffocating. Not in

some metaphorical way. I mean I slept on Rhett's couch the wrong way, and folds of its soft leather covered my face so I literally couldn't breathe.

"Ahh!" I shouted, clawing my way out. I rolled onto the floor, gasping for air, thinking that Rhett would run out to help. But it was just me, a fresh pot of coffee, and broad waves of sunlight pouring into the living room. Without a phone, I was disconnected from everything I wanted to avoid: Ma, Soraya, the news. It felt good.

I took my time getting dressed, grabbing one of Rhett's expensive button-ups, denim joggers, and even a pair of his calfskin Maison Margiela high-tops. I devoured the plate of blueberry pancakes, eggs, and sausage that Rhett had left out for me, tossed his wretched excuse for coffee, and found a cab.

When I got to Sumwun, the sales floor wasn't its normal, chaotic, in-need-of-a-large-animal-tranquilizer self. Instead, everyone quietly fiddled on their keyboards, rearranged their desks, and occasionally looked around before gluing their eyes back to their monitors. Even Clifford the pig looked like someone had died.

"Yo," I whispered to Charlie, quietly putting my bag down. "What's going on?"

He leaned in closer, his voice barely

audible. "You didn't see the video? Shit, where have you been?"

"I don't have my phone, man. What's going on?"

Charlie grabbed his phone, handed me earbuds, and pressed play on a video. It was of a shirtless Rhett at a club, probably from a month ago, standing on some couches. He was rapping along to Ja Rule and spraying bottles of Dom P everywhere like a madman.

"Fuck," I whispered.

Charlie shook his head. "Yeah, he could've at least picked a better song than 'Mesmerize.'"

I played it again. Rhett had two attractive women sucking his nipples as he sprayed champagne all over them, exposing their own hard nipples through tight white shirts. Rhett's eyes were barely open, and the neon lights exposed the outline of a large hard-on.

"Who?"

"A fucking bottle girl, dude. Supposedly she tried blackmailing him, but when he didn't budge, she sold the video to fucking Bonnie Sauren, and PSST News uploaded it to YouTube."

"So why is it so quiet in here? Shouldn't everyone be on the phones?"

Charlie shrugged. "Rhett's in Qur'an with the board. The windows are all covered."

I turned toward the frosted doors.

"Lucien and all of them flew in on a red-eye. They're in there right now, tearing him apart."

The elevator bell rang. Two figures with bulky silhouettes stepped out and paused in the elevator bay before heading through the transparent doors.

"Not this again," Charlie said, pushing his seat out and walking over to Clyde.

Porschia and the two men, definitely cops, emerged from the far corner of the floor and walked in our direction. They were staring at us. Then I realized they weren't staring at *us,* they were staring at *me.*

"Um, Buck," Porschia whispered.

"Yeah?" My heart was beating so loudly, I could hardly hear; it felt like I was underwater. *What is this? Did Jason tell them something? Do they think I was somehow responsible for Donesha Clark's murder?*

"These two men want to speak with you," she said, avoiding eye contact.

I followed the three of them to Bhagavad Gita, my stomach full of wasps.

"I'll leave you all to it," Porschia said, closing the door.

"Take a seat, son," the tall Italian-looking

one with a strong jaw said.

"I didn't do anything." I slowly lowered myself into the seat while maintaining eye contact with him.

"Why haven't you picked up your phone?" the other, red-haired, blue-eyed copper asked.

Fuck. They're going to beat me down like Rodney King. This is how it happens.

"I broke it," I said, shifting in my seat. When it came to cops, Ma always said to "cooperate, but don't incriminate."

"We've tried calling you all morning, son," the Italian one said. "Even your neighbor, Mr. Rawlings, said he couldn't get in touch with you."

"For what? Like I told you, I didn't do anything. And unless you're going to charge me" — I stood up — "I'm leaving."

"Son," the Italian one said. "Your mother died this morning."

I was suddenly standing outside Bhagavad Gita looking through the glass wall at the scene inside — me, laughing in disbelief. The red-headed cop leaned against a window, biting his nails. The Italian one stared at me sympathetically.

I heard the Italian cop say, "I'm sorry, son. So, so sorry," as he kneaded his chin with his hairy knuckles.

I saw myself shaking my head, saying, "No, man. My mom isn't dead. Can't be. I just saw her the other day. Stop fucking lying to me."

I saw the red-headed one walking toward me and placing a hand on my shoulder, saying, "Everyone has been trying to get in touch with you all morning, Darren. She had lung cancer, didn't you know?"

Lung cancer? "No," I heard myself say through the glass. "My mom didn't have lung cancer. She just had a little cough, felt a little tired, but she didn't have lung cancer."

"I know it's hard to believe, son," I heard the Italian one say. "I've been through it too. It may be hard now, but —"

I saw myself push the cops. "Get the fuck off of me!" I heard myself shout. "You fucking pigs come here and start telling lies. You're the enemy, trying to get in our heads and make us lose the war!"

And then I saw myself with my back against the dry-erase wall, sliding down, taking whatever grand plans were written on it along with me down to the floor. I saw my head drop into my hands; saw tears, snot, and spit cover my face; heard a deep, guttural, desperate sound emerge from my throat.

"Ma isn' dead," I heard myself whisper. "Ma can't be dead."

The cops drove me to Woodhull, where Ma's body was. After I confirmed her identity, the staff left me alone to process. But when I looked down at her, already cold and stiff, I felt like I was going crazy. This couldn't be real.

"Hey, Ma," I said, stroking her hair. "I — I came as fast as I could, but I guess it wasn' soon enough."

I traced her wrinkles, which had been slick with tears the last time I'd seen her. "Ma. I'm sorry about —" I laid my head on her cold stomach, wishing there was some way she could hold me and say that everything would be all right, that we'd still have to-morrow.

I cleared my throat and stared into her gray face, seeing no light. Her eyes would never open again. Her mouth would never smile again. Those hands, the hands that took care of me all my life, would never hold mine again.

"You lied to me, Ma," I said, my tears leaving dark stains on her clothing. "Why was it so easy for you to lie to me, Ma?"

I saw the signs: the weight loss, how her hands couldn't grip a mug, the blood-covered napkins in the trash, how she inhaled before she lied about being fine. *But she told me it was nothing.*

"How could you leave me, Ma?" My voice shook uncontrollably. "You said you would be there, to root for me when I made it, Ma. Didn' you see that I only did all of this for you? You lied!" I realized I was yelling when an attendant entered and put a hand on my shoulder. "Calm down, please. I know it's tough, but we have a room where you can sit and gather yourself."

"Get the fuck off me!" I shouted, shoving him backward.

I'd done everything she asked. *The future you spoke of always had both of us in it, Ma. Why'd you leave me?* As the questions multiplied, so did my anger. At her. At the world. And most of all, at myself, because I was helpless. I'd never felt more alone in my life.

When I got outside, I saw Mr. Rawlings sitting on a bench outside, wearing green slacks and suspenders.

"Where you been, boy?" he said, looking up, covering his eyes from the sun. "Been lookin' for you for days. Your momma went to the hospital Wednesday night, but no one could reach you. I tried callin', but your phone was off."

I didn't sit. I just stared at him sitting there with a wrinkled hand over his eyes. "Did you know?"

He lowered his hand, rubbing it on his pants before grabbing his rosewood cane.

"Did you know?" I repeated.

Mr. Rawlings gripped his cane tighter, rocking back and forth. He let out a lungful of air and nodded. "She tol' me not to say anythin'. I tol' her you needed to know, but she made me promise."

I tried to swallow but felt my throat catch like I was choking. Once the air was able to pass, I looked at him, but he couldn't look at me. "After the funeral," I said, "on Sunday, I want you to take your things and go."

He looked up at me for a long while, sucked his teeth, then waved me off. "Boy, I know it's a tough time, but stop playin'."

"Who's playin'?"

"What, you mad because I didn' say anythin'? Maybe if you wasn' runnin' 'round day and night, gettin' into trouble with those white folk in Manhattan, you woulda seen that she was losin' weight, havin' trouble breathin', and forgettin' things. Don' put none of that on me. Be a man and accept responsibility."

I gritted my teeth, shoving my fist into my

pocket instead of crashing it into his face. "I am a man," I spat.

"Then act like one." He got up and leaned onto his cane, coming face-to-face with me. "I been livin' at that house from before you was born, boy. From way before you was even a glint in your daddy's eye. I ain' goin' nowhere."

"You will," I said, anger taking hold of me.

He reached out for my hand, but I pulled away as if he were diseased. "Please, boy. I got no people, nowhere to go. I been good to you your whole life, was friends with your momma and your daddy and your momma's people before they passed."

I didn't say anything, didn't move. Just stared at his face, his trembling lips.

"I'm an old man," he begged, leaning toward me. "I can' jus' get up and move my life somewhere from the place it's always been. I been like a grandfather to you. Please don' do this to me."

"I'm not doin' this to you," I said. "You did it to yourself. And I expect you and all of your things to be gone by Monday."

"But where will I go?" He brought a crumpled napkin to his eye. "I have nowhere to go, boy."

"Figure it out," I said, walking away from

him, from the hospital where Ma's frozen body was, from everyone who had ever hurt me.

I made arrangements with the church on Saturday, then spent the rest of the day in bed with the shades drawn, replaying the last few months in my head, but this time, the truth was superimposed on every scene. Ma telling me she was okay when she knew she wasn't. Mr. Rawlings asking me about Ma when he knew she was dying. Soraya telling me she'd always be there for me only to turn into someone else once I tried to better myself. Jason claiming he was looking out for me when he was actually trying to bring me down the minute I began to succeed.

When I realized it was Sunday, I got dressed and walked to the church. Dozens of men and women sat in the pews. Mr. Rawlings sat in the front row across the aisle from me. Since Ma and I didn't have any living relatives, I was alone. Then I felt a hand on my shoulder.

Rhett, Frodo, Marissa, and Eddie were standing there. I asked them to sit next to me, and Rhett held my hand, not letting go.

Before the sermon began, Soraya, Mr. Aziz, Jason, and Wally Cat took a seat next to Mr. Rawlings. Jason looked at me and turned away after our eyes met. Soraya rested her head on Mr. Aziz's shoulder, crying as she stared at the casket.

After we buried Ma at the gravesite, a few women tried pushing food on me and said they'd like to come over to talk. I declined. I didn't know these people and certainly didn't want to entertain them back at the house. Instead, I hopped into an Uber SUV with Rhett and the other Sumwunners and headed home.

"Sorry, bud," Rhett said, gripping my knee as we sat in the living room.

"Yeah, I'm real sorry," Frodo said, stuffing his face with something.

Marissa cut her eyes at him. "Where'd you get that?"

"I heard some of the women discussing all the food they made, so I offered to bring a few trays over so, you know, it didn't go to waste."

I went up to my bedroom and collapsed onto my bed. I felt grateful for the Sumwunners being there, but I was exhausted.

There was a knock at the door. *It's probably Frodo with a plate of food.* I told him to come in.

But when the door opened, it was Soraya standing there in a long-sleeved black dress, staring at me. "Why haven' you been pickin' up your phone?" she asked, sitting on the bed next to my legs.

"My phone broke," I said, unable to look at her. I wanted her to leave.

"So why didn' you come by the shop? Why did I have to hear about all of this from Jason, who had to hear it from Wally Cat?"

"You're seriously goin' to fuckin' press me? Now?"

She stared at her lap. "You're right. I'm sorry, D. About all of this. But what are these people doin' here?" she asked, pointing toward the door. "You didn' even invite me, my dad, Jason, or Wally Cat over. And Mr. Rawlings was outside with empty boxes sayin' you're kickin' him out. After all these years, you're gonna do him like that?"

"It's not your problem," I said, unfazed.

She moved closer. "Look me in the eye."

"For what?"

"Because I wanna see who I'm lookin' at. I wanna see who you are today."

"Not this fuckin' shit again." I stood up, walked into the bathroom, and slammed the door.

She yanked it open. "Look me in the eye," she repeated, wiping dark watery streaks from her cheeks.

"What?" I faced her. "What the fuck do

you want from me?"

"I want you back!" she shouted. "The real you! The you who promised me you wouldn' change no matter what happened. But here you are, lookin' like someone I don't recognize, like someone Mrs. V wouldn' know."

I gripped the sink so tightly, I swore the porcelain would crack. So many thoughts were racing through my head: the first time Soraya and I kissed; Ma and me at the park when I was younger; Jason shoving shaved ice down my back one summer; Nicole, Brian, and Carlos at Starbucks; everything that existed before Sumwun. But I couldn't go back to who I was. Not now.

"Fuck you," I said, staring her in the eyes. "Fuck you, Soraya."

"Don' say that, D. Please don' say that."

I pushed her away, repeating it. Again. And again. Louder. And louder. She couldn't wipe her eyes fast enough as she rushed out of the bathroom toward the bedroom door.

"If you walk out on me again, Soraya," I said, as she paused at the threshold of my room, "we're done."

She gripped the doorknob tighter, exposing the whites of her knuckles, and inhaled deeply. "I know that, D," she said, and pulled the door shut behind her.

19

"Darren, baby, this is your mother," Ma said on the voice mail. Her voice was shaky. I could tell it was hard for her to speak. Her lungs whistled like a creaky wheel after every few words. "I'm sorry, Dar. So sorry for everything. And I know you're mad, but please call back when you can. I'm not feelin' too good, so I called an ambulance like I promised. I love you."

I played the voice mail over and over again throughout the night. After everyone had left, I went out for a new phone and anxiously transferred my old SIM card, wondering what I would find. Every time I listened to it, it felt like someone was twisting a knife in a wound that would never heal. And I can tell you, even now, writing about this years later, the wound is still as fresh as it was when she first died.

Without any sleep, I rolled out of bed on Monday, got dressed, and walked down the stairs into the kitchen with my eyes closed, hoping that, somehow, she would be there when I opened them. But I already knew what I'd find. There was no smell of coffee, no humming, no sound of Ma's slippers padding across the floor. No Ma.

Not wanting to give up, I walked downstairs, took a breath, and knocked on her bedroom door, praying she'd be inside, curled to the side of her bed and coughing, but still there. No answer. "Ma," I said, slowly opening the door, my fingers repeating the motion they'd made thousands of times, my mind not even contemplating that she wouldn't be there. But when I opened the door, all I saw were crumpled bedsheets with blood on the pillow she always slept on; a half-drunk glass of water on her bedside table with the faint print of her lips still there; her TV remote on the other side of her bed; all of her favorite books on the shelves, right where she left them, waiting to be held.

"Ma," I repeated, lying down on her side of the bed, grabbing fistfuls of her sheets and bringing them close to my face. They absorbed the tears I hadn't realized I was releasing. "Please come back, Ma. I'll be better, I promise."

Lying in her bed, I pressed play on the

voice mail again and listened to her words, trying to travel back through time to figure out how this all happened so quickly, but I already knew. *Darren, baby, this is your mother.*

When I went back upstairs and reentered the kitchen, I noticed two envelopes sitting on the table with my name written on them in Ma's handwriting. I had seen them when I got back on Friday, but I still hadn't opened them. I took a breath, lowered myself into a seat, and grabbed one. I sighed with relief when I realized that it was the unsigned contract to sell. Ma hadn't gone through with it. The house was still ours.

In the second envelope I found a letter written by Ma. The letters dragged up and down like a jagged line graph. I held it tightly.

My Dearest Darren,
Baby, I know you're hurt. Hurt because I never told you. Hurt because we had to lose each other this way. And hurt because life has been hard for you lately, and the world hasn't made it easier for you. A mother's love for her son is end-less, and I decided that the best way for me to show my love to you was by hid-ing my own pain even if it hurts you

now. I didn't want it to become a burden to you on your own journey.

From the day I brought you home from the hospital, you've been my guiding light, Dar. After your father died, I had no one to turn to except you and God, and seeing your smiling face greet me every morning was what kept me alive. In the same way I gave you life, son, you gave me life, too.

Darren, I want you to know that I am proud of you, that I've always been. No matter if you were working at Starbucks or at Sumwun, you've always been my proudest accomplishment and you always will be. You were born to lead, son, not follow. And I want you to remember to stay true to yourself and help others like you live the best life they can. It's the duty of every man and woman who has achieved some success in life to pass it on, because when we're gone, what matters most isn't what we were able to attain but who we were able to help.

I'll always be with you, baby. Never forget that. And when the world beats you down, when you feel like everyone is against you, think of me, because I'll always be thinking of you until the day we meet again, my beautiful boy.

Be good to those who need love most. Don't be too hard on the world, especially yourself. And remember that the time we all have on this earth is but a brief flash of beauty, like a shooting star, and that we have to do all we can to live our dreams. You were the best dream I ever had, Darren. May God bless you until I can hold you in my arms again.

Love always,
Ma

The letter, feeling heavier than before, dropped from my hands. I gripped the sides of the table, trying to balance myself. I couldn't stop shaking. Sadness was transforming into something else, something blisteringly hot like lava, and I couldn't stop it from engulfing me.

I flipped the table, sending the letters soaring like paper birds into the air. I threw the coffee pot across the room, glass shattering in every direction. I slammed a wooden chair onto the floor again, and again, and again until it broke into splinters. Heavy mugs crashed against walls. Pots and pans clanged like a brass band as I threw them toward windows. I blasted my fists, one by one, into a wall, my knuckles becoming caked with blood and plaster. When I saw the photo of Ma, Pa, and me on the living-room wall watching it all, I walked over and spit in Pa's face. "If you hadn' fuckin' died, Ma wouldn' have had to work in that factory inhalin' all those chemicals, you stupid motherfucker!" I never knew him, but that didn't matter. I hated him for his absence.

When I finally collapsed onto the floor, my lungs working double time, I couldn't stop thinking: *What next? What next? What next?* What could I break next? What could I do next? What would happen next to my life that was already so shattered? As the questions piled up like an accident on the freeway, I decided to do the only thing that made sense: get up and go to Sumwun.

Down the stairs. When I reached the bottom, Mr. Rawlings's door was open. I walked in. His entire apartment was empty except for abandoned packs of seeds, stray furniture, letters, and ladybugs floating through the air. I walked into the backyard, finding rows of tomatoes, heads of lettuce, carrot tops, and yellow, red, and purple flowers covering the whole yard. He was gone, just like I told him to be. The feeling that I had made a mistake began to bloom in the pit of my stomach, but I quickly killed it. *What kind of man lets a mother hide her illness from her son?*

Turn the corner. When I passed Mr. Aziz's bodega, he was sweeping out front. He looked at me, shook his head, and turned away before heading back inside. The gargoyles were where they always were. It was the first time I saw Jason back on his corner since the hospital. Everything felt like it was moving in slow motion. Our eyes locked and he spit on the ground. Across the street, Wally Cat fanned himself with his fedora, staring at me. There was no longer an empty crate next to him. I ducked into the subway.

When I arrived at 3 Park Avenue, I headed to Starbucks. Carlos was mopping, Nicole was arranging new cardboard cutouts, and Brian was stacking cups. But when I tried opening the door, it was locked. Brian looked up, his eyes met mine, and he went back to setting up. Nicole turned around, frowned, and returned to her cutouts. And Carlos paused, and said, "Not open yet," then dropped his gaze back to the wet tiled floor. *Brian must have said something.*

It was 7:05 a.m. and the entire sales team was in Qur'an. As I stepped into the elevator bay, I felt all two-hundred-something eyes on me. But instead of turning left, I went right. It was officially Deals Week, and the floor was empty.

I dropped my bag, booted up my computer, and looked for a Post-it in my file cabinet, the one from Hell Week. Then I found it, a crinkled purple Post-it with three names.

1. Bernie Aiven, head, Hinterscope Records
2. Stefan Rusk, CEO, SpaceXXX
3. Barry Dee, owner, DaynerMedia

"Yo," Charlie said, pushing open the frosted doors, walking toward me. "Um, you know it's Deals Week, Buck. Everyone's in Qur'an waiting for you."

I typed Bernie Aiven into our lead database and found his number.

"What's this?" Charlie asked, picking up the purple Post-it. "Your wish list? You can call them after the meeting, dude. Let's go," he said, grabbing my arm. I yanked it away, glaring. He flinched and walked back through the doors.

I dialed the number and grabbed the receiver. After a few rings, a woman picked up. "Good morning, Bernie Aiven's office, how may I help you?"

"Hi," I said, clearing my throat. "This is Buck Vender calling from Sumwun, is Bernie there?"

"Sorry, where did you say you were calling from?"

"Sumwun. I've exchanged emails with Bernie for a while now and wanted to catch him before the day started."

After a pause, she said, "Okay, one second."

Eddie walked through the doors, confused. "Buck, hey," he said, placing a hand on my shoulder. I shrugged it off.

"I'm sorry about everything with your mom, but you have to come into the meeting. Rhett's about to flip and Clyde's going to come in here and it's just going to be bad. You know everyone's on edge."

I didn't look at him. I just clutched the phone tighter. "Sorry, honey, but Bernie said he's never exchanged any emails with you and he's a busy man, so maybe send him another and he'll respond if interested."

"Wait."

"Thank you." *Click.*

I found Stefan Rusk's number. It went straight to his secretary's voice mail.

Eddie sighed. "Alright, Buck," he said, and walked off the floor.

I clicked the button for Barry Dee's office. The phone rang.

Clyde and Rhett flung the frosted doors

open and stormed toward me. "What the fuck are you doing?" Clyde shouted, nostrils flaring, looking like an animal ready to attack.

"C'mon," Rhett said, ending the call. "Everyone's waiting, Buck. I know you've been through a lot, but if you're going to be here, you need to be here."

Without looking at them, I dialed Barry Dee's office again. When Clyde reached over to end the call, I smacked his hand away, and said, "If either of you touch that phone, I'm going to send you to the hospital."

"I'm calling the cops, Rhett. He's having a mental breakdown and is liable to do anything," Clyde said, as he charged out the doors.

The phone kept ringing. Rhett leaned closer. "Don't do this, Buck. I can't save you if you don't get in Qur'an now. The board's done with us and I'm going to be canned at the end of the week. Don't do this. Not now."

Someone picked up. "Hello, Barry Dee's office, this is Tracy speaking."

"Hi, Tracy, this is Buck Vender calling from Sumwun. Barry in?"

Rhett shifted behind me, staring at my monitor. "Why're you calling Barry Dee?"

"Yes, he is, Buck, but he's incredibly busy. Can I take a message?"

People poured through the doors, surrounding my desk. Clyde smiled, shouting, "This is what happens when you think you're bigger than the company! Cops will be here any second now."

"No," I said into the phone. "No message. But can you please grab him and let him know Buck Vender from Sumwun is on the line? I have incredibly important information for him that he's going to want to hear, Tracy. Trust me. If he doesn't take five minutes to talk with me *right now,* he's going to regret it."

"Um," she said, sounding afraid. "Is . . . is Barry in trouble?"

"No, but we need to speak. *Now.*"

"Okay, hold on." Classical music filled my ear and I turned to see the crowd of salespeople staring at me with mixed expressions: some looked around, confused; others had fear in their eyes and were biting their nails; a few dialed into my line to listen, signaling for others to do the same.

"Just hang up, Buck. Please," Frodo said across from me. "Whatever you're doing isn't worth it."

But it was. At that point, I had nothing else to lose. The company was going down.

Ma was dead. Everyone I knew in Bed-Stuy hated me. And even my soldiers at Starbucks couldn't face me.

"What do you want, Mr. Vender?" an energetic, raspy voice said on the other end.

"Is this Barry Dee?" All of the salespeople's eyes widened, and everyone who wasn't already listening on my line jumped to their phones. Even Rhett had a phone pressed to his ear.

"It's not fucking Willy Wonka," he said. "So you have five seconds to tell me why I *have* to talk to you right now at this moment."

"Well, Barry, like I said, it's Buck Vender calling from Sumwun and —"

"Hold up," he said, laughing. "Vender? The kid who was on *Rise and Shine, America*? And the company with the, uh, what is it? The therapy that fucking kills people? Yeah, that's it. Why the hell are you calling me?"

"Yeah," I said, "that's me. And I'm calling to make a deal with you, Barry."

"And why would I want to make a deal with you, Buck? I have hundreds of people trying to sell me shit every day. So why the fuck would I want to work with you and a company that no one from here to San Francisco wants to touch with a ten-foot

342

pole? You all have startup syphilis. And no one, no matter how hot a girl once was, wants to get syphilis."

I took a breath. There was no turning back now. "What did you think when you saw me on *Rise and Shine, America,* Barry?"

"I thought your CEO was smart enough to use someone like you as a human shield and that you were pretty smooth."

"And why do you think I'm calling you?"

"Because you have no other options and need someone to rehabilitate your image. But I'm getting real fucking tired of playing twenty questions with you, Buck. You better start saying something that keeps me on the line or I'm gone."

"I have nothing to lose, Barry. Nothing. My mother died last week. As you said, Sumwun has startup syphilis, and everyone I've ever known hates me. So that's why I'm calling you. To ask you to take a small risk and buy a couple thousand licenses for your employees and those in your portfolio companies."

I could hear him breathing on the other end. Everyone at Sumwun leaned in closer, wiping sweat off their brows, hyperventilating. The elevators rang open. Two police officers pushed through the doors.

"Him," Clyde said, pointing at me.

343

"How'd your mother die?" Barry asked.

"Lung cancer. I didn't even know she had it."

"Fuck," he said, exhaling. "My mom died a few years ago. Also cancer. I knew she had it, so we were able to make the most of her time, but it was still a bitch."

Rhett went over to speak with the cops, giving me time.

"Does it get easier?"

He laughed. "Not really, kid. Sorry. But distracting yourself with work helps."

"Yeah. That's what I thought. Anyway, man, I appreciate you taking the call. I figured it was worth a shot, but I also understand why you don't want to be associated with us."

The cops headed back to the elevators, and Rhett walked over, bringing a phone to his ear. Everyone looked deflated. Some, realizing defeat, stopped listening and walked off the floor.

"Wait," Barry said. "What'll five hundred K get me?"

Rhett dug his nails into my shoulder.

"Twenty-five hundred licenses," I said, my heart beating faster than Uma Thurman's after her adrenaline shot in *Pulp Fiction*.

"That's not good enough," he sang.

I looked at Rhett. He wrote something on

a Post-it and shoved it in my face: ANY-
THING.

"What else do you want?"

He laughed again. This time deeper,
longer, and slower. "I want you, my man. I
want you."

"What does that mean?"

"It means that every second you're not at
Sumwun you work for me."

My hands were shaking. I couldn't believe
what was happening. I was ready for him to
yell, "PSYCH" before hanging up. But I had
to keep going, just in case. "And what does
working for you entail?"

"Oh, a lot of things. Helping me with
investments. Running errands. Putting some
of your raw potential to proper use. If you
make me money, I'll make you money, but
it'll come at a price. And I'm not talking a
measly five hundred grand. Doing this deal,
Buck, the deal I'm bringing to the table,
means I own you."

I didn't know Barry aside from his reputa-
tion as an energetic, ruthless, and pompous
businessman, which made the prospect of
being "owned" by him as appealing as
chewing nails. But when I looked at Rhett, I
already knew what I'd have to do. He gave
me the opportunity I'd always wanted but
didn't know I needed; despite managing

hundreds of employees, he made me feel as if I were the only person in the world when he looked at me, and I couldn't let that go, especially now, when I'd lost everyone who had ever meant anything to me.

"Okay, Barry," I said. "We have a deal."

"And what does having a deal mean, Buck? I want to hear you say it."

I took a deep breath and looked around the room. Everyone stared at me, nodding. Back during Hell Week, they went to bat for me when I needed it most, and I needed to do the same for them. I truly believed in this company, so I had to give myself to it, to do whatever it took to save it.

Reader: In the same way there's no such thing as a halfway crook, there's no such thing as a halfway success. In sales and life, you're either all in or you're not. And if you're not, then step the fuck aside before you get run over by someone who is.

I closed my eyes and gripped the receiver tighter. "It means you own me, Barry. I'm yours."

■ ■ ■ ■

IV.
DEMONSTRATION

■ ■ ■ ■

For what shall it profit a man if he gain
the whole world and suffer the loss
of his soul?

— JESUS CHRIST

IV

DEMONSTRATION

For what shall it profit a man if he gain
the whole world and suffer the loss
of his soul?

—JESUS CHRIST

20

6 MONTHS LATER

"Rise and shine, America! This morning, our guest is someone you may recognize from six months ago. When he was last with us, Darren 'Buck' Vender was defending his company, Sumwun, after an incident with a young girl and one of the service's assistants. But today, Buck's here to discuss how he went from a young no-name cold-caller to what every major news outlet, blog, and magazine is calling the best salesman in New York City. Buck, thanks for joining us."

"My pleasure, Sandra. Thank you for inviting me back on, especially after the fun time we had last year," I said, looking into her eyes, chuckling on cue.

"So," she said, crossing her legs, leaning toward me. "How did you do it?"

"Do what?" I asked, grinning.

"Well" — she waved her hands in front of me — "this. The expensive suit. Slicked-back hair. Everyone in New York knows about how you single-handedly saved Sumwun from certain death. You've spoken to crowds of hundreds of people; written articles for the *New York Times, Forbes,* the *Wall Street Journal,* and countless others; and you're basically the poster boy for New York City tech sales. Plus, everyone knows you're Barry Dee's protégé. Tell us about that."

I laughed, self-consciously pulling my cuff over my Rolex. "I wouldn't say I single-handedly saved Sumwun, Sandra. That's a bit of an exaggeration."

"That's not what *Wired* magazine said a few months ago. They say you cold-called Barry Dee and closed him for half a million dollars."

The audience of middle-aged white women were all on the edge of their seats, expecting a show.

"I can't say they're wrong, Sandra. But, candidly, I don't read magazines, blogs, or the news. I don't even watch *Rise and Shine, America,*" I said, playfully covering my face.

"How dare you!" she said, slapping my hands with index cards. "We'll forget you said that. So, after you closed Barry Dee, it seemed like everyone from New York to San Francisco wanted to work with Sumwun, as if they'd forgotten about everything that had happened. How did that feel?"

"It felt great, what can I say? It's hard to believe, but that's what happened," I said, pulling my cuff up. "Once we had Barry in our corner, especially after he joined our board, people realized that what happened was a one-time thing. We've since instituted rigorous vetting processes for all of our assistants, quarterly assessments, and more."

"Yes, I read about that. It's all impressive, but tell us about what's going on in your life, Buck. You've accomplished so much in less than a year, and you're only how old?"

"I just turned twenty-three," I said, sitting up. "But, yeah, everything is still surreal. Working with Barry feels like I'm getting my MBA."

"Which must feel like a lot since you never even went to college."

"Exactly. It's the best education I could receive. I'm helping him with the venture capital arm of the business, finding and funding the next startups that'll have a large impact on the world. And everything at Sumwun is going really well."

"Is it?" Sandra asked, narrowing her eyes. "Didn't Rhett Daniels fire cofounder Chris Davids and a handful of other employees who supported the board wanting to fire him?"

"You're right, he did. It's incredibly difficult to work in an environment where you know people don't have your back. So, as you said, Chris and a few others had to go, but everyone parted on good terms."

"So what's next?"

"I'm not sure, Sandra. I'm just enjoying the ride right now."

"Well, we'll all be watching, Buck. Thank you for your time." She smiled into the camera until the greasy operator cut to a commercial.

"Always a pleasure," Sandra said, removing her mic and her heels.

"The pleasure was mine. Thanks for inviting me back."

"As long as you keep on making headlines, we'll keep bringing you onto the show."

I pushed my way through the crowd outside, hopped into the back of a black Tesla Model S, and waved to a few cameras from the window. Since it was still winter in New York, it was cold as hell out, but I guess not cold enough to keep tourists away from Times Square.

"Where to, sir?" Chauncey asked, his African accent thick.

"DaynerMedia," I said, rolling the window

back up. I pulled a small vial from my suit pocket.

"You must be very busy today, sir," Chauncey said, driving down West Forty-Third.

"I am." I poured the vial's contents onto my phone and rolled up a hundred-dollar bill.

"But please, Chauncey." I inserted the bill into my nose; took a quick, violent snort; and jolted my head back. "Stop with the 'sir' shit. You're old enough to be my father."

He handed me a tissue, and I wiped my nose before leaning my head back onto the seat and watching the city pass by.

"In my country, it is the duty of a chauffeur to refer to his employer as 'sir,' sir, so I only do it out of respect."

"Then call Barry 'sir,' Chauncey. He's your employer, not me."

His eyes met my mine in the rearview, and he scrunched his eyebrows together, moving his thick dark lips into a frown. "Even so, you are a Black man, like me, who has made it in America despite how they treat us. I have respect for you."

Respect is for suckers, Chauncey. Power is the new black, baby.

I closed my eyes and sighed, felt my veins opening up wider, my heart pumping faster, and all of the confidence from the show returning. "As you wish. But let's get to the office as quickly as possible, please. Barry's waiting."

"Yes, sir." He honked the horn as if he were performing CPR.

Hudson Yards, I thought, craning my neck to see the top of the building DaynerMedia was in. *Just when you think there's no more space in NYC.*

When I got up to the twenty-ninth floor, I bypassed the main receptionist and found myself face-to-face with Tracy, Barry's executive assistant, sitting in her private area. She allowed only a few chosen ones unfettered access to the boss.

"The camera really caught your good side, Buck." She looked up from her computer with a wink.

"Thanks, Trace. Has he been waiting long?"

"No, he was watching the interview too. I think he liked it, but I wish you would've mentioned how Barry's radiant, intelligent, visionary EA was the one who let you through to him on that fateful September day. You know you wouldn't be here without me," she said, half smirking, half making puppy-dog eyes at me.

"When you're right, you're right, Tracy. And you? You're always right," I said, paraphrasing *Spaceballs*.

"Truest thing you've said all day."

Barry's office was twice the size of Rhett's but had half the shit. Floor-to-ceiling windows revealed the Hudson River and a crystal-clear view of the Statue of Liberty, which Barry prayed and masturbated to every morning. There was a plain oval table surrounded by padded chairs; a wall adorned with six long shelves holding trophies, books, and sports jerseys, which served as the backdrop for the daily videos he recorded; and some other random crap he said added to the ironic, postmodern, prehistoric ambiance he was looking for.

"My man," he said, rising up from the table, giving me a dap that reverberated off the windows. *White guys always love to give overzealous daps.*

"What'd you think?"

"I think Sandra Stork was legit creaming her underwear. Was it me, or did she keep crossing and uncrossing her legs to prevent her sweet juice from dripping onto the floor?"

I took a seat across from his shrine. An autographed football encased in glass from the last Giants' Super Bowl win stared at me. Even though it'd be hard to tell from his typical outfit — a solid-colored T-shirt, faded jeans, and sneakers — Barry Dee was filthy rich, but not rich enough to buy the Giants, which was his life's aspiration.

"Yeah, I did see that. I also got her number afterward."

He jumped across the table and punched me in the chest, lifting the front of my chair inches off the ground. "You fucking salty dog, Buck! But what happened to Katrina?"

"Who?" I asked, grating my knuckles across my forehead. "I don't remember any Katrina."

"That fucking smokeshow you brought to Beauty & Essex the other night."

"Oh," I said, shaking my head. "That was Natalia, the bottle girl from Avenue."

He spread his palms across the table. "Okay, well, what happened with Natalia the bottle girl? Or Veronica the Brazilian model? Or Naomi the Japanese lawyer? Or —"

"Alright." I put my hands up. "I get it. You know I can't sleep alone."

"It's called Ambien, Xanax, and some cough syrup mixed with Sprite," he said. "Shit will knock out an eight-hundred-pound gorilla. But, alright, enough of the bullshit. Did you look over those portfolios?"

My head was pounding, and my hands started to shake. I slid them below the table. "Yeah," I said, flipping through the companies on my phone. "They were all dogshit, man. Straight dogshit."

"You need to stop thinking every startup actually needs to make money in order to be valuable. That's old-school, kid. Gotta think about the Instagrams of the world. The companies that are legit worth billions of dollars not because of any real value but because of the cool factor. Like that winner you picked when I first brought you on. You saw the cool factor in pork-free pork for Muslim millennials who want to eat BLTs without being, um, what's the word?"

"Haram."

"Yeah, without being haram. We made like five mil on that, and you took home a couple hundred thousand for yourself. So keep thinking outside the box and stay open-minded."

"Alright. Anything else? I gotta head to Sumwun for a bit and I'm beat."

"Yeah, one thing. This company we just acquired, something to do with funding hip-hop videos with a roster of tried-and-true sponsors — you know, like Hennessy, Beats, and whichever company makes those heavy-duty metal dog collars. They need an SDR.

You know anyone?"

I went through my mental Rolodex. "No, not right now. But I'm sure I can find one."

"Yeah, do that," he said. He pulled down the blinds and sat down in a padded gray chair that faced the Statue of Liberty. "But think outside the box. This company is going to be the future of partnering with rappers, and we need someone strong in the position."

"Sure," I said, rising to my feet, steadying myself. "I'll find someone."

"Where to, sir?" Chauncey asked, jumping out and opening the back door.

"Chauncey," I said, rubbing my forehead as I entered the car. "Please, man. Don't get up and open the door for me like I'm one of these white tech millionaires. The only reason I agreed to you driving me around is because I like you."

"Okay, sir," he said, looking at me in the rearview mirror. "I like you too, sir."

"Good." I pulled out my little vial and went to town on a few lines of medicine. "Now, I just need to get you to call me Buck instead of sir."

He laughed. "Baby steps, sir. So, where to?"

I leaned my head back and dripped Visine

into my eyes. "Sumwun, please."

We headed up Tenth Avenue and turned right onto Thirty-Fourth Street. The Sumwun I was headed to was different than the Sumwun of six months ago. Eddie was an AE, Charlie had become a sales manager, Marissa had replaced Charlie as SDR manager, the Duchess had quit to work for her pops, Frodo was still an SDR, and I, of course, had been promoted to AE. But since I closed such a huge deal, I skipped the normal sales hierarchy and became an enterprise AE, which meant Clyde, now VP of sales, was my direct manager.

If you're wondering, I made a hundred K off the deal with Barry. And even though we missed our number for September, having his endorsement brought other wary prospects back to our side. The damage was done, but we forgave them once the money poured back in. And with the money, we started to hit our monthly goals for real this time, which put Rhett back in good standing with Lucien, who not only conveniently forgot about ever having wanted to fire him but also used his connections to stop the FBI investigation. So between the salary bump from raising Sumwun from the dead, the hundred K from closing Barry, and the two hundred K I made from the pork-free

pork startup that turned a quick profit for
Barry's firm, I became wealthy overnight. It
was weird as hell, but you could say I got
used to it.

When I stepped out the elevator, Porschia
rushed through the doors and grabbed me.
"They've been waiting for more than an
hour," she said, distressed.

"Who?"

"Those executives from London. The
Tesco deal."

"*Oh,*" I said, squeezing my eyes to stop
them from throbbing like a subwoofer.

She pushed me through the doors toward
Qur'an. "You okay?"

"Yeah, just a little tired. Can you bring
me a coffee? Maybe something from Starbucks, like a Pike Place Roast."

"Okay, I'll be back in a few."

Everyone in Qur'an stood to greet me.
Three brown-haired white men in cheap
suits were beaming, Rhett, wearing a white
button-up and designers jeans, was sweating bullets, and Clyde, in his typical startup
vest-khakis-and-plaid-shirt douchebag attire, mean-mugged the hell out of me.

"Hello," I said, shaking hands with the
men.

"It's such a pleasure to meet you, Buck,"
one man, whose name I don't remember,

said with a posh English accent, holding my hand longer than necessary. "I've only seen you on TV, but has anyone ever told you that you look like Morgan Freeman? You must charm all the ladies, eh?"

"Something like that," I said, getting a strong cuckold vibe from him. I unbuttoned my jacket and grabbed a manila folder off the table.

"So," Rhett started. He looked from the three men to me and back to them like he was about to piss himself. "We were just talking about the pilot, Buck. And what we can do to make sure it's extra special so the five thousand Tesco employees we're starting off with get the most out of Sumwun."

"Great," I said, leaning back in my seat and closing my eyes. Within seconds, I heard myself snoring.

Rhett nudged me in the ribs. "Buck."

"Huh, yeah?" I said, startled.

Rhett, Clyde, and the three men stared at me in suspense.

"So," I started, clearing my throat and smoothing out my jacket. "What were you all thinking?"

"Well," the closeted cuckold said. "We're thinking of creating some posters to rouse the troops, right? And maybe a short video from you, someone they've read about in the newspapers, would help make sure they took advantage of Sumwun. If we can get —"

"I don't get it," I said, taking my steaming cup of coffee from Porschia and setting it on the table.

The cuckold tilted his head, narrowing his eyes. "Apologies, but what don't you get?"

"Why a video from me will make your employees more likely to use the service. People use it because it's going to help them, not because someone they don't even know tells them to."

"Right," he said, twisting his freckled hands. "But every bit helps."

I shook my head and straightened up, staring the cuckold directly in his eyes, piercing his feeble little soul. "Not in this case. You don't want your employees to rely on me to get, I don't know how you say it across the pond, excited —"

"*Chuffed* works," one of the other Three Stooges chimed in.

I winked at him. "Thanks. You don't want your employees to rely on me to get *chuffed* about using Sumwun. That's lazy and, frankly, not my job."

"Well," the cuckold said, getting red, looking to Rhett and Clyde for assistance. "We just think it'll help get them behind the deal.

362

A million dollars isn't a light investment for us."

"Bollocks," I said, smirking at him. "You're one of the world's biggest grocery chains and brought in over two-point-five billion in profit last year alone. In *pounds.* So don't tell me a million greenbacks is going to put you and your friends in" — I turned to the stooge who'd helped me before — "what do you call public housing over there?"

"Council estates," he said, smiling at the attention I was giving him.

"Yeah," I continued. "So don't tell me a million dollars is going to put you and your friends in council estates. Do we have a deal or not?"

After Clyde walked them out, he stormed into Qur'an and slammed the heavy wooden door shut.

"What the fuck was that?" He got so close that pieces of foamy spit landed on my nose.

"Jesus," I said, plopping down in my seat, rubbing my eyes. "Ever hear the phrase, 'Say it, don't spray it,' Clyde?"

He swung around the table and grabbed Rhett's shoulder. "Rhett, enough of this shit. This guy has been acting like he owns the place ever since he closed that lucky deal with that maniac and —"

I coughed loudly and theatrically stuck

my index finger in the air. "Ahem. Lucky deal that produced other baby deals," I said. "Many of which I handed off to you because you couldn't close shit when we were going down. Don't forget about that."

"Do you hear this crap?" Clyde turned to Rhett. "He shows up when he wants to, takes all kinds of risks with high-profile prospects, and is one thousand percent on cocaine right now. He looks like fucking Tony Montana slumped over in his chair after he snorted that mountain of blow in the last scene of *Scarface.*"

"Me?" I asked, standing up and pounding my chest. "I want what's coming to me . . . the world, Chico, and everything in it."

Clyde knelt beside Rhett, looking him in the eye. But Rhett had his eyes closed and was whispering to himself. Clyde pushed him and he slowly came to and looked around the room. "Rhett," he begged. "Say something. This can't continue."

Rhett took a deep breath and shrugged. "But at least they signed the deal, Clyde. That's a million dollars. It's huge."

Clyde stood and walked to the windows. "I can't believe I'm hearing this shit." He shook his head. "I can't believe we're trusting the fate of the company to some uneducated, gallivanting" —

Go ahead. Say it. Say the word you've wanted to call me from day one, so I have a reason to bust your pretty white nose open like a coconut.

— "*thug*. This fucking thug. He's a charlatan who's going to bring us down, Rhett. I know it. You know it. I mean, look at how he's fucking dressed." Clyde waved his hand in front of my Armani wool-blend Sablé Soho suit and locked his eyes onto my Rolex Oyster Perpetual.

"It was refurbished and under five Gs," I said, sticking my wrist in his face.

"Fuck you."

"Let's discuss this later," Rhett said. He started gathering the signed contracts. "We closed the deal and that's what matters most."

Clyde walked over and slammed the door shut before Rhett could leave. "No, that's not what matters most. This whole thing is exhausting," he said, hands on his hips. "So it's either him or me."

Rhett groaned and grabbed the nearest chair. "C'mon, Clyde. It's already been a long day. Buck," he said, looking at me across the room. "You'll stop coming late to meetings and make more of an effort to tone everything down, right?"

"Sure," I said, winking at Clyde.

"I'm serious, Rhett." Clyde hovered over him like a thick cloud ready to shoot lightning from his skinny gut. "Who's it going to be? The guy who helped you build all of this or this two-bit clown?"

Rhett shut his eyes and gripped the table. " 'Brothers . . . do not slander one another. Anyone who speaks against a brother . . . or judges them speaks against the law and judges it. When you judge the law, you are not keeping it, but sitting in judgment on it.' James 4:11."

"Amen," I said, clapping. "Stop slandering me, bro."

"I don't want to do this." Clyde placed a hand on the door, lowering his head. "But I have to. You have five seconds to make a decision, Rhett. One."

Bullshit.

"Two."

"Cut this out, Clyde," Rhett ordered. "Seriously."

"Three."

Rhett stood and grabbed Clyde's shoulder, bringing them face-to-face.

"Chill, Rhett," I said, my feet on the table. "There's no way he's leaving. He has nowhere else to go."

"Four," Clyde counted, visibly shaking as tears fell from his bluer than blue eyes.

"Clyde," Rhett pleaded, gripping both of his shoulders. "Stop it, please. Just stop it."

"Five." Clyde stared into Rhett's eyes.

He turned around and opened the door. But before Clyde walked out, he smiled at me. "We'll see each other again, Buck. You can count on that."

21

"Ma!" I shouted, bolting up in bed, a mix of salty sweat and tears running down my face, my chest vibrating like an animal that knows it's about to be murdered.

"What is it, Buck? What's wrong?"

Caught in the space between the world of dreams and waking life, it took me a second to realize what day it was, where I was, and who was lying next to me. It was Monday. I was in my loft, the top floor of a brownstone on Seventeenth between Second and Third Avenues. But the white woman, who looked like a Nike model, was a blur.

"I'm sorry." I jumped up and headed to the kitchen. "But who are you?"

Fuck, fuck, fuck. I hoped I hadn't had sex with her. I had a strict no white women policy, a policy I'd never violated before on account of what Wally Cat said all those months ago. I wasn't superstitious, but I preferred being on the safe side.

She sat up and ran a pale hand through her hair, laughing. "All of you guys are the same, I swear. We met last night? At Up & Down? You said I looked familiar and you somehow knew I was a model?"

I chugged a glass of cold water and prayed I'd passed out before anything happened. "Melanie, right?"

She rolled her eyes. "Lexi, actually."

"My bad. I just had a bad dream. I'm a little confused right now."

"Yeah," she said, twisting around in my silk sheets like a snake in the sun. "You were talking in your sleep all night. You said 'Ma' a few times, but who's Soraya?"

Shit. So it was Soraya last night. Some nights it was Jason. Others it was Mr. Rawlings. Every night it was Ma, which was one reason I never kept any woman around for long. I hated the questions.

"No one. But listen, this was fun. I gotta take a shower and head to the office. So . . ."

"So that's it? Giving me the boot already?"

"It's more like an expensive alligator-leather loafer." I smirked.

"Asshole. Can you at least lend me your driver?"

"Lend you my driver? Who do you think I am? Here," I said, quickly tapping my phone. "An Uber's arriving in five minutes."

369

She jumped out of the bed, punched her arms through her white maxi dress, and stomped across the kitchen. "So how do I get in touch with you?" she asked, a perfect hand resting against the bathroom door.

"You don't," I said, pulling the door shut.

"I hope you don't treat every girl you have sex with like this!" she screamed all the way into the elevator.

"Morning, sir. Where to?"

"Sumwun, Chauncey. Thanks. And don't drive too quickly," I said, absorbed by my phone.

"Yes, sir. Everything okay? You seem tense."

"Everything's fine, Chauncey. Let's just get to Sumwun in one piece."

I flinched when my phone vibrated. It was Barry.

Find that SDR yet? It's been a week my man.

On it.

When we got to 3 Park Avenue, I tiptoed up the stairs. I was fiending for caffeine, but I didn't want to waste time going upstairs, giving Porschia my order, and then waiting, so I walked right into Starbucks.

Brian stood behind the register. The morning rush was just over. But instead of the same green apron he'd worn for years, he now wore a black one.

"Damn, Brian, when did you become a coffee master?" I hoped my cheery tone masked my anxiety. I hadn't been in there in months.

"Last month." He avoided my eyes. "Jared got fired for spitting in people's drinks, and they had no one else."

"Congrats. What happened to Nicole and Carlos?"

"Carlos disappeared two months ago. I think he got arrested or something. And Nicole had a baby a few weeks ago and moved to Iowa with her wife."

There was something different about Brian. But I wasn't sure what it was.

"You gonna order anything?" He clutched fistfuls of black apron with one hand, tapping the counter with the other like a wartime telegraphist.

"Pike Place Roast."

He nodded to an Asian kid, who immediately got to work. I pulled out my card, but he waved it away. "On the house," he said, still staring at the floor.

"Thanks, man. Must be nice to be the boss now, right? No one to tell you what to do, and it looks like you have some good soldiers here."

"I guess. Just took your advice and decided to stick to Starbucks for life. It could be worse, I think."

"That's right," I said, feeling sick. I bent over, gripping my stomach, trying not to throw up everywhere.

"You okay?" He leaned over the counter.

I threw my hand up. "Yeah." As I knelt on the ground, I realized what was different about Brian. He wasn't screaming random obscenities every five seconds.

I got up and straightened my suit. "What happened to your Tourette's?"

"Not exactly sure. But I started going to behavioral therapy and meditating a few months ago, and I don't have tics as often as I used to."

"Thanks, Leah," he said, grabbing my coffee from a white girl and handing it to me. "Here."

"Listen, Brian," I started. "My bad for being so harsh last year. I was just stressed out, you know?"

"No worries, Darren. You were right. I was stupid to think I could ever do what you do. I'm making more money than before, and that probably wouldn't have happened if I hadn't listened to you and focused on being the best barista I could be. So I guess I should thank you."

Shit, I must be the best salesman in the world if I actually convinced someone that slaving away at Starbucks should be their life's ambition. But what if I could help Brian and find Barry's SDR at the same time?

Reader: Always keep your eyes open. Your next opportunity could be staring you right in the face.

"Fuck that," I said.

He finally looked at me. "Huh?" he said, confusion squishing the pockmarks around his eyes.

I yanked him over the counter. "Forget everything I said before, Brian. I was fucking wrong, man. Do you still want to learn to do what I do?"

He looked down at my hands — gripping his apron, shirt, and probably some chest hair — and then at me, eyes wide and full of fear. I could feel his heart thumping.

"I can't do what you do, Darren," he said, swallowing hard. "I gave up on all of that. You were right. Plus, this isn't so bad. It's like *Green Lantern* issue one hundred eighty-one when Hal Jordan retires for good."

"This isn't some superhero shit, Brian. So I'm going to ask you once more," I said, focusing every square inch of my power directly into the whites of his eyes. "Do you. Want to. Learn to do. What I do? To sell?"

He scratched the back of his head. "But how can I?"

I let go of him and took my phone out. "You still have the same number?"

He nodded.

"Okay, I just texted you my new address. Be there at six-thirty. Tonight."

"For what?"

"For class," I said, and stumbled out the doors.

After a long day of meetings, I finally arrived at my apartment. "Thanks, Chauncey," I said, exiting the Tesla.

"Have a good night, sir. I will see you tomorrow."

I walked up the stairs, inserted my key into the door, and was stepping inside when someone grabbed my arm.

This is it. This is what I get for having sex with a white woman. I'm about to die. Trembling, I turned around only to be face-to-face with Brian wearing a black leather trench coat.

"Fuck, man. Don't ever sneak up on me like that again. What's wrong with you? And why are you dressed like Shaft?"

"My bad," he said, retreating down the

stairs. "I was waiting across the street until you got home. You take an Uber every night?"

"Something like that. Come on, let's go. You probably scared all the white people on the block just by being here."

"Damn," he said, stepping out of the elevator into my apartment, his head on a swivel like a horny teen in the Museum of Sex. "This all yours?"

"All the furniture, art, and shit? Yeah. But I'm renting. You want something to drink?"

"No, thanks," he said, carefully sitting on a tall white chair at the marble island.

"Coke it is." I tossed a cold can in his direction. It landed on the floor behind him.

He quickly got up and grabbed the can. "Sorry."

"No, don't!"

The can's violent hiss sent brown sugar water all over the white walls, white chairs, and white floors. Brian looked like a dog that had just taken a shit on the floor.

"Okay, okay, okay," I said, rubbing my forehead. "I'm going to go get changed and you're going to clean this up. Then" — I handed him a roll of paper towels — "you're going to take a seat over there." I pointed to the white couch in the living room across from the plasma TV. "And please, Brian, don't touch anything else."

Ten minutes later, I found him cross-legged on the couch, eyes closed, breathing deeply.

"Let's go, Buddha. Time for class."

He slowly opened his eyes. "Where do we start?"

I rolled out the dry-erase board Rhett and I used for weekend strategy sessions and went through the basics: the role of an SDR, the anatomy of a cold call, objection handling, and more.

"Any questions?" I asked, wiping sweat off my brow and turning to Brian. He was still cross-legged, scribbling notes like a cartoon character who's actually not taking any notes.

He shook his head.

"Two hours of this shit and no fucking questions, Brian? That makes me nervous, man."

He just stared at me blankly, his hand still scribbling in his composition notebook. I walked over and snatched it out of his hands. The asshole hadn't taken any notes. It was just paragraphs of wavy lines, random circles, and other ridiculous shapes.

"Brian," I said, chucking the notebook at him and trying to steady my breathing. "What the fuck is this?"

"I can't do this, Darren," he said, defeated. "None of this — DICK! — excuse me, I'm sorry. None of this makes sense to me. This is a waste of your time, and I'm really sorry."

I won't lie; I wanted to hit the mother-fucker right in his face.

"Why didn't you say anything, man? I've been up here for hours after a long-ass day at work, and you're here just scribbling gib-berish to make it look like you're following along? What the fuck, Brian?"

He looked down at his notebook. "I know, I'm sorry."

"Stop fucking saying that and speak up. You know how much shit I have to do? I'm here, with you, right now, investing my time in you."

"I know," he said, forcing back tears. "I just wanted you to think I could do it. I'm —"

"Don't you fucking say it," I said, point-ing a finger at him. "I don't want to hear you ever say you're sorry again. It's a waste of your time and mine."

I plopped down next to him, taking a deep breath. It was night one, and this shit wasn't working. Fear wouldn't work with Brian; it would cause him to be like that guy who ran out of Qur'an on day one never to be seen again, so I'd have to find another way.

"I'll leave." He uncrossed his legs and got up from the couch.

"Sit," I ordered, eyes closed, running through a list of possibilities.

What did I know about Brian? He was a few years older than I was. He was from Connecticut. He had a hard-on for D&D and comic books. He'd never had a girl-friend but wanted one. He worked at Star-bucks and was pretty good with people face-to-face, especially when doing something he loved.

"Got it," I said. I jumped up, grabbed his coat, and threw it at him.

The solution I found was so good, I couldn't contain my smile. "Put it on."

"Okay. Thanks for trying anyway, Darren. I appreciate it. I'll see you around." He slipped his coat on and grabbed his bag.

"What? No. I have an idea, a way for this all to get through your thick skull. But it's going to be uncomfortable. You down?"

"Anything."

"Good. So I want you to go to every deli from here to First Street. And you're going to try to sell them a magazine subscription."

"You own a magazine? I didn't know."

"No, you moron. That's the point. You're going to sell them a subscription to a magazine that doesn't exist. The goal is to get as many of them as possible to give you money for a year's worth of magazines."

His crooked smile quickly disappeared. "I don't know about that, Darren. It seems illegal. And, like, fraud."

"Let me worry about that," I said, pushing him toward the elevator. "We can return the money tomorrow if you want. The point is for you to get comfortable selling something, and there's no better way to do that than trying to convince a stranger to buy something they've never heard of, especially face-to-face late on a cold night."

"What do I even say the name of the magazine is?"

"Hmm, good question. Let's call it" — I paused — "let's call it *Blackface.*"

"What's it about?"

"Oh, you know," I said, massaging his shoulders. "Same as most magazines. White cooks appropriating Black dishes, white musicians appropriating Black music, white designers appropriating Black fashion, et cetera, et cetera. Use your imagination. And don't take no for an answer. That's an order from Sensei Buck."

"Sensei Buck, I don't know if —"

"GO!" I shouted, pressing the elevator button and smiling as he descended into the frigid depths of New York City.

An hour went by, and I figured he must've been doing pretty well, probably chopping it up with deli owners and taking their money, playing them for the chumps they were. Then another hour passed, and I shot him a text. All G?

No response. I started to worry, which reminded me of all the times Ma would text me after my phone would die, and I'd find her in the kitchen, up late, waiting to make sure I made it home okay. "Darren Vender," she'd say. "Haven' you ever heard of a charger?" I swallowed hard and pushed the memory out of my mind.

Another thirty minutes passed until I heard the buzzer. "Who is it?"

"Me." He sounded exhausted.

When the elevator opened, Brian stumbled out with a bloody lip and a pair of eyelids that looked like a Macy's Thanksgiving Day Parade balloon.

"What the fuck happened to you?" I asked, helping him to the living room. "You better not get any blood on my couch."

He took his shoes off and leaned his head far back on a pillow. "Got a steak?"

"A steak? What do I look like?" I walked over to the fridge only to find a freezer full of pork-free pork.

"Thanks," he said, resting a piece on his

swollen eye.

"Now tell me what happened."

"Well, I did what you said. I started off at one deli, on Fourteenth, and the owner didn't speak too much English. He kept thinking I was asking for a black iPhone case, so I left. Then, at the next one, this Hispanic guy seemed curious, but a fight broke out with two customers and he took a knife out, so I ran. I thought about going back, but he seemed on edge. At the third, there was an Indian woman who kept saying, '*Blackface?* What is this blackface? I have brown face! When you have magazine called *Brownface,* I buy. Get out.'

"I kept on walking, grabbed a slice of pizza because I got hungry, then stopped at a deli on Fifth. There was a Black guy behind the register, so I figured this was the one. When I told him about the magazine, and what was inside, he looked at me like I was crazy and told me to leave. But, like you told me, I wasn't going to take no for an answer, so I kept telling him I wasn't leaving until he bought a year's subscription. After that, he leaned over the counter and punched me in the eye. Then, when I was down on the ground, he punched me again in the lip and said if I don't get my

Uncle Tom ass up out of his deli, he'd lynch me."

The frozen fake pork thawed in his hand, dripping water.

"So," I said slowly, covering my face. "You're telling me you didn't sell one fucking subscription all night? And all you have to show for it is a black eye? Jesus, Brian. Did you learn anything tonight? Fucking anything at all?"

He sat up, smiling, dried blood turning a crusty maroon around his bulging mouth like a lip injection gone wrong. "I think . . . I think I learned that no one will be able to punch me through a phone, so selling that way will be a lot easier than this."

I picked my head up and stared at him. He was right, and he had managed to learn a sales lesson after all. I put my feet up on the white oak coffee table and nodded. "Exactly, Grasshopper. I wasn't sure if you'd get it, but you did. Now get the fuck out and be here tomorrow at 6:30 p.m. sharp."

When we pulled up to my apartment on night two, I saw Brian sitting on the steps, shivering and looking over his shoulder like he was going to get in trouble just for being there. In all honesty, I wouldn't have been surprised if one of my neighbors had called the cops on a "suspicious individual."

"Yerrr!" I shouted from the Tesla. The bass from Kendrick Lamar's "Swimming Pools" shook the car. Brian squinted, confused. I let the chorus play on, deciding if my plan for the night was a good one.

"Turn it down, Chauncey!" I screamed over the song. "Yo, Brian. Get the fuck in, man. Can't you tell it's me?"

He looked up and walked down the steps toward the car. "No, yeah, I knew it was you. It just looked like you were having fun, that's all."

"I was, and we're about to have even more. Get in before Chauncey hops out and tries to open the door for you. You must be colder than Jeffrey Dahmer's freezer."

Reluctantly, he got in and sat next to me.

"Hello," Chauncey said, greeting Brian with his big ivory smile. "Pleased to meet you."

"Nice to meet you too. I gotta say" — he laughed — "this is the nicest Uber I've ever seen."

"It's because it's not an Uber," I said, patting Chauncey's shoulder. We started toward Third Avenue.

"So," Chauncey said, looking in the rearview. "Where to, sir?"

"The Belfry, please. It's on Fourteenth between Second and Third."

"Yes, sir."

I grabbed Brian's thigh and he flinched. "Relax, man. How was your day? Any crazy shenanigans at Starbucks?"

"The usual," he said. His black eye somehow had gotten blacker and shined like a recently polished bowling ball. "What's the Belfry? I thought we were going to continue with the sales training."

"We are. But not at my place. The whole 'Good Will Hunting dry-erase board' routine wasn't working, and even though you got a nice shiner last night," I said, poking the lumpy bag under his eye, "the hands-on

384

experience was effective."

He looked forward, gripping his knees, and his Adam's apple bobbed in his throat.

When we arrived, I hopped out and held the door open for Brian, who was still glued to his seat. "After you."

"This looks like a bar," he said.

"An astute observation, Brian. If you keep this up, you'll be a master salesman in no time."

"Why — why are we at a bar, Darren?"

"Come and you'll find out. And stop calling me Darren, man. It's Buck now."

He stared at me like a trapped animal, wide eyes laced with fear. Like any good villain in one of those PETA propaganda videos, I reached in and violently dragged him out, causing him to trip and fall on the sidewalk.

As Chauncey drove away, Brian's eyes followed the Tesla with obvious sadness. "Get up," I said, and offered my hand.

The bar had an old-time saloon feel to it. It was dimly lit, with low circular wooden tables, flickering candles, exposed brick, and lanterns that stretched across the ceiling all the way to the back, where neo-yuppies gorged themselves on pickles, craft beer, and the possibility of getting laid.

"Why are we here?" Brian looked around

as if he'd never been in a bar before.

"Relax, man. We're just going to get a drink and kick it. The stiffer you are, the worse this will all be. Two Delirium Tremens," I said to the thick Asian woman behind the bar.

She glanced at Brian, who looked like he was about to throw up, then at me, and asked, "You sure?"

"Sure as steel."

"Darren, I mean Buck, please tell me why we're here. It feels like I'm gonna get punched in the face again."

"First," I said, smiling at him and raising my beer. "Cheers."

We clinked glasses and I drained half of mine in one gulp. Brian took a tiny sip and set it back down on the cork coaster, his hand shaking like he needed a fix.

"We are here," I said, scanning the room with my finger, "forrrrrrrrr . . . her." I settled on a racially ambiguous girl with high cheekbones, a nice smile, frizzy hair, and olive skin that glowed in the candlelight. She was, without a doubt, a solid ten. And she was sitting alone.

Brian turned to me and took a heavy gulp of his beer. "Uh, is that a friend of yours?"

I laughed and shook my head.

"Someone you're looking to do business with?"

I shook my head again.

"This isn't what I think it is, is it, Buck?"

I took my eyes off her and turned to him, placing a hand on his shoulder. "It is, Brian. You're going to pick her up."

The guy just stared at me like I had said something in a foreign language and he didn't know if I was complimenting him on his looks or cursing out his mother. After a second, he decided it was the latter. "No. No way. I'm not going to embarrass myself, Buck."

"You're right, you won't. As long as you follow the plan."

He threw his arms out to the side. "Plan? Look at me. Take a good look at me. I'm wearing an old hoodie, faded jeans, a ripped T-shirt, and dirty Converses."

"Then you're right at home, man. Look around. Everyone here is dressed just like you."

He surveyed the room, grabbed a napkin, and wiped the sweat off his forehead. "It doesn't matter. This is too much. What's the point? I thought you were going to teach me about sales."

Reader: Watch closely and take notes.

Sales isn't about talent, it's about over-coming obstacles, beginning with yourself.

"*This is sales,* Brian. You think you're just going to call up random strangers and they're going to give you the time of day out of nowhere? You need to learn how to build rapport, open people up, and keep them interested."

"And how do I do that?" He drained his glass and waved it toward the bartender.

"By disarming them and establishing common ground as quickly as possible. The surest way to do that is to get them talking by asking open-ended questions. Like 'What brings you here?' 'Where are you from?' 'Oh, nice tattoo. What's it mean?' Anything, man. Get creative. Just don't be boring."

He grabbed his second pint and gulped half of it down, visibly shaking like he was experiencing an earthquake no one else felt. "Look at me," he said, finding my eyes with his own.

"We already went over this, man. Your clothes are fine."

"No, Buck. I mean how I look. My face. It's disgusting."

I took a breath. "Don't ever say that, Brian. Don't you ever fucking say you're disgusting. Do you understand?"

He raised his glass to his lips, and I grabbed his wrist before he could knock it back.

"You know how many people around the world, or even in this very fucking country, would kill to have your life? To be healthy and free? How many people, Black people, from only fifty years ago, wouldn't believe that we'd be in this bar, drinking at a counter while white people sat around us?"

I thought of Mr. Rawlings. It was something he would say.

"I know, but —"

"But fucking nothing, Brian. Nothing you can ever say will justify you thinking that you're less than. That because you have some acne you're not worthy of a happy life. That you should be afraid of talking with a girl like that. So don't ever give me that again. Because if you do, I won't just stop investing my time in you, but I swear to God I'll also give you another black eye. Now go over there and get that girl's fucking number."

Without a word, his hands still shaking, he got up and slowly walked toward her.

"Damn," the bartender said behind me. "You're like the Black Tony Robbins or something. Do you think he'll get it?"

"A shot says he will," I said.

"And if he doesn't?"

"Then I'll take you to dinner."

"Deal."

Brian tapped the girl on her shoulder. And when she turned around and smiled up at him, his shoulders relaxed a bit, and he cautiously took a seat. His face began to lose the cryogenically frozen look, thawing into a smile, then laughter, followed by raised eyebrows, smirks, and, I shit you not, a solid wink.

"It looks like your brother is killing it," the bartender said. "I may end up owing you that shot."

"He's not my brother," I replied. But I can't lie; I did feel like a proud teacher.

The girl traced a polished nail across his wrist, then I saw it: the close. He took out his phone, handed it to her, and her face glittered in the candlelight as she punched in her name and number. A second later he leaned over, and they exchanged a kiss on each cheek. Then he got up and floated back toward the bar, a goofy-ass smile stuck to his face that made him look like a drugged-up tiger in a Thai zoo.

"So?"

"Yooooo," he whispered, his eyes bulging out of their sockets like wet cotton balls.

"Act cool, man, act cool. What happened?"

Laughing, he scratched the back of his head. "I don't really know, Buck. Honestly. I went over there, then she said I could sit because her friends had ditched her. I noticed a French accent, and I studied a little French in school, so we got to talking. She's an au pair. Then she said I looked like a baby seal, which was weird, but I let it go, and we just kept talking until" — he took a gulp of water the bartender handed him — "until I took out my phone and we exchanged numbers!"

"Fuck yes. See? I told you that you could do it." We bumped fists under the bar. "But listen, I don't think she was calling you a baby seal. I think she was saying you look like a younger version of Seal."

"Who's that?"

"A singer."

"Well, is he good looking?"

"He's married to Heidi Klum. But remember, sales isn't about how you look, man. It's about the confidence you hold."

He leaned back, sighing with relief. "Okay, but it's still cool. So she's into me. This is crazy. Can we do this every night?"

I laughed and slapped him on the back. "It gets old after a while, man. But sure, we can do this again. *After* your training is done."

He left to go to the bathroom, and the bartender handed me my well-deserved shot. "It's a shame you won't be taking me out," she said, pouting.

I raised my shot glass to hers. "I think I can work something out."

"To your brother picking up his first girl," she said, tapping my glass with her own.

"Listen, he's not my —" I turned toward the far end of the bar and watched him rub his wet hands on his jeans and walk toward us like a new man — like he had just realized that he was someone who deserved to be happy.

"Fuck it," I said, downing the shot. "Cheers to my brother."

23

The buzzing woke me up. Without opening my eyes, I grabbed my phone and swiped it open. "Hello?"

It was Rhett. At six in the morning. He told me to meet him at Cafeteria on Seventeenth and Seventh in an hour. Nothing else and no explanation.

After I kicked the bartender from the Belfry out and chugged half a liter of bubble gum Pedialyte, Chauncey drove me across town.

When I opened the door to Cafeteria's brown vestibule, there was a line of glittery drag queens in heels, fur coats, and wigs. One turned around and slowly eyed me up and down. "Well, don't you look delicious."

"I'm not in the mood." I pushed past them and the porcelain-skinned host toward the back, where I spotted a seated Rhett wearing a beige turtleneck sweater and scrolling on his phone.

"What's up with this place?"

He put his phone down and looked up at me. "What do you mean?"

"Look around. It looks like everyone just left the club."

"That's because they did," he said, straight-faced. "This place is open twenty-four hours and attracts a certain type of crowd. Swanky, beautiful, fabulous. You know."

"I see." I ordered the lemon ricotta pancakes and a green smoothie, hoping I'd be able to keep both down. Rhett ordered truffled eggs.

After the modelesque waitress left, we sat there in silence. My hands were sweating, my legs were shaking, and no amount of water I could drink would cure my cotton mouth. I could hear the veins in my skull pulsing with the previous night's cocktail of debauchery, and I had the feeling that I, at the age of twenty-three, was going to die from a heart attack right then and there. Rhett just kept staring at me.

"Alright," I said, shakily setting a glass back on the table. "Please, whatever this is, just tell me. I can't take this shit, man. I feel like you're about to drop a bomb on me. Just do it already."

"Bomb?" he said, spreading a cloth napkin

over his lap. "I don't know what you're talking about."

"C'mon," I said, like a fiend begging for a drug dealer's mercy. "Please stop with the games."

"Games? Again, not sure what you're talking about, Buck. You okay?"

I brought the cold glass to my lips, but it slipped and crashed to the ground, shattering like ice. "Fuck, my bad." I started to bend down when a waiter appeared out of thin air with a mop and a dustpan before grabbing me a new glass.

I closed my eyes and tried to steady the pounding in my head.

Rhett laughed. "Relax, Buck. Listen, I've been thinking about the sales team. Since Clyde left, things haven't been the same. Charlie's overwhelmed and people don't respect him as a leader. The company's doing well, better than ever, but we're not growing as rapidly as I want us to."

"Okay," I said, as our waitress set plates of steaming food in front of us. I inhaled the warm vapors, hoping they'd ground me. "And?"

He placed a forkful of eggs into his mouth. "Are you worried about something?"

"I'm worried about a lot of things. Like what Clyde's going to do. He's well-connected and angry. He won't even answer my texts or calls. And we all know how vengeful he is."

"I don't get it," I said, gulping down my smoothie. "How does Charlie play into all of this? Or the sales team?"

"There's just an obvious gap. And I want to take care of it ASAP."

"So why don't you demote Charlie and put one of the other AEs in charge?"

"I *am* going to demote Charlie, and I *am* putting one of the other AEs in charge."

"Perfect. Who?"

"You," he said, finally smiling. "I want you to be our new director of sales."

I choked on the thick mix of pancakes and smoothie. When I could finally breathe, I said, "That doesn't make sense, Rhett. I haven't even been with the company for a year. No one will respect me."

"You've done more in less than a year than most people do in their entire careers, Buck. And every AE not only *respects* you but is *inspired* by you. Plus, they're all looking forward to grabbing some of your connections through Barry."

"How do you know?"

"Because I already spoke to all of them. When you walk into the office today, you'll be the youngest director of sales in New

York City, maybe in all of America. At least that's what *BuzzFeed* and the *Huffington Post* are saying."

My headache and the feeling of impending death slowly returned. I chugged more smoothie. "Wh-why would they be saying that, or anything at all, Rhett?"

He winked, smirking like a bandit. "Because we sent them a press release last night. The news just broke!" he said, reaching his hands toward me.

"Rhett. I don't know about this, man. It's just that —"

"Just what? Anyone would kill to be in your shoes, Buck. I thought you'd be more grateful."

I swallowed. "I am, Rhett. I really am, but —"

"But fucking what? I can't believe what I'm hearing right now. Why do I always have to push you to accept a golden opportunity? Do you think you're too good for this? For us? Are you trying to start your own thing, is that it?"

"What? No. What are you talking about?"

"You know, Buck. Maybe Clyde was right. Maybe I backed the wrong horse, and you're not cut out for this anymore. Maybe I was wrong to think you still cared about the company, about me."

The waitress walked over and refilled our glasses. "Can I get you two anything else? Coffee? Tea? It's past eight now, so maybe a mimosa?"

"No, thanks," I said, forcing a smile.

"Just the check, please," Rhett said.

We sat in silence as a busboy cleared the table. Rhett picked up the check, and we silently pulled on our jackets and gloves. When we got outside, Chauncey was waiting across Seventh.

I turned to Rhett, who slowly exhaled a plume of breath into the cold air. "Want a ride?" I asked.

"I'll walk."

"Okay. See you at the office."

I took a step into the crosswalk, then felt a firm hand on my wrist. When I turned around, Rhett was shaking like he was going to cry.

"I meant what I said, Buck. Whether you like it or not, when you walk into the office, you *will* be Sumwun's director of sales, and you *will* give more time and attention to the company. It's the least you can do for everything I've done for you. For picking you over Clyde. Understood?"

I stared at his white knuckles tightening their grip on my wrist, burning in the late winter's chill. "Yeah, my bad. Thanks for always looking out for me, Rhett."

The buzzer rang. I got up from the couch and walked over. Then it rang again, long and obnoxiously. It was around six-thirty, so I figured it was Brian and let him up without checking.

Barry was also blowing up my phone.

Got the SDR yet? ;)

Almost, I typed. Unsure why this is so important though?

Don't worry bout that. Just don't fk it up. If u do, we're done

When the elevator opened, I stabbed my head inside, and said, "What the fuck is wrong with you?" I saw Brian, but I also saw the face of an elfish Black girl. She was wearing a black leather jacket and had a pixie cut, black ear gauges, and one of those bull-like septum piercings.

"You're shorter than you look on TV," she said, hands on her hips and a face full of disappointment.

I turned to Brian. "Who the hell is this?"

"I'm right here," she said, pushing past me into the apartment. She took her jacket off and I saw tattoos running the lengths of her arms. "If you want to know who I am, why'd you ask him? You're probably not used to women speaking up for themselves, but I assure you I am capable of doing so."

"Brian," I whispered, looking over my shoulder to make sure she wasn't stealing anything. "Who. Is. That?"

"Um, that's Rose Butler."

"Okay," I said, squeezing my eyes. "And?"

"And we play poker together. Usually on Wednesdays. When I told her I couldn't make it, she asked why, so I told her."

"And?"

"And she said it sounded fun. That she saw you on TV and wanted to meet you . . . and see what you could teach her."

I grabbed his collar and yanked him out of the elevator. "Are you out of your fucking mind? You think you can just bring anyone here? That this is some sort of a game? And I didn't know you played poker or even had the money for it."

"He doesn't," she said, grabbing a Perrier out of the fridge and cracking it open. "I have to spot him since I took all of his money last month. But this looks fancy, is it French?"

"Put that down," I ordered. She chugged half and left the opened bottle on the counter before plopping down on the couch and putting her dirty leather boots on my white oak coffee table.

"I'm sorry," Brian said, wearing his abused

puppy-dog face. "She won't get in the way, I promise. I told her this is serious."

"Don't ever invite anyone here again. Got it?"

Still staring at the ground, he nodded.

I looked across the room. She was digging her heels into the coffee table, working stains into it that I'd likely never get out. I stormed over and shoved her feet off. "Get out. I don't know you, and I don't want to. Plus, you're ruining my shit."

"Oh, like this?" she asked, swinging her feet over the length of the couch, holding them there.

"Don't you dare. I swear to God. If one piece of dirt gets on that couch, I'm going to have you arrested."

"You have two choices, Buckaroo. Either let me stay and your couch stays just how you probably like your women, white and pretty, or you kick me out and I drive my muddy boots into the cushions before you have a chance to forcibly remove me. Which will it be?"

I turned to Brian in disbelief. He just shrugged. *Who the fuck is this girl? And why does she have bigger balls than I do?*

"Okay. I'll let you stay on one condition."

She placed her feet on the floor and relief washed over me. "What is it?"

"We role-play. If you last more than a minute, you stay. If you don't, you leave. Sound fair?"

"Sure, but what kind of role-playing are you referring to? Doctor and patient? Cop and robber? Some weird phone-sex-operator fantasy you no doubt have?"

I felt myself getting hot. "What, no? This is Sales 101. You need to try to sell me something or at least keep me on the line."

"And what am I selling you?"

I searched my mind for something impossible, something that would allow me to get rid of her ASAP. "Okay, got it. You're selling me a dildo."

She threw her head back onto the couch, letting out a hard laugh. "A dildo? Seriously? I didn't know you swung that way. Looks like we're more alike than I thought."

"I *don't* swing that way, you fucking goblin. That's the point. Now say 'ring ring' and call me up."

"Whatever you say, Buckaroo. Ring ring."

"Hello, this is Buck."

"Good evening, Buck! This is Rose calling from Diamond Dildos, how are you?"

"Diamond Dildos? I think you have the wrong number."

"No problem!" she said, smiling with closed eyes. "Happens. But since I have you

402

on the line on this beautiful, wintry New York City night, let's chat. I'm sure you have a few seconds for a new friend. How's your evening?"

"Not great," I said. "I have an unexpected houseguest I'm trying to get rid of."

"Oh, poo." She mimicked a sad clown. "That's never fun. Anyway, I'll be quick. Do you have a girlfriend?"

"No."

"Do you have sex?"

"Of course, what kind of a question is that?"

"A good one, trust me. Do you prefer men, women, or like me, both?"

"Women," I said firmly, unsure of where she was going.

"Would you say you make them orgasm every time? That you're a pro?"

"Yeah, I'd say I'm better than average."

"Most men say that, Buck, but do you know how many women fake an orgasm? Just to get it over with?"

"No," I said, now genuinely interested and a little nervous. "How many?"

"Take a guess."

"I don't know, three out of ten?"

"*Higher,*" she said, looking up from the couch, pointing that impish grin at me.

"Five out of ten?"

403

"Higher."

"Seven out of ten?"

"Almost there. So close, I can feel it. Almost."

"Eight out of ten?"

"Ding, ding, ding! That's right, Buckaroo. Eighty percent of women fake orgasms, which is why we at Diamond Dildos are in business. Our dildos are guaranteed to increase the number of real orgasms you give women and take the guessing out of all of it."

I walked to the kitchen to grab a drink. I was suddenly dying of thirst, and this little fucking girl was making me sweat, but I couldn't let her see that.

"I'm a man," I said from the kitchen. "Why would I want the help of a dildo?"

"Why wouldn't you?" she asked, standing up now.

"Because I'm capable of making women orgasm all on my own, thanks."

"You can lie to yourself," she said, laughing now. "But numbers don't. Are you so self-conscious that you're afraid of a little hand-blown glass dildo?"

"Of course not."

"Then what are you afraid of? Why not think of someone other than yourself?

Someone else's pleasure instead of your own?"

"Fine!" I shouted, slamming the fridge door. "I'll buy one if it gets you off the fucking phone."

She cut a smile at me, exposing a set of straight white teeth. "All I need is your credit card and an address to mail the hardware. You've made a wise and empathetic choice, sir."

I plopped down on the couch, and she took a light bow, rubbing my head before sitting next to me. "So, can I stay?"

"Whatever."

Brian sat in the corner, his mouth hanging open as if he'd just seen Superman get beat up by some middle-aged average joe. "Um, what's next?" he asked.

I closed my eyes and thought through a dozen sadistic things I could make them do while also, of course, teaching them about sales. I could make them try selling *Blackface* magazine again, but this time in Harlem. But I wanted something more fun, something that would make me laugh, especially after this girl, whoever she was, just passed a role-play on her first try.

"Dancing," I said, chuckling to myself like some maniacal villain. "We're going dancing."

"So what club are we going to?" Rose yelled, excitement bathing her face like a cucumber mask. "I hope they let me in with my dirty boots."

As we stood in Union Square subway station, all I could do was smile. Packed trains passed us going uptown and downtown, commuters forcing their way in and out like desperate sperm.

"We've been here for like thirty minutes, Buck," Brian shouted over the mechanical screeching. "Shouldn't we get on one?"

I let a few more pass until they became emptier. Then, when an Uptown 6 pulled up and the platform extensions stretched to meet it, I pushed them inside.

"Uptown?" Rose asked, confused. "I thought all of the swanky spots were in Chelsea or the Meatpacking District. Shouldn't we be taking the L?"

"You know, you would be right if we were going to one of those. But the club I'm taking you both to is much closer than you think."

"Okaaay," she said, cutting a sideways glance at Brian. "Why are you being so strange and mysterious, Buckaroo? Where is it?"

"One second." I scanned the train, which was weirdly crowded for seven-thirty at night. Exhausted men with stained construction boots and stiff Carhartt jackets nodded off to sleep; teenagers in basketball sweats with Nike gym bags bobbed their heads to hypnotic beats; night nurses heading for Mount Sinai, Lenox Hill, or Henry J. Carter chewed on protein bars; old-money white folks wearing fur coats but too cheap to take a cab rested gloved hands on ivory canes.

"Ladies and gentlemen," I shouted. "Please excuse the interruption, but this evening I have a special treat for you all."

Rose grabbed my arm. "What is this?"

"This is the club," I replied, winking.

"I have two young and promising dancers from Juilliard — Monte Negro and the Duchess of Philly — here with me to do a new routine they're working on called 'Don't Take Another Step, Whitey,' which is an avant-garde, modernist interpretation of America's Reconstruction in which two newly freed enslaved people come to terms with the obvious struggle of Black liberation. Please put your hands together for them!"

The construction workers looked up with puzzled faces; the athletic teens removed oversize headphones; the nurses paused their dinners; but it was the elderly white folks who looked up with eyes full of joy and clapped loudly.

"Buck," Brian whispered, sweat making his skin shine like an enslaved man on the run. "Why are you doing this?"

"I'm not doing this," I said. "You are. And you" — I poked Rose's arm — "you better get this minstrel show hopping. I need big bills — no dimes, nickels, or quarters."

She scowled. "What the fuck does this have to do with sales? I refuse."

"If you refuse" — I leaned closer — "then you can kiss coming back tomorrow good-bye. Your ride on the rollercoaster of Sales Sensei Buck ends now, which is fine with me. Plus, sales is about staying loose, enduring humiliation, and being flexible."

Reader: I know, this was a bit extreme, but when it comes to sales, you either sink or swim.

I removed a portable speaker from my backpack and put on "Say It Loud — I'm Black and I'm Proud." "C'mon everyone," I yelled, running down the aisle. "Clap with the beat."

Once James Brown hit his *Uh!* the residents of that particular Wednesday night's New York City Uptown 6 train loosened up and pointed expectant faces in the direction of Brian and Rose. I pushed them forward, but they were as stiff as sculptures.

"The road to greatness ends for you both right here, right now, if you don't start dancing. No sales. No better life. No cash money or freedom. No escaping the game. You have a choice. To die as an enslaved person or live as a freeman and freewoman. Hit it."

James Brown wailed into the subway. Brian slid forward like a spastic middle school nerd and turned around, extending a hand toward Rose. She mouthed some obscenity at me, placed her hand in Brian's, and twisted her body into his.

As the hardest-working man in show business sang about Black people finally working for themselves, Rose pushed herself away from Brian. He stumbled back on his heels, grabbing a metal pole to steady himself. And she hit a series of dance moves — the running man, the tootsie roll, the sprinkler, the robot, and even the YMCA — to the raucous applause of the entire train. By the time the song finished and the train hit Grand Central, stunned passengers walked on to fifty white people clapping and shouting, "Say it loud, I'm Black and I'm proud, huh!"

"Okay," Rose said after we got off, hands on her knees, catching her breath. "That was pretty fun."

"Yeah," Brian echoed, wiping the sweat off his face with a puffy sleeve. "I didn't even know I could dance."

"You can't," I said, laughing. "But at least you didn't make a complete fool of yourself. And you both managed to not only convince a subway full of white people that they were Black but also that they were proud of it. If that's not sales, I don't know what is."

"Psh," Rose said. "That's not hard. Rappers who let white people sing 'nigga' at their concerts do it every night."

"She has a point," Brian said.

I waved a heavy hat in front of them. "Anyway, by the time this went around, we made almost fifty dollars."

"Ohhh, gimme!" Rose dug her tiny fingers into the hat, pulling out the big bills. "I'll take this as payback for the money you owed me from poker, Brian."

"Perfect," he said, relieved.

"What's next?" Rose asked, her voice softer than it was hours ago.

"What's next is I'm grabbing an Uber and going to bed," I said. "I'll drop you each off on the way. Where're you going, Brian?"

"East Village, thanks."

"And you?" I asked, looking beyond my phone at Rose, who shrank back into her hardened shell.

"Oh, I'm okay."

"C'mon, you earned it," I insisted. "It's on me."

"Thanks, but no thanks. Uber is a predatory company that takes advantage of immigrants; ignores safety precautions for its riders, especially women; and is everything that's wrong in a world run by narrow-minded, solely profit-driven white men."

Brian and I stared at her, blinking. *"Well,"* I said. "When you put it that way."

"But tonight was fun," she said, reaching up, wrapping her arms around my neck. "Same time tomorrow?"

"Yeah, my place at six-thirty. Are you sure you —"

Before I could finish, she was up the stairs and out of sight.

24

Thursday at Sumwun was my day for one-on-ones, which meant utter chaos. I drank about six coffees, ate almost nothing, and spent the entire day from 8 a.m. to 6 p.m. meeting with as many AEs as possible.

After escaping, I barreled into the Tesla and locked the doors before some brave soul decided to badger me with "one last question."

"You look exhausted, sir," Chauncey said, concerned. "How are you?"

That question. I couldn't remember the last time someone had genuinely asked me how I was. Ma used to. Wally Cat used to. Soraya used to. Jason used to.

"I'm okay, Chauncey," I replied, slumping over in the back seat, swallowing memories of a past life. "Thanks for asking. How're you?"

He smiled in the rearview. "Me? I am good, sir. Always good if you are good. You know, when I look at you —"

I had to tune him out. I liked Chauncey, but he was suddenly reminding me of Bed-Stuy and all of the people who had hurt me. They'd all cared, but what had that amounted to?

"I have a meeting at my place, Chauncey," I said, once he was finished. "Let's just go there. And turn the heat up, my nipples are sharper than Michael Jackson's nose."

"As you wish, sir."

We arrived at my building, and I saw a group of people huddled on the sidewalk. It was dark, so I couldn't tell who it was, but I faintly made out Rose's pint-size silhouette in the streetlight's orange glow. *Fuck, what is this?*

"Chauncey."

"Yes, sir?"

"Can you work tonight? I'll need a ride somewhere in a few minutes."

"Of course, sir. Whatever you need."

I hopped out, and after getting closer, I saw Rose, Brian, and two — yes, two — other fucking people.

"Please tell me you all just met outside and that you don't know these people," I said to Rose and Brian, nodding at the newcomers.

"I hate to break it to you, Buckaroo," Rose

said. "But I know 'these people,' as you so rudely called them. This is —"

"I don't give a shit who they are," I snapped, turning to Brian, who was visibly shaking. "I told you last night not to invite anyone else, Brian. The whole thing is off," I said, my voice rising. "I don't have time for this shit!"

Rose stepped between us. "Hey," she said, composed. "It wasn't his idea; it was mine. We had so much fun last night and learned to, you know, loosen up and be flexible, so I thought it'd be good for others to join and learn from Sensei Buck."

"Well, you were dead fucking wrong." I pushed through them and walked up the stairs.

"Each one teach one, Mr. Buck," someone with a soft Southern accent said.

I turned around and saw a lanky light-skinned fellow sporting long tied-back dreadlocks and a brown leather aviator jacket with the trim looking up at me.

"What?"

" 'Nslaved people use' to say it. You see, masters 'n' other people in power knew that in orda to 'nslave the body they had to keep the mind ignorant. 'N' since 'nslaved people weren' allowed to learn how to read 'n' write, when one of 'em somehow managed to become educated, it was his or her duty to teach as many as they could."

I slowly clapped from the top of the stairs. "Bravo, Jed Clampett, or whatever the fuck your name is. What does this have to do with me?"

"Everything, Buckaroo," Rose said. "Brian told them how you promised to teach him how to do what you do, to sell, so that he can quit his job and have a better life."

"I didn't promise shit," I said, opening the front door. "And I don't owe any of you anything."

Brian ran up the steps and grabbed my arm. "What was all of that stuff you said at the Belfry? About us not being able to even be in the same places as white people fifty years ago and like how we need to do what we can to get ahead, to be happy?"

I looked down at Brian's hand on my arm. *Was he actually trying to sell me?* Despite being pissed, I was proud of his newfound assertiveness.

I shrugged him off. "I just said that shit to pump you up, Brian. To give you the courage to take a leap."

"But it's true," the other intruder, a tall androgynous white guy with a long serious face, wire-framed glasses, and wearing what looked like a green woman's parka, said in

415

an accent that sounded both Southern and British. "In fifty years, a whole lot has changed for us, but we still have a long way to go. And from what Rose and Brian preached, you can help."

I looked around to see if anyone else thought it was weird that this white motherfucker was trying to tell me about the plight of blacks in America, but no one moved. I walked down the stairs, stood right in front of him, and said, "Us? We? What the fuck is this white guy talking about? And why do you both sound like you walked barefoot across the Mason-Dixon line?"

Rose doubled over. Then Brian did, then the lanky guy with the locks — the three of them leaning onto one another, holding their stomachs as plumes of cold air billowed out of their mouths into the street like a dense fog.

"What the fuck is so funny?"

Rose eventually collected herself and pointed at the straight-faced white guy in front of me. "First, *he* is a *she*. Second, she looks white, but she's Black. I can assure you of that."

"Ellen Craft of Georgia, Pennsylvania, Massachusetts, England, and a host of other places," the tall girl said, taking a bow, a long brown mane tumbling out of her beanie. "Pleasure to meet you."

I looked her over in the light. She gripped my hand and her handshake was as firm as any grown man's I'd encountered. I won't lie; it was intimidating.

"And this is Jacob D. Green of Kentucky," Rose said, motioning to the lanky guy.

I reluctantly shook his hand. Chauncey rolled down the window. "Shall we go, sir?"

The four of them looked at me, eyes full of anticipation. "What do you have to lose?" Rose asked, grabbing my shoulder. "This is it. Just us four learning how to do what you do. To sell. I promise, Buckaroo, I won't invite anyone else."

My phone buzzed. Barry. Better have someone ready for an interview on mon morning. 9am. SHARP!

"Fine," I said, opening the Tesla, nodding for them to get in. "But only if you each promise to do everything I tell you to. No matter how wild, unorthodox, or potentially illegal it may sound."

Everyone nodded, and the five of us piled in.

"Where to, sir?"

"Just drive, Chauncey. I'll tell you when to stop."

"Here," I said, in front of a 7-Eleven on

Twentieth and Third.

"Y'all sure?" Jake asked, a wrinkle forming between his eyebrows. "Lotta of cops 'round here. Doesn' bode well for five Black folk."

"This isn't the 1920s," Rose said. "Chill out."

"Fooled me," Ellen said.

"I'm with Jake," Brian added.

"Everyone out," I ordered.

Bells clanged as the 7-Eleven's doors opened, and the Indian man behind the register stared at us one by one.

I walked to the back, pulled open a beer fridge, and grabbed a different tall boy for each of them. "PBR for you because you're dressed like a Black hipster and sound like a hillbilly," I said, throwing it to Jake. "Coors Original for you because" — I handed it to Ellen — "you're as white as the Rocky Mountains on the can but probably change colors when the sun hits you."

"It's true," she said, turning over the cream-colored can in her hand.

"Bud Light for you," I said, tossing one to Brian. "Because you're a lightweight." He frowned, disappointed.

"And the best for last," I said, grinning at Rose. "You, little one, get a Busch Light."

"Busch Light!" she shouted. "This crap is

418

the bottom of the barrel and tastes like piss."

"Now, now, Rose, beggars can't be choosers. You agreed to do whatever I asked. No complaints."

I paid for the beers and we walked outside. "Wait here," I said to Chauncey, who was parked in front of the store.

"Yes, sir."

"Now," I said, facing the group. "Follow me."

"Shouldn't we at least put these in brown paper bags?" Brian asked, his voice cracking in fear.

"No."

"We gon' get arrested," Jake said.

"We won't."

"But we're heading toward the police precinct," Brian added.

"Exactly. Tonight's lesson is all about tone, confidence, and delivery. What you're going to do is make a right there," I said, pointing at Twenty-First Street. "Crack open your beers, walk toward the group of cops hanging outside the precinct, and then you're each going to casually walk past them. One by one."

"Dang, Mr. Buck," Jake said, blinking hard. "I'm on probation. Can' do that."

"Listen. You said you wanted to learn to do what I do. To sell. And that you'd do everything I told you to. No one is going to get arrested. One of the first rules of sales is that it's not what you say, it's how you say it. So when the cops stop you and ask what the fuck you're doing, you drink your beer slowly right in front of them, and say, with chests out, strength in your voice, and a raised head, 'Just drinking a beer, officer.' "

"Are you out of your mind?" Rose asked. "You have to be if you think they're not going to arrest a bunch of Black people parading in front of the precinct with open beers. We're giving them a reason to do something when they shoot people for less."

"Open your beers," I ordered.

They turned to one another, stalling. Brian's hands trembled, but then two quick hisses came from beside him: Rose and Ellen.

"Fuck it," Rose said, taking a sip of her piss-flavored beer.

Ellen raised her can to Rose's, poker-faced. "Catch me if you can."

Brian and Jake followed suit, nervously pulling on aluminum lids, sending sprays of foam into the air, then taking hurried swigs.

"Single file," I commanded. People on the sidewalk stared before turning their strolls into light jogs.

"Now march."

The group, led by Rose, walked up Third Avenue and turned right onto Twenty-First Street. A crowd of policemen stood in front of the precinct smoking and laughing.

"Onward," I ordered, watching their bodies shake with fear in the freezing winter night.

"You sure about this?" Brian asked, turning around for one last glance.

"Nope."

Once they reached the cops, they each took a swig from their cans. I moved closer to get a front row seat.

"Hey," a short Black cop with a moustache said, turning away from his pals toward Rose and the others. "That's not beer, is it?"

The four of them froze, at least twenty cops staring them down. Then Brian, like a moron, said, "Just, just — PUSSY! — drinking a beer, officer."

The cop turned to his buddies, laughing, then spun back around gripping a taser.

"Run!" I shouted, reversing direction and bolting down Twenty-First Street.

Jake, with his Gumby legs, stretched past me; Brian, asthmatic, wheezed behind me; Ellen caught up to Jake; Rose zigzagged in the middle of the road like she was dodging bullets.

Chauncey saw us running toward the Tesla, started it up, and four of us hopped inside before he peeled away.

"Brian!" Rose shouted, pointing to a shadow on the corner, hands on his knees.

"Open the door!" I screamed.

We grabbed him before the cops caught up, slamming the door shut. Chauncey pulled an illegal U-turn and drove down Third Avenue toward Union Square. We collectively exhaled after we realized the cops weren't chasing us. Cans clinked. Laughter ensued.

"Woohoooo!" Rose shouted, hanging her head out the window like a dog in the wind.

"Dang, that shit was wil'," Jake said, biting his fist.

"I thought I was done for," Brian said, traumatized.

Ellen stared out the window, unfazed.

We headed back to my place and whiteboarded basic sales theory for a couple of hours. Believe it or not, Jake and Ellen were naturals just like Rose. They still had things to work on — Jake needed to enunciate more, Ellen needed to be less stiff — but they were solid. Even Brian was taking what he learned and applying it with finesse.

Eventually, they all knocked out, so I ushered them out of my place into the Tesla.

I hopped in to make sure they didn't take advantage of Chauncey's kindness by asking him to make random stops at fast food spots or anything else like that.

After dropping Brian and Ellen off in the East Village and Jake in Williamsburg, there was only one left.

"Where to for you, miss?" Chauncey asked Rose. She was passed out on my shoulder in the back seat.

I nudged her, and she shot upright, hands in the air. "Relax," I said. "Chauncey just asked where to drop you off."

Rubbing her eyes, she looked around the dark car as we crossed the Williamsburg Bridge back into Manhattan. "Oh, you can drop me off at the bottom of the bridge, thanks."

"But where do you live?" I asked.

"Not far from there. In" — she paused — "FiDi."

"FiDi? Why would we drop you off in the Lower East Side then? We got you, sit back and relax."

"No!" she shouted, sitting up. "I mean . . . no thanks. I can walk. Seriously. You've done enough, spending all of this time on us."

I stared at her, trying to figure out what the deal was, why she was so guarded, but I gave up. "Fine, have it your way."

She hopped out at the bottom of the bridge, and we turned up First Avenue.

"Long night, huh, Chauncey?" I asked, stretching out in the back seat.

"Yes, sir," he said, his eyes staying closed for a few seconds, then fluttering open. "But it is not over, at least for me. When I go home, I will wake my daughter to sing happy birthday to her."

"Oh, when's her birthday?" I looked down at my phone; it was past midnight.

"Yesterday, sir."

"Yesterday as in a few minutes before it turned twelve or the day before?"

He laughed, flashing those ivory teeth in the rearview. "As in a few minutes ago."

Whatever I ate earlier turned to concrete in the pit of my stomach. I grabbed it and pushed my head to the front of the car, turning to Chauncey. "Why didn't you tell me? I wouldn't have asked you to drive all night if I knew it was your daughter's birthday."

Without taking his eyes off the road, he gripped the steering wheel, holding his smile. "It is okay, sir. My job is with you; she understands."

"How old is she?"

"She just turned seven, sir."

424

"What's her name?"

"Amina. It means 'trustworthy.' My wife and I hope that this means she will be a lawyer or a big executive like you, sir," he said, turning to me, laughing.

"Wife? You're married, Chauncey?"

"Yes, sir. Ten years now. I brought her and Amina over four years ago."

"From where?"

"Senegal, sir. It is where I am from."

I fell back and rested my head on the seat, breathless at the fact that Chauncey had driven me for six months, yet I didn't know anything about him. I'd never cared to ask. "Pull over."

"Sir? We are almost home."

"Pull over," I repeated. "Please."

He crossed Fourteenth and pulled to the side of the empty avenue.

"Now out."

"Sir?"

"Out," I ordered.

He slowly opened the door and stood to the side. I hopped out, grabbed his driver's cap, and took his place. "In the back," I said, pointing behind me.

His eyes went white in the cold orange light of the night, as if he'd seen a ghost. "No, sir. I cannot do that. It is not proper. Please, sir, please step out."

Without a word, I closed my door, reached back, pushed open the one behind me, and adjusted the seat. Chauncey was a few inches taller than me.

He reluctantly grabbed the door handle, looked around the street, then quickly stepped inside, shutting the door.

"Where to, Chauncey?" I asked, looking at his tense face in the rearview mirror.

"Please, sir, you cannot —"

"Where to?"

He leaned forward, gripping the collar of his shirt and holding it there for a while; but he eventually loosened his tie and sat back. "Harlem, sir. One Hundred Thirty-Fourth Street and Malcolm X Boulevard."

I drove the car at a snail's pace all the way up to Harlem. Chauncey told me about life in Senegal, about the famous people from his land, like the father of African cinema, Ousmane Sembene, and about *ceebu jën,* also known as thieboudienne, which is basically their version of paella. Before moving to America, Chauncey had completed his PhD in renewable energy, but when he arrived here, no university would offer him a professorship, so he got a job as a driver through his cousin.

Thirty minutes later, we were there. I handed him the keys. He kissed his hand

and raised it to the sky. *Damn, is my driving that atrocious?*

"Tell Amina I said happy birthday and that I'm sorry for keeping you away from her."

"I will, sir, but no apologies necessary."

I started walking down the street, hoping I could catch a cab all the way up there.

"Sir?" he called, holding the Tesla's open door.

"Yeah?"

"I do not know what you are doing with all of these new people, but whatever it is, I know it is good. You are a good person, sir."

I quietly saluted him, turning back down the street. I already knew what I was doing with "all of these new people." One of them would be the ticket to getting Barry off my back. After that, Sensei Buck would cut the rest loose.

25

"Where's Rose?" I asked, looking around the Time Warner Center's lobby. It was seven. "I said 6:45 p.m., didn't I?"

Earlier in the day, I'd met with Barry, who finally explained why getting this SDR was so important. He said that the CEO of the hip-hop sponsorship company, X-Ploit, was the son of a wealthy Arab who could use his connections to help Barry get closer to a minority stake in the Giants. It was stupid as shit, but Barry wasn't the type of person I'd want as an enemy, so I told the troops to meet at the Time Warner Center that night.

"You did," Brian said.

Jake pointed toward the glass doors as Rose walked in. "Ova there."

"Why are you late?" I asked, as she strolled over wearing black leather from head to toe.

She patted my shoulder, unconcerned. "Because I'm late. Is there anything I can

428

say that'll really make you feel better?"

"No."

"Exactly. So what's the plan?"

I scanned my motley crew. "Tonight is a celebration of all of your hard work over the past couple days. I want to thank you for making this an exciting week and for trusting me to lead the way."

"This jus' the beginnin', Mr. Buck," Jake said, slapping my shoulder with his oversize hands.

"Yeah, so we're going to go up to the fourth floor to enjoy a delicious and expensive meal at Per Se," I said. "But before we do, I want all of your wallets."

"For what?" Rose asked, hesitantly reaching into her back pocket.

"Because Sensei Buck says so, that's why."

They each threw their penny-thin wallets into my bag and we entered the elevator. Four floors later, we reached a pair of royal-blue wooden doors. The four of them, wearing nothing even reminiscent of fine-dining attire, stood speechless before I pushed them inside.

Tables full of people lined the windows overlooking Columbus Circle, Central Park, and the skyline. A pretentious, likely hazardous, fireplace crackled behind glass. Six or seven white-clothed, candle-lit tables stood on a level higher than the others. After a little trouble, we were shown to one of them.

"Where are the individual prices?" Brian asked, scratching his cheek as he scanned the menu.

"There are no individual prices, it's a fixed menu," I said.

"Down there." Ellen pointed to the bottom of Brian's menu. "See that? It says three hundred forty per person. Service included."

"Dang," Jake said, looking over at me. "You sure you gon' pay for all this?"

"Of course, it's my pleasure."

After I ordered a bottle of one of their most expensive champagnes, explained what prix fixe meant, showed Brian how to lay his napkin across his lap instead of shoving it into his collar, and told them to ignore all of the rich white people staring at us, everyone lightened up.

"So what we gon' do with these new sales superpowers?" Jake asked, smelling his champagne before taking a sip.

"What do you want to do with them?"

"Make loads of money, obviously," Rose said, swinging her head around the table for confirmation.

"Now tha's a plan," Jake said.

Brian silently nodded.

430

Ellen wiped her mouth, and said, "Of course money. But also use them to get ahead and help others do the same."

The rest murmured agreement, and I slapped my hands together. "Perfect, that's exactly what I wanted to hear. Because I have an opportunity. But for only one of you."

"Who gets it?" Rose asked.

"It's only right that it goes to Brian, since he was here at the beginning."

"Will there be others?" Ellen asked, her blank stare seeing right through me.

"Maybe," I said. "We'll see. But either way, at least you all have learned something useful, right?"

Of course, Barry needed only *one* SDR, but that wasn't my fault. The way I saw it, if the rest of them wanted to better their lives, they were now more equipped to do so. I didn't owe anyone anything.

Reader: This is called *information asymmetry,* which basically means that one person has more information than another, giving them an advantage. It used to be more prevalent in sales before potential buyers could google everything, but it still exists, and the sleazier types of salespeople exploit it

whenever possible. Don't be that sales-person.

Everyone nodded, the air heavy with disappointment.

Brian's eyes darted around the table, ashamed. "What's the opportunity?"

"An interview. Monday at 9 a.m. You in?"

He took a sip of water and nodded. Everyone took turns rubbing his head, pulling his ears, and shaking his shoulders.

"You got this, boy!" Jake said. "I also want to thank you, Mr. Buck, for takin' us all in as family."

"Of course. No problem."

"Not to get all sentimental, but it's never been the easiest for me to make friends 'n' keep 'em, since I spent most of my teenage years in 'n' outta juvie, 'n' doin' all other kinds of foolishness, so I'm grateful for you," Jake said, looking at me before addressing the table. "For all y'all."

"Same here," Ellen said. "I've moved around most of my life, seen terrible things, and sometimes still forget who I really am, but I feel grounded with all of you. To Buck." She raised a glass of champagne.

"To Buck!" everyone echoed.

After we devoured and drank everything in sight, the waiter appeared. "Will there be

432

anything else?" he asked, refilling everyone's water glasses.

"Just the check," I replied.

He bowed and walked away.

"This check 'bout to be big as fooook!" Jake shouted, obviously drunk, tipsy, or whatever they call it over in Kentucky.

I doubled over, laughing. "That's right." I gripped my stomach in pain.

"What's so funny?" Rose asked.

"You didn't think this was going to be that easy, did you? A free meal, and one, two, three" — I snapped three times — "you passed?"

"Whatchu mean?" Jake asked, now sober.

"For your last test" — I waved them in closer as if I were the quarterback in a huddle — "you have to convince the waiter that we're not paying."

Brian, as black as asphalt, turned a few shades whiter.

"You're a sadist," Rose said, knocking back the last of the champagne straight out of the bottle.

"Regardless of what I am, none of you have your wallets, the bill is going to be bigger than your monthly rent, and I'm sure as hell not paying, so . . ."

"So we have no other choice," Ellen said. Her face turned red and tears began forming in her eyes.

Jake wrapped an arm around her. "Dang, Ellen. It's okay."

"I'm not seriously crying," she whispered. "It's for show."

"One of the most important part of sales is objection handling. You need to do everything in your mortal power to overcome the hurdles others place in front of you."

The waiter returned with the bill, stood behind me as I reviewed all 2,830 dollars and 75 cents of it, then remained where he was, waiting for us to pay up. I handed the bill to Ellen, who handed it to Brian, who, with trembling hands, handed it to Jake, who, like a kid playing hot potato, tossed it to Rose.

She looked at the bill, then up at the waiter, and said, with a straight face, "We're not paying this."

The waiter let out a theatrical gasp like everyone does at the end of a mystery movie when you find out it was the butler who murdered the queen. "Is there an issue?" he asked.

"The food wasn't good," Rose said, holding his stare.

"But, madam, you already ate the food. Every last bit of it. Plus, all of the champagne is gone. How can you expect not to pay?"

"It — DICK!" Brian shouted, not even attempting to cover his mouth. "It wasn't good. It got my friend sick," he said, pointing at Ellen.

Ellen, who was now full on crying, held a napkin to her mouth, nodding.

" 'N' your atmosphere's racist," Jake added, leaning back in his chair, gesturing toward the portraits of various white men and women on the walls. "Where the Black folk at?"

The waiter, seeing that I was the best dressed of the group, shot a terrified, pleading look of desperation my way. I shrugged.

"I see." He straightened out his shirt before retrieving the bill. "If you're not going to pay, then I'll have to get the host."

The waiter power walked toward the host, who swung his head at us, baring cigarette-stained teeth. Red-faced, he whispered into an earpiece.

Three oversize goons in suits started toward the table, getting closer with each passing second.

"What do we do, what do we do, what do we do?" Brian asked, sweat pouring from his face.

"The elevators!" Rose shouted.

We each took off in different directions, causing the three bouncers to separate. Jake knocked one over on his ass, and two pale-faced, powdered-donut-looking women shouted as he crashed into their table, sending their trout into the air like it was jumping for joy.

Rose, with her dirty boots, leapt from table to table, as if she were making her way across a rocky river. Ellen blended in with the crowd, acting like she was talking with various similarly skinned patrons, stealthily making her way out of the sliding glass doors untouched.

They were all in the elevator by the time I got there, and Rose slammed the door Close button with her fist. Just like in every action movie, the doors closed right when the three bruisers showed up.

"Tha's what it is!" Jake screamed, wrapping his large arms around the four of us. But after exiting the elevator, we realized that someone was missing. Brian.

"I thought he was right behind us," I said, watching subsequent elevators arrive without Brian.

"Dang," Jake said. "What now?"

I took a deep breath and let it out. *This wasn't supposed to happen.* "Everyone go home. I'll wait here for him and talk to the cops. It'll be fine."

I returned all of their wallets and everyone except Rose left. "You should leave," I said, looking back at the elevators, anxiously waiting. "I can give you some money for a cab or something."

"I'm okay."

"Where do you live, anyway?"

"Here and there," she said, avoiding eye contact.

"Here and there? C'mon, Rose. You force your way into my life, I go along with it, and that's all you're going to give me? 'Here and there'?"

She plopped down on the floor and started to play with her shoelaces. "Why are you so fucking nosy?"

"Because I don't even know you, and I'm investing my time in you."

She laughed and looked up at me, her eyes shining like bubbles in sunlight. "Your *precious* time," she spat. "I'm fucking homeless. Is that what you want to hear? How I spend some nights in a shelter, others with friends, playing a big game of musical chairs around the city hoping I always land on my feet?"

What the fuck? I thought, unsure if it was a joke, just another way for her to press my buttons. But it'd be some cruel joke. I knelt down beside her. "I didn't know."

"Of course you didn't. No one knows, and I like keeping it that way. I never want to be the girl people pity. Just another sad Black girl in need of saving."

It was crazy to see how she looked then, on the floor of the Time Warner Center, hands tangled in dirty shoelaces, eyes heavy with pain. This wasn't her typical tough self.

"Come on." I extended a hand to her. "You'll come home with me."

"Like I said, I don't want your pity."

"It's not pity; it's just a place to stay. Once you get a job, you'll be making a ton of money in no time and can move out."

"What about Brian?"

"He'll be fine," I said, unsure. "He probably left another way. I'll call him tomorrow, and if things somehow didn't work out, I'll fix it. I promise."

"No. I'm not leaving Brian."

I kept my hand out. "Rose, he will be fine. Trust me on this. Brian's a lot tougher than you think."

She stared at my hand for a few seconds and eventually took it. "Fine. Maybe you're right."

We walked outside and grabbed a cab. As she leaned her head against the window, the lights of New York City traveling across her face like faded spotlights, I turned to her, and asked, "What do you want out of life, Rose? Aside from money?"

"A family," she said, letting out a lungful of air into the cab. "What about you? World domination? Best salesman in the world? Trophy wife who sucks you off every night?"

I shook my head. "No. I just want to make my mom proud."

"I wasn't expecting that." She finally faced me. "Is she hard on you?"

"Yeah," I whispered, looking out the window at all of the buildings blurring into one sloppy mess of a city. "She was."

Having Rose stay over felt like what I imagined having a younger, messy, foul-mouthed sibling was like — one who raided your fridge, left dirty clothes everywhere, and watched endless amounts of Netflix, HBO, and, weirdly, the History Channel until five in the morning. She was annoying as hell, but I can't front, it was nice having some platonic feminine energy around.

"We're low on Cap'n Crunch," Rose announced on Sunday morning, sitting cross-legged on the couch and staring with zombie-like fixation at the TV.

"You mean *you're* low on Cap'n Crunch," I said, shoving her over so I could sit on *my* couch, in *my* apartment, to watch *my* television.

"Weren't you the one who said, 'What's mine is yours, Rose, treat this like it's your own spot'?"

I stared at her, impressed by her relentless wit. But before I could respond, my phone rang.

"Hello?"

"Hello," a robotic voice said. "This call will be recorded. This is a prepaid collect call from" — then I heard, "Brian Grimes," in Brian's trembling, panic-stricken voice — "an inmate at a New York County detention facility. This call is subject to recording and monitoring. To accept charges, press 1."

"Who is it?" Rose asked, still staring at the TV.

"No one." I pressed 1 and shot up from the couch.

From the way she turned and looked at me — eyes narrowed, face scrunched — I could tell she knew I was lying. "Is it Brian? Is he okay?"

"Thank you for using T-Netix," the robotic voice said. "You may start the conversation now."

"Buck?"

"Brian, where are you? We've been wor-

440

ried sick, and Per Se wouldn't give me any information about what happened or where you are. It's been almost two days, man."

"I'm scared, Buck."

"Scared? We just skipped out on the bill, Brian. Relax, it's not like we killed someone. I'll get you out and pay whatever the fine is."

There was a pause, and I imagined Brian dressed in an orange jumpsuit with INMATE in black block letters over his heart, shaking with the pay phone in his hands. "It's not that simple, Buck. I'm at Manhattan Detention Complex, and they *do* think I killed someone."

"Shut the fuck up," I said. "Stop playing. Where are you? I'll come get you."

"I'm not playing — VAGINA! Sorry. I'm serious. I ran down some stairs in the back of Per Se and the cops were there. They grabbed me, read me my rights, and said I'm under arrest for the murder of some guy I'd never even heard of. They brought me in and finally let me have my phone call, so I'm calling you. I don't know what to do, Buck. Tell me what to do. I feel like Wolverine when he was locked up in *Weapon X*."

Tell him what to do? I had no fucking clue. Who was I, Johnnie Cochran? "Brian, just try to relax. Everything will be fine. You

441

didn't do it, so they can't hold you. Let's wait one more day, and if you're not out, I'll speak with someone, maybe Barry, and get you a lawyer. Can you do that? Can you hold out for one more day?"

I heard him fill his lungs and let it out. "Yeah, Buck. Okay. Sounds like a plan. Thank you." *Click.*

"What the fuck is going on?" Rose stood behind me in my bedroom, hands on her hips.

"Brian's in jail somewhere in Manhattan," I said. "They think he killed someone, but he'll be okay. If he's not out tomorrow, I'll get him a lawyer. They can't keep him; he's innocent."

Rose shook her head. "What, you think we live in a world where innocent Black men don't spend five, twenty, or thirty years in jail only to be let out with an apology? Get real, Buckaroo."

"Alright, alright, alright," I muttered, pacing around the apartment, running through every possible scenario. Brian being let out. Brian being falsely imprisoned. Brian committing suicide because he couldn't take prison life. Brian being shanked for a piece of meatloaf.

"What now?" Rose asked. "You're the man with the plans, right?"

442

My phone buzzed. Barry. 9am tomorrow my man. He better be a star. I'm talkin out of this world superstar. Not one of those dwarf stars. He better bring the heat! The fire!

I could think about Brian later. He wasn't going anywhere. This, Barry, was the priority. "The plan is you have an interview," I said to Rose. "Tomorrow. 9 a.m. And you better not fuck it up."

She popped open a soda, chugged half, let out a belch, and smiled. "I thought you'd never ask."

26

We spent all of Sunday reviewing messaging and interview questions, role-playing, and strategizing about how to make sure she got an offer and secured a fair salary that any man, no, any *white* man, would receive.

Come Monday, she was ready, except she didn't have any clothes to wear other than dirty boots, ripped jeans, holey hoodies, and T-shirts emblazoned with names of heavy metal bands. No clothing stores would be open before I had to be at Sumwun for the 7 a.m. meeting, so I called the only person I could think of who was about Rose's size and wouldn't ask too many questions: Marissa.

"Any last words of advice?" Rose asked, leaning into the Tesla's window moments after Chauncey had let her out in front of the Flat-iron Building. She looked more like a deer in headlights than I expected. Good thing she had more than two hours of waiting time to sort it out.

"Never look a baboon in the eye," Marissa said from the far end of the back seat. "They take it as a challenge and will attack."

Rose and I exchanged confused looks. "Anything *else*?" she asked me.

I grabbed her hand. "Always be better."

"Better than who?"

"You know."

We held each other's eyes for a moment, then she pulled away, straightened up, and walked into the building.

At twelve, I got a call. It was Rose. "How'd it go?" I asked.

"I'm not sure," she said. "The VP of sales, some chick from California, asked a ton of questions. The CEO popped in and was ultra-aggressive, but I just stared him in the eye and didn't back down. I met a few of their AEs, two twins who looked like extras from *Entourage.*"

"But did they give you an offer?" I asked, about to faint. "Did they discuss salary?"

"No," she said. "Does that mean I didn't get it?"

FUCK! Barry was going to destroy me. Everything I had, the cushy lifestyle, the power, the freedom, it was all gone. If she didn't get an offer on the spot, she didn't crush it, meaning she failed.

"I don't know," I said, coughing, trying to perk up. "It could mean anything. But, uh, as long as you did your best, that's all I can ask for."

"You sound like the Black Mister Rogers," she said. "Have you heard from Brian?"

"No, not yet." I was going to throw up. Between her bombing the interview and Brian still being locked up, I couldn't take it. "I gotta go, Rose. I'll see you at home."

A few hours and a toilet bowl full of vomit later, Barry called.

"Hey, Barry," I whispered, afraid.

"Buck, my man. What's shakin'?"

"Nothing, at Sumwun. You know."

"Fuck yeah, that's why I love you. Always working. Listen —"

"Listen, Barry," I said, interrupting. "Before you lay in on me. There was a mix-up. I was supposed to send someone else, but he got arrested, and I know she wasn't ready, but she was the only other one I could send. I thought she would be good, but —"

"What the fuck are you talking about? I didn't know you were sending a girl, but she blew them away!"

"What?" I asked, gripping my phone tighter with my sweaty hand. "Are you serious?"

"Serious as cholera, homie. The CEO was so happy he said he had to call the board before giving the offer to make sure they could afford her. Said something about them both being metalheads and legit being afraid to look her in the eye. Like a baboon. You're never supposed to look a baboon in the eye, my man, did you know that? They think it's a challenge and will attack."

"Yeah," I said, relieved. "I heard that before. So you're saying she's hired?"

"As hired as one of those expensive escorts politicians need to pay off with hush money. As hired as a Mexican on the side of the road who's looking —"

"I get it, Barry. That's amazing to hear, man. I'm gonna call and give her the good news. Thanks for letting me know."

"No," he said, the sound of metal clinking against metal, like a belt unbuckling. "Thank *you,* Buck. The CEO already made an intro to his dad for me, so I'm one step closer to buying the Giants. Do you have any more SDRs? I know he'll need more. Hell, we can staff all of our portfolios with them if they're as good as this girl."

I laughed. "I think I can do that. Let me get back to you."

When I got home, Rose and I cracked open a bottle of wine and celebrated with some feature on the History Channel about all of the US presidents who fathered mulatto babies with their "Black wenches." In the middle of it, I got a collect call. Brian.

"Yo," I said, drunk and weary.

"Buck, thank God," he said, speaking quickly. "I'm getting out tomorrow. They called a lineup for someone who supposedly witnessed the murder, and it was just me and five other guys who looked nothing alike except that we were Black and had bad acne. They say I'll get out tomorrow once they complete the paperwork."

I bolted off the couch, spilling an entire bag of nacho cheese Doritos all over the floor. "YES!" I shouted, pumping a Black Power fist in the air.

"What is it?" Rose asked, her face covered in orange cheese, eyes as red as Lucifer's balls. "Is he free?"

I nodded, and she started doing some weird dance that looked like she was in a mosh pit at a country hoedown.

"I'll have Chauncey get you tomorrow and bring you straight to my place. He has an extra key," I said, smiling so hard, my face hurt.

"Thanks, Buck. For everything," he said. "Don't know what I'd do without you, big bro."

"Of course, Brian. See you soon."

After work on Tuesday, I got home and found Brian on the couch, rocking back and forth in the fetal position like he was in a trance.

"Yo," I said, grabbing his shoulder.

"Fuck!" he shouted, staring at me with a face full of fear as if he had just realized I was there.

I knelt beside him. "Brian, you good? It's all over, man. You didn't get turned into a punk in a few days, did you?"

He turned away from me, hugging a cushion tighter. "No, but I've never been — *SHIT!* — sorry. I've never been that scared in my entire life, Buck. People were screaming all night, the food was just stale PB and J sandwiches, and it felt like, I don't know — *COCK!* — like the people in charge didn't care what happened."

"That's the American judicial system for you, Brian. But you're good, man. I'm sorry that happened."

"It's okay," he said, sniffling into the pillow. "It wasn't your fault."

I scratched the back of my head and looked around the room. "I mean, it sort of was, but I won't let anything like that happen to you ever again. I promise."

449

"I know, Buck. I know."

It was a little corny, but I didn't know what else to do, so I just sat on the couch and held him for a while, realizing that the consequences of my actions were real and that I had to be more careful.

Reader: The things we do and say on this earth, whether as salespeople or just people, matter. As do the things we don't do or say. To be a salesperson is to believe that you are the master of your own destiny, something never to be taken lightly.

Rose was supposed to get back after I did since she had to sign her formal offer letter. We invited Ellen and Jake over to celebrate the first of the bunch getting a job and Brian getting out of jail, and to talk about who would get the next interview and other logistical questions.

The buzzer went off.

"Hello?"

"Buckaroo, it's Rose. The papers are officially signed, sealed, and delivered."

"Rose? Why are you buzzing?"

"Just come downstairs," she said. "There's something I want to show you."

Brian and I grabbed our coats, and

hopped into the elevator. When we stepped outside, no one was there.

"Over here!" someone shouted from Stuyvesant Square Park. I looked over and saw a group of about fifteen people huddled around the flower garden in the park's center.

I turned to Brian. "You know anything about this?"

"No, how could I?"

We crossed the street and entered the chilly, dimly lit park. As we neared the group, I made out the shapes of Rose, Ellen, and Jake standing near other people wearing puffy jackets, beanies, and scarves.

"Okay," I said, shivering. "What's going on?"

The three of them smiled at one another.

I nodded at the small crowd behind them. "Are you with them?" I took a closer look and realized that the people wearing the beanies and scarves all shared something in common: black and brown skin.

"Yeah," Rose said, stepping forward. "And so are you."

"What the fuck are you talking about? It's freezing. Cut the shit and let's go up. It's time to celebrate."

"Each one teach one, bruh," Jake said, lining up next to Rose.

451

"Why do I feel like I'm being ambushed?"

"What you did," Rose said, tears pooling in her eyes under the orange glow of the park's lights. "You've changed my life."

"You've given us a gift," Ellen said, joining Jake and Rose.

"None of you except Rose even has a job." I turned around and walked back toward the apartment. "So quit whatever this is and let's go."

"These people," Rose said, nodding to the group behind them, who were staring at us. "They want to learn from you, just like we have. They want to learn how to sell."

"You promised you wouldn't invite anyone else."

"I didn't. Well, not really. After I signed my offer letter, I posted on Facebook, saying, 'I got a job! This girl is one happy camper.' After that, friends, mostly people like me, who are smart but need help, started to ask questions about what the job was and how I got it. I didn't think it'd do any harm, so I told them about my 'sensei,' and I may have accidentally said a few of us were meeting tonight."

I looked at the group of people, who were still staring at us, then at the four of them. "You four. My apartment. Now."

Once we were all in the living room, I

rained fury on them. "You're taking advantage of me!" I shouted. "Each and every one of you. I'm not some sort of charity. This isn't Buck's Sales Bootcamp for the Downtrodden. Who do you think I am? Tell them, Brian; tell them how wrong this all is."

"I mean" — he shrugged — "why not, right?"

"Why not?" I stormed toward him and shook the shit out of him. "Why not? Because I have other responsibilities. I have Sumwun, everything with Barry, my social life, my —"

"What?" Rose asked. "The women, the drugs, and the fame? C'mon, Buckaroo, we all know that shit leaves you empty inside. Last week was the most fun you've had in a long time, and you can't even admit it."

"We all here with you for a reason, Mr. Buck," Jake said. "This, us, you, it's no coincidence."

"I agree," Ellen added. "You have the opportunity to change lives."

"To make your mom proud," Rose said, standing up. My heart tightened at her words.

"Come here," she said, staring out the window.

I slowly made my way over. "What do you see?" she asked.

I looked out and saw more than a dozen people still huddled outside, looking up at the window toward us, toward me. "I see people."

"*Your* people. And you have a responsibility, Buckaroo. Whether you realize it or not."

In that moment, I thought of something I'd been trying to block out for months: Ma's letter.

I looked out the window, closed my eyes, and heard Ma's voice. *It's the duty of every man and woman who has achieved some success in life to pass it on, because when we're gone, what matters most isn't what we were able to attain but who we were able to help.*

She was right. And I guessed Rose, Ellen, Brian, and Jake were too.

"We need rules," I said, facing them. "No one can know I'm involved."

"Done," Jake said. The others nodded.

"What will we call it?" Brian asked.

"How 'bout the African Society of Salespeople?" Jake said, scanning the room for agreement.

Rose palmed her face and shook her head. "That spells A-S-S, you ass."

"Okay, what about the Salespeople of Color," Ellen said. "S-O-C doesn't mean anything."

"That's wack," I said.

454

Brian clapped his hands. We all looked at him. "Rose, what was it you wrote on your Facebook status? You were one what?"

"One happy camper."

"Yeah, that," he said, looking around the room. "Why don't we call ourselves the Happy Campers? It's fun, and if anyone accidentally lets the name slip, no one will have a clue who we are."

"Fine," I said. "We can change it if we need to."

" 'N' it's only for Black folk, right?" Jake asked.

"People of color," I said. I thought back to Sumwun and every other tech startup sales team out there. They weren't missing just Black people, but *all* people of color.

"Perfect," Rose said. "Now that that's settled, I think it's time to invite all of these freezing Happy Campers inside."

When we got back to the park, the group stared at me like starving refugees. "Rule number one," I shouted, making them all straighten up. "Only friends are allowed in, and they must be people of color. We're not against white people, but we are simply ignoring them. They've had a mile head start and we're only a few feet off the starting line.

"Rule number two: you may know me

from the news or some other way, but no one else can know I am involved in this. Letting outsiders know I'm leading the charge will only attract unwanted attention.

"Rule number three: you will use what I teach you for good and to get ahead. Not for manipulation nor the mental, emotional, financial, or social harm of others.

"And rule number three-point-five, because, as Jeffrey Gitomer says, you always have to give a little extra: if this is your first night with the Happy Campers, you have to role-play, which is our version of bare-knuckle fighting. The main difference is that the wounds you receive won't heal as easily.

"If you break any of these rules, any at all, not only will you cease to be a Happy Camper, but the entire group will be dissolved," I said, wiping my hands. "Understand?"

They all nodded.

"I need to hear you say it, that you understand."

"Yes," a few of them said, others eventually echoing.

"Any questions?"

"No," they replied, shaking harder than before, the hunger in their eyes and bones obvious.

"Good," I said, stretching out my hands. "Who's ready to learn how to sell?"

"Good," I said, stretching out my hands. "Who's ready to learn how to sell?"

27

On Saturday, twenty Happy Campers descended on Bed-Stuy to set up our headquarters, which was none other than 84 Vernon Avenue, the brownstone I grew up in. I hadn't been there since the day I closed Barry Dee, having immediately moved in with Rhett before finding the spot on Seventeenth Street.

"Dang, what in the world happened here?" Jake asked. There was broken glass all over the kitchen and living-room floors, yellowed pieces of paper lying on the overturned table, smashed chairs, fist-size holes in the walls, and a thick sheet of dust covering every surface.

"Let's open these windows," Rose said. The new recruits jumped into action.

I walked over to the kitchen and picked up the two letters I had tossed there six months ago — the one from Ma to me and the unsigned contract to sell. Since Ma had never signed it, and I sure as hell hadn't, the place was still ours; all I had to do was pay the rising property taxes that seemed to be whitening up the neighborhood day by day. Till taxes do us part.

"Dry-erase boards over there," Rose ordered, pointing to the wall across from the old couch. "Someone sweep up that glass and toss out anything else that's broken — mugs, plates, these tables and chairs."

I folded the letters and placed them into their envelopes. I felt a hand on my shoulder. "Huh?" I asked, seeing Rose looking up at me, confusion on her face.

"I asked if it's cool for us to throw out a bunch of stuff. We're going to start unpacking the U-Haul. You okay?"

"Oh, yeah. It's just that I haven't been back here since my mom died, so . . ."

"Can't be easy. But let me take care of all of this. Go do what you have to do. We got it under control."

"Thanks," I said. I remembered that I had exactly two things I needed to do.

Down the stairs. Turn the corner. I stared at Mr. Aziz's bodega and saw a steady stream of Saturday-morning traffic entering empty-handed and exiting with egg sandwiches, Arizona iced teas, and cigarettes.

Only one gargoyle was out: Wally Cat.

"What up, Wally Cat?" I asked, my nerves banging like bells in the wind.

"That you, Darren? I ain' seen you in what, half a year, nigga? How you doin'?"

"I'm aight." I wished there was an extra crate for me. Like before. "What about you, man? What's good over here?"

He shot a stream of spit into the street and looked over his shoulders. "Ain' shit, you know. Same ole same ole. More whities movin' in, niggas movin' out. It's the damn circle of life out here."

I had to do something, say something, to let him know I was sorry. About everything. I planted my ass on the curb and looked up to meet his eyes. "Yo, Wally Cat, I'm —"

"Don' you dare say you sorry, nigga. Everyone makes choices, you know that. And you gotta live with yours, 'specially whatchu did to Percy. You know you was wrong for that, right?"

Mr. Rawlings. I saw him only in my nightmares.

I tried to gather some spit and clear my throat, but it was bonedry. "Yeah," I whispered, looking away from Wally Cat. "I know."

"Good, 'cause every action has an equal and opposite reaction, nigga. And you betta hope he's aight so you don' get yours. But"

— he placed a hard hand on my shoulder — "I been watchin' you on TV, seein' you pop up in the newspaper. Seems like you made a new life for yourself in the WWW. So I'm proud of you. Yo' momma would be too."

I can't lie; hearing that made me feel a little better, but the feeling didn't stick. Wally Cat was an OG and having his respect meant a lot, but I still had bridges to rebuild. And he couldn't do that for me.

"Thanks, Wally Cat. I appreciate that more than you know." I stood up and dusted my ass off. "Where's Jason at? He still on the corner?"

He nodded at Jason's corner. "What it look like?"

"Where is he?"

"Mickey D's," he said, finally breaking out his big-mouthed smile. "Boy stopped tryna be a gangster and became a man."

"And Soraya?" I asked, trying to be casual. "You seen her around here lately?"

Wally Cat sucked his teeth and leaned back on his crate, nodding at Mr. Aziz's bodega. "She over there, you fool."

"Thanks, Wally Cat." I dapped him up and he pulled me in for an embrace, holding on longer than he ever had before.

"You didn' fuck no snow bunnies, did

461

you?" His grip was tight, with grave concern in his voice.

"Nah," I quickly whispered.

He laughed. "Good. Seven years bad luck, don' forget now. You gon' be stickin' 'round a while?"

"Somethin' like that," I yelled back as I crossed the street, opting to begin with the easier of my two tasks.

There were two McDonald's about the same distance from us — one on Broadway and the other on Fulton — and I knew that Jason would never work at the one on Fulton because he once said he found a fully fried chicken head in his six-piece McNuggets. But then again, I never could've pictured him working at a Mickey D's, so what did I know?

I jogged to the one on Broadway, looked through the window, and found him behind the counter clad in a short-sleeved blue button-up, a black hat with a big McDonald's *M* on the front, and a "*Please* kill me now!" face as he surveyed the endless line of Black and brown families waiting for their Sausage McGriddles and burnt coffee.

"Yo," I said. He looked up from the register, surprise flashing across his face, then anger.

"Whatchu doin' here, nigga? Tryna buy a McFlurry?"

"What are *you* doin' here?"

"What it look like? Makin' an honest livin'. Prolly more than I can say for you."

He looked the same but slightly older. He stood up straighter and moved his body with more control.

"Whatever, man. Listen, I'm here with an opportunity. To help."

He stretched his head over the register, scanning the line snaking out the door. "I don' need your help. If you ain' gonna buy anything, step up out the line. You holdin' it up."

"Tha's the truth!" an older heavyset man said from behind me. "This ain' no barbershop. Cut the talkin' and get to walkin! I'm hungry as a motherfucka and got diabetes."

"Then why are you at McDonald's?" I asked, silencing him. "Anyway, what I got will beat eight whatever an hour and help you get your moms out the projects faster than this. If you're down, meet me at my place on Vernon in two hours. Soraya will be there."

"Get to steppin'," the heavyset man shouted, muttering about kids these days, no respect, and blood sugar.

I jogged back to the corner and leaned on

463

Wally Cat, catching my breath. "One down," I said, plastered in sweat. "One to go."

"Damn, nigga!" Wally Cat shouted. "You wetter than a drug mule in front of TSA. Wipe yourself off and go do the damn thing 'fore you freeze up."

I wiped my face, straightened my clothes, and set off for the bodega.

The bells clanged as I opened the door. Soraya was behind the candy-and-cigarette-filled display, but she didn't see me. She was leaning over the counter, smiling as she twirled this tall, fair-skinned, almost-white-but-not-quite guy's beard. Not knowing how else to interrupt whatever the fuck was going on, I walked out, then back in, pushing the door open harder so the bells clanged louder.

"D?" Soraya said, eyes wide as she yanked her finger out of the guy's beard. "Are you okay?"

"Yeah, hey," I said, walking closer. She was wearing a mustard-colored sweater with the initials ZNH written in white cursive on it.

"What's up?" the guy asked, cutting his eyes at me before turning to Soraya.

"Jalal" — she peeled her eyes off me — "this is Darren, I mean Buck. An old friend. Buck, this is Jalal, my —"

"Boyfriend," he said, and extended a beige hand. I grabbed it, then turned back to Soraya.

"What happened to nursin' school?"

"I dunno." She rubbed the back of her head. "I don' think it was for me. I probably couldn' be a real nurse."

"Why not?"

"Because I have responsibilities, like the stores and . . . other stuff. I also gotta firsthand look at what achievin' your dreams can do to a person."

A chill ran down my spine, and it took everything inside me to hold her stare, that piercing gaze that turned me from flesh and bone straight into glass.

"She's always busy," Jalal interjected. "Busy, busy, busy. It's why I love her, but I still don't know why she loves me."

His words sounded like a threat.

"Can you come over to my spot? In two hours? Jason will be there, and I wanna show you somethin'. Jus' as friends," I said, a little louder so Jalal would back off.

"Who said we're friends?" she asked, her face turning into stone.

I swallowed hard. "Nah, I'm jus' sayin' —"

"Jus' sayin' what? Why're you even here?"

"Yeah," Jalal said, stepping between me

and the counter. "I think you gotta leave."

I looked him up and down, and laughed. "I think you don' know who you're talkin' to, *halal.* Now back the fuck up before I show you."

He stared at me for a second before turning to Soraya.

"Jus' step outside for a second, babe," she said, rubbing his arm. "He's harmless, I promise."

"Whatever." He bumped my shoulder as he pushed past me, bells clanging on his way out.

She rounded the display and stood in front of me, level with my shoulders but grilling me as if she were seven feet tall. "Now what the fuck was that, huh?" she said. "You think you can come here, outta nowhere, and act like you run the place?"

"Nah, I —"

"Nah is right, Darren, Buck, or whoever the hell you wanna be today. You got ten seconds before I grab my broom and clean the floor with you. Speak."

I took a breath, realizing that this would be harder than I thought. "Listen, I'm jus' tryna make things right, Soraya. I know I did a lot of fucked-up shit, and I'm not comin' here tryna start any trouble, but jus' come through so I can show you what I'm

466

doin'. If you're not about it and still hate me, I'll never speak to you again. But I'm the same person you used to know."

She turned away from me and went back around the counter. "No, I don' think so."

"Please, Soraya. Jus' gimme ten minutes. I promise it'll be worth it."

She clenched her jaw and fixed her eyes on mine as if she were trying to find a piece of the old me. Then she closed her eyes and shook her head. "I don' think it's a good idea, but you said Jason's goin'?"

"Yeah, he'll be there," I replied, unsure if he was actually going to show.

"Fine. If he's goin', then maybe I'll join him. But if you try to pull any slick shit, I'm out and we're never talkin' again. Got it?"

I sighed with relief. "I got it."

Two hours later, the house wasn't spotless, but it did have new tables, chairs, dry-erase boards, a few telephones, and even a couch.

"So," Rose said, standing in Mr. Rawlings's old living room. "This garden level will be for basic theory, the first floor will have a room where people can practice calls, and another where they can sleep if they're tired. The second floor is mostly for role-playing, the kitchen for food, and the living room can be like a meeting space. Upstairs, we basically kept your bedroom like it was but turned it into more of an office for you."

I looked around the room, now empty save for a few piles of trash.

"Who was this?" Rose asked, inserting a half-torn photo into my hand. "You, your mom, and grandpa?"

I quickly tossed the photo onto the trash pile. "No, must've been someone the previous tenant knew," I said. "But, wow, HQ is starting to look good. You sure this is all gonna work?"

"It will if you want it to."

"And what about the garden in the back? What're we going to do with that?"

"Leave it as it is. We can use it as one of those little home farms that're every hipster's wet dream."

When we got upstairs, people were already role-playing. There were half a dozen "Ring ring"s going off, and Brian, Jake, and Ellen screamed, "*Click!* Nope! Try again!" with glee.

"What's all this?" someone said from the door.

Soraya and Jason stood there, stretching their necks to look around the room.

"This some Black Panther shit?" Jason asked, stepping inside, scanning the room. He was still in his uniform and smelled like

French fries.

"Something like that," Rose said, stepping forward. "Who the fuck are you, the Black Ronald McDonald?"

"Chill," I said. "These are old friends."

"Not really," Jason said.

"Then get the fuck out of here," Rose snapped, burning a hole in Jason's head.

"Let me have a moment with them, Rose." She looked up at me, concerned. "Please."

She turned around, clapping at the recruits. "C'mon, c'mon, c'mon. You want to be broke forever? Put some energy into these role-plays. Spit!"

"New girlfriend?" Soraya asked, nodding in Rose's direction.

"Nah. She's like a little sister."

"Aight, nigga. I don' know why you invited us here, or what this all" — Jason waved his hands around — "even is. But if you don' get to explainin' real quick, we out."

I took a breath and slowly let it out. "Okay. First, I asked you here to apologize."

"For?" Soraya asked.

"For bein' an asshole. Actin' like I was better than both of you. Forgettin' where I came from. For —"

"Sucker punchin' me like a li'l bitch," Jason added.

"For sucker punchin' you," I whispered,

469

"like a li'l bitch."

Soraya slowly clapped. Everyone in the room stopped what they were doing and stared at us. "Who knew this day would come? The mighty Darren, I mean Buck, Vender would admit he was wrong. He mus' be in trouble," she said, turning to Jason.

He smiled. "Mus' be."

"I'm not. The second reason I asked you here was to see if you wanted to join us."

"Who's us?" Jason asked.

"The Happy Campers," I said, waving my hand around the room.

"Happy what? Nigga, I sell Happy Meals all day. I don' need no more happy anything in my life."

"It's jus' a name," I said. "It can change."

"And what do the *Happy Campers* do?" Soraya asked.

"We sell. I'm teachin' all of them how to do what I do so they can get better jobs, make money, and get ahead. To fix the game."

Jason shook his head and laughed. "And what's the catch, huh? We become twenty-first-century enslaved people to some white man on Wall Street?"

"There is no catch. All I'll do," I said, looking back at Rose, Jake, Ellen, and Brian. "I mean all *we'll* do is teach you and set

470

you up with opportunities. If one is right, you take it and hopefully help others along the way."

"What makes you think I wanna learn how to do what you do?" Soraya asked, looking like she was about to swing on me. "That either of us wanna be a parta the world that turned you into an asshole?"

"Because neither of you wanna stay here forever. Jason," — I turned to him — "you wanna sell Chicken McNuggets for the rest of your life? Or go back to pushin' weight?"

He clenched his jaw, and said, "Of course not, nigga. I'm tryna get my momma out the projects ASAP. Not tryna be stuck here like every other nigga who never got out."

"Tha's right. And you, Soraya, you're tellin' me you *really* wanna run Mr. Aziz's stores until you're forty? I get it if you don' wanna be a nurse, but what we'll teach you will allow you to be free to do whatever you want. It's about more than workin' at some tech startup in Manhattan forever. Once you learn how to sell, to truly sell, anything is possible."

Reader: Quote that last sentence.

I looked down. My shirt was drenched with sweat. My heart thumped like a bass drum. "I can't go back in time," I whispered. "But I can help make your future better."

They looked at each other for a long time. Jason whispered something to her, then she whispered something back. They turned around and headed for the door.

I bent down and sat on the floor, exhausted. I'd given it my all. I understood why they didn't trust me, why they wouldn't want to have anything to do with me.

"Aye!" Jason called.

When I looked up, they were both standing in the doorway, smiling.

"We're in," Soraya said. "But only as long as you keep it one hundred with us. The minute this goes south, we're out. You got it?"

"Yeah," I said, finally feeling like I understood who Ma was talking about when she said she wanted me to be who I was always meant to be. "I got it."

"And I gotta boyfriend now. So don' think this means there's anything between us."

"I got that too."

"So where the fuck do we start?" Jason asked, taking off his Mickey D's hat and dunking it into the garbage. "I'm tryna make that Daddy Warbucks paper."

■ ■ ■ ■

V.
CLOSE

■ ■ ■ ■

The good and the great are only
separated by the willingness to sacrifice.
— KAREEM ABDUL-JABBAR

V

CLOSE

28

6 MONTHS LATER

I know. The turns in this story are half absurd, half jaw-dropping, and a whole heaping of crazy. But I assure you, every single line is true. I've taken countless hours to teach you how to get ahead, to unshackle yourself from the fetters of the twenty-first century, and my job is almost done. But before I go, you must be curious as to how I ended up where I am today — writing to you from the penthouse of a one-hundred-one-year-old building worth millions of dollars that overlooks Central Park.

Well, I suppose all good things must come to an end, including the picture I painted for you when we met. Because, while I am writing this cautionary memoir from the highest floor of my building, the room I'm sitting in is six by eight feet. And if you need me to spell it out, that means I'm in prison — Lincoln Correctional Facility. Inmate number 8121988, nice to meet you. And now I'm sure as hell that you have more questions than a kid with ADHD watching porn for the first time, so let me explain how I became one of the one in three Black males who finds himself locked up. It all came down to one night.

Once we got the Happy Campers up and running, which took no time with the help of Rose, Brian, Ellen, and Jake, our numbers grew by twenty new recruits a week. That was even with us all working on it only part-time. Rose was in charge of making sure everything ran smoothly. Ellen created "homework," which consisted of dangerous and almost life-threatening assignments for the recruits to execute. Brian was a counselor, ensuring that everyone found jobs. Jake took care of our financial and legal apparatus. And what did I do? Well, I was our fearless leader, the HNIC, and my job was to rally everyone behind our mission, be the final say on disputes, and ensure that we spread faster than syphilis in the sixties.

You see, in addition to directly bringing Happy Campers into Sumwun, the way it all worked was that I'd recommend Happy Camper SDRs to Barry and his portfolio companies. After surviving our top-notch sales boot camp, the SDRs would, of course, destroy the interview and get hired. Once hired, they'd recommend one or two other Happy Campers to the company, who would, of course, also be the best SDRs the company had ever laid their pretty blue or green eyes on.

At tech startups, there's this ridiculous thing called a referral fee. So if I refer a friend to a job at my company and they get hired, I get a few thousand dollars, maybe more. The Happy Campers had a tradition of always donating half of your first paycheck to the organization as well as at least twenty-five percent of any referral fees you earned. And if the average SDR was getting paid a base salary of $40,000 a year, average referral fees were $5,000 per referral, and we had more than 250 Happy Campers, well . . .

This is getting more technical than it has to be. But all you need to know is that within six months we had close to half a million dollars in our bank account, a dozen chapters in every major American tech hub — New York, Boston, Austin, San Francisco, Raleigh, Seattle — and were expanding internationally to places like Dublin, London, and Tel Aviv, all while remaining anonymous. You know what? Let me shut the fuck up and just show you how it would go.

Picture two people, Mary and Denmark. Mary's a senior SDR, maybe even a manager, at some bullshit startup in San Francisco. And Denmark just moved there from, say, Harlem. They don't know each other, but through the network, Mary heard there may be a brother heading her way. Denmark walks into the bullshit startup, and since Mary is one of the few Black people there, if not the only one, some pigment-deficient higher-up, of course, micro-aggressively suggests she meet with Denmark to "you know, make him comfortable enough to show you the *real him.*"

Mary is sitting behind a desk. Denmark enters. Now watch closely. Mary, smiling, well dressed, and confident as a boss-ass bitch (BAB), will say, "How are you today?"

Denmark, breathing a sigh of relief as he hears the cue, answers with something like "Happy, thank you. How are you?"

Mary, now understanding that she is among family, says, "Happy as a camper," before offering Denmark her right fist. To seal the deal and fully verify who Denmark is, Denmark bumps Mary's fist and they each bring it to their chests — left side over the heart — twice. They'll laugh, chat about mutual connections, and Mary will give Denmark the lay of the bullshit company's land — fair starting salaries, who's ass he needs to kiss in the interview, overseerlike folks to watch out for, and everything else he needs to know in order to navigate that instance of the Hundred Acre Peckerwood. *Whoosh! Bang! Poof!* Another young person of color is on their way to fat-pocketed professional success. And so the cycle continues.

"But — but that's unfair!" someone might cry, blue blood running through protruding veins on their white neck. "This is worse than affirmative action!" they shout, asking themselves how this happened, how good white folk like themselves managed to let a group of elite minority salespeople slip through the cracks. Well, to that I say, think of this as long-overdue reparations. But instead of waiting for the government to give it to us, we took it. But don't fret, because we eventually found ourselves under attack, which is where I'll pick up our story. This would be six months after the founding of the Happy Campers, in September, still in the clutches of a humid, swamplike New York City summer.

It was a Saturday morning, which meant it

was time for Hush Harbor: the weekly meeting where every Happy Camper around the world gathered to hear the latest updates, air grievances, welcome new recruits, celebrate wins, and, of course, grill me during a fifteen-minute Q&A.

I was in my old bedroom — which, thanks to Rose the Builder, was now my office — reviewing updates and issues, and trying to memorize every member's name when there was a knock at the door.

"Come in," I said, not making an effort to look up.

"D," Soraya said, holding herself as she slowly walked in, her cheeks damp with tears.

I jumped up and ran toward her, making sure not to touch her. It was a rule we'd established when she joined. "What's goin' on, Soraya?"

Within a week of joining the Happy Campers, Soraya had landed a job at a healthcare startup and was making more money than most of the other people we placed. I'd even apologized to Mr. Aziz for being an asshole, and he accepted it, so I had no idea what could've been troubling her.

"I jus' dumped Jalal," she said, plopping down on my bed, which Rose had kept in case I ever wanted to crash.

I won't lie; seeing Soraya sitting on my bed and hearing that she just dumped that clown made me smile, but I quickly wiped it off. "Why? I thought you were two were straight?"

"Me too. But he couldn' keep up. The new job, new friends, new money. All of it was a lot for him, and he became insecure and controllin'."

I laughed. "Sounds familiar."

"Shut up," she said, punching my shoulder. "But, forreal, I'm sad because I thought he was the one. I try to be strong, but I feel like I'm gonna wake up and be fifty and alone with an apartment full of cats."

Before I could think, I grabbed her shoulder. "You're one of the strongest people I know, Soraya. If the guy couldn' cut it, he wasn' right for you. People either bring you up or down, and if it's down, they gotta bounce. No matter how hard it is. But" — I lifted her chin — "don' sweat it. You'll find the right guy. You're young, beautiful, out of this world intelligent, and only a li'l bit of a punk."

"Asshole." She slapped the shit out of my arm.

Another knock at the door. "Yeah?"

The door slowly opened, and a short light-skinned kid with glasses two sizes too big poked his head in. "Um, S-s-ensei Buck, sir, I'm sorry to b-b-other you, but —"

"Come in, Trey. What'd I tell you about looking shook all the time? This is how you ended up as my assistant instead of getting a real job."

"Y-y-yes, sir," he said, looking at his feet. "But I like being your assistant. I like helping the m-m-move—"

"Movement," Soraya said, smiling as she patted a space next to her. "It's okay, Trey. You know he's harmless."

Treyborn Percival Evans, clutching a notebook to his chest, sat down and smiled at Soraya. The kid stuttered worse than a scratched CD and always meant well.

After hearing us getting rowdy one day, he just knocked on the door and asked what was going on. Rose, seeing this small kid with ripped clothes and dirty sneakers who reminded her of herself, brought him upstairs, gave him some food, then presented him to me.

"What's your name?"

"Tr-tr-treyborn Percival Evans, sir," he said, avoiding eye contact.

"Okay, Trey. Nice to meet you. How can I help you?"

He stared at his shoes. "I d-d-on't know,

sir. But I need a j-j-j—"

"Job? You need a job?"

He nodded.

"Maybe I can help you, Trey. But I'm going to need you to pick your head up. No one we work with ever hangs their head, cool?"

He looked up and finally made eye contact even though it was obviously uncomfortable for him.

"Good. Quick learner."

I told him about the Happy Campers, and he said he'd love to join. But after a month of training, we realized that he was one of the few people we encountered who didn't take to sales, so I asked him to be my assistant, and he'd been my right-hand man and friend ever since.

"What is it, Trey?"

"It's t-t-time for H-h-hush Harbor, Sensei Buck. Everyone's w-w-waiting for you."

"Well, let's not make them wait any longer then. Tell them I'll be right there."

"Yes, sir," he said, beelining out of the room.

"Big Bad Buck," Soraya said, wiggling her fingers at me. "Such a scary, scary guy. Who knew?"

I laughed. "Right?" She got up and made her way to the door, but I grabbed her wrist.

"You gonna be okay?"

"Yeah. It'll be fine. Thanks for bein' here."

We stared at each other for a while, electricity crackling between us. I swore we were about to cross another line, but she quickly turned around and walked out. Her scent of cinnamon and cocoa butter lingered in the air — a cloud in the shape of her body.

The living room and kitchen were bursting at the seams. Happy Campers of almost every color, religion, sexual orientation, and gender presentation sat on tables, chairs, the kitchen counter, windowsills, and the floor, forming a circle. In addition to the faces that streamed in from our branches around the world, Happy Campers on the other floors of 84 Vernon also videoconferenced in. I swear, when you walked in and saw a bunch of Ugandan, Mexican, Jamaican, Chinese, Bolivian, Indian, Iranian, and other young men and women sitting in one room, you'd think you were at a Model UN meeting.

I put on my new glasses, stood behind a mahogany lectern in the middle of the circle, and said, "How are you?"

"Happy!" they shouted, like it was Christmas.

"Happy as what?" I asked, beaming from ear to ear as I swung around the podium like some overpaid, overnourished, and oversexed Southern preacher.

"A camper!" they replied, smashing fists into their chests twice.

"That's what I like to hear," I said, peering at the papers in front of me. "This has been an exciting week. With the expansion of our London chapter, we now have almost three hundred Happy Campers worldwide. Let's give it up for Joe Knight, Jimmy Somerset, and Mary Prince for leading the charge across the pond."

Three floating heads smiled from each of the many screens on the walls as the room exploded in applause.

"Okay," I continued. "We're growing at an insane clip, which is excellent. Almost all new recruits find a job within a month of joining. And from the looks of all of you, our diversity efforts, headed by Rose, are going well, so let's clap it up for her."

Rose kissed Dolores, a Mexican transplant from California, on the lips, stood, and bowed to applause before taking her seat.

"Question." A tall Chinese girl stood, wiping black bangs out of her face.

"Wu Zhao?"

"What about the recent video?" she asked.

"I'm pretty sure all of our growth has also attracted" — she paused — "hostility from others."

"You mean white people?" a dark round Ghanaian named Kujoe said from the kitchen counter behind me.

I turned to Trey. "What're they referring to?"

"I-i-it's nothing, Sensei B-b-uck. Seriously," he said, widening his eyes at Wu Zhao.

"Definitely something," someone said through one of the screens.

"This is why we should let whites in!" Diego, an Afro-Colombian sitting on the floor, shouted. "It's the twenty-first century. I get that we always say they had a head start, that —"

"That they created the game, like the Parker Brothers and Monopoly, while we minorities" — I stepped from behind the podium and walked toward him — "constructed the pieces even though we weren't able to play. But when we were allowed to, we realized the game was fixed with all kinds of rules that were created to handicap us, to make us never able to win.

"But there was a certain knowledge imparted to the people who worked with their hands and built the game from the ground up, like our parents, their parents, and their parents, going back to wherever we come from. And now it's up to us to fix the game and help others, like you, Diego, to learn how to do the same to get ahead. So what were you saying?"

"Just. Just that maybe that video, you know, uh, that group maybe formed because we, we didn't let white people in."

I walked back to the podium and nodded to Trey. "Throw it up."

On the screens appeared a dozen almost identical white guys and girls sitting on miniature thrones, one leg crossed over the other; wearing red velvet jackets; and staring straight-faced into the camera.

"America is under attack," a disembodied narrator bellowed. "But to be more specific, White America is under attack. Today" — the Ivy League–looking fraternity bros in ties and sorority sisters in skirts stared straight ahead — "it is a crime to be white. A crime to have money. A crime to be straight. A crime to be Christian and everything else our beautiful land was founded on two hundred thirty-seven years ago."

"What the fuck is this?" I asked, looking around the room. Everyone's eyes were fixed on the screens.

"J-j-just keep watching, Sensei Buck,"

Trey said.

"Every day, we who built this country with our bare hands, we who defeated the British with nothing more than perseverance and —"

"Enslaved people!" someone shouted.

"Yeah, fuck them!" someone else said until a wave of shushes silenced them.

"One of the arenas where we're being majorly attacked is the world of sales. Yes, the very profession that many of us blue-blooded Americans have occupied for years in order to earn an honest living, provide for our families, and move up in the world. The main antiwhite proponent in this battle is an anonymous group called the Happy Campers, who hide behind a grotesque logo depicting a Black Power fist clutching a telephone receiver. Well, I say enough is enough. If they want war, we are going to give them war. And we're not going to hide behind any logos."

How do they know our logo? Our name?

The sound of footsteps echoed throughout the speakers, and when another one of these Skull and Bones clones appeared on the screen, my heart dropped like someone in a dunk tank.

No way.

"Hey," Brian whispered in my ear. "Isn't

that —"

"I'm Clyde Moore the Third," the guy on the screen said, smiling like Patrick Bateman in *American Psycho.* "President and founder of the White United Society of Salespeople. We started our organization in response to the racist and, frankly, terroristic likes of the Happy Campers, and I extend an invitation to every white salesman and saleswoman in America to join us in our fight for the right to be white, happy, and successful.

"We're growing every day, we can use all the help we can get, and we have an extensive professional network connected with every Ivy League secret society, Fortune 500 company, and even the Illuminati." He laughed, motioning to the group of now smiling people seated behind him. "Just kidding, the Illuminati is for amateurs. We're connected with the Freemasons. Anyway, feel free to give us a call, visit our website, or follow us on social media. We have big plans and are just beginning. We'll be waiting."

Silence. In one swift motion, everyone turned to me. But I was frozen.

"WUSS?" Rose shouted, standing up, flipping two birds at the screens. "We should be afraid of an organization that's too stupid to even check their acronym? Really? I say we forget them, but what do you wanna do, Buckaroo?"

I swallowed deeply, two hands gripping the shit out of the podium.

Fuck.

29

It turns out we didn't have to wait long for WUSS's first move. And if you're wondering how a few Happy Campers, like Trey, knew about WUSS while I and the other top brass didn't, it's because we were too damn distracted with our own shit and they were too afraid to let us know.

The following Tuesday, every major newspaper, channel, and blog was talking about them, which is, I guessed, why Rhett called me into his office first thing that morning.

"Sit." He gripped a pool stick, and I felt like he was going to either ram it through my eyeball or hit me upside the head with it.

"Did you see this?" He nodded toward a YouTube video on his screen. It had been posted the day before.

"See what?"

He pressed play. There's a large group of people, mostly tourists, crowding around a platform. Behind it are people jogging and biking along the East River; you can see parked yachts, the Brooklyn Bridge, and a hot, clear-skied New York City day.

If this were any other day, it wouldn't be alarming. But it wasn't any other day, because on the platform stands a lanky man with sun-toasted dark skin, toothpick-thin arms, and a salt-and-pepper beard that he can't stop scratching. A dozen people of various sizes and shades of brown stand to his left, waiting their turn. On stage with him is none other than Clyde, dressed in a three-piece suit, with a monocle, top hat, pocket watch, and shiny wooden walking stick.

"What you see here!" he shouts, sticking his cane out toward the smiling crowd, "is one of New York's finest. This here man" — he exchanges whispers with him — "John Casor, hails from the rural jungles of North-ampton County, Virginia. And instead of leeching off tourists, John is willing to work for his keep. He knows how to clean and will do whatever you need for three hots and a cot. Let's start the bidding at twenty-five dollars. Do I have twenty-five?"

The tourists look at one another, puzzled, likely wondering if this is one of those crazy New York City shows they heard about. A few raise their hands.

"Thirty, do I see thirty?" Clyde calls. A shifty-looking Asian man closes the bidding out at seventy-five dollars for a month of John's services. Clyde claps his hands. "Sold to Bruce Lee in the back!"

The show went on for another twenty minutes, with homeless men and women — all minorities — auctioned off for next to nothing. Then the video cuts to Clyde and none other than Bonnie Sauren, who sticks a microphone in his face. "So, Mr. Moore, can you tell us what this is about?"

"Surely," he says, grabbing the microphone. "But, please, call me Clyde. So the White United Society of Salespeople and I went around Manhattan asking homeless people if, instead of being lazy, freeloading barnacles stuck to the great ship that is America, they would be willing to work if given the chance. Surprisingly enough, most of them said yes, so we decided to help them by auctioning off their services. In exchange, they'll receive a place to stay, warm food, and, most importantly, they won't be stinking up our subways and streets. It's a win-win for all."

"Genius," Bonnie says, staring up at Clyde's blue eyes as if she'd never met such an innovative man. "Utter genius. And does this have anything to do with that Happy Camper group you mentioned in your video last week?"

"It has everything to do with them," he says, looking directly into the camera. "Honestly, they're not all that different from the bums you just saw on stage. In fact, they're worse, because you don't know who they are and just how dangerous they can be. But, all the same, you can smell their fetid stench, and my organization and I plan to find out who's behind them and expose them for the racist, white-hating terrorist organization they are."

"We'll be watching, Clyde. You can count on us. Back to you, Chet."

Reader: Hell hath no fury like a white man scorned. Especially in the world of business. If you're going to do something to piss them off, be prepared for them to strike back sooner or later.

Rhett turned to me. "What did I tell you?"

What did he tell me? He told me a lot of things, almost too many to keep track of. I shrugged.

"I told you," he said, balancing the pool stick on his neck like a peasant carrying water buckets, "that Clyde was well-connected and angry, that he could either do something very good or very bad. And now he's like the sales version of Hitler. Who knows what he's capable of."

"You're right. But what does this have to do with me?"

He paused, placed the pool stick down, and stared at me. "That's a good question, Buck. What *does* this have to do with you?"

My heart beat harder than a racist cop in Kentucky. I was doing all I could not to choke, sweat, or fidget. "Stop with the games, Rhett," I said, steadying my voice. "What is it you want to know?"

He rounded the coffee table in front of the couch and bent forward at the waist until we were eye to eye. "I want to know whether you're involved with these Happy Campers. I want you to look me in the eye and tell me you're not behind this. Because if you are, you're compromising everything we've done here by bringing race into the mix. If you hadn't noticed, race isn't all that popular a topic these days, especially for startups."

Funny. Race was popular when he brought me on Rise and Shine, America *for "optics."* I gripped the black leather couch, held his stare, and said, "I am not in any way involved with the Happy Campers. I have enough on my plate with you and Barry, man. You think I have the time to go play Huey Newton? Come on, Rhett."

He stared a moment longer, searching. Then he smiled and walked toward the windows. "Good, that's all I needed to hear. Especially because I'm going to need you now more than ever."

"What's going on?"

"The business is doing well, we're growing and closing a record number of deals, but it feels stale around here," he said, staring out a window overlooking the East River. "We're not innovating anymore, Buck. The board's contented with the positive growth, but that's not what's going to take us to the next level."

"So what is?"

He turned around, grinning. "A conference. Every major player has one. HubSpot, Salesforce, you name it."

"Great," I said, happy he'd have something other than me and the Happy Campers to focus on. "When is it?"

"End of this month. Friday, September twenty-seventh. We're going to bring in A-list speakers, have a concert, and cement ourselves as the premier thought leader in SaaS therapy."

"That all sounds expensive, man. And a

few weeks isn't a long time to make this happen."

He laughed. "You're right, which is why marketing has been on it for the past three months behind the scenes. And all I need from you is to show up, give a presentation on why diversity matters, and make everyone fall in love with you."

I shifted on the couch, failing to get comfortable. "I don't get it. You just said race isn't popular. Why would I present on diversity?"

He walked back toward me and placed a hand on my shoulder. "*Race* isn't popular, Buck. It's a dirty word. But *diversity* isn't. Everyone's talking about it. And the more people talk about it, the more attention it'll bring to whoever's leading the charge. And since you've hired more than a handful of" — he paused — "people of color, who better to present on this than you, right?"

I began to pity Rhett then. He was so smart and saw so much, yet he was still a prisoner to his limited worldview. But it wasn't my problem.

"Right," I replied. "I get it. Great idea. Can't wait."

"Now that's the Buck I know."

A week later, the Talented Fifth, which was

497

what everyone called HC's leadership — Rose, Brian, Ellen, Jake, and I — met to discuss how we were going to fight WUSS. The ideas ranged from too moderate, like writing blog posts and sending them to major news outlets, to too extreme, like doing a drive-by on their headquarters. So we all decided that something in the middle would be an appropriate first line of attack.

When we shared the plan with all of the Happy Campers on Wednesday, they were as divided as white teens after reading *Twilight*. But instead of #TeamJacob and #TeamEdward, we had #TeamTooSoft and #TeamJustRight. Jason, the main voice for #TeamTooSoft, stood after we explained our plans, and said, "Y'all niggas are straight pussy, I swear, bro."

"No need for that, bruh," Jake said, stepping toward him.

"Nah, y'all actin' like a bunch of Uncle Toms and mammies. We need to go Nat Turner on these crackers and blow they whole shit up. If not, it's jus' gonna get worse. Watch."

"I d-d-disagree," Trey, a member of #TeamJustRight, said, stepping between Jake and Jason. "This is a good f-first attack to see what we're dealing with. And to see how the public r-r-reacts."

Jason looked down at Trey and laughed. "Aye, Buck, get your li'l mans out my face before I stuff him in a garbage can."

Trey, despite Jason standing a full foot above him, didn't back down. Even though he usually walked around like a kid who'd lost his mommy in the supermarket, when it came to defending me and my ideas, he always had my back. I couldn't have had a better partner.

"Alright, everyone chill. The good thing is that it doesn't matter what any of you think," I said. "It's decided. And we're doing it tomorrow night. If you want to be here for it, then be here. If not, be gone."

I stared at Jason and his followers looking salty as hell in the corner. Despite still being hotheaded, Jason was doing well for himself. Unlike most of the Happy Campers, he landed a job with one of the few Black-owned startups in New York City — some Ancestry.com-like company specializing in Black DNA.

The next night, a group of us gathered in the living room. One of our veteran Happy Campers, Kujoe, typed away on his laptop, his typing displayed on every screen. The plan was to hack WUSS's website and social media, replace their logo with swastikas, post a bunch of racist articles from far-right, neo-Nazi news outlets, and, we hoped, find some incriminating bigoted emails from Clyde and the rest of WUSS's leadership.

Kujoe had graduated with a PhD in computer science back in Ghana and had been hacking corrupt politicians from the age of twelve. He was also a skilled SDR and worked with me at Sumwun.

"Okay," he said, flexing his fingers. "Let us begin."

People passed around buckets of popcorn, bags of Twizzlers, and boxes of Milk Duds.

Kujoe happily narrated as he typed. "So, last night I used a Trojan on him."

"Damn, nigga," Jason said. "I knew you was gay, but you into white dudes? Say it ain' so."

Kujoe kept his eyes on his laptop. "Not a Trojan condom, American idiot. A Trojan *horse* attack. I sent Clyde an email acting like I was someone interested in joining WUSS. The email contained a download link, and the *obroni* was dumb enough to download it, giving me access to his computer."

His fingers flew over the keyboard as if they were dancing.

"So he has no idea?" someone asked.

Kujoe smiled. "None. We are going to take these bastards down. So now I am scanning for open ports on his computer, which" — he shimmied in his seat from left to right — "I just found. Gotcha, *kwasia*. Okay, we are in!"

Everyone clapped their hands, high-fived, and watched the screens open up to Clyde's computer. His desktop photo was a portrait of Ronald Reagan.

"So," Kujoe said, winking at Jason. "Where should we start?"

Trey stood, pointing at the screen. "Wh-wh-what's that folder? Up-p-p-pity Campers take-d-d-down?"

"Oh, fuck these motherfuckers!" Rose shouted. "Kujoe, open that shit up and let's blast them to pieces."

"Your wish is my command, Queen." Kujoe spun around, cracked his neck, and clicked open the folder.

Two seconds later, a grotesque photo filled the screen, accompanied by cartoon-villain-like HA! HA! HA! HAs.

"What the fuck?" Jason said. He grabbed one of the screens and almost yanked it off the wall.

There was a black-and-white photo of six Black men hanging from trees with broken necks as a crowd of white men, women, and children looked on with glee as if they were at the circus. The laughter looped on and on, then the screens began to go black.

"No!" Kujoe shouted. Seconds later, his laptop's entire screen was dark. He kept punching his keyboard but nothing happened.

"What is it?" I asked, peering over his shoulder.

"A honeypot," he whispered, shaking his head. "That folder was a trap. They just fried my laptop."

"What do you mean?" I pressed. "For them to have set a trap, they had to have —"

"Known we were coming," he said.

Rose walked over, hands on her hips, fire in her eyes. "So he downloaded that thing, the Trojan, on purpose? And we just walked into an ambush?"

Kujoe nodded and closed his laptop.

"But how could he have known?" Brian asked. Lines of confusion mixed with sweat on his forehead.

"Doesn' matter," Jason said, standing in the center of the living room with his arms stretched out. "This is what the fuck I was talkin' 'bout. Niggas ain' playin' out here with this cyberwarfare shit. We need to get physical. I'm sayin' we gotta get our Malcolm X on and stop these honkies by any means necessary."

"No," I said. "That's what they want us to do. Once we get physical, we expose ourselves. Once we're exposed, they can attack every single thing we've achieved. And I'm not about to let that happen."

"So then what are we going to do?" Rose asked.

I took a second, trying to think of how to hurt Clyde where it would sting most, but drew a blank. "Listen," I said, turning to Jason. "I know you wanna get violent, but as corny as it sounds, violence isn' the answer. I'm sure between the two of you" — I looked at him and Rose — "you can uncover some shit about Clyde. So get creative and we'll base our next move on that."

"Aight." Jason nodded at Rose. "We'll get on it."

30

"Okay," I said, wrapping up the Monday sales meeting. "Anything else before we break?"

Hundreds of eyes stared back at me, too many to count. Among them were Brian, Kujoe, and almost fifteen other Happy Campers I'd hired in the last six months. And despite what segregationists would have you think, things were as smooth as a baby's ass. At least I thought they were.

"Yeah," Tiffany, the blonde, sadistic former senior SDR — now an enterprise AE — said from the back of Qur'an. She was wearing a white button-up blouse with maroon high-waisted pants.

"You have the floor, madam," I said from the head of the table. Rhett was no longer in these Monday meetings, so I was the Lord and HNIC of the sales team.

"I know we have a bunch of snowflakes who are going to be offended," she said, standing up. "But I have to call out the fact that a lot of the newer SDRs are handing over shit that never closes."

"Really?" I asked, surprised.

"Yes, really. And since none of the other AEs want to come out and say it, I will. It's all of the new *minority* SDRs who are handing over shit."

Whoa, whoa, whoa. "Hold up, Tiff—"

"Funny," Kujoe said, also standing up. "All of us *minority* SDRs have felt like the *obroni* AEs have been scrutinizing our hand-offs harder than those of the other *obroni* SDRs."

"*Obroni?*" Tim, a newer white AE said, getting in Kujoe's face. "This is America, not Mali or whatever shithole country you're from. We speak *English* here."

"I'm from Ghana!" Kujoe shouted, shoving Tim back.

More white AEs stood, getting in minority SDRs' faces, and other white SDRs crowded the AEs, picking their allegiances based on skin color. Brian looked over at me, nervous, and I had no idea what was happening or where this was coming from. I just knew I had to stop it before a race riot broke out.

"Hold the fuck up!" I shouted. Everyone froze. "And sit the fuck down," I ordered, scanning the room. "Now!"

Everyone sat, but now the room was literally divided by minorities on one side, leaning against the glass that looked out onto the hallways, and white salespeople on the other, leaning against the floor-to-ceiling windows overlooking Park Avenue.

"What is going on?" I asked, looking at Tiffany.

"What's going on is that we're finally standing up for our rights, just like Clyde would have done if he were still here. Ever since you got in that seat, we've seen how you favor the Black SDRs and how much time you spend with them. White lives matter, too."

"Okay," I said, standing with my hands out, surrendering. "I'm sorry if some of you feel like I've played favorites or that" — I looked at the minority SDRs — "certain people are out to get you. But we are one team, and the company is doing better than ever, so we can't become divided now. Please, just go get some food and let's start the week off right."

I sat with my head in my hands as everyone poured out of the heavy wooden doors. Then I felt a thick, burly hand on my shoulder.

"Yeah?" I said, trying to smile as I looked

into Frodo's concerned face. He was still an SDR, having plateaued months ago. However, he had upgraded his wardrobe from football T-shirts to pastel-colored polos with the collars popped. *Some people are hopeless.*

He grabbed a chair and sat next to me. "Buck, is everything going to be okay?"

"Yeah," I said, rubbing his back. "You just focus on getting promoted, man. Don't let this shit bring you down."

He nodded. "I will, but I'm hearing things, Buck."

"Hearing things? Like voices, Frodo?"

"Yeah, but not like, uh, in my head. Just, um" — he looked toward the window — "more talk about race and stuff. Ever since that video with Clyde and his group. I think he has followers here."

Clyde. The gift that keeps on giving, like hemorrhoids.

"Okay, Frodo," I said, helping him up. "What I need from you is to be my eyes and ears. If you hear something, say something. I don't want to be caught with my pants down, you know?"

"What do you mean, Buck? Do you, uh, need a belt?"

I looked at him for a while, knowing he meant well but that he was still as dumb as rocks. "Yeah," I said, laughing. "You'll be my belt, man."

So much for a belt. On Tuesday morning, all hell broke loose. I was at Sumwun reviewing the AEs' Q3 pipelines when Rose texted me.

Washington Square Park. The arch. NOW!

"Sorry," I said, rising from the table in Qur'an. "I have an emergency. Eddie, keep it going."

By the time I got to Washington Square Park, there was a crowd in front of the arch. I planted myself on a bench near the fountain close enough where I could see what was going on but far enough where I'd be hard to recognize, especially with the oversize hoodie and sunglasses I'd bought.

From where I sat, I saw balloons, smiling teenagers, and tourists munching on cupcakes, cookies, and pie. Rose stood off to the side, enraged. A PSST News truck was parked beyond the arch, which could only mean one thing.

Here, I texted Rose. Black hoodie. To the left of the fountain facing the arch.

She looked up and walked over.

"Sit," I said, trying not to draw attention.

She gripped her hips, shaking her head. "No, fuck no. Do you know what's going

508

on over there?"

"*Please,* Rose. We have to lay low. Sit."

She looked back at the crowd, then slammed her ass down. "Go to PSST News. There's a live stream of this shit. That Missy Anne–looking bitch Bonnie Sauren is in the middle interviewing Clyde."

I pulled the stream up on my phone. There was a shot of a plastic folding table featuring different baked goods. Behind it were WUSS members, smiling, taking cash, and handing out cookies and donuts. Some of them, I noticed, were Sumwunners who were conveniently out sick, but who obviously didn't care enough to hide their allegiance to Clyde by standing off camera.

"Fuck," I said. "I see some people from Sumwun, but this just looks like a normal bake sale."

Rose scrunched her face in disgust, like she had stepped in a pile of shit. "Keep watching."

"So, Clyde," Bonnie said, wearing a slim-fitting white blazer and white skirt to match her I-can't-believe-it's-not-bleached! blonde hair. "For all of the viewers who just joined us, please explain what's going on here."

"Of course," he said, smiling directly into the camera. "We're throwing a bake sale. But not just any bake sale. No, ours has a

509

more modern component to it. To truly reflect the times. You see, the costs of our baked goods depend on who's buying them. If you pan over to here, you'll see our list of prices."

The camera focused on a sheet of paper propped up on the table.

- Donuts: 50¢ each for Blacks, 75¢ each for Hispanics, $1.50 each for Asians, $2.50 each for Whites
- Cookies: 10¢ each for Blacks, 25¢ each for Hispanics, 75¢ each for Asians, $1 each for Whites
- Pie: $1 slice for Blacks, $1.50 slice for Hispanics, $2 slice for Asians, $3.50 slice for Whites
- Coffee: Free for Blacks, and only for Blacks

"No fucking way," I said, gripping the phone so hard it hurt.

"We figured that with affirmative action being such a hot topic — since it's basically a tool for reverse racists to fill top institutions with kids who don't belong there — we'd boil the issue down to something more tangible so people can understand the real harm that reverse discrimination inflicts on those who have nothing to do with the actions of their ancestors."

Bonnie nodded, mesmerized. "And what has the response been?" she asked, grabbing a vanilla cookie.

"Extremely positive. People agree with what we're doing and what we stand for, which is putting an end to all of this color crap. We're all Americans and need to do our part to get ahead. No special treatment for anyone. And if there are people out there like those Happy Camper terrorists who think that they deserve special treatment, they're in for a very rude awakening."

I looked up from the phone. Rose was gone. She was already halfway to the crowd. I yelled after her.

She turned around and saluted me, pushing her way through the crowd. Seconds later, baked goods and coffee flew in the air as if they were bouncing off a trampoline, followed by screams and shouting. I wanted to go and get her but couldn't. If Clyde saw me, he'd know that I was involved, which would destroy everything.

One of Clyde's soldiers, a barrel-chested guy with a buzz cut, wrapped Rose in his arms and let her go once police arrived. PSST got all of it.

That night, Jake sent Trey to get her out,

and when she returned to HQ, everyone clapped and whistled, a true soldier's homecoming.

Fuck this. "Shut up!" I shouted. The party paused.

"Chill, D," Soraya said, grabbing my arm.

I yanked it away. "No. There is no fucking reason we should be celebrating." I swung my head around the room and stopped at Rose. "What you did today. You could have fucking ended everything we've worked for. For what? To flip a table?"

"To stand up to those peckerwoods," Jason said, standing next to Rose.

"Which is more than you've done," she added.

The entire room stood still as if stuck in time. "I'm just trying to make sure we survive this," I said, softening my voice.

"What's the point of just surviving, Buckaroo? It's what we've done since we were first brought to this country. Me?" Rose said, turning to the group. "I'm tired of surviving. I want to thrive."

Behind Jason and Rose stood fifty Happy Campers reflecting the same murderous desire for action. I knew what was up. Fuck a mutiny, this was a coup.

"Think," I said, desperately appealing to reason. "If we do anything we can't take

back, this all goes up in flames."

"Maybe so," Jason said. "But I'd rather go out free in a burnin' buildin' than alive and shackled in the basement." Tired, furious heads nodded.

"Everyone out!" I shouted, and turned to Jason and Rose. "Except you two."

"Even us?" Brian asked, nodding toward Ellen, Jake, and Soraya.

"Even you," I said, holding my eyes on Jason and Rose.

Once the floor was empty, Jason stretched out on the couch lengthwise, and Rose grabbed a beer.

"Are you trying to ruin us?" I asked, watching Rose plop down next to Jason.

"We tryna save us," Jason said.

Rose smiled up at me. "Not trying, Buckaroo. We are," she said, extending a phone in my direction.

"What is this?" I saw a photo of a sweaty white guy making out with a Black guy in what looked like a dingy club.

"Look closer," Rose said, increasing the brightness on her phone.

It took me a second, but I saw it. The sweaty white guy was Clyde, but I couldn't identify the Black guy.

"What the fuck is this?"

Jason and Rose looked at each other and

laughed. "You said to get creative. But, honestly, it was luck, because this fell from the sky. I was at Cubbyhole with Dolores, you know, doing our date-night thing, when we overheard some guy, the Black dude in the photo, crying to his friend about his 'lover,'" Rose said, with air quotes.

"So I moved closer and got the whole scoop. Clyde and this dude have been secretly dating for years, but this WUSS stuff is tearing them apart. So I just lifted his phone, found a handful of photos of them, texted them to myself, deleted the texts, and then returned the phone as if nothing happened. He doesn't even know. Now we can send these to the media and blow his whole, closeted, self-hating, racist spot up."

"Shit's genius," Jason said, sitting up. "We luckier than a motherfucker. 'Bout to send these off first thing in the mornin' and get shit poppin' like Vietnam."

I looked down at the phone, scrolling through the handful of photos of Clyde and his boyfriend: in a jacuzzi, smiling with champagne in their hands; holding each other in a hotel room overlooking the Hudson; with fat pieces of cheesecake in front of them, forks ready to dig in. This was what we were waiting for, what we needed to get the upper hand, but it wasn't right.

"Nah," I said, deleting the photos, emptying her trash folder, and handing the phone back.

"What do you mean, 'Nah!' " she shouted, furiously flipping through her phone for the missing photos. She turned to Jason, fire raging in her eyes with her mouth half open. "He just fucking deleted our leverage!"

Jason jumped off the couch and stood eye to eye with me, ready to tear me apart. "What the fuck? I thought you was about this shit. Whose side are you on?"

"It's not right," I said. "Outin' Clyde to embarrass him? That shit's too low for us."

Rose took a breath and looked up at me. "This is war, Buckaroo. Anything goes. The point is to win, and you just brought us one step closer to losing. Why would you do that?"

I turned to her, wondering where the girl who had no place to call home six months ago went, the girl who told me that what she wanted most in the world was a family. I supposed she got what she wanted, and she was doing everything to protect it.

"We gotta have some integrity, Rose. This isn't a game; it's people's lives."

Jason sucked his teeth. "Not a game?

Tha's all you talk about, nigga. That we gotta 'fix the game,' 'the game's rigged and we gotta even the playin' field,' 'we gotta do whatever it takes to get ahead.' Now you here with this conscience and integrity bullshit? Miss me with all that, son. If you not gonna do what it takes to hold this shit down," he said, looking at Rose, "we will."

Reader: Life, like sales, comes with an endless amount of opportunities to do the wrong thing to win. But understand that whether you take those opportunities or not, consequences still follow. And they won't always be in your favor.

31

Despite the week's crazy start, peace reigned for all of Wednesday and Thursday. I was now breathing just a bit easier.

I'd promised Eddie, Marissa, and Frodo I'd grab lunch with them on Friday, to catch up, but as I headed out of Sumwun to join them, Rhett pushed open the frosted glass doors, grabbed me by the arm, and shoved me toward his office.

"What the fuck?" I asked once we were inside.

"That's what I'm asking myself, Buck," he said, thrusting a piece of paper into my hand.

I looked down and saw about fifty signatures on it, with PETITION TO REMOVE BUCK in bold letters at the top.

"Huh?" I scanned the list of names, beginning with Tiffany and including people from all levels of the sales team.

"You have at least fifty people there,"

Rhett said, jabbing the paper, "who want you out. They say you're unfit to lead. How could you let it get to this?"

"It's not me, Rhett," I said, shaking my head in disbelief. "It's Clyde! He's somehow invaded the ranks with his white supremacist shit."

"White supremacist shit? Buck, I need you to be honest with me now more than ever. You remember our promise, right?"

"Yes," I said. "Of course."

"And you know I love you like a brother, right?"

"Yes, Rhett," I said, the paper shaking in my hands. "What is it? Just say it."

"Are you part of the Happy Campers? I can't see you being involved in something like this, but I need to be sure."

Something told me to just get out with it then and there, but I didn't know what the consequences would be. And there was still a part of me, despite everything, that didn't want to disappoint him. In many ways, he had given me a brand-new life.

"I already told you, Rhett. I am not a part of the Happy Campers and have no affiliation with them. The last thing I'd want to do is get Sumwun caught up in this race mess."

He sighed with relief and sat down, signaling for me to do the same. "Good. I know you're too smart for that, but I had to be sure. What I think would be best is for you to denounce the Happy Campers in front of the entire sales team, so everyone knows whose side you're on."

My mouth went dry. "What do you mean 'side,' Rhett? If I denounce the Happy Campers, won't that make it seem like we're supporting Clyde?"

He scratched his forehead. "Maybe so, but you have fifty people right there on that list who are ready to quit if you don't win them back. And we can't have that type of media scrutiny, not again. It's a matter of survival, Buck."

"Whose survival, Rhett? A lot of the Sumwunners of color look up to me, and to denounce the Happy Campers would make me look like an Uncle Tom. I can't do that."

He snatched the petition from my hands and stood up. "It's not about race, Buck! Stop being so simple. It's all about the company. No one cares about the color of your skin. Frankly, you're being narcissistic."

I thought back to my first day at Sumwun and saw myself covered in white paint, the bucket hanging above me as everyone laughed and laughed and laughed. I'd come a long way since then, had gained the world, lost it, and was setting it right again — for Ma, myself, and the future generation — so there was no turning back.

"Whatever, man," I said, heading for the door. "I'm not going to do what you asked, but I will figure out a way to fix this."

"You better."

"What was that all about?" Eddie asked as I approached their table at the Shake Shack in Madison Square Park.

"That petition," I said, taking a seat. "You guys know about it?"

Eddie looked at Marissa, who looked at Frodo, who turned to me, fear on his face. "Uh, yeah, I did, Buck, but I didn't think it was anything important, so I didn't bring it up." He nervously inserted half of a Shack-Burger into his mouth.

"So much for being my belt."

Marissa reached across the table and placed a hand on my shoulder. "Don't worry about any of this, Buck. Half of those people are mad about deals or something else that has nothing to do with you."

"It has everything to do with me. They want me out."

Eddie laughed, tossing a fry at me. "That'll never happen, so stop sulking. But, hey, what about Clyde, huh? He's going off the rails."

"Yeah," Frodo whispered. "He's like, um, taking this all to another level. Who knows what he'll do next."

"But those Happy Campers sort of came out of nowhere too, right?" Eddie said.

"Yeah," Marissa agreed. "It's like some top-secret organization. I wonder if they do human sacrifices."

Eddie placed a single fry into his mouth. "It's the Illuminati. I just know it."

I laughed, trying to lighten up. "You ever hear that Kendrick line about Black men and the Illuminati?"

Crickets and stares.

"Never mind." I shook my head. "But seriously, guys? You think there's some conspiracy going on? It's just a bunch of Black salespeople who started some club to feel special."

Eddie narrowed his eyes across the table, beheading a fry. "Hmm, sounds like you're on the inside. Got something to tell us, Buck?"

I forced myself to breathe, then laugh. "Me? They must think I'm part of the system, because I never got an invitation."

"Just like my letter from Hogwarts," Frodo muttered.

"Well *I* actually know a Happy Camper," Eddie announced.

"Stop lying," Frodo said. "How would *you* know a Happy Camper?"

"I won't say where we met, but we recently started dating," he said, leaning in now, whispering. "After I open him up with a few drinks, he becomes *really* talkative. He swears he'll tell me who's behind it all if I let him hit it."

Frodo looked around. "Hit what, Eddie? If anyone hits you, I'll strangle them."

"Thanks," Eddie said, rubbing Frodo's hand. "But, yeah, this guy says things are tense over there, real tense. Like there's a civil war going on in response to Clyde and his cronies. It's all *v* juicy."

Motherfucker! I twisted my hands beneath the table. *Whoever's talking to Eddie must also be the one who tipped Clyde off about our plans to hack him.* I ran through all of the gay, bi, or possibly questioning guys in the group. There were more than a few.

"Who's the lucky guy?" I asked, taking a sip of my shake, trying to be casual.

Eddie pinched my cheek, smirking. "You know I don't kiss and tell, Buck. But I will say he's incredibly intelligent, good with computers, and" — he opened both hands like a magician — "he's *African.*"

Kujoe. That rat motherfucker. Right in my own house, at Sumwun, in front of my own face. How did I not see this? He must have warned Clyde about the hacking and told him about us in the first place. Right before I tried to get more info, my phone rang. It was Jason.

"One second, guys," I said, getting up, unclenching my fist.

"Hello?"

"Yo, come to HQ."

"For what?"

He laughed. "I gotta surprise for you."

A surprise? I didn't want any surprises, especially from him. "What is it?"

"Man," he said, sucking his teeth so hard my ear vibrated. "If I *told* you, it wouldn' be a surprise, now would it? Stop playin' and get over here."

"Aight."

I walked back over to the table and said I had to go.

"Come on," Frodo pleaded, his lips as glossy as a freshly waxed floor. "We never get to hang anymore."

"I'm sorry. This was fun, though. Let's do it again next month."

"See you, Buck," Marissa said, planting a greasy kiss on my cheek.

"Peace, Eddie," I said, leaning in for a

hug. "Good luck with your guy. What's his name again? Prince Akeem?"

He sealed his lips with his fingers, twisted them, and threw the key over his shoulder. "Nice try."

I stood at the base of the stairs and saw the second-floor lights on before stepping inside.

"Yo," I called, looking into an empty room full of phones on the first floor. There were usually people there, but it was a Friday. I guessed Rose had sent them home early.

As I walked upstairs, I saw a dark figure standing on the second-floor landing.

"Who the fuck is that?"

"Mr. Buck? It's Jake. Dang, Jason lost his goddamn mind, I swear. There's somethin' goin' on in there, but he's not lettin' anyone in. It's jus' him 'n' Rose, 'n' they tol' everyone to leave. If somethin's goin' down, I gotta know. It's my job."

I moved him aside and knocked.

"Who is it? I told y'all to bounce."

"Jason, it's me."

"Finally."

He cracked the door open and looked around. "Jus' you," he said, keeping his eyes on Jake. "And don' speak too loudly."

The kitchen and living room were empty

save for Rose and someone tied to a thick plank of wood propped up by two sawhorses. A black cloth bag covered the person's head, and there was a large empty bucket underneath.

"What the fuck did you do?" I pushed past Jason and stood in front of the man. "Who is this?"

Rose laughed. "It's Justin Bieber," she said, slapping the man's head so hard it sounded like heavy water hitting pavement.

The man twisted his body and screamed, his voice muffled like he was underwater.

"We gagged him with some sock we found under the couch and jammed in ear plugs so he can't hear shit," Jason said proudly. "But keep your voice down. Don' know the quality of the ear plugs. Prolly some knock-off shit."

"No, I think they're industrial," Rose said.

"What. The. Fuck. Is going on here?" I whispered, looking back and forth between them.

"What do you think, Buckaroo? We're fighting back. That whole hacking thing was a dud. And since you vetoed our plan to blackmail Clyde with his Black male, it's time for some real action."

I looked at Jason, standing with his arms folded over his chest, grinning like someone about to cannonball into a pool and make a mess.

"This isn't who I think it is, is it?"

Rose shrugged. "It's not *not* who you think it is."

"Tha's right," Jason said, eyes popping like Malcolm McDowell's in *A Clockwork Orange.* "And we 'bout to go straight Guantánamo on his ass."

"Spanish Inquisition," Rose corrected. "I think they did it first."

"Are you both out of your minds?!" I shouted. "This is serious as fuck, man. If we get caught, we're not only done but we're also going to jail."

"Since when did you get so pussy, nigga? I wan' that guy who punched me in the face las' year. It was a bitch move, but at leas' it was a move. *Damn.* Plus" — Jason placed a hand on my shoulder — "you not really runnin' the show anymore, bro."

Rose reached under the black bag and removed the dirty sock from Clyde's mouth and the plugs from his ears. He sucked in a huge breath of air. "You're all going to die for this," he coughed. "You think you can just kidnap whoever you want? I'm Clyde Reynolds Moore the Third! The fucking Third. Do you know what that means?"

"Not really," Rose said. She rolled the

black bag up to the bottom of his nose and laid a rag over his mouth. "But I'm sure it means your daddy's daddy's daddy probably owned some enslaved people. And that the land your daddy's daddy's daddy owned was passed down through the years, accruing generational wealth along the way and lining your pockets with money made from cotton picked by the very enslaved people they owned."

She went to the fridge and grabbed a gallon of Poland Spring. "Is that what you were going to say?"

"What do you want?" he asked, twisting his head around. "Money? I can give you that."

"Don' need it," Jason said.

"Okay, then what? I'll do anything."

I won't lie; seeing him like this, desperate and vulnerable, made me feel good despite all the shit it was going to land us in.

"For starters," Rose said, uncapping the jug, "you can stop all this white supremacist bullshit you've been spewing for the past couple of weeks."

I opened my mouth, but Jason clamped his palm over it. He shook his head. I understood. Clyde knew my voice. If he could identify me, we were in trouble. Jason switched on some jazz; a saxophone's wail filled the room.

Rose poured water over the rag covering Clyde's mouth, causing him to shake like he was undergoing electroshock therapy. "I'm sure you're used to Evian, but I hope you don't mind Poland Spring."

"Please!" he screamed. "Please stop."

"That's what we want you to do," Rose said. She tilted the plastic jug again and poured water on his head for ten, maybe twenty seconds.

"What you're experiencing," she shouted over the music, lifting the jug up for a moment as Clyde coughed, then resuming, "is the sensation of drowning."

He jerked his head in every direction, his hands and feet convulsing as if he were possessed. Before, it was fun, even exciting, but now this was real one-hundred-percent bona fide torture. My heart was beating faster and faster.

"You see, the water soaks the rag," Rose continued, "causing it to cling to your face, making it harder to breathe. The water enters your mouth, runs down your throat and nostrils, making you feel like you're really —"

"Drowning!" Clyde shouted after she emptied the last of the jug and removed the rag. "I can't! I can't breathe," he said, spitting water all over the kitchen floor.

"Are you gonna stop this Nazi bullshit?" Jason asked, kneeling next to Clyde's drenched body.

Clyde twisted and pulled on the damp plank before nodding.

"Are you gonna get rid of the White United Society of Sadists?"

A whimper escaped his mouth — the sound of an abused animal.

"What was that?" Rose asked. "Louder."

"Yes," Clyde whispered.

"Louder!" Jason said, pulling out his phone, recording the scene. "Say 'I am Clyde Reynolds Moore *the Third,* and I am wrong for what I've done. The White United Society of Salespeople is racist, bigoted, and evil.' "

"I," Clyde started, choking on his spit.

"Shout it to the heavens!" Rose ordered. "So loud your precious white God and blue-eyed, blond-haired Jesus can hear you!"

"I," he said, louder now, "Clyde Reynolds Moore the Third, am wrong. The White United Society of Salespeople is racist, bigoted" — he paused and Jason squeezed his leg — "and evil."

Jason and Rose bumped fists. I stood there speechless. I went to the fridge, grabbed a beer, and chugged the entire thing in one gulp, trying to taste something, anything.

"If we hear anything from you again," Jason said, rolling the black bag back over Clyde's mouth, "we will take you, jus' like we did today. But you won' live another day to talk about it."

"I understand," he said, soaking in fear. "N-n-now what?"

"You're going to go to sleep for a while, and then you'll wake up like nothing happened," Rose said.

"Huh?"

She delivered a swift kick to his head, knocking him out.

"Start the van," Jason instructed her. "We'll carry him down."

As we carried him down the stairs — I held his legs while Jason held his arms — Jason whistled as if everything were normal. We shut the doors to the van Ellen usually used with the new recruits, and Jason hopped into the driver's seat. Rose took shotgun.

"Don't worry," Rose said. "We got this."

Jason smiled from his window. "Yeah, Superman. Go home and get some sleep. You can finally rest easy now that this is all over. Told you this was the only way."

They peeled off down the street. I waded

through the thick humidity of a summer night, heading for the subway, wanting the underground to take me as far away from what just happened as possible. We had crossed a line and there was no going back — especially not with someone like Clyde.

Before finding sleep, I called Kujoe, who denied being the rat but admitted to discussing the Happy Campers with Eddie. Did I truly believe that he wasn't the rat? No, not at all. Anyone who broke our primary rule of not discussing the Happy Campers couldn't be trusted, so I told him he was banned from HQ until further notice and to keep to himself at Sumwun or I'd fire him.

With that done, I mentally prepared myself for whatever was going to happen next, even though I could have never anticipated the lengths Clyde would go to to win. But sleep was pulling me into its abyss, and I had to surrender, at least for the night.

32

Nights later, HQ was buzzing. Just like the sadists at Gitmo and Abu Ghraib, Jason and Rose made no effort to hide what they had done. The video of Clyde's confession looped on the screens, and the Happy Campers celebrated as if we had truly won.

"Aye, lemme getchyour attention," Jake said, raising a beer. "I know it's been a rough coupla weeks 'n' that we all been a bit divided, but here's to the enda that."

"And to Jason and Rose for doing what they had to do to keep us safe," Ellen added.

"As well as t-t-to Sensei Buck," Trey chimed in, winking at me. "For remaining our f-f-f-fearless leader."

"To Jason, Rose, and Buck!" everyone shouted, clinking cans, downing flutes of cheap champagne, and passing joints around like they were at Burning Man, Woodstock, or one of those events where white people suspend all law and fuck themselves senseless.

I didn't feel like celebrating — not yet. It all felt too soon. I was headed upstairs when someone grabbed my hand.

"Hey," Soraya said, not letting go. "Not in the mood to celebrate?"

"Nah, not really. Mad tired. Jus' gonna knock out, but have fun."

"If you say so." She sounded disappointed.

A few hours later, as I was finally settling into sleep, my phone went off, snapping me awake. I picked up without looking at it, betting it was Kujoe calling to beg me to let him back.

"Hello?"

"Buck?"

It was a woman's voice. It sounded familiar, but I couldn't place it. "Who's this?"

"Sandra Stork. I'm calling because you're in trouble."

"Trouble?" I asked, turning the light on. "What kind of trouble?"

"Buck." She paused. "Everyone knows. The media is already drafting their articles to drop tomorrow morning."

"Everyone knows what?"

"Listen, we could play games or you could be straight with me. An anonymous source reached out to all major outlets an hour ago saying that you're behind the Happy Camp-

533

ers. They sent a video of you addressing a large group of people, discussing plans for combating that group of Nazi salespeople. There are also other clips."

Kujoe, that motherfucker. He must've been recording the Hush Harbors.

"Even if that were true," I said, closing my eyes, "why are you calling me?"

She laughed. "Because I can't stand to see smart young brothers used for target practice. So I want to give you a chance to get ahead of this. Come on *Rise and Shine, America* tomorrow and present your case before it's too late. I won't go easy on you . . . because I can't, but at least you'll be able to control part of the narrative."

I had known the war wasn't over; it couldn't have been. People like Clyde — rich, white, and powerful — don't succumb to physical threats, and they also don't make them. Their warfare is institutional, psychological, and strategic. In chess, you don't beat your opponent by rocking them in the jaw, you back them into a corner until they have nowhere else to go.

"Thanks, but no thanks," I said, clutching a pillow to prevent myself from breaking something.

"Are you sure, Buck? This may be your

last chance before everything gets out of hand."

I took a breath and replayed the last week in my head: Clyde's videos, the bake sale, our failed attempt at cyberwarfare, the race riots at Sumwun, Clyde's kidnapping; everything was already out of hand, and the only thing I could do now was face the music instead of trying to control, control, and control it.

"Yeah," I said, exhaling. "I'm sure. But thank you for looking out, Sandra. I appreciate it."

"Of course, Buck. Good luck."

After that, sleep was impossible. I walked downstairs and people were passed out all over the place, looking like bodies on a battlefield. Except for one. Soraya stood in the kitchen nursing a glass of wine.

"Hey," I said. "Got one for me?"

She forced a smile and poured me a glass of red. We clinked glasses. But there was enough pain in her eyes to let me know the smile was a front.

"What's wrong?"

"I was jus' thinkin' about Mrs. V, that's all. It was only a little over a year ago when me, you, her, Jason, and Mr. Rawlings were in here eatin' pizza and laughin'. But now" — she waved her glass around — "everything, I mean *everything*, D, has changed. This room, this house, you, me, us. Sometimes I think, *Man, this is all so great, I'm somewhere I never thought I'd be,* but then I remember the past, your mom, and I jus' miss it all so much."

I put my glass down and took her face into my hands, wiping as many of her tears away as I could. "I know the feelin', *habibti.* Trust me."

She brought my hand to her lips, holding it there before looking up at me. "Whatever happened to Mr. Rawlings, D? Did you ever go look for him? Did you try to help him?"

I tried to speak, but there was a lump in my throat. Ever since I kicked him out, I hadn't been able to stop thinking about him.

I looked at her and shook my head; tears blurred my vision.

"He didn' deserve that," she said as she rested her head against my chest. "He didn' deserve any of that."

"I know." I wrapped my arms around her, trying to fight my way back to the past. "I know."

It was exactly as Sandra had said it would be. The next day, I was all over the internet. My face was on every major newspaper, with some people even calling me a terrorist. Texts and emails caused my phone to overheat so badly that I just shut it off.

"Good morning, Chauncey," I said, climbing into the back seat. "Let's go to Sumwun."

He swallowed hard and looked at me in the rearview. It was only after we crossed the Williamsburg Bridge and made our way up First Avenue that he spoke. "I read the newspaper, Buck. Are you okay?"

I looked out the window at Black nannies pushing white kids in strollers, food cart owners stacking blue paper cups, dogs shitting on the sidewalk without a care in the world. "I'm not" — I closed my eyes — "but I will be. Nothing lasts forever, right?"

"Yes, that is true." Chauncey smiled at me. "But you are one of the strongest people I know, Buck, and strength lasts forever."

"Thanks, Chauncey. I hope so."

I pushed the revolving doors open and looked into Starbucks; everything was just as it had been a year ago except I didn't recognize anyone working. People were frantically shouting at one another and spilling drinks as they tried to keep up with the morning rush. *Fuck, everything's falling apart.*

I exited the elevator, paused in front of the frosted doors, and took a deep breath before pushing them open. The floor was bubbling with chaos — balls flying in every direction, people screaming, slamming their phones, dogs sprinting, salespeople pacing around the rows — a fearsome cacophony for anyone not used to it.

But when I walked in, everything stopped. It became so silent that I could hear the wall clocks ticking in a dozen different time zones. *Well, the cat's out the bag. At least now I won't have to denounce the Happy Campers.*

Rhett's door opened, and he stepped out. "What the hell is going —" Seeing me, he stopped, then said, "Everyone get back to work." But no one did. Their eyes followed me as I walked past their desks toward Rhett, a few of them coughing out "traitor" as I traversed the floor. Only when the door shut behind me did the deafening roar return.

It was a Wednesday afternoon, but Rhett's office had the feeling of that first Deals Week when he'd been a nervous wreck, sure of Sumwun's demise. He sat on his leather couch, a glass full of gin in his hand, ice clanking around like rattling chains.

"Hey," I said, standing in front of him, unsure if I should sit. His button-up was wrinkled, which could only mean the worst.

He silently nodded, peering into his drink like he was trying to find an answer in it. Seeing him like that, deflated, sucked all of the confidence right out of me.

"Rhett," I said, finally sitting next to him. "Look at me, man. Please."

He wouldn't. He took a sip and turned toward the window, squinting in the bright September light.

"Where did I go wrong?" he finally asked. He stood up and walked to the windows.

"What do you mean?"

"I mean what did I do to you, Buck? Where did I mess up?"

I got up and stood next to him, watching boats glide across the East River and the tips of buildings reflect the sunlight like diamonds. "I don't understand, Rhett."

He shook his head and emptied his glass in one shot. "Me neither. I gave you everything, Buck. Every opportunity I never had at your age. The sun, the moon, and the stars. But now look at you." He finally faced me.

" 'If an enemy were insulting me, I could endure it. If a foe were rising against me, I could hide. But it is you, a man like myself, my companion, my close friend.' Psalm 55, Buck. Verses twelve and thirteen." He grabbed his bottle of gin and took one long gulp directly from it. "Do you know what it means?"

"Rhett, I —"

"Go," he said, turning away from me, pain rising in his voice. "Just go, Buck. I don't want to see you again until the conference. After that, you're free to leave, like I know you want to. So please, just go."

I felt like shit. Rhett had given me the opportunity of a lifetime, but it came at the cost of my freedom. And it was then, as I walked out of his office past the hundreds of salespeople laughing as they saw their fearless leader fall, that I realized it was freedom that had motivated me from the very beginning. Not money, power, the need to prove myself, or even to make Ma proud, but the freedom to breathe where I want, when I want, how I want, and with whom I want in my beautiful brown skin.

Reader: By this point, you should know nothing in life is free, especially freedom.

33

"Buckaroo! Buck-a-fucking-roo!"

I opened my eyes. Rose stood in my bedroom. Light fought its way in through the drawn shades.

"Why the fuck aren't you answering anyone's calls?" she asked, throwing a T-shirt and pair of pants at me. "Get dressed," she shouted. "Now!"

"What? What time is it?"

"It's Thursday afternoon, and someone fucking lit HQ on fire. Chauncey's outside. Get up, now!"

I got dressed and jumped into the elevator so quickly that Rose had to chuck a pair of shoes at me.

"What's going on?" My heart was pinballing around in my ribs.

"Are you fucking deaf? I said HQ is on fire. It had to have been those WUSS motherfuckers. Where have you been?"

We jumped into the Tesla and Chauncey

peeled off before the doors shut. "I cannot believe this," he shouted, as we sped down Second Avenue. "These are the real thugs!"

"Where have you been?" Rose repeated, furiously chewing a piece of gum. "We were all waiting for you last night. We had balloons, confetti, fucking everything to celebrate you finally being out to the world as our leader, but you never showed."

"I went home. If you couldn't tell, a lot's going on. I'm a terrorist now, didn't you know?"

"You can't just do this, Buckaroo. You can't just abandon us when we need you."

"Abandon you? It seemed like you and Jason had everything under control."

She rolled down the window and spit her gum at an unsuspecting pedestrian. "Are you crazy? We're just the muscle. You," she said, pointing, "are the heart."

We could see the black smoke rising once we got off the Williamsburg Bridge. Chauncey pressed on the gas, blowing through as many red lights as he could without injuring anyone. But when we passed Marcy Playground and reached the four corners — Wally Cat's, Mr. Aziz's, and Jason's old corners — there were cop cars, fire trucks, and ambulances blocking the street.

We jumped out of the Tesla and ran

toward the corners, but two heavyset cops blocked our path. "Stay back!" one yelled, and gripped his holster.

"It's my house!" I shouted, pushing past him.

"No, you don't," the other said, grabbing me. "We got a million kids like you out here saying it's their house. Whose fucking house is it?"

"It's ours!" Rose kicked the cop in the balls, which forced him to let me go. The other restrained Rose. I ran for the house and ducked under the blue wooden police barriers and the caution tape that stretched across the street like a finish line.

A crowd stood on the sidewalk across from HQ: Happy Campers.

"Buck," Brian said, running toward me. "We don't know how it happened — BITCH! It must've been Clyde and them. This is some Magneto work, I know it."

Bright orange flames shot out of every window. Walls crumbled, glass shattered, and the black smoke was so heavy, it resembled burnt cotton candy.

"Is anyone in there?" I asked, watching my house, the house of my mother and father, crumble right before my eyes.

Brian looked at me, his chest rising and falling, and nodded.

"Who?" I shouted, panic exploding in my stomach.

There was a hand on my back. Jason. "Trey, Superman. Li'l nigga wen' in there to save what he could and never came out."

I made a break for the house and jumped the steps two by two, screaming his name. I ran upstairs, but the smoke was so thick, it burned my eyes, blinding me. I kept calling him, but all I got was black smoke barreling down my throat, choking me as it grabbed hold of my lungs.

I fell to the floor. It felt like hot coals were burning every surface of my body. The heat entered me, and I couldn't do anything to push it out. But before I took my last breath, I heard something coming from the kitchen. A familiar laugh, one I hadn't heard in a long time but could never forget.

"Ma?"

"Dang, he in a coma?"

"Funny, last time I was the nigga in the hospital. Looks like the tables have turned. Superman is strong, though. He'll be aight."

"C'mon, Buckaroo. Stop playing around and wake up. We need you. I swear to God, if you die on me, I'm bringing you back to life just to kill you myself."

"He'll be fine. Buck's like me, nothing can

stop him."

"Ring ring, D. We're all here for you, *habibi*. Open your eyes if you can hear us."

"COCK! Um, sorry. Stay strong, Buck. I guess fire is your kryptonite."

I felt tubes in my nose and tried to pull them out. The beeping, the shuffling feet, and the sensation of burning lungs made me think I was in purgatory. But when I opened my eyes, the Talented Fifth, plus Soraya and Jason, were staring at me.

"Mornin', D," Soraya said, removing my hands from the tubes. I was so weak, all she had to do was pick them up and drop them like lead weights into my lap. "Don' do that. It's helpin' you breathe."

"There you are, Buckaroo," Rose said, placing a cool hand on my forehead.

"I," I started, trying to sit up, coughing like I had just chain-smoked a pack of old turds. "I thought I heard you say something about killing me if I died. I couldn't let that happen."

Everyone laughed. One big dysfunctional family. My family. "What day is it?"

"Friday," Brian said, as he inserted a straw into my mouth. "Drink this." Water never tasted so good.

"What happened?" I searched their smiling faces for answers.

"You wen' all supernigga," Jason said. "Ran into the spot like you was invincible, like that shit wasn' on fire."

"Yeah, Mr. Buck," Jake said, resting a large hand on my foot. "Firefighters said they found you on the floor right before it collapsed 'n' that you, uh" — he looked down — "kept yellin' for your ma."

Ma. I remembered hearing her laugh, right in the kitchen, as if she were sitting there before work, making coffee, and waiting to greet me.

"Where's Trey?" I asked, extinguishing their smiles.

"He —" Rose took a breath, squeezing her eyes. "He didn't make it."

"What do you mean 'He didn't make it'? Where is he?"

Soraya grabbed my hand and rubbed it. "The house collapsed, D. And once the firefighters found him, the body was" — she brought the back of her hand to her mouth — "they could only identify it by bits of Trey's sneakers."

No. There was no way. My lungs burned again. I pulled the tubes out of my nose, pulled the taped IV needle out of my hand, and tried to get out of the bed, but Jason restrained me.

"Don't," he said. "Jus' don', bro. Can't do

nothin' 'bout it now except move on."

"Move on? How the fuck can we jus' 'move on'? What was he even doin' in there? Why didn' one of you stop him?"

"After the fire started," Brian said, hugging himself, "he was outside, where you saw us. But then he said he had to get something and ran back in. A few seconds later, the whole fire got crazier and they wouldn't let us inside."

"What did he run in to get?"

The six of them looked at one another. The fire inside of me spread even further. "Someone," I said, coughing up a storm, "better talk now or I'm kicking you all out."

Jason nodded at Rose. She took something, a little burnt piece of paper, out of her jacket and handed it to me. The edges were burnt to a crisp and flaked all over the bed, but part of it was still intact. When I turned it over, I saw what it was. A photograph.

"He was probably looking for something else, but the firefighters found this in the backyard," Rose said.

It was a photo of Trey and me, taken a month after he showed up, on the day I asked him to be my assistant. He was so scared that we were going to kick him out of the Happy Campers because he stuttered too much to ever be on the phones. When I told him I still had a place for him, he hugged me harder than anyone ever had in my life. Later, we took the photo I held in my hands: he was smiling like someone graduating from high school, and I, like a proud big brother, had my arm around him.

Salty tears singed the burns on my cheeks. All of the anger I had, all of the destruction I wanted to inflict on Clyde, dissipated like steam rising off a cup of coffee.

"Whatchu tryna do?" Jason asked, revenge already burning in his eyes.

"There's only one thing we can do," Rose replied. "Fight fire with fire."

"No," I said, staring at the photo in my hands. "No more."

"But, Buck," Brian said. "They can't get away with this. It's like when —"

I lifted my head and looked at them. "No more violence. We've had enough. And we've worried too much about other people instead of focusing on why we started the Happy Campers in the first place."

They looked at me as if I was joking, as if Trey's death could only be met with more death. But we weren't a gang, and we weren't killers.

Reader: A good salesperson knows

who they are, but that's only half of the equation. A great salesperson knows who they are *and* who they're not. Corny but true.

"Jake, how much cash do we have?" I asked, my strength slowly returning.

" 'Bout four hundred K."

"Good." I sat up. "Start looking for a new building. And put out a press release saying that the war is over, that we have no plans to find out who did this or retaliate in any way. That we're focusing on growing our organization and helping as many people as possible."

"Done," he said.

"Ellen. No more crazy, illegal homework. Think of other ways to teach new recruits. It draws too much heat and we can't afford any of us going to jail."

"Sure, Buck. Understood."

"Jason and Rose. If you do anything, or if any of you do anything" — I scanned the room — "you're out. No questions asked. Do you understand?"

"Aight," Jason said, looking at Rose.

"Fine, Buckaroo. If that's what you want, that's what we'll do."

"Thank you. Now can all of you get out? I need to rest." I laid my head back on the

pillow and closed my eyes, trying to understand what happened, what Trey actually
went back inside for.

"Not you," I said, calling to Soraya. "Can
you stay? Please?"

"Of course."

She looked down. "We're gonna have to
call a nurse to put all those tubes back in,
D. Can't have you dyin' out here."

"Okay," I said. "But not yet. I wanna tell
you somethin'."

"What?"

"What Jake said before? About me callin'
out for Ma? It's because I heard her laughin'
in the kitchen, like she was sittin' there, forreal, as if it were a normal day and she was
gettin' ready for work. You think tha's
crazy?"

She sat on the bed and took my hand in
hers. "No, D. I don't. Maybe she was there,
protectin' you."

I stared into her dark eyes, remembering
how she was there for me whenever I
thought I couldn't do it, whenever I didn't
believe in myself, whenever I needed someone to hold me in the right way.

"I love you, Soraya. And I'm so sorry for
everything that happened. For how I took
you for granted. For how I was never around
when you needed me most. For how I

turned into a —"

"Big asshole?" she said, running her fingers over the cuts on my cheek. I inhaled, and even with burnt lungs, I could taste the cinnamon and cocoa butter on her skin.

"That," I replied, laughing.

"I love you too, D. And even though you lost yourself for a bit, I love who you are now, who you've become. Mrs. V would be proud."

"Then kiss me," I said, pain pulsating through my cracked and splintering lips.

She leaned in. I rose to meet her, my entire soul bending in desire. But before our lips touched, she poked me in the chest, laughing like a hyena.

"Huh?" I opened my eyes.

She was grinning at me. "Kiss you? You're crazy, D. I said I love you, but that doesn' erase everything that happened between us. If you want me, you're gonna need to earn me, little by little. And even if that does happen, I'm not kissin' you until you take a test for every STD under the sun so I know you didn' catch anything from all those girls you were runnin' around with. Deal?"

"Damn. Aight," I said, lying back down, defeated. But then I smiled, remembering that, after everything that had happened, she was still there. "Same team, same "dream?" I asked.

"Always."

34

I got out a few days later, and we held Trey's funeral at the same church as Ma's; it was open only to Happy Campers. We looked everywhere for Trey's people but couldn't find anyone. Between Facebook and the white pages, there were tens of thousands of people with Trey's last name, Evans, across the entire country. It was like looking for a shell in the ocean. We announced his death across social media and even took out an ad in the *Daily News,* but no one followed up or ever claimed his body — it was like he hadn't existed until he walked into HQ off the streets.

Rhett knew what had happened, but I assured him I'd be fine for Friday. The plan was still to speak at the conference, then quit Sumwun and go Happy Camper full time. Surprisingly enough, after the media told the world that I was the leader, hundreds of people asked if they could join or set up their own chapters in places like South Africa, Italy, and Brazil. After I told the Talented Fifth about going full-time, they all thought it would make sense to join me, so they planned to quit their jobs at the end of September.

On top of all of that, I promised to downsize my life. There was no reason I needed a fancy apartment, expensive clothes, and other flashy shit. We were going to be models of how the twenty-first-century salesperson should live — not like monks, rejecting all material possessions, but also not like rock stars who lived only for themselves. We were going to run workshops and travel the world building the foundation for our other chapters. Man, the plan was perfect. It really was. All I had to do was speak at Sumwun's conference, then I'd be free. Even Barry had texted me after the news broke and said he was proud of me or, in his own words: Luv the blk pnther shit! Keep the SDRs comin and we're good. Once you go blk, u cant go back!

"Where to, Buck?" Chauncey said, wearing a light-green linen suit I'd recently bought him as a thank-you for all of his hard work. "I know it is a big night."

"That's right, Chauncey. After tonight, I'll be a free man. And so will you, if you want."

554

Chauncey cut his eyes at me in the rear-view, wrinkling his brow. "What do you mean?"

I laughed. "I mean that, if you want, you can quit driving me around and come work for the Happy Campers."

He looked back to the road and nodded. "What would I do?"

I rolled down the window and took in a big breath of New York City: trees blowing in the late summer, early fall air; the stench of garbage and cigarettes; the sounds of the subway screeching below.

"Whatever you want. We can discuss logistics later. You can run security, cook up some of your delicious Senegalese food, or shit, I could even teach you how to sell."

He rocked in his seat before breaking into his signature smile. "Ah! Buck. You are too good to me. I will discuss with Fatou tonight. Maybe I would like to sell. When I was a kid, I used to catch fish with my father from the ocean and sell them in the market, so maybe I already have some skills?"

"Yeah, I bet you already do," I said, steadying my heartbeat, excited and afraid of really being free to live on my own terms without Rhett or anyone else telling me what to do. "First stop is the conference, Madison Square Garden. Then back to HQ to celebrate."

As we arrived, Chauncey looked around, and said, "Well, this does not look like much of an event, Buck."

He was right. Madison Square Garden didn't look any different than on any other day. People rushed in and out of Penn Station; taxis lined up for those old-school enough to take them; sweet and salty smoke billowed from food carts; and, of course, there was classic New York City honking mixed in with "Fuck you!"s.

Contrary to what I expected, there was no gang of reporters loitering outside ready to attack, not even huge signs bearing Sumwun's logo. Just Frodo and a few of the newer SDRs pointing people in the right direction.

I made my way toward Frodo and the other SDRs who, on seeing me, began whispering. They stopped once I was within earshot.

"Hey, Frodo," I said, extending my hand, tense.

He looked at it, then up at me, and pulled me in for a tight hug. "Oh man, Buck. Oh man."

"I know. It's okay, Frodo. Everything will be okay. I promise."

Frodo wouldn't let go of me, and I felt

my shoulder getting wet. "No matter what happens, Buck. I want you to . . ." He squeezed me tighter and bawled like the big baby he was.

I patted his back, hoping he wouldn't throw up on me. "It's okay, man, it's all okay."

"People are saying the worst things about you, Buck. That you, uh, are like the Black Osama bin Laden. And hate white people. And, um, hate America. And a lot of things worse than that. I can't take it."

I freed myself from his grasp and held him in front of me. His eyes were red, his nose runny, and freshly cut pieces of hair covered his face; he had gotten a fade, the same style as mine. Not just that — I also realized that Frodo, however stupid and ridiculous he could be, was a real friend.

"I want to thank you, Frodo."

"For what?" he asked, wiping his eyes with the back of his hairy arm. "It's you who's done so much for me, for all of us. The company wouldn't — wouldn't be around without you. I wouldn't be around without you."

"Maybe so, but I want to thank you for being a loyal friend. And for always accepting me as I am, not for who you wanted me to be."

"I, uh, I appreciate that more than you'll ever know, Buck. Does this" — he paused — "does this mean I can join the Happy Campers?"

"No, Frodo, it doesn't."

I stepped inside. There were no lines of people waiting to get in. The place was empty, and I shit you not, I pinched myself to make sure I wasn't in some weird nightmare where I'd wake up and have to do this all over again.

"Buck," Marissa called, skipping down the hall toward me like she was at a hippie festival. "Everyone's waiting for you. Magic Johnson just finished the keynote speech, and you'll be up soon! How excited are you?"

"Magic Johnson?" I asked, stunned.

"Yeah! Isn't it crazy?" she said, looking more pumped up than Arnold Schwarzenegger on roids. "He spoke about how Sumwun is the embodiment of him. You know, overcoming life's crazy and kooky obstacles, rising to the top, like cream, and making enough money so not even an extremely lethal disease can kill you."

"Uh-huh, interesting. So where should I go?"

"Follow me!"

We walked down a long empty hallway.

She pointed me to the green room behind the stage. "Ten minutes, Buck. Break a leg!" She reached up and kissed my cheek.

I opened the door and entered an underwhelming room that had a few chairs, standard windows, and a turned-off television hanging from the ceiling. The only shock was that Rhett was sitting there, facing the windows.

"Hey," I said, walking over to him.

He didn't move. He just kept sitting there with his eyes closed. A minute later, he looked up at me. "Hey, you ready?"

"If you mean did I prepare something, no, I'm not ready."

"I'm sorry I didn't visit you at the hospital. And I'm sorry about your friend."

Trey, man. Fuck. Just hearing Rhett's condolences made it all real again. The life I was entering after this day wouldn't just be for me, Ma, or the people we'd help. It'd also be for the guy who always had my back and looked at me as if I could do no harm. For Trey.

"Thanks," I said, sitting next to him.

More silence. Then he said, "Are you leaving Sumwun?"

I nodded without returning his gaze.

"It's probably for the best."

"I'm sorry, but I can't be who you want

me to be, Rhett. I just can't."

"The only thing I've ever wanted was for you to be as great as I knew you could be. But now" — he stood up — "you've become someone else. Someone I no longer recognize."

"So what does this mean for us?" I asked, pain spreading from the pit of my stomach. "Am I no longer your brother?"

He refused to look at me. "It means that you broke your promise, Buck. You said you'd never lie to me, but you did. So I can't be there to protect you anymore no matter what happens."

"What's happening?" I asked, standing in front of him, no longer able to prevent myself from crying. I knew that everything I was doing was right, but choosing the Happy Campers over Rhett still hurt.

He cared more about Sumwun than anything or anyone else. He chose to see me as a *man* or a *Black man* when it was convenient to him. He likely picked me over Clyde because it was a better business decision. Still, I loved him with all that I had. He gave me the greatest gift in the world, one I can now give to others: an opportunity. And nothing, including what was about to happen, could ever take that away.

He dropped his head. "We have to distance ourselves from you, Buck. You're poisoned."

"What do you mean?" I pressed, grabbing his shoulders.

"It's the only way."

A thin man wearing a headset walked in. "Ready? Follow me please."

As I exited the green room, I looked back, finally finding Rhett's eyes. "I'm sorry, Buck. But you did this to yourself."

"Up there," the man said, gesturing to a small set of stairs leading to the stage.

I made my way up the stairs before two things stopped me in my tracks. One was the sight of a packed theater. There were easily five thousand people sitting there, laptops on their knees, phones in their hands, and complete silence as they focused their eyes on the stage, which held surprise number two: Bonnie Sauren.

She was sitting in one of two blue chairs, sipping bottled water, and smiling when she saw the shock on my face. On the oversize screen behind her was the title of our session: DIVERSITY GONE WRONG: BUCK VENDER IN CONVERSATION WITH BONNIE SAUREN.

"Look who showed up," Bonnie said, flashing her white teeth toward the crowd like blood diamonds. "It's the man of the hour, Buck Vender. Let's all please give Buck the welcome he deserves."

It started in the nosebleeds — a faint buzzing. But as it made its way toward me, like a towering tsunami complete with deadly white froth at the top, the wave of boos crashed into me with merciless ferocity.

Fuck me. This is an ambush.

The booing intensified as I made my way over to Bonnie, the sheer hatred it was laced with was a living, breathing, dangerous organism. I felt it in my bones, like the way you can feel the bass in your heart at a concert. I closed my eyes, waiting. But when the booing settled down, five thousand people began chanting, "RACIST! RACIST! RACIST! TERRORIST! TERRORIST! TERRORIST!" Bonnie, pleased, sat in her seat as snug as a white bug in a rug.

After a few minutes of this, which felt like a few days, she gripped her microphone, smiled, and said, "I'm with each and every one of you. But we're here for a conversation, so please let us get on with it."

Conversation? More like a modern-day lynching. When I looked out into the crowd, all I saw was a sea of red-faced men and women out for Black blood — *my* Black blood.

"You know?" Bonnie said, turning to me with that same plastic smile plastered to her plastic face. "We've actually never met before. But I met your friend Jason, right? That guy with the ski mask who said you both used to rob ice cream trucks together?"

"THUG!" someone shouted not too far from the stage.

"But," Bonnie continued, "the two of us have never had the pleasure of meeting. Has anyone ever told you that you look like Drake? I'm Bonnie," she said, extending a hand toward me.

"Buck." I shook her hand. She wiped it off on her skirt.

"*Buuuuuck,*" she said, drawing it out. "What an interesting name. Why don't we start there, hmm? How did you get the name Buck?"

"It was a nickname I got when I started at Sumwun."

"And who gave it to you?"

I flashed back to that day in Qur'an. "An old colleague," I said, straightening up.

Bonnie nodded. "Old indeed, huh? I heard it was Clyde Moore the Third, president of the White United Society of Salespeople. Is that true?"

I grabbed my bottled water from the little table between us and nodded.

"And it was because you had worked at Starbucks for, what, four years?"

I nodded again.

"My, hiring standards sure have dropped over the years," she said, turning to the audience. Laughter spread throughout the theater faster than the Paris Hilton sex tape.

"Okay, so you used to work at Starbucks. Clyde Moore hired you —"

"Rhett Daniels," I said, my voice cracking in all the wrong places, forcing me to take another sip of water. "He hired me."

"That's not what he says. He says it was Clyde's idea to take a chance on you, that he was just there to try to mentor you. And look at how you repaid him. By proving to be a closeted racist and founding a terrorist organization."

"It's not a —"

"Which brings us to the topic of today's conversation. Diversity gone wrong. When power is placed in the hands of the wrong people and abused, just as you abused yours. So, tell us, why do you hate white people, Buck?"

Everything slowed down, and the only thing I could hear was my heartbeat, ticking like a bomb. It pulsed in my ears, and in the veins in my head, arms, hands, legs, and feet.

I turned toward the audience. There was so much anger on their faces — red, fiery, heart-stopping anger. I truly didn't understand it. I didn't understand why they looked like they wanted me dead when they didn't even know me. And if they didn't know me and already hated me, I had nothing to lose, so I reached for my water, drained half of it, and took a deep breath.

"I don't," I said. "But let me ask you something, Bonnie. How many Black people are employed by LinkedIn, Facebook, Instagram, YouTube, Google, Twitter, and Tumblr?"

She rolled her eyes, looking to the audience, and laughed. "Oh, *come on.* Not the race card. That is so played out, Buck."

"You played the race card when you asked me why I hate white people, which I don't, so humor me. How many people, say, out of a hundred, are Black at those companies?"

"I'd say thirty, maybe forty," she replied, annoyed.

"It's two. At each of those companies, only two in a hundred employees are Black. For most of them, only four in a hundred employees are Latinx."

"Boo-hoo," she said, pretending to rub her eyes. "You know why there aren't more? Because they don't have the skills, buddy. If more Black and Latin-whatever people were competent enough to get these jobs, they would. Look at Asians. You don't see them crying and blaming the white man for not succeeding. No, they just buck up, get good grades, and reach for the American dream."

"YEAH!" a man shouted, rising from his chair and clapping. The rest of the crowd clapped along with him.

"I'm not here to convert you," I said, facing them. "And I'm not here to, as you say" — I turned to Bonnie — "play the race card. I don't want to waste your time. So just humor me for a second and close your eyes."

"What is this?" Bonnie asked. "I thought you just said you weren't here to convert us."

"I'm not, I promise. And I'm tired of arguing, defending, and everything else you brought me here for. You win." I addressed the crowd now. "You all win. But before I go, just close your eyes. It'll only be for a second."

I turned to the side of the stage where the man with the headset stood. "Dim the lights, please."

As the lights turned down, I closed my eyes and brought the mic closer to my mouth. "I want you all to think back, way back to when you were a kid. Think back to where you lived, to your parents or whoever raised you. Think back to the school you went to, your first crush, what you loved to do on Saturday mornings, your favorite types of snacks.

"Think about what you wanted to be when you were younger. Maybe it was a firefighter, nurse, actor, police officer, doctor, lawyer, hell, maybe even president. Try to remember what that feeling felt like, when you *really* believed you could be anything you wanted. That not even the sky was the limit. And now hold that feeling in your chest. Feel it in your heart — its warmth, how it lifts you up like your mom or dad carrying you on their shoulders.

"Now I want you to think about the moment you realized you wouldn't be what you wanted to be. Maybe you never saw anyone who came from where you did achieving what you wanted. Maybe it was a teacher, or one of your parents, who told you to get real. Shit, it could've just been as small as a friend laughing at you when you told them your dreams, and that little laugh, that seed of doubt, crushed you. You felt less than, like you weren't worthy of being more, of being better. Like who you were wasn't good enough.

"That is why we started the Happy Campers. Not to be labeled as terrorists, racists, or anything else the media loves to portray us as, but because we wanted to help others — people who, maybe even like you said, Bonnie, usually don't have the skills for those jobs — get ahead. Because we know that when you lift others up, regardless of their skin color, your arms get stronger. And what I want for those Happy Campers is the same thing I want for you all here today. To never, ever, feel less than again."

I opened my eyes and saw the men and women in the crowd opening theirs too. When I looked into their faces, everything that had been there before — the red anger, electric violence, and blistering hatred — was still there, but it was softer. Like they remembered the children they were, the dreams they had, and when they'd lost themselves.

I turned to Bonnie. Her face was trembling as if she were fighting a war inside of herself. She slowly raised her mic, and said, "I wanted to be an actress, but my . . . my mother said I was too fat, that Hollywood would never let someone as large and clumsy as me in any movie."

She paused. A tear of mascara rolled down her cheek, staining her signature white dress. In that moment, I didn't care that Bonnie Sauren was an evil white supremacist who probably wished the South hadn't lost the war. I got up and did what I would've done with anyone else: I gave her a hug.

The crowd didn't applaud, but they also didn't boo. Bonnie, rendered defenseless, sobbed into my chest in front of five thousand people who may have still hated me but also, I hoped, saw my humanity, which was a win. The wars I had fought to get there were over, and now, no matter what happened, I was finally, truly, and completely free. *Whoosh! Bang! Poof!* Every day is deals day, baby. Every day is deals day.

Reader: There's nothing like a Black man on a mission. No, there's nothing like a Black *salesman* on a mission. And don't you forget it.

35

"How did it go, Buck?" Chauncey asked.

I laughed. "I guess as well as it could've, Chauncey. I'm still in one piece and no one broke out a noose."

"Of course you are still in one piece. I told you, strength lasts forever. So, if you are free tonight, maybe you could join Fatou, Amina, and me for dinner at my home?"

"Sounds like a plan. Is Fatou going to make —" My phone buzzed. "One second."

It was Kujoe. "Kujoe," I said, anger bubbling in my stomach.

"Buck, I know you told me not to call, but —"

"But *what,* Kujoe? Don't fuck up my perfect day, man. Especially with all of the shit you've pulled. Trey is fucking dead, and it's probably your fault."

"But, Buck, I'm calling to —"

"You're calling to get me heated, Kujoe. Listen, you're done. HQ is destroyed, and we need to start over, and it pains me to say it because I liked you, but you're not going to be a part of it. You only get so many chances in this life, Kujoe, and your time with the Happy Campers is over," I said, and hung up.

"Like I was saying, Chauncey, I really hope Fatou's making some of that stuff, what was it? With the chicken, vegetables, and rice in peanut sauce?"

Chauncey laughed, slapping the steering wheel. "*Mafé,* Buck. You are really becoming an African! I think my job is done."

I laughed too, my mouth already watering at the thought of the delicious food we were about to have. "Yeah, maybe." My phone buzzed again. I quickly picked it up.

"What the fuck did I just say, Kujoe? Don't fucking call me again or —"

"D?" It was Soraya. "What are you talkin' about? What did Kujoe do?"

"Oh," I said, sitting back, relaxing my muscles. "Sorry. Nothin', he's jus', it's nothin'. What's wrong?"

"You're lyin'," she said. "But it doesn' matter. Jason's in the hospital."

"Hospital? What happened?"

I tapped Chauncey on the shoulder. "Turn back around, Chauncey."

"Okay, Buck. What is going on?"

"Yeah," Soraya continued. "He's okay, but he has a broken leg and some bruises. He's at Beth Israel. I was jus' there but came to your place to rest. He's really okay though, D, trust me, but he's askin' for you, so can you go and see him?"

"Yeah, of course. I'll see you right after. But what happened?"

"He jus' said he was randomly attacked in Chelsea."

"But what was he doin' in Chelsea?"

"Won't say, maybe you can get it outta him. But I'll see you soon. I love you."

My heart jolted. It would take me some time to get used to hearing her say that, or maybe I never would, and every time would feel like the first. All I knew was that it felt good. Really good.

"Well," she said, a smile in her voice. "I'm waitin'."

"I love you too, *habibti.*"

"That's what I thought," she said, hanging up.

I told Chauncey to hang outside once we got there. If Jason wasn't really messed up, then I'd just go check him out before scooping Soraya and heading to Harlem for some of that *mafé.* This was just a small hiccup.

A nurse directed me to his room, and on seeing him lying up in bed and scrolling on his phone, I said, "Damn, son. Looks like you've upgraded your hospital game since I put you in Woodhull."

"You think you so funny, nigga. Funny for someone who I was jus' visitin' in the hospital."

I sat next to him and examined his leg, which was already in a cast and elevated by some hanging ceiling contraption. He had a few bruises on his face and scratches on his arm, but he seemed okay overall.

"What happened?"

"Motherfuckers came outta nowhere, bro. There was like four of 'em rockin' some scary-ass cryin' baby masks. One hit me in the head, and I managed to knock two of 'em down, but then one guy, some shorter nigga, took out a bat and caught me in the leg. Doctor said my tibia's fractured, so they put a metal rod in me and now I'm here, talkin' to you."

"*Okay,*" I said, trying to piece everything together. "You're sayin' four dudes jumped you . . . in Chelsea . . . while other people were around?"

"Yeah, nigga. You tryna say I'm lyin' or some shit? I don' need that."

"Nah, man. I'm jus' sayin' it's weird. Shit like that doesn' happen in Chelsea. What were you doin' there?"

He picked his phone up and started scroll-ing again.

"Yo." I snatched the phone out of his hands. "What were you doin' there, going to SoulCycle or some shit? Why're you bein' so sus?"

He snatched his phone back. "Funny, ha-ha-ha. I was buyin' some high-end wine and cheese, nigga. Tryna elevate myself, you know."

"Did you jus' pick the whitest things you could think of and lie to me?"

"Basically," he said, laughing. "But, okay, Imma keep it real with you, because you my boy and I need your help. But you gotta promise not to flip, aight?"

"Aight."

"I was bustin' a trap."

I shot up from my chair, using every inch of force I had not to strangle him. "You were *what*? I hope you're fuckin' with me, Batman. I really do."

He shrugged.

"Why?" I looked up at the ceiling and paced around the room. "Why, after joinin' the Happy Campers, gettin' a job, and everything you've done, would you still sell drugs?"

He put his phone down and looked at me. "It's not that simple, G. The money I was

574

makin' was okay, but my momma is in some serious debt with some serious people. I've been workin' for, what, a coupla months? I know the money I need will come, but I had a few opportunities to make some *real* loot, and I wasn' tryna pass 'em up."

"So, what, you were dealin' to someone in Chelsea? How long you been doin' this for? How many clients you have, man?"

Jason sat up, laughing. "I thought you taught us to only ask one question at a time, nigga. Look atchu."

I clenched my jaw.

"Aight." He took in a lungful of air. "It was jus' one client. Some rich guy who would only hit me up every coupla weeks for some serious weight. Must've been supplyin' all of lower Manhattan or maybe steppin' on it and flippin' it himself. But I've only been doin' it for about a month. Matter fact, I was done dealin', bro. Trey's the one who said he knew someone that wanted, and when he told me how much, I'm sayin' like ten stacks' worth, I said hell yeah I could do it. So I hit up Malcolm, he hit me with the weight, and I made the money easy."

"Why didn' you stop then? Ten Gs mus' be enough to clear your moms's debt."

"Nah, bro. It's some killer debt, and not

the kind you pay the government, you feel me? So when homie called me for this flip, I was like, 'Bet. This is the last time Imma do this. After this, plus my savin's, her debts will be cleared, and we'll be set.' So when those niggas jumped me, I texted the guy and said I'd have to bring it in a coupla days, but he said he didn' have a coupla days, that it was now or never. And I'm not about to be on the hook with Malcolm for ten Gs, so I gotta get it to the guy tonight."

He reached over the side of his bed, grabbed a black backpack, and threw it at me.

"I can't trust anyone else," he said. "This guy is straight, bro. I promise. All you gotta do is ring the buzzer, take the elevator up, drop it on the floor, grab the money from a little table, count it, and be out. You never see him; he never sees you. I don' even know what this nigga looks like."

Fuck! I knew the night was going too perfectly. I wanted to say no, but I didn't because, if the tables were turned, Jason would have done it for me without a question. Plus, he didn't seem too worried about it, so I didn't either. *It'll be quick and easy.*

"Text me the address," I said.

"If I don't come out in fifteen minutes,

Chauncey," I said, slinging the backpack over my shoulder as I leaned into his window, "leave and don't look back. Okay?"

He laughed. "What are you talking about, Buck?" He shook his index finger at me. "Are you trying to get out of dinner tonight? We can always do it another time."

"No. There's nothing I want more than some of Fatou's food, but seriously, if I'm not out in fifteen minutes, leave. Okay?"

The light in his face went out. He bit his lower lip and shook his head. "I do not understand, Buck."

I extended my hand through the window. "Promise me, Chauncey. Promise me that you'll leave."

He looked at my hand for a minute, as if he didn't know what to do, then shook it. "I promise, Buck."

The building, on Twenty-Third and Tenth, was like others in the area: tall as hell, made out of brick, and sitting in front of trees with low black fences that dogs love to piss on. I buzzed 818 and the door clicked open.

I found the elevator and entered the room number on some high-tech digital display. The doors opened directly into the apartment, like at my place. I stepped out into an empty hallway and saw the little table Jason mentioned, with a white envelope on top. I picked it up, counted the bills inside, then put the bag down.

So far, so good. Sweat poured down my brow. I quickly turned and pressed the elevator button, wondering if the guy was in the house or if he was somehow watching me from a hidden camera. A bell rang, the elevator doors opened, and as I stepped in, something heavy crashed into my head.

"Fuck," I whispered.

Everything went black.

When I woke up, I was in what I guessed was the living room, tied to a chair with dried blood sticking to my head, hands, and clothes.

"Yo!" I shouted, struggling with the ropes on my wrists and ankles. "What the fuck!"

"Calm down," a voice said from behind me.

"Who the fuck are you?" I tried to turn around. "What do you want?"

"That's a good question," the voice said. "What will you give me?"

"Money, you want money?"

The voice laughed and punched me in the back of my head. My wrists and ankles burned against the fibrous ropes. The voice forced a plastic bag over my head. As I coughed, the bag became tighter to the point where I was only sucking in plastic.

No air. My mind went blank. I was certain that I was going to die.

By the time this had begun to sink in, the voice yanked the bag off, and I was left gasping like I'd been brought back to life. The voice just laughed, and laughed, and laughed.

"Please," I said, my throat feeling like someone poured hot gravel down it. "Please stop." I hated the desperation in my voice, how I was begging whomever, whatever, this was, but I had no choice. I didn't even know where I was. There was just a nondescript hardwood floor beneath me and a white wall in front of me.

"Fine," the voice said. "As you wish." A white hand dangled a knife in front of me.

"FUCK!" I shouted, twisting in the chair, trying to break free.

"Relax," the voice said, turning the knife in front of me. "Or I will drive this through your fucking eyeball faster than you can say Harriet Tubman."

The voice brought the knife to my ankles, cutting the rope. Then my wrists. Even though I was now free, or at least thought I was, I stayed glued to the seat, afraid of what the voice would do next.

"Go ahead," it said. "Stand up and face me."

Trembling, I slowly rose, my eyes fixed on the wall in front of me, then quickly turned around.

"Hello, Buck," Clyde said, grinning from ear to ear. "Welcome to my home."

"You?" I said, wondering how the fuck Clyde had become Jason's customer without him ever knowing, how any of this added up. *Did Jason set me up?*

"Me," he replied, walking to his kitchen. "Drink?"

"No, thanks. What the fuck are you doing, man? You're crossing a line, over what? This white-salespeople shit? C'mon, Clyde."

He grabbed a bottle of white wine out of the fridge and poured himself a glass, slowly smelled it, brought it to his lips, sipped, and let out a sigh of satisfaction before sitting down at a dining table. "Sure you don't want any? It's expensive."

I stayed where I was, deciding when to knock the shit out of him or worse. He had left the knife in the living room, so I could just grab it and force him to let me leave.

"Fine." He shrugged. "Suit yourself. But if you want to talk about crossing lines, I think you and your friends crossed a line when you waterboarded me. But that's just my opinion."

"I don't know what you're talking about."

He poured himself another glass. "You don't? C'mon, Buck. That dyke Rose and your drug-dealing friend Jason? That cute stunt where you tried to hack me. I gotta say, you all are creative, but not smart."

Kujoe. It had to be him. How else would Clyde know all of these details?

"I don't know what you promised Kujoe," I said, walking toward him. "But it had to be good for him to turn his back on us. You fucking asshole."

Clyde looked up, confused. "I don't know a Kujoe, but if you're wondering how you got here, I'll let him tell you himself."

"Him?"

Clyde turned toward the hallway. "You can come out now."

I couldn't believe my eyes. I stepped backward, tripped over a chair, and looked up from the floor. He stood in the kitchen, staring at me with fire in his eyes.

"Trey?"

"In the flesh," he said.

"But you're —"

"D-d-d-dead?" he said, laughing. "Looks like I'm pretty alive, Buck."

He walked over and extended a hand to help me up, but when I grabbed it, he brought his other one around and slammed a cane into my face.

"What the fuck, Trey!"

"That must've felt good," Clyde said, looking up from his wine.

Trey turned to Clyde. "You know what? It did. It felt *so* good."

Trey. Clyde. They knew each other. And the truth of everything started to unfold. Kujoe wasn't the snitch — it was Trey. The whole time. But how?

Trey stood over me, still laughing. "You seem confused, Buck, so I'll help you out. You see, it was you who actually did this to yourself. When I first joined the Happy Campers, all you'd talk about was that — what did you call him? — 'pigment-deficient pussy, Clyde.' Yeah. So I figured if you hated someone that much, he and I would get along. When we met, it was obvious we shared the same goal, so we hatched a plan to" — he stretched his hand toward me — "put you on your ass, so to speak."

"But, Trey. You're dead, man. We found the body. Pieces of your shoes."

"Body brokers," Clyde said, handing Trey a glass. "You'd be surprised how easy it is to buy cadavers, especially Black ones."

Trey took a seat at Clyde's table and crossed his legs. "That's why I ran back in. I planted the body and the shoes. I ran out the back through the garden and even dropped that photo there, as a nice touch, long before the building collapsed."

I still didn't get it. "Why would you do this to me, Trey? After everything I've done, everything the Happy Campers have done for you?"

"Because you are everything that's wrong with this world, Buck," he said, and banged his cane on the floor. "The person who lives like they can do whatever they want without any consequences. Consider this a consequence of past sins committed."

"Trey." I got up and walked over to him. "What are you talking about?"

He seemed unfazed. "What is my name?"

"It's Trey."

"No." He shook his head. "My full name."

"Treyborn Percival Evans. Why?" I placed a hand on his shoulder, but he flung it off. "It's me, Trey. It's Buck, man. What the fuck?"

"Does my name sound familiar to you? Any part of it?"

I closed my eyes, trying to think, but I couldn't connect it to anything. "No, it doesn't."

He stood and faced me. "When I was younger, people used to call me Percy." He paused. "After my grandfather."

"And what does that have to —" I stopped, the blood in my veins turning to lead. I did know a Percy once. Mr. Percy Rawlings. *Rosewood, of course.* I recognized that cane.

Trey smiled. "Now you see, huh? You kicked my grandfather out of the home he had lived in for decades, you piece of shit. Do you know what happened to him when he left? Where he went?"

All I could do was shake my head.

"He went to an old people's home. He and my mom didn't speak anymore, but when a nurse called our house, I picked up and said I'd go to see him. Even though my mom never let him visit us, I remembered and loved him. He was the kindest man I knew. Not one!" He was shouting now. "Not one bad bone in that man's body.

"But when I went to see him, all he could talk about was *you*. The kid he wronged by not letting you have a last word with your mom. He would say your name in his sleep and repeat it all day, tears covering his wrinkled face as he stared out the window. Within a few weeks of me getting there, he had a stroke. Nurses said he was under a lot of stress. That his body just couldn't take it.

"So I went to where he used to live, to

confront you, but when I saw what you all were doing, I figured I could make my revenge even sweeter — that I would hurt you *and* everyone you loved in the process."

"And when he came to me," Clyde interjected, "I didn't hesitate. It was Trey's idea for me to start WUSS, and he always helped me stay one step ahead of you . . . except when your friends went all *Taken* on me."

"That was the only thing I missed," Trey added. "But it didn't matter. Jason was always running his mouth about his drug-dealing past. So, knowing he wouldn't be able to pass up a quick buck, I convinced him to start dealing to Clyde without knowing it. He always just came here, dropped the bag off, took the envelope, and left without ever seeing Clyde.

"We were the ones who got people from WUSS to jump him and told him he had to deliver the cocaine today or that we were done," Trey said, looking at me with a face full of satisfaction. "This was chess, Buck, not checkers. You never knew what game you were playing, but all roads still brought you here. And that's what matters most."

"That's right," Clyde said, rounding the table and getting so close that I could smell the fermented grapes on his breath. "You took Rhett away from me!" he shouted, spitting in my face. "The only brother I ever knew. You're scum, which is why I named you Buck. Because I knew you'd never be worth more than that."

I looked from one to the other, wondering what they were going to do to me, if there was some staircase I could run down, or maybe even a window I could jump out of and somehow survive the fall. I needed time to think. "What now?"

Clyde unclenched his jaw, sat back down, and poured himself another glass. "You just delivered a quarter pound of coke to me, Buck. What do you think?"

"No," Trey said, opening up a cabinet, taking out other packages. "He delivered a few pounds of it, actually. And we have it all here."

"You both are insane. I never did that."

"No?" Clyde said. "We have you walking into my apartment, placing the bag on the ground, and taking the money. When we told my dad's DEA buddy that we knew about a big drug dealer parading around as some civil rights activist, he jumped at the chance."

Clyde took out his phone and brought it to his ear. "You can come up."

I turned to the elevator, saw the numbers slowly rising, and ran to the window. I stuck my head out and saw tiny people pausing on the sidewalk as more cop cars arrived, sirens blaring. It was a long way down — there was no way I'd make it. And even if I did, they'd be there to stop me. I looked back at the elevator — the numbers kept climbing.

"Trey," I said, running over to him. "I'm sorry. I'm sorry about Mr. Rawlings, man. About everything."

"I'm sure you are," he said, hard eyes boring into me. "I would be too if I were about to go to jail for a very, very long time."

"Clyde," I said, rounding the table.

"No, Buck," he laughed. "It's too late for —"

I blasted my fist through his face, breaking his jaw, nose, and some other smaller bones in that blond head with those bluer than blue eyes.

Just then, when the elevator rang and the doors opened, I could think of only one thing. A question.

Was it all worth it?

Reader: You tell me.

EPILOGUE

On May 8, 1973, New York Governor Nelson Rockefeller signed what are known as the Rockefeller Drug Laws. If you were caught selling two ounces or more of narcotics or weed, or even just possessing four ounces of either, you were going to prison for a minimum of fifteen years and a maximum of twenty-five years to life. I know, fifteen years of your life gone for just two ounces of weed. The prison population in New York tripled, and ninety percent of those incarcerated under the drug laws were Black and Latino males.

In 2004 Governor George Pataki signed into law the Drug Law Reform Act, which reduced the minimum sentence from fifteen years to eight. So now a Black or Latino male would spend only eight years of his life in prison for selling or possessing drugs that had seemed to them like the only way out of their circumstances.

In 2009 yet another governor, David Paterson, removed the minimum sentences and left prison time for drug possession and sale up to judges' discretion.

So how do I fit into all of this? Thanks to the video Clyde had of me dropping the backpack off and taking the money — and his framing me for the two pounds that Jason had delivered — I was charged with an A-I felony.

My lawyer threw everything she had at them, including entrapment and a whole host of other shit, but nothing stuck. And since I refused to snitch on Jason, a jury found me guilty. Despite being a first-time offender, I was sentenced to a healthy eight years without bail. I suppose it didn't hurt that the judge and prosecutor played squash with Clyde's pops on weekends. Or that I'm a young Black male who successfully bucked the system that was created to keep them in power and minorities like me subservient. But that's just a hunch.

The rest of the Talented Fifth, plus Jason and Soraya, held marches. People from all over the world made posters saying FREE BUCK. Others lobbied Congress. But I eventually told them to stop. The Happy Campers were bigger than I was, and they would be able to thrive without my presence, proving I'd done something right.

I've been in here for two years now, and my lawyer continues to fight for me. But to tell you the truth, it's not so bad. After the whirlwind I experienced, the past two years have given me time to think, analyze, and finally internalize everything that happened: Ma's death, Mr. Rawlings's, Sumwun, Rhett, Barry, the Happy Campers, and all of the other events that feel like a dream that happened far too quickly to someone that young.

Plus, I receive about a hundred letters every week from new Happy Campers and other admirers around the world, so I have my hands full responding to them, calling in to different talk shows, and taking about a dozen visits a week from friends and strangers. Just last month Frodo showed up with Marissa and told me they're having a baby. Life is weird as fuck. I would have never guessed Frodo knew what a vagina looked like. Even Brian has a girlfriend — the French woman he picked up at the bar during his sales training.

As for the others, Jason cleared his mom's debt and still lives with her in Bed-Stuy, although in a much nicer and larger apartment that he owns. Rhett's still going strong at Sumwun, Barry continues to move up the Forbes list, Bonnie Sauren came out with a *New York Times* bestseller, *White Offense: Why Being White Is Quite All Right,* and the rest of the Talented Fifth have their hands full with thousands of Happy Campers worldwide. Trey, unfortunately, has never reached out to me and I don't know what he's up to now. I hope that it's something good.

At the beginning of this book, I told you that my aim was to teach you how to sell in order to fix the game, to realize that life comes down to a handful of key negotiations, and that you're either selling someone on "amen" or they're selling you on "hell no." If I taught you something, skills that you can take into your own life to get ahead, I hope you'll make good on your end of the deal and share this book with someone who needs it. Don't give them your copy; I want you to wear it out, reread your favorite passages, and understand the tactics that worked and the choices I made that didn't. Buy your friend a new copy, open up the first page, and write the thing that you wish most for them. For me, what I want most for you is to be free.

As for my life, I am happy. I am locked up in a cage but have never been freer. I also apologize if I tricked you; it's just that you probably wouldn't have wanted to sit through hundreds of pages written by someone locked up who was trying to teach you how to be free.

But I'll end this on a happy note, and I do hope that we'll see each other again. The highlight of every week I've spent in here for these two years is Sundays. A correctional officer — who, I should add, has a niece who's a Happy Camper — says I have a visitor. He unlocks my cell, we shake hands, and he leads me to the visitor center. When I sit down, the first thing I notice is the smell: cinnamon and cocoa butter.

We never say anything for the first minute or two. We just stare, taking in each other's faces across a table. Then, my visitor turns her hand into a phone — thumb up, pinkie down, index, middle, and ring fingers curled toward her palm — and raises it to her ear. It's my signal to do the same.

When I bring my own hand to my ear, she smiles, but there are some days when I don't — when I just sit there for as long as I can, staring at her in her scrubs, thinking about how much better a man she makes me, how she is my rock, my foundation, my everything, even though I don't deserve her after all the shit I've done. But on the days I do reciprocate, and we speak with our hands to our ears, do you know what she says? Do you know how she starts our conversations?

She says the two words that translate into opportunity, that mean the possibility of a better life is calling you, and that you better pick up before it's too late. Two words that, like a rooster crowing, the sun rising, or coffee brewing, signal the beginning of a new day.

Two words that, if you pay close attention, can open doors that will make you never, ever feel less than again.

Ring ring.

ACKNOWLEDGMENTS

Ayo! We're here! As J. Cole said in "Note to Self," which I'm paraphrasing, for legal reasons (you see that, Cole?!): *acknowledgments are like movie credits. If you're not down to sit through them, get your ass up and leave the theater!* Truth. Picture this acknowledgments section as a freestyle — pure stream of consciousness. If you're reading this, you're a real one, and I want to start off by thanking you for purchasing my book, consuming it, and taking the time to let it digest. But whether it gives you energy or indigestion isn't on me!

Aside from you, the reader, the first person I need to thank is my agent, Tina Pohlman. Tina, we did it! Whew. Feels like just yesterday when we first spoke. I knew from our first conversation that you were the one. Seriously. When you said, "This sounds like a sales manual," I was knocked flat on my ass because someone other than me understood what I was doing. Thank you for being my confidante, my therapist, and for being a true partner I can always rely on.

Pilar Garcia-Brown. Pilar! Missing my flight in San Francisco and taking my call with you in a dingy hotel room was one of the best decisions of my life. This book would not be what it is without you, and I am indebted to you for your calming manner, how patient you are, and for how you've helped me become a better writer and literary citizen. Thank you, Pilar.

Other folks at Houghton Mifflin Harcourt I've relied on — Taryn Roeder, Lori Glazer, Michael Dudding, Matt Schweitzer, Jenny Freilach, and everyone else working to get *Black Buck* into as many hands as possible — thank you, thank you, thank you. Shout out to the sales team, too. It's an honor and a privilege to publish my debut novel with HMH.

Shout out to David Hough, who copyedited the hell out of this! David, whether you know it or not, you helped me become a better writer through your encouraging edits. For real.

Pat Mulcahy and Matt Sharpe, two of my early readers whose notes helped this book puff its chest out and gain some good mass,

I thank you. Same to Julio Saenz and Gow Mosby, two close friends who read early drafts and let me know I was on the right path.

Again, stream of consciousness, so let me express my deep, really bottomless, love for my family. Words won't do this justice. But, Mom, Sonia Askaripour, I love you so much. I have tears in my eyes as I write this. You always believed in me, even when I was lost, and I wouldn't be here without you. Pops, Aziz Askaripour, same to you. You taught me what it means to work hard and never let up, no matter the obstacles, and I will never be able to thank you enough. *Doostet daram, baba.*

My brothers — Darius, Dave, Khalik, and Andrew — you four have been my greatest teachers, supporters, and friends. I know that when everyone and everything else in the world fades away, you will always be there for me, and I will always be there for you. Sometimes it feels like the earth is getting ready to split when we're together, and I'm grateful for that feeling. When the five of us are aligned, nothing can stop us. I love you with all that I am.

To my aunts, uncles, and cousins — from the United States to Jamaica to Iran to Canada to England and everywhere else we are — thank you. I feel your love and send you my own. RIP to Uncle Dicky and Aunt Sheri.

Grandma Clarine Emily Case and Grandpa William Rochester Case, I am proud to have your blood running through my veins. The blood of enslaved people, yes, and so much more. The blood of teachers, of politicians, of dedicated community members who uplifted the lives of so, so many. Thank you for teaching me how to read, Grandma. Thank you for teaching me how to lead, Grandpa. I hope that you both are proud.

Johania Dinora Ramos. My first love. My Soraya. My first reader. Thank you for allowing me to read you new chapters every night, as well as for your candor in what you liked and didn't. Thank you for our history. Thank you for still being in my life. I hope everything has been worth it.

Quemuel Arroyo. YO! We did it, Q! Damn, man. I truly understand the limitations of language when I try to express how I feel about someone like you. You've held me down from day one. Whether it was introducing me to Moet and ice cream from Trader Joe's, letting me indefinitely cohabitate with you, or just being there for my manic ups and downs, yo, I love you, man.

I don't need many people in this world, but I do need you. Thank you for always leaving the door open . . . except that first time.

Geetanjali Toronto and Adam Vinson: two homies who have been there for me and supported this book from way back when. I thank you. Same to Michael Esposito. A real one.

Thank you to Delaney Poon and the whole Poon gang for your support when everything — getting an agent, a book deal, selling the film/TV rights — was popping off. The time we spent together was meaningful, and I am glad to have met when we did.

Grovo. Grovo. Grovo. I know, all of this is crazy. I can't wait to hear what you think of this book. I don't know what to say. Working with you all was one of the best times of my life. Also, one of the craziest. Thank you for allowing me to lead, as well as for forgiving me, at times, for my inability to do so — I, too, was just trying to figure it all out as best as I could. Special shout outs to Nick Narodny, for being there for me after I left and remaining a true friend; to Jeb Pierce, for making sure we kept in touch, even when I fell out of it with so many others; to Ben Contillo, yes, you, Ben Contillo, for always saying I was your #1 draft pick;

to Dan Levine, for helping to edit a book manuscript that will never see the light of day, and for doing so with an open heart and enthusiasm; to the SDRs, the other founders, for giving me an opportunity; and everyone else who made Grovo one of the "best places to work in NYC tech."

Big ups to the team at MACRO. They are not only a pleasure to work with, but also committed to creating works by and for people of color — thank you all for your hard work. And thank you, Anna DeRoy, my film/TV agent! *Black Buck* couldn't have a better shepherd in Hollywood. Also shout out to Jay Ellis, who has become a real friend and source of guidance. Thank you for entering my life, brother.

Speaking of people who enter your life, yo, the biggest of shout outs to the Rhode Island Writers Colony. I can say with the surest conviction: the road to publication would have been so much lonelier and more difficult without all of you. You were the writing family I needed but didn't know it. Jason Reynolds, bro, thank you for all of the game you've dispensed and continue to pass to me. Miss Dianne, I love you so much. John and Mary, thank you for always making Warren feel as welcoming as possible. My 2018 cohort — Lena, Carla,

Qurratulayn — I am so happy to know you. All of the other RIWC fam, especially those who allow me to vent like a madman, Candice Iloh and Irvin Weathersby, I thank you. RIP to Brook Stephenson. Your spirit lives on, brother.

A couple of people in the literary community who helped me out when I truly had no idea what I was doing, whether through meeting up, sharing information, or just giving me kind words of encouragement: Jess Mowry, Danya Kukafka, Viet Thanh Nguyen, Kris Jansma, and Arvin Ahmadi. Morgan Jerkins, too, who gave me my first opportunity to have an essay published, which set off many more. Same to Joe Keohane, from *Medium,* who extended help when he didn't need to. And shout out to Corinne Segal, from *LitHub,* with whom I published many of my favorite essays.

Also, Jake Dunlap, from Skaled, for helping me to avoid being a starving artist as I wrote this book — thank you, man. Startup consulting was a godsend. Thank you to Tanya Fadlallah and Rahman Berrada who double-checked my Arabic. *Shukran jazeelan!* And to Thomas Mailey, from the now thankfully closed down Lincoln Correctional Facility, who answered some of my questions. As well as to Sally Wofford-

Girand, who is working to sell *Black Buck* overseas as I type this — thank you, Sally!

This is roll credits, man. If you're still reading, I love you. I do. I want to extend the highest gratitude to some of my biggest inspirations, many of whom are no longer alive: Nina Simone, Malcolm X, Gordon Parks, Jean-Michel Basquiat, Fred Hampton, Frederick Douglass, Miles Davis, John Coltrane, Richard Pryor, Maya Angelou, Dave Chappelle, Oprah Winfrey, Nat Turner. I would look at your photos every day before writing *Black Buck.* Thank you for the lives you led, and lead (talking to you, Ms. Winfrey and Mr. Chappelle).

Some know that I would watch two to three hours of music videos and movie trailers every day before writing *Black Buck,* and while I can't list all of the artists whose videos I watched, a few that stick out: Nipsey Hussle (RIP, King), Boogie, Buddy, Kendrick Lamar, J. Cole, Aminé, Jessie Reyez, Joey Bada$$, Teyana Taylor, Kanye West, Tai Cheeba, Chance the Rapper, Towkio, Kid Cudi, Dave, Stormzy, KOTA the Friend, Sinéad Harnett, ScHoolboy Q, Childish Gambino, Tyler, the Creator, Jay Rock, Kyle, Russ, Drake, YBN Cordae, Megan Thee Stallion, Nas, Wu-Tang Clan, Capital STEEZ, Radamiz, Snoh Aalegra,

Dot Demo, Anderson .Paak, Meek Mill, Pusha T, Black Thought, slowthai, Vince Staples, Big Sean, Mac Miller, Duckwrth, The Game, Mereba, and ODIE.

Man, this could go on forever. I didn't even touch on composers, TV shows, films, or other writers (go read some John A. Williams, Toni Morrison, Chester Himes, Iceberg Slim, Percival Everett, Paul Beatty, Colson Whitehead, Chimamanda Ngozi Adichie, Nafissa Thompson-Spires, Brit Bennett, and Mitchell S. Jackson, though). I just wanted to pay homage to only a small number of the people who helped me write this book. I was alone in a room, you know. No coach over my shoulder saying, "Write that shit, son! Yeah, yeah, keep going!" So these people and their incredible artistry, as well as my brothers, parents, and close friends, were my coaches. But a writer writes alone — no one is going to put your fingers to the keys or pen and guide them for you, unless you believe in otherworldly guidance, which I often do. Point is, you need to draw inspiration in any way possible, and above are some of my mine.

Shout out to a few teachers from Bellport High School who saw me as a human and not a burden, and who built me and others up instead of tearing us down: Mr. Boes,

Mrs. Budd, and Mrs. Bavosa.

That's it. The next book I publish won't be anything like this one, and I hope you still support. But in case I don't see you, "good afternoon, good evening, and good night!"

ABOUT THE AUTHOR

Mateo Askaripour was a 2018 Rhode Island Writers Colony writer-in-residence, and his writing has appeared in *Entrepreneur, LitHub, Catapult, The Rumpus, Medium,* and elsewhere. He lives in Brooklyn, and his favorite pastimes include bingeing music videos and movie trailers, drinking yerba mate, and dancing in his apartment. *Black Buck* is his debut novel. Follow him on Twitter and Instagram at @AskMateo.

The employees of Thorndike Press hope you have enjoyed this Large Print book. All our Thorndike, Wheeler, and Kennebec Large Print titles are designed for easy reading, and all our books are made to last. Other Thorndike Press Large Print books are available at your library, through selected bookstores, or directly from us.

For information about titles, please call:
(800) 223-1244

or visit our website at:
gale.com/thorndike

To share your comments, please write:
Publisher
Thorndike Press
10 Water St., Suite 310
Waterville, ME 04901